RIGHT OF THE FIRST NIGHT

Alison J Butler

This novel is dedicated To **Lynne Caulfield** and **Jean Butler**

My thanks go to:

Stuart S. Laing for editing/proofing the novel and adding some wonderful Scottish dialect.

Brian Murray for his expertise, and invaluable information regarding Scottish eighteenth century mining. Thanks also for a copy of Scotch mining terms, and kindly providing an extract from History of Newton Parish.

I'd also like to thank my immediate family – my wonderful husband - **Dave Butler (chief editor)**, and three of my children - **Belinda, Isabella** and **Oliver** for all their encouragement and support.

Apologies go to my readers for taking so long to write book 2, I will be sure to make sparks fly from my pen in future!

Re: The Scottish Serf Collar: this is not fiction, a real example of this kind of collar can be viewed at the Nation Museums Scotland: This brass serf's collar was found in the River Forth at Logie in Stirling. It dates from the early 18th century.

You can contact me at:

AlisonJaneButler@hotmail.co.uk or

@halfhangitmaggy on twitter.

I'd love to hear from you :)

*A*fter the Reformation, the barons became heritors of

their parish church and strictly upheld church discipline. At
Stichill, in 1696, delinquents who broke the Church's law
were sentenced by the Baron's Court to be chained in the
stocks or placed in the jougs during the laird's pleasure.

*F*or the slightest offence, or imagined misdemeanour,

punishments including torture, which was legal in Scotland
until 1709, were used. Men were hung up by their thumbs,
hung by the feet in a room filled with nauseous smoke and
had knotted strings tied around their head. Women had red-
hot tongs placed between their shoulders and under their
armpits until the tongs went cold, fingers were broken, faces
branded and backs lashed with a whip. The barons had
epileptics gelded and lepers burned alive.

Droit du seigner/ Right of the First Night - *also*

known as jus primae noctis, refers to a supposed legal right in medieval Europe, and elsewhere, allowing feudal lords to have sexual relations with subordinate women on their wedding night.

LIST OF CHARACTERS

Baron William Bothwell
> Laird/Baron/Lord of Castle Wood

Lady Matilda Bothwell
> The Baron's Wife

Robbie Bothwell The Younger
> The Baron's Son

Baron Robert Bothwell The Elder
> The Baron's Father (Deceased)

Elisabeth Bothwell
> Sarah & Magnus's Child (Adopted by Matilda)

Magnus Styhr
> Land Serf/Collier/Eldest Son of Erik

Eleanor Styhr
> Magnus's Mother/Wet nurse/Cook

Sabine Styhr
> Magnus's Sister/Land Serf

Erik Styhr
> Master Mariner/Land Serf

Harold Styhr
> Magnus's Brother/Land Serf

Sarah Campbell
> Magnus's Sweetheart

Jeannie Campbell
> Sarah's Mother

Klok Gumma/ Getrud Hakansson
> Castle Wood Wise woman

Greta Hakansson
> Getrud's Daughter

Hanne Hakansson
> Greta's Daughter

Falmouth
> Ghillie/Gamekeeper

Morice McDonald
> Castle Steward

Bradley McKenzie
> The Baron's Manservant/Valet

Black Friar John
> Minister of Black Friar's Kirk

Lang Sandy
> Surgeon

Donald
> Surgeon Apprentice Boy

Sister Louise Valois
        French Nun/Prioress

Abbess/Mother Hoppringle
        Abbess of Magdalene Chapel

Captain Pepper
        Ship Captain - Leith To Calais

Angus Parker
        Ship Cabin Boy

Jacob Poste
        Quaker/Castle Wood Dungeons

Sir John Stuart
        Coal Master of Newton Colliery

Jimmy Mole
        Collier

Effie Hume
        Fremit / Coal Bearer to Magnus

Thomas Hume
        Trapper / Effie's Brother

Tiny
        Giant Collier

Betty
> Pregnant Coal Bearer

Mr Moffat
> Old Collier

Mrs Moffat
> Coal Bearer

Angus McCain
> Blacksmith

CHAPTER 1

At Castle Wood, a boy stood on the brae, among harebells and ling, looking down across the wild Scottish moors. At his feet was a bow, a fine piece of weaponry, made from yew sapling and strung with animal gut. Beautifully crafted, it was an object completely unappreciated by young Robbie, who really would have been happier with a sling and stone. A breeze rustled the trees, Robbie closed his eyes and sniffed up the air. He could smell moss and the tang of fresh bark. He picked up the bow and heaved a great sigh, conscious of his father behind him. But before he'd even lifted it to chest height, a rough hand shoved him. 'Not here, laddie, you're too exposed. Follow me. I'll find the perfect spot.'

Father and son trekked across a cold and wild terrain, the landscape a blur of marshes, nettles, and twisted trees ravaged by a howling wind. Upon a soft mound of heather, Robbie made an awkward attempt to shoot an arrow, not a good one. But with his father standing close by, he swallowed his pride and tried again. His second attempt was worse than the first. With the muscles in his jaw twitching, and nostrils flaring, Robbie had the look of a wild creature as he flung his bow to the ground. 'Pick it up. Try again,' his father commanded.

Robbie stamped a foot then stooped to recover the weapon.

His father placed a hand upon his shoulder and said: 'Stand with your eyes to the arrow shaft. Now step back with your front foot a wee bit. This is your shooting stance, remember it.'

Robbie nodded and curled his fingers around the bow, and as he did so he imagined himself to be a fierce hunter hidden within the forest, invisible amongst bursting colours of brown, green and vermillion red. The earth seemed to vibrate below him, sending a tingle up his legs.

His father ranted: 'You hold the bow like a lassie. Hold it steady or I'll clap you round the lugholes. Now nock an arrow in the centre of your bowstring and let the shaft of the arrow rest on the bow. No – not like that. Like this.'

Robbie glared at his father. 'All right, leave me be,' he held the bowstring with his first three fingers, and used his thumb to stabilise the arrow.

'In a V, keep your arm locked straight. Christ, you're useless. Lift your head and face in line with the target. Now raise your bow arm and keep it locked, draw the string back until your thumb is against your jaw line. Careful now, that's how you do it.'

Robbie scanned the horizon, an old barefoot serf and his mangy dog ambled up a mossy trail. He watched them for a moment, and then complained: 'There's nothing for me to aim at.'

Robbie continued to complain, only quitting when his father puffed out his cheeks and pressed a finger to his mouth, before looking powerfully into his eyes. 'Hush. Be patient, laddie or you'll scare everything away. Put the bow down for now, let's follow the mossy trail. Perhaps there's something beyond the nettles.'

Robbie moaned and cursed all the way, and cried like a wee bairn when a nettle stung him. Before long, his legs developed an itchy rash, prompting him to search for a dock leaf amongst the nettles. 'I want to go hame.'

His father shushed him and turned his head to the side so that one ear rested on his shoulder, just like their hunting dogs when they caught a trail. Suddenly, a rustling sound prompted them to hide within tall weeds, and together they crouched like soldiers, till a dark shadow sliced through the twilight.

'Now laddie - aim now, before it's too late.' He ordered.

'But Father...'

In one swift motion Robbie leapt up and took aim. With steady hands, he once again imagined himself to be a hunter, his shoulder and back muscles straining as he tested the string. The bow made a creaking noise, like the sound of a corpse swinging from a gallows, and as one eye closed to line up his prey, the arrow hissed through the air.

'I got him, I got him,' Robbie jumped up and down on the damp earth, his eyes sparkling with pride as his father shook his hand.

'Good shot, son, you should aim for the heart next time, you got it in the stomach and it'll take longer to die.'

'Why's the old man weeping, Father?'

'Probably fond of the old mutt. But I expect you did him a favour, did you see the size of it? It must have taken some feeding, a mammoth hound such as that? Anyway, let's be off, 'tis getting cold.'

***

Baron William Bothwell, to the best of his ability, applied himself with much devotion to the teachings and divine providence of the Lord. He was particularly concerned with the wellbeing of his mortal soul, and so now and again, he had his footman grind up a page of his bible, to mix with water and gulp down in one. Today was page 197, and the baron, in partaking of his pious beverage, hoped to ward off all manner of great evils to which he was prone. How else would he preserve his mortal soul? He was above all a man, and in moments of weakness a sinful one at that. In short, to his mind, temptations were everywhere. Such enticements were not within the power of human nature to resist. Thus, he fell from grace many times, *so what* he thought, *wasn't it folly to deny impulses? What was the sense in denying one's basic urges? To deny one's primitive inclinations was to deny the very thing that made one human.* And yet, sin however delightful and decadent at the time, seemed to eat away little holes, like wormwood burrowing into his soul. As night fell, hands clasped together, William prayed to God to be guided by the hand of Providence. He prayed for the soul of his father, a wicked and lecherous man. A man he was determined not to become. Many years ago, when feudal rights were endemic, William's father claimed the right of hereditary jurisdiction - fossa and furca, which allowed him to have his own pit, prison and gallows and be answerable to no one. This right was granted by the King, in return for military service. A service Baron Bothwell was obliged to continue.

Through the window of his private quarters, he looked out of his castle. It was a classic baronial sandstone structure, topped by a riot of turrets, crow-stepped gables and conical roofs. The castle grounds sloped gently down to the river's brink, its silver sheen overshadowed by overhanging boughs of yew and ash and nodding birch. Due north, across the Lowlands, several peasant cottages dotted the horizon, their dwellings so weak in structure they could have been torn down by a child. A bucolic image of run-rigs and miserable tenants performing back-breaking work, come rain or shine.

The baron smiled when he spied his son, Robbie, handling his new bow and arrow. He was glad the boy had made his first kill, it was about time. For a while he observed him, then knocked on the window and waved. 'I won't be a moment,' he shouted through the glass, and beckoned for his son to wait for him outside. The little soldier boy waited patiently near the door. His laddie's eyes brightened at the sight him: 'Ah, I expect you're hungry, Robbie after today. Let's remedy that shall we?'

From the east wing they walked along a screened passage, until they reached the great hall. The room bustled with activity, servants rushed here and there; some of them ushering father and son to a dais, where they settled on benches. A delicious aroma lingered in the air. Placed in the middle of a great dining table, were a selection of cold meats, beef, venison and mutton, as well as partridge and a selection of vegetables and soups. The baron ignored the food and examined the jugs: syllabub, claret and small ale.

Robbie shook his head. 'The pease-soup is cold and there are no sweet meats.'

William nodded and summoned a kitchen boy. 'Why hasn't cook prepared the master's favourites?'

The ragged kitchen boy began to shift from foot to foot, his flushed face suddenly turned pale. 'Cook's legs are bad again, Baron Bothwell, they're all swollen up like and she keeps getting dizzy spells.'

'That idle wench. Well get her a chair to sit on so she can continue with her work. Tell her I insist that she prepares more sweet meats for the young master.' In one smooth motion, the baron leant back on the bench and stretched out his long legs in front of him, then raised his boots into empty air. 'And take these off before you go. I want you to clean them. And do it properly or I'll hammer your ears to the whipping post.'

Much to the baron's displeasure, Robbie ate his food like a ravenous dog; William at once chastised him and commanded him to eat slower. Furthermore, thrice he had to warn him not to scratch at the table and not to pick his teeth. A wave of revulsion surged in his stomach, he could not abide bad table manners; at least the boy had the grace to stand when his mother, Lady Matilda approached the dining table.

'Help your mother into her seat, boy.'

4

Robbie twisted his face. 'That's what the servants are for.'
'I'll not ask you again, laddie.'

In a short while, as appetites became sated, servants came to snuff out candles, take away food, or fetch more claret and so on. During this activity, without much enthusiasm, William grimaced and forced himself to glance in his wife's direction. She sat with her hands resting in her lap, eyes staring down at them as though searching for the answer to some invisible clue. Just once she looked up to catch his eye, her little mouth quivering as she babbled some nonsense. The weaker sex in his experience rarely had anything useful to say.
'Wherever have you been today, husband? I've been looking for you all day.'
With one brow raised he groaned. 'Must I always account for my whereabouts, Matilda? Do not trouble me with your feminine curiosity.' He turned to his son. 'Women need a firm guiding hand, Robbie, remember that and you will be spared much inconvenience.'
Matilda blushed and wrung her hands in her lap.
'If you must know, I was teaching our boy how to hunt.'
'William, how could you? Heaven above, he's too young for pistols…'

'Nonsense, woman, he's old enough to learn whatever weaponry he chooses. Besides, we weren't using pistols – were we, Robbie? It was just a wee bit of target practise with a bow and arrow. Ask him yourself.'
Matilda turned to her son. 'How was it, Robbie?'
'William slapped his son on the back. 'Well, speak up, laddie. Was it clean or messy? Tell your mother about your first kill.'
'I got him right in the stomach – he was bleeding all over the ground.'
'Are you proud of our little hunter, wife?'
'Of course, of course,' she answered. 'Well done, Robbie. Perhaps we can eat it for supper – I do adore a good stew.'
'But, but, mother…'
The baron slapped Robbie's leg and cackled. 'I'm sure cook will find a cooking pot big enough for the job.'

***

Sarah was a hopeless maidservant. She could not perform the simplest of tasks and therefore needed constant supervision, much to the annoyance of her sister, Maggie. It didn't matter how many times Maggie demonstrated to Sarah how to sweep, do laundry, wash vegetables, make a good fire – Sarah had to be shown again and again. In short, Sarah was a nuisance. When Maggie was not around to look out for her sister, two things generally occurred... Sarah made an almighty mess, or she shirked her duties. By dusk, Maggie had had just about enough of her lazy sister and sent her home, surmising it would be quicker to get her work done alone.

***

It was in a miserable state that Sarah walked barefoot home. Her back ached, and her arms and feet were sore. All day she'd been fetching and carrying – collecting water for cooking or cleaning, or gathering wood to make up fires. Why was it that Maggie was allowed to sleep in the great hall with all the other servants and she was not?

No sooner had she set out towards the run-rigs, did she feel queerness settle into her bones. Twilight was upon her, light fading with every single step she took. Through a field of golden crops she traipsed for what felt like an eternity, with the sound of rustling grass in her ears, and the breeze feeling like the breath of a thousand feverish souls upon her tired body. As her toes curled into prickling sward damp with dew, she entered a pasture and stopped at the sound of something snapping. Sarah's mouth went dry.

'Lord don't let it catch me,' she whimpered, imagining a savage beast behind her. Like a field mouse she burrowed into a patch of weeds. She crouched in the darkness, her ears alert to every sound, her heart thumping beneath her breast.

'Sarah, Sarah. It is I, Magnus. Come out from your hiding place, I know you are there.'

For just a moment hoary clouds uncovered a half moon, allowing just enough light to enable Sarah to make out the silhouette of Magnus, holding a bunch of wild flowers in his coarse hands. From her crouched position on the ground his person took on an almost giant-like state, and in her distress she found herself clambering out and clutching to his legs like a small child.

'Oh. It's you, Magnus. I thought you was a beast or the devil himself ….'

''Tis me, you little fool.' Magnus reached down to scoop her into his arms, then buried his face into her soft neck.

'You frightened me half to …'

Magnus hushed her and tightened his grip. 'Shush, Sarah. Have you decided?'

'Decided what?'

'What we talked about.'

'Oh,' she tittered with a mixture of fear and embarrassment, 'I am not sure I know what you mean.'

With a strange feeling in her belly, Sarah allowed Magnus to push her to the ground, and as he did so wild flowers scattered beneath them to form a bed of fragrant bluebells and weeds. No moonlight, no sweet words of love, just pitch black – and Magnus and Sarah. It was not what she expected this first time with a man, in fact, to Sarah, it felt wrong… as though she ought not be with him at all, like kissing her brother or father. In the absence of moonlight, Magnus was spared the look of revulsion on his sweetheart's face, as he covered her body with his own. She whimpered as he placed his weight upon her, her cries muffled by his torso blocking out the night air. Couldn't he hear her distress, her cries? She thought not as he placed one knee between her thighs. A wave of terror seized her as he pushed her legs wide… can I change my mind, she thought? But it was too late. Of a sudden all she wanted was to be home with her mamma, preparing the night oats and filling her father's pipe. Even the detested spinning wheel would be preferable to this – sprawled on her back, fingers pinching at her soft thighs, her face squashed against Magnus's broad chest. Sarah yelped with pain as virgin blood seeped into damp loam, and as she did so the eerie cry of a fox echoed into the night.

'It's done. You belong to me now,' his panting breath tickled her ear.

'Does that mean I am safe?' Sarah pulled down her skirts and wondered why he took so long to answer. Perhaps he hadn't heard. She repeated: 'Am I safe now, Magnus?'

'Of course you are safe. I'll protect you.'

Sarah scratched her head and tried to remember what she was about to say. Then it came to her, this matter that irked her so. 'So he won't claim his right – what do you call it?'
'The *right of first night.*'

Magnus clutched his sweetheart to him; Sarah suffered his embrace in the hope that he wouldn't want to take her again. In truth, it hadn't been a pleasant experience, and she was stinging down below. It took all her strength of will to stop herself from crying like a wee bairn. She couldn't wait to be away from him and his fierce embrace.
'What do you think, Sarah? Have you not a brain in that pretty head? Bothwell's just like his father, he would never miss the chance of deflowering a young maiden. He will lie with all the young brides of his vassals…'
'The laird lies with his serfs?' Sarah's eyes near popped from her head.
'Where have you been, Sarah? Hasn't your mother ever warned you?'
It was her fourteenth summer. Mother had not yet given her the talk she promised. 'Perhaps he'll not want to bed me.'
'Ah, lass, if only that were true, but there's not a man in Scotland who would not want you.'

***

The baron woke early, as was his custom, then prayed to Almighty God for His help and guidance. For many nights now, nightmares had plagued his sleep. Thus, he was in a dismal condition, eyes bloodshot, head aching and hands shaking liking a man seized with barrel fever. His condition caused him to reach for a claret jug upon his desk, and so with no one about to see him, he supped it straight from the jug, without spilling a drop. In spite of his poor state, he searched for his book of accounts. Once he found it, he began to examine it. Yet again he had accumulated a gambling debt. Soon his creditors would demand him to settle. He groaned and pinched the bridge of his nose before weighing up his options.

After more claret (the alcohol helped him to think clearer), and a little deliberation, he traced a finger down one page of his accounts book. Henry Deaton. How many cows did he have? Three cows, a horse, and a fat wife – and wasn't she the one who made the warmest blankets of uppermost cloth? If memory served him right, Deaton was a wretched man. Not long ago he had the audacity to cut himself a walking stick from the branch of a covin tree, the very tree that stood at the front of his castle, a trysting place that marked the spot where he received and took leave of his guests. A quantity of claret sloshed from the jug as he drained it clear. With the back of his hand he wiped his mouth and shouted to his manservant.

'You – stop what you're doing right now and fetch my steward. I have a very important task for him.'

***

The day was fine, and the air pungent with a mixture of damp loam and ripened crop. Across the moors, the serfs began the day's toil, bent over double, working the soil. Blackbirds and crows sang near and far, competing with the groans of disgruntled serfs and the grunts of an enormous ox as it pulled a cart. Sunbeams covered one half of the run-rigs in horizontal strips of light. At the sunny side, Magnus took his place among the men, clutching a well-worn spade between calloused hands. There was a rhythm to the men's work, and in no time at all their bodies gleamed with sweat. At noon the cries of a hungry child echoed into the warm air prompting a young woman to abandon her work and flee in the direction of her wean, one milky white breast exposed in anticipation of the task ahead. Directly above Magnus, a bird of prey swooped in the bright sky, its sharp eyes scanning the field in search of its quarry. For a while Magnus stood quite still, his face turned up to the sky, to observe the majestic flight of the winged hunter, before turning away – and where the eyes look the heart follows. Magnus spied her on the shady side talking to her mama and a strange man. A tightening sensation squeezed within his chest as he tried to catch her attention.

'Sarah. You're wanted here, I'm parched, lassie - bring us a drink,' he shouted across the field.

But Sarah didn't seem to hear him; he shouted louder. Before long and with no sense of urgency, she proceeded to walk towards him at a snail's pace, picking up her skirts as she crossed the mud.

'Hurry, Sarah, for God's sake I'm growing a bloody beard here, lassie.'

'All right, all right I am coming,' she whined.

All Magnus's frustration and anger vanished as she appeared before him, pretty as a rose, carrying a drinking horn filled with small ale. His eyes never left her as she stretched out one arm to offer him the ale, and as their hands touched for just a brief moment his gaze dipped to the peaks of her breasts, that were clearly swollen. Sarah had missed two monthly courses; soon he'd have no choice but to approach the baron and ask for permission to wed. The days were getting shorter, and in next to no time the harvest would take up all of their time. Magnus had to act soon.

'Who's the stranger talking to your mother?'

'One of the baron's henchmen.' She looked down. A moment passed before she met his eyes.

'Is he bothering you?'

Sarah shook her head. 'He's no bother, but this is. Mother says that I'm to have a bairn.' She prodded her stomach. 'I know nothing of weans, Magnus. I'm a simple maid. I don't want a baby. I've changed my mind.'

For just a moment Magnus glimpsed beneath the glowing skin and fair hair, the essence of Sarah concealed within a facade of beauty. In earnest he tried to see beyond the thick lashes and full mouth and peered deep into her eyes… and as he did so his stomach turned. Hers was an empty expression, eyes vague and startled like some dumb beast. Why hadn't he noticed how young and dim-witted she was, his fair Sarah? He shook his head and shivered as though someone walked upon his grave. Magnus knew really, deep down. If truth be told, he'd overlooked Sarah's flaws, precisely because of her fair looks, that so resembled his first love…Greta.

'You can't change your mind, Sarah. The thing is done now and cannot be undone. Don't you understand? Better my child than the laird's bastard.'

10

'Nae I don't understand and I like not your tone. I have felt quite ill this two month, and would rather not have a …'
'Surely you realise how a baby is made?'
'Nae and I have no idea how it will get out.'
'The same road it got in.'
'Oh dear.' Sarah began to weep.

Magnus pulled her to him, then, not caring about nosy folk and wagging ears. A sprig of heather stuck out from the thick tangles of her honey-coloured hair, he removed it and inhaled its sweet scent.
'Oh. I see,' she said, her brow furrowing. 'So when we – you know – that night. We…we made a baby?'
It took all his composure not to sigh, sometimes he wondered if she was of this world or away with the fairies. Magnus didn't want a changeling child.
'Sarah, why do you think I bedded you so soon? Don't you take heed of anything I say? You're just a young lassie, too young perhaps. 'Tis a pity we didn't have more time for courting and walking out, but I couldn't chance leaving it too long. I had to be your first. I had to.'

The midday sun streamed into Sarah's eyes turning them a liquid amber colour, like a jug of fine ale; there was bewilderment behind those pale eyes, like a small child observing a thing of wonder.
'I don't like courts. Why would I want to go courting?' she asked.
'Never mind, Sarah. Stay away from the baron till I have his permission to marry. Can you manage that?'
'Aye.'
'Good lassie.' He kissed her small nose and held her small body to him. To his mind they were a perfect fit. Magnus could have stayed like that forever, young Sarah in his arms – dim and yet so beautiful.

CHAPTER 2

The baron could not sit still for long. He was the kind of man that if you sat him down and tried to have a conversation with him, before long, he'd look completely uninterested in anything one had to say. Furthermore, he made no effort to hide his disinterest, in fact he made a great display of it - yawning, rolling his eyes, and tapping his fingers and his feet. He was not a man to be pinned down. Folk who tried to hold his attention were doomed to fail, after a few minutes he began to look like a caged animal. Inevitably, not long after folk sought him out, he scarpered. In short, the baron was a restless soul… and this restless spirit governed him and filled his veins with poison and longing. His actions, the majority of them reckless, only sought to a fill a void - a void that was yet to be filled. In truth, he was a profligate, a debauchee of the highest order. And yet, unusually for a man of such character, he struggled to make sense of it all. What was he looking for? Why couldn't he find happiness? What would become of his immortal soul?

The baron forgave himself frequently. The gambling, women, sins of the flesh… he dismissed as moments of weakness and nothing more. After all wasn't it just human nature? Temptation for many was indeed hard to resist. So what if he fell down once in a while, well that was natural. For the baron, justification for such behaviour was always easily found. His wife for instance, she pleased him not, never had done really. Matilda bored him. Just the thought of her caused him to curse and think unpleasant thoughts. Then there was the new ghillie , he was a disappointment too. The wretched man was an upstart, did as he pleased. Upstarts had to be punished.

'Damned ghillie.' He cursed loudly - his jaw twitching as he poured claret into one of his favourite air twist wine glasses. The baron knocked the claret back in one. How dare he take an axe to his covin tree, the blasted fool. Upon his desk sat his accounts ledger. He opened it, traced a finger halfway down a page and then stopped. A list of names filled the parchment, scrawled beautifully in midnight blue ink. With a steady

hand William drew a line through the ghillie's name. ~~Henry Deaton.~~
~~Occupation Gamekeeper~~. Once it was done he summoned his steward.
'Morice. Get in here man. I need funds and I need them quick. It's his
fault that old bastard.'
'Who my Lord?'
'My father - damn well sold off most of our land before he succumbed
to the pox, taking my poor mother with him… he's practically left me
a pauper. How am I supposed to settle my gambling debts?'
'Aye well I expect there's a painting you can sell.' Morice nodded.
'No no. Father sold most of the old masters… I'll not part with another,
especially the Dutch ones. Now take heed, I refer to the ghillie, you
must turf him out, and his fat wife, in fact throw out anyone who dwells
within that miserable abode,'

William stared at his steward hard, as though daring him to react, but
the steward was a canny one, he displayed neither surprise or horror.
Morice was a sharp, and was chosen precisely for his obedience,
shrewdness and loyalty.
'All right and his position here at the castle?'
'His services are no longer required. '
'And what am I to do with his family, his possessions?'
'Banish them all. Sell all his livestock and possessions, his wife makes
a good cloth I'm told, so there's some money to be had from that. Get
as much as you can, then burn anything left. I really don't care. He
should not have cut down my best tree. Oh and Morice, arrange for a
new gamekeeper will you, I haven't the time.'
The steward nodded again and promptly left. Soon after, William sent
for his valet to help prepare him for kirk. William hated to dress in
finery, he preferred his riding clothes. All those damned buttons and
pins were a nuisance for sure. Final alterations were hastily made to his
new coat and breeches, all made from the finest silk, embroidered with
silver thread and lace. Another manservant man powdered his periwig
with a mixture of flour, nutmeg and starch.

At Kirk, William took his place within a raised and partitioned
platform, well away from the serfs and common folk, a handkerchief to
his face to shut out the stench. Matilda and Robbie sat beside him,

staring ahead as the Minister delivered a fine speech from his pulpit. When the sermon ended, and the poor box was handed out, many a bad coin ended up inside the box, as most folk used it as a receptacle for bad copper money, which was constantly refused at market. Thus, in an effort to secure a place in Heaven, the baron left a most generous donation, that more than made up for any bad coin.

***

As Sarah's stomach grew, so did Magnus's unease. There was no sense in trying to hide the fact for much longer, the time had come to ask the baron permission to wed. With great trepidation Magnus grabbed his coat and set out for the castle. He walked slowly, small steps, but with each step closer, his neck became tense and his stomach knotted. As he entered the castle walls his shoulders lowered and his breath shortened. The place seemed to fill him with dread. When he reached the cobbled pathway that gave entry to the castle, Magnus had to dodge a number of geese and swine, not to mention the dung that littered the floor. The sound level was louder here…the majority of noise from unhappy servants and serfs summoned to work, covered in filth and sores, their children barefoot and hungry. Magnus recognised most of them except an unusually tall man, who walked shoulder to shoulder beside him carrying a small, ailing child. At the main gate he entered a large court-yard, in its centre a battered old covin tree; his palms suddenly grew damp as he glimpsed a gallows and whipping post.

'You. State your business.' A henchman prompted Magnus to the castle door.
'I wish to see Baron Bothwell.'
The henchman looked him up and down and sneered. 'Are you sure, serf? Name?'
'Magnus Styhr.'
'I thought so. Come with me,' the henchman beckoned for him to follow.

The temperature dropped inside the castle walls, the air thick with damp and mould. Under foot, the floor was wet and slippery. Magnus trod carefully, head bowed to avoid bumping his head upon the low ceilings. There seemed to be a never-ending series of draughty corridors to walk through before they reached a winding staircase; the stone steps of which were very uneven, some generous in size, others tiny and narrow. To climb the majority of them, Magnus had to place his large feet sideways in an awkward manner. At the top of the staircase they entered a small circular room, glazed with one small window. Flanked by two henchmen; the baron sat at an old desk peering into an enormous leather bound book, a feather quill in one hand, a large apple in the other.

'Sit down, Magnus. I've been wondering when you'd pluck up the courage to see me,' he said, his eyes never leaving the pages of the book. 'It's been a long time – too long.' He closed the book with a thud, sending a thousand dust particles floating into the air.

'Now then, within these castle walls are lots of clacking hens. Do you get my meaning? Lots of good-for-nothing sluts spreading gossip and telling tales, and if memory serves me right there's a rumour going about… a rumour about *you*. Do you know of any rumours, Magnus?'

Magnus shifted in his seat and shook his head.

'Would you like me to reveal this rumour to you, Magnus?'

'Aye.' Magnus swallowed back sour bile.

The baron continued in a flippant manner, but of a sudden his tone changed and his face became grave. 'Haven't I been a good laird to you, Magnus? To you and your mother with her bad legs… and all you other mongrels?'

'Aye my Lord.'

The baron's face reddened. 'Yes. Yes. So imagine my disappointment when I learn that you have a sweetheart Magnus, and that behind my back, you and this lassie have sinned before the eyes of our Lord. How dare you fornicate with one of my serfs… damned scoundrel, can't you see this is a serious matter? Man and girl unwed…what say you?'

'My Lord, I …'

'I've seen her; I know why you've chosen her for yourself…the lassie has a likeness for…'

'Greta.' Magnus completed his sentence for him, his chin jutted upwards in defiance.

'Do not speak her name.'

Without warning, the baron raised his arm backwards and hurled an apple at Magnus, catching him square in the eye. 'Feckless fool. Did you really imagine that I would allow you make your own choice? Hah!' the baron spat on the floor. 'Speak up, man.'

Magnus gasped and pressed a hand to his eye socket, the pain that surged through him near took his breath away. With one eye, he stared out and looked at his oldest childhood friend, searched for some compassion, sympathy...but there was nothing. His shoulders stooped as a sense of doom seeped into his bones. 'Please forgive me my Lord, I am sorry if I have offended you, but I meant no malice. Weren't we friends once, William, you and I?'

'Do not presume to call me by my Christian name. You are not my equal and never will be.' The baron scoffed and turned to one of his henchmen. 'The fool thinks we're friends because we shared a tit... his mother was my nursemaid once, so what!'

Magnus bowed his head and felt his stomach churn. With all his heart he wished he was home with his family, and not here with his Laird. But here he was, all he could do was await his fate and likely punishment.

The baron stood. He then walked from one side of the room to the other, pacing like a expectant father outside the birthing chamber. After a while he stopped and faced Magnus. 'Does your mother know of this?'

'Nae. She knows nothing.'

'Yes, she's more sense than you. But she is getting old, Magnus, half the time she can't even stand upright in the kitchen and has to sit in a chair. What to do? What to do? Must I replace her with Sabine?'

''Tis her legs, they swell on occasion. It will pass. Do not punish her for my sins.'

A moment of silence passed, tension crackled in the air. Magnus removed the hand from his swollen eye. A feeling of dread bubbled within him, it started in the pit of his stomach and travelled upwards towards his throat, constricting and threatening to choke him.

16

'Magnus.' the laird barked. 'Take heed of my words. I have waited a long time for this opportunity.'

***

Magnus's sweetheart was a beauty true, but in truth, she was really just a plain country girl, and a naive one too. Sarah knew little of the world and the ways of men…she hadn't sought out Magnus's affection; in truth it had been all his doing. To be honest, she would have accepted any man, for Sarah followed the wind and did as she was told. Even her own mother thought she was like the sheep in the fields, following the herd, only bleating when cold, hungry, or in pain.

Soon she would have a child, and the thought of nursing it terrified her. Sarah knew nothing of weans and how to care for them. All that crying, feeding and attention, how was she going to manage that? Perhaps she could give it to her mother to look after once it was born, she thought smiling. Aye, that was the answer, her mother would take the child and she could go back to work at the castle with her sister, Maggie. So intent was Sarah in her thoughts, suddenly a voice startled her.

'Mother, you frightened me to death.'

Sarah's mother stoked up the peat fire and laughed aloud. 'Silly girl. You're too busy daydreaming to pay attention to your surroundings. I've finished the blanket – look, it's for your kist. Now fetch the spinning wheel so we can prepare more linen for your bottom drawer.'

'Yes, mother.'

'Are you happy, lassie? He's a fine young man, no doubt one of the strongest at Castle Wood.'

'Well I'm not sure, mother…I suppose.'

'Suppose! Where's your gratitude? You look as though you're about to be wed the miller. Magnus Styhr is a good catch, his mother was wet nurse to the laird as a wean, did I tell you that?'

Sarah shook her head. 'Will I have to feed the bairn when it's born?'

'Well who else do you think will feed it, silly girl? The wean can't feed itself now can it? You know how it is with babies. You've been blessed if it lives passed two moons. Now stop talking nonsense and fetch me some yarn for the spinning wheel.'

When they came it was a complete surprise. Six fine soldiers on milk-white horses kicking up a swirl of dry dust. And as their hooves galloped along the sandy ground, a violent wind blew feverishly into the cottage, prompting mother and daughter to venture outside. Instinctively, Sarah gravitated towards them with her country girl smile, the sound of her mother's shrill voice ringing in her ears as she accepted one of their outstretched hands.

**

Magnus remained locked in the tower room. He'd been ordered to stay put, but was more than tempted to leave, it was preposterous - he hadn't done anything wrong…not really. A guard hovered nearby, scowling at him once in a while. With trepidation, Magnus asked him for something cold to press to his swollen eye, but the guard ignored him. So Magnus sat with his face in his hands, his eye so swollen now he could no longer open it. He racked his brains, tried to remember something - anything that could have caused the baron's wrath. He thought back, and in his mind's eye he saw them all… Greta, Sabine and the young baron all playing in the woods. How they'd loved the freedom of the forest; their favourite game pretending to be out-laws. Boys against girls, the boys highly spirited, the girls screaming like banshees.

A door creaked open.

'Ah – I do apologise for the delay, Magnus, I had a matter to attend to. Goodness me, that eye looks horribly swollen.' The baron tutted and sat in his chair. 'I expect you're wondering what all this is about?'

Magnus nodded and tried to focus through his one good eye.

'Ah, Magnus, Magnus. Magnus the great, what am I to do with you? Come here, stand before me.' The baron pushed his chair away from him, and stood up to face him.

They stood barely inches apart, nose to nose, they were of equal height. The laird cleared his throat. 'I presume your reason for visiting the castle today was to ask something of me… my permission to marry your

18

sweetheart perhaps. Am I right? Well here's your answer. I will not. I refuse.'

Magnus opened his mouth to speak, but one glare from his tormentor changed his mind.

The baron continued. 'I've waited a long time for this, Magnus. And now I expect you're perplexed and want to know the reason why I refuse your request to wed. Well hear me now – I' m *not* going to tell you. Do you hear me? I'm *not* going to tell you.'

'I do not understand ...'

'Silence. The answer is for you to ponder in isolation, away from distractions. Not so great now are we, Magnus?' With a wave of the hand, he motioned to his guards, and then uttered five words that made Magnus's chest feel as though it was about to collapse inwards.

'Take him to the dungeons.'

***

Sabine stood dead centre of the fields, a hoe in her hand and a face like thunder. Other folk were already hard at work, bent over double, to free their crops of stones or weeds.

'Where are you Magnus?' Sabine muttered to herself. It was not like her older brother to be tardy, he was usually here at the crack of dawn to greet her with a smile. Magnus never slept late, or shirked his share of the work, he was a man who could be relied upon - always. She gazed across the grassy fields, her shoulders sagging at the prospect of hard labour. There was much toil to be done, of the back-breaking kind. It irked her that she'd now have to suffer it alone. Across the field she caught a glimpse of her father and younger brother, Harold, busy with an ox team…they'd not long returned from fishing, without Magnus - Magnus avoided water. It was pointless asking them for help, and mother was busy as usual in the castle kitchens. Of a sudden Sabine felt weary. Everywhere she turned mud and earth covered the ground; it clung to her clothes, her skin, and beneath her finger-nails. And yet this miserable existence was all she'd ever known.

At that moment a fresh south west breeze swept across Castle Wood. Sabine gathered her plaid around her and stared ahead, her eyes narrowed, a bright spark of light illuminated the horizon before fading away. There were little prospects for the likes of her kind beyond the fields and mud…never would be, or the serfs that came after her. But her brother Magnus, he thought different, oh dear Lord he was a foolish boy - he always talked of trying new things, or worse still *changing* things. The crops for instance - all their lives they'd grown oats, but this year, to her amazement, Magnus had persuaded their father to try growing barley, on condition that they grow it as a second cereal in rotation. Sabine had her reservations, but in truth, the going had been good - so far, what with the cold and damp conditions. The barley in truth seemed to thrive in such a sun-deprived climate, and at this rate a good winter yield was expected in July, when the time would come to pick up a sickle and cut down the ripe spiky grass.

The day was slowly ebbing away, Sabine really needed to be getting on. With haste she wiped her hands on her apron and picked up a weeding hoe. Two hours later she paused for a break, shaking her head at a farm laddie offering his help. No doubt he'd want something later for his kindness and she hadn't a mind for that. Her back throbbed. For relief she massaged the base of her spine and arched backwards. In the act of stretching, Sabine looked into the distance…then her mouth was dry. They appeared suddenly on the horizon, as though out of thin air, the laird and his young son. Worse still, they seemed to be walking straight towards her. Sabine's stomach turned, she backed away and near tripped on a barrow in the process. To her relief they changed direction and crossed to the infield, to greet Sabine's mother, who presumably had just finished her work.

'Sabine, Sabine. Come greet the baron and his wee boy, Robbie. Hasn't he grown into a fine boy, Sabine. Sabine.' She shouted.

Sabine wondered if she could feign deafness. Pretend that she had simply not heard. But then to her horror, her mother called out again.

'Sabine. Stop what you're doing and come here right now.'

But Sabine's legs had turned to mush. Her limbs simply would not move. She froze. The baron unnerved her, he always had done, even when they were just children…somehow he always made her feel awkward and clumsy and something more…fearful. The kind of fear that crept up on you in a stranglehold, a sixth sense of sorts, that all was not well.

His voice cut through the air. 'Come come girl. Do not be coy. It will please me to see you again after all these years. I cannot remember when I saw you last. It's been too long.' A few powerful strides and he was standing before her, the top half of the sun framing his head like a fiery halo. In one hand he held a hessian bag, and for whatever reason he suddenly dropped it and held out his hand.

'Yes it has been a while, my Lord. Unlike my mother, I prefer the fields to the kitchen,' Sabine hesitated and shook his hand, all the while keeping her eyes on the bag, wondering what was contained within it. It was to remain a mystery, because he gave no clue to it.

The baron pressed his lips to Sabine's ear and whispered. 'Ah that's part of the reason I am here. Your mother has been sent home early again. Do you know why?'

Sabine shook her head.

'Swollen legs.'

Sabine grimaced and stepped back, keen to distance herself from the laird. 'Oh dear.'

The baron moved in again and whispered once more into Sabine's ear. 'Yes girl. Your mother is getting old, she needs rest. We've another cook on hand, but she's not a patch on your mother. I was hoping she'd passed her culinary skills on to you…'

'My cooking skills are basic I'm afraid, and I prefer the fields.'

'Pity. We're lost without your mother, Sabine. We simply can't do without her. I'd like it if you could take her place one day… I would make it worth your while,' he said grasping her arm. 'Perhaps we could talk of this again another time?'

Sabine sucked in her breath as long, tapered fingers pinched her skin. 'Perhaps. Well I must return to my work. Your bag, sir.'

'Ah yes. Must not forget that.' The baron picked up the hessian bag.

Sabine watched him walk away, the further away he travelled, the better she felt. How she despised him with his smug and haughty expression, the kind all aristocracy seemed to possess around poor and common people. And yet, Sabine's mother seemed to adore him, and even linked the baron's arm for a while as they walked away. Why, oh why?

'Goodbye Eleanor. Off you go now. And rest those legs you useless woman or I'll have you fed to the dogs.'

'Ah be off with you or you'll feel the back of my hand… Laird or no - and don't you be thinking of fetching my Sabine for kitchen work, she's an out-of-doors girl like her father… happier in the fields she is my lassie.' Eleanor laughed.

Only mother could talk to him that way and get away with it, Sabine knew that for sure. They had an odd relationship her mother and the baron, Sabine never could understand why her mother tolerated him. Personally, he made her skin crawl.

The baron placed his hands in an inverted v around his mouth and shouted across to her, 'Sabine. You look not a day older I swear. Remember what I said, be sure to get your mother to take some rest, I want her fit for work on the morrow. '

For just a moment Sabine forgot herself and screwed up her face, then quickly tried to conceal her displeasure. She thought the baron grotesque and monstrous even. His fine looks didn't fool her, never had. True, the years had been kind to him, and he was handsome as ever with his chiselled features and fair hair. But his features were that of a temperamental man, irritable, changeable. All high brows and stormy expression, forever set in a perpetual scowl, as though angry at something or someone.

***

'Who was that peasant girl, father?'

'That was cook's daughter. Strange girl. Prefers to toil in the fields like a man instead of working aside her mother in the kitchens. Never mind her; put your hat back on, there was no need to take it off for the likes of them.'

'The maid seemed frightened of you.'

'Sabine? Nonsense, we grew up together. She's just a wee bit shy.'

They crossed a burn and then a meadow. Soon they came to a dry stone wall and abandoned watch-tower, the area all around covered in gorse, ling and weeds. Near a willow tree, the baron dropped his hessian bag and removed his heavy coat.

'What's in the bag – a bow and arrow?'

'No.'

'Are we going to practice hunting again?'

'No. You'll see.'

William threw open the hessian bag and pulled out a heavy metal contraption. With great care he placed the strange device upon the soft earth. 'It's something I had the blacksmith fashion for me. It's like an animal trap but bigger, work of art isn't it. Look at the lines on that and the craftsmanship.'

'Are you trapping foxes, father?'

'No. Trespassers and poachers on my private land, look at the damage they've done to our boundary wall. I'd like to string them up if I found them.'

'Ah, so is it a mantrap?'

'Aye. You could call it that.'

'How does it work?' Robbie bent over the contraption to peer at it with inquisitive eyes. His hands hovered over the terrifying implement itching to touch it.

'Careful, laddie, don't be tempted to handle it mind, it has quite a bite on it. Can you see the plate? Well that will be hidden under a covering of earth or leaves. When someone steps on it the spring will close tight. And the springs see are armed with teeth and will lock on the leg like this.' He clapped his hands together for effect. 'And once it does nothing will wriggle its way out of it.'

'Will it kill the poacher, father and will his blood and guts spill?' Robbie asked.

'No, of course not laddie. Most likely it'll break his leg. Come on. Let's set it up over there, near the hole in the wall.'

They set the trap together; William positioned it while Robbie collected earth and leaves. After a while they stood a distance away from it, eyes squinting past the harsh rays of the sun to examine their handiwork.

'Can you see it?'

'No, father.'

'Well if you can't see it, neither will the trespasser. Our work here is done. Let's go eat.'

CHAPTER 3

Magnus couldn't catch his breath, he was terrified. Once or twice he near fell on his backside as he descended slimy stairs into a gaping black mouth. A foul and desolate cavity beckoned. His hands trembled, and his chest felt tight, as though a great weight pressed upon it. He squinted his eyes and peered into the darkness, here awaited the promise of a miserable existence, where all days and nights merged into one. Magnus sniffed up and almost gagged, the stench was nauseating, and as they descended further into the putrid hellhole, rats scurried here and there. The gaoler found it quite amusing when one fat rodent ran up Magnus's leg and caused him to scream.

'You'll get used to that soon enough. They're everywhere. Sleep with your good eye open or they'll chew off your ears.'

Magnus's lips curled with contempt. 'Sleep here?'

'Aye.' The gaoler sniggered.

'But why?'

'How should I know?'

Magnus's shoulders slumped. But worse was to come. Before the gaoler put him to the gad he gave Magnus what he called 'the grand tour,' and in hindsight Magnus would have preferred to stay within the miserable confines of his cell. In the bowels of the castle, a complex maze of corridors crawled with vermin, mould and lichen. In vain, Magnus staggered through this maze, struggling to keep up with the gaoler, encumbered by chains, his one good eye peering through murky light. They passed a deep pit, an emaciated creature languished within it, the man had neither tongue nor testicles.

'Epileptic,' explained the guard. 'Wait till you see this,' he pushed Magnus through a barred door.

In the centre of a chamber a naked woman lay in a foetal position covered in filth and sores. Arms tied behind her back: a thick rope circled her wrists and passed over a pulley system to the roof. The guard without delay walked over to her and proceeded to fondle her breasts.

24

'Do you want her? You can stick in your yard for a few coins if you want to – might be the last chance you get.' The gaoler rubbed his manhood.

Magnus looked at the gaoler then the woman, it was hard to decide which sight revolted him more. His stomach churned and bubbled, before long bile worked its way up into his throat. He swallowed hard, then turned to the gaoler. 'Nae, I do not want her. Take pity on the poor woman's soul. What on earth could she have done to deserve treatment like that?'

Magnus shivered as the gaoler sniggered and then shrugged his shoulders. To Magnus's disgust he observed the man had a disgusting habit of hawking up great globs of mucous and spitting it onto the floor. How on earth was he going to suffer this awful place was beyond him. The gaoler clapped his hands together. 'All right. So you're a shy one, you don't want her hey… I expect only because you haven't any coin on you. Please yourself, there are other ways to enjoy her.'

The woman began to weep and the sound distressed Magnus. He tried to close his ears to the noises, but it was no use. The lassie cried softly, and then pitifully she began to beg and plead for mercy, to let her be… all in a pathetic attempt to appease the gaoler, who couldn't care less. She was a plaything, *his* toy, an object to torment. The gaoler ordered her to stand, but she was too weak and couldn't keep her balance. The poor lassie kept falling to the ground. Magnus ached to go to her aid, after a while he could stand it no longer and shuffled towards her. But one look from the gaoler changed his mind, and so he did nothing.

'Get up,' he hissed and kicked her in the stomach. 'Strappado it is for you then.'

The gaoler reached high and pulled on a rope, and as he did so he grunted with exertion and then laughed as the woman became suspended in empty air. The poor woman hung from her wrists in exquisite pains of agony. She screamed till her voice became hoarse, and her chalky face became gaunt and immobile.

Magnus's head drooped; he placed his hands over his ears to muffle the sound of the lassie in torture. With a sick heart he peered through a

sickly amber light to peer at her, and in truth he thought for her to die would be a merciful thing. It broke his heart to hear the lass suffer.
The gaoler cut her down once the girl became unresponsive and silent. It was as though there was no fun in it once the girl was out cold.
'Take me out of here,' Magnus begged. 'I've seen enough.'

The blow when it came knocked him sideways, a great whoosh of air whipped from his mouth as he collapsed to his knees. An eddying darkness came after, followed by a searing ache right across his stomach. Magnus writhed upon the dirt floor in pains of agony, clutching his belly. *I'm stuck, he's stabbed me*, he thought, and like a crazed animal he rolled onto his back and felt his belly for blood.

***

Once a week, the baron, his wife and son dined together in the great hall. After their meal they retired to the solar to gather around a roaring fire. Matilda insisted it was a perfect opportunity to be together as a family, and to have discourse with their son. William loathed these get-togethers and sought every opportunity to avoid them. As a rule, the baron always made up some excuse to either not attend - or leave early. He found such occasions to be a terrible bore. But his wife, being the minx that she was, sometimes tricked him into it.

Today was one of those occasions. William twitched and fidgeted. He felt stifled, cornered like a fox trapped in a chicken coop. For a while he watched Robbie playing some game or other with a dice, but before long he became bored. To get through the tedium, he turned to the healing charms of claret. As he poured himself a glass, Matilda's favourite maid entered the room. The girl kept her eyes focused ahead and seated herself beside Matilda near the fire. Two pale complexions safely screened from a blistering fire. The baron observed the maid in secret, noting the little smile she gave his wife. It amused him the way she sat daintily in her seat, crossing her legs and offering a tantalising glimpse of one stocking. A tingling sensation shot up his legs, travelling higher and higher towards a swelling in his groin. In spite of this, the baron continued to stare and wickedly imagined the young maid in a

state of undress. It was whilst in the midst of this fantasy William wondered if she could somehow read his wicked thoughts, because before long the said maid began to shuffle nervously upon her seat, as busy little fingers twitched all the while beneath her embroidery hoop.
'Does something trouble you, husband?'
William loosened his collar and shook his head, irritated that his wife had disturbed his reverie. 'Tis too hot in here, Matilda. You know how I hate to be indoors. I must take some air.'
'Then open a window dear husband. The air will do us all good.' She looked to her maid and gave her a nod. 'Do open the window, Alice.'
The baron stood up and stated in a loud voice: 'That won't be necessary. I really don't know why you insist on us all coming together in this stuffy little room, it's nothing but a frightful bore, I'd much prefer the time spent with my hounds, Matilda.'
Robbie's ears pricked up at the sound of his father's raised voice. 'Oh father please may I come with you... I'm bored too?'
'Another time laddie.' And off he went.

Matilda turned in her seat so that her knees knocked the maids' embroidery. 'Sorry my lady.'
'Oh Alice. It's not your fault. 'I swear he cares more about those hounds than he does for Robbie and I.'
Alice tried her best to conceal a smile. But the baroness caught it from the corner of her eye.

***

Much like his father, Robbie loathed family time too. He much preferred to be out of doors with his favourite hound, or running across the heather, or better still climbing trees. The family room was after all awfully dull. Mother and father hardly uttered a word to one another, and father always looked for an excuse to leave as soon as he could. Less than half an hour, after supping half a bottle of claret, Robbie's father rose as expected from his chair and left the room. Now it was just him, mother and a silly maid.
'Mother – may I go with father?'

'No, you heard what he said, leave him be, Robbie. I expect he has some business to attend to.'

'No he hasn't. He said he was attending to his hounds.'

'Do not answer me back, boy. I said leave him be.'

Robbie sulked. In spite of the dreary situation he found himself in, he decided to make the most of it, and set out to amuse himself in one way or other. So off he trotted to the middle of the room, arms outstretched and head bobbing up and down like a duck apple, his arms flapping frantically like a bird of prey amidst clouds. Above him dangled a chandelier, Robbie focused his eyes on it and began to spin and spin. But somehow what with all the spinning, he lost his balance and landed with a crash right atop his mamma's feet. He giggled when she let out a sharp cry.

Matilda chastised him. 'Oh dear me, child, please be careful. You've hurt my feet again. Goodness, time after time I've warned you to keep away from my feet – my poor toes, look at them they're black and blue. Aren't you getting a wee bit old for all this nonsense, Robbie, you'll soon be a man?'

'I am a man already, there's hair beginning to grow on my lip.'

'That does not make you a man.'

'Well what does then?'

'Heavens, how should I know, ask your father.'

'I would if you'd let me go to him.'

Matilda puffed out her cheeks and groaned. 'Oh I've had just about enough of you today, Robbie…Alice, please take him outside for some air and take your time. I wish to sew in peace.'

The maid sighed and dropped her sewing, a face like thunder as she reached out a hand for young Robbie. Mischievous as ever, he stretched out his hand to her, but at the last moment snatched it away and raced out the room, yelling for her to follow. Halfway along the corridor he glanced backwards, his lips curving at the sight of her. He liked the way her breasts jiggled as she ran, that and her hands lifting her petticoats high to sprint along the corridor behind him. Robbie deliberately slowed his pace and allowed her to catch up with him, but once she did, he bolted away through the main doors to the garden and beyond. Out-of-doors, Robbie ran like a deer, his scrawny legs leaping across heather and gorse, his own laughter ringing in his ears.

'Master Robbie. Please slow down.'

Robbie hadn't even broken into a sweat when the maid called out to him, her voice breathless and forlorn. He halted, and as he did so a deep furrow marred his brow. To his utter annoyance, the lassie had sat down upon a stone bench and was now hunched forward over her knees, one hand held up to her heaving chest. The view of her bosom was glorious, but all that gasping for air reminded him of a salmon that had leapt out of the riverbed gulping for breath. Still scowling, Robbie shook his head and strutted over to the girl, placed his fingers upon her soft arm, and then pinched with all his might.

'Ouch. What did you do that for, Master Robbie?'

'I care not for your idleness…'

The maid slapped his hand. 'I will not go anywhere with you until you beg for my pardon, Master Robbie…'

'I will do no such thing.' His chin jutted upwards, and pointed towards a stormy sky.

Robbie's cheeks flushed as the maid stared at him, as if to take in his image and remember the ill deed she had just received. He began to fidget, feet shuffling through soil and yellow leaves, until at last she turned and called out to him: 'Master Robbie, I shall tell your mother you have acted like a beast…'

'Och, I was just jesting with you, lassie, come on,' he took her hand, so soft and warm and nearly as small as his.

'This is the way, nearly there,' said Robbie as they crossed a golden meadow towards a crumbling wall. 'Do you like frogs?'

'Nae, they're slimy,' the maid grimaced.

'Well what about snails then?'

'Nae, why do you keep asking me silly questions?' she replied.

'Worms?'

'Nae,' she puffed out her cheeks.

'Master Robbie, must we go any further? I should like to go home. I am cold, I haven't even got a proper coat to wear for a walk. And will you look at my new shoes, they're ruined, I'll never be able to wash the muck and stains off them now. 'Tis all right for your mother, if her shoes are ruined she can just buy another pair… but me, I cannot afford to…'

Robbie stuck his tongue out. 'Oh Alice, do stop whining. Don't you know you are mother's pet? She will buy you another pair. I don't want to return yet. We've only just set out. Besides, I've something I need to show you, nearly there – here it is.' Robbie stood before a dry stone wall, all of its footing stones intact. Although above the boulders, a small section of the wall had caved in, so that the filling and coping stones spilled in all directions onto the ground.

'That wall is crumbling.' The maid said.

'Aye it's the creep hole that's collapsed.'

'Creep hole?'

'Aye, a place for sheep to jump through from one field to another. Father thinks poachers have been using it to access the land.'

'Really?'

Robbie nodded. 'Aye, not to worry though, father has a remedy for that.' Robbie rubbed his hands together and walked over to a pile of mossy stones, towards a slight mound of decaying leaves, twigs, and withering weeds. 'Girl come here to me.'

'I've no time for your foolishness, young Robbie. What are you up to? You are scaring me.'

'What you scared of? Just stand here by me - face that way, look at the trees yonder.'

Robbie stooped to pick up a stick, stabbed at the earth, and all at once a terrifying noise sliced through the air, as metal scraped against metal, and razor-sharp teeth snapped together, and tearing through the maids' skirts.

Alice screamed, and pulled her skirts away from the trap, and all the while Robbie laughed and laughed.

***

William rolled off the woman. Now that the deed was done, the lassie ceased to exist. He sat up, yawned and stretched, bounced to his feet, then told her to get out. Once the slut had gone he walked to a window and glanced outside. In the distance he could see stallions, five or six of them. They were some of his finest horses. After a while, the group came to a halt outside a small cottage. He presumed this to be the home of Magnus Styr's sweetheart. He cupped a hand over one eye in an effort to focus. A blurred figure mounted one of the horses, a thick cloud of dust soon trailing them, as the stallions galloped towards the castle. His heart raced. Soon she would be here. He reached for his breeches.

It didn't take him long to dress. His riding clothes lay in a heap on the floor, casual, nothing too fancy with cumbersome pins or buttons. Fancy clothes he favoured not, he much preferred his tricorn to a powdered wig. Once dressed, he banged the door behind him and descended a staircase. William took the steps two at a time, all the while resisting the urge to scratch his privy parts. If that kitchen slut had given him the pox she would swing. He cursed her out loud, not caring who heard him. At the bottom of the staircase he tried to remember where he'd arranged to meet them. After a wee think, it came to him. The covin tree. So, off he went with a spring in his step.

At the tree, William passed a young stable boy and groom attending his stallions. The smaller of the two, the wee laddie had the boldness to complain that he was thirsty, and asked could he drink from the horses' pail. William's eyes shifted from stable boy to groom, the two of them looked alike, horrendous orange hair, both covered in freckles.

'That your lad?'

'Aye.' The groom placed one protective hand on his son's shoulder.

'I suggest you teach him to keep his mouth shut, you're here to work not complain. But, let it not be said that I am a hard-hearted laird. He may drink from the pail if he must.'

'Aye, I mean yes Master. Thank you Master.'

'Get back to work.' He swished one arm as though swotting away a fly and patted one of the horses, and it was then, that he spotted the girl… a small lassie with fair hair. So this must be Sarah, the lassie Magnus had bedded. For now, William kept his distance and made her wait. To pass time he talked to his henchmen, bawdy talk, the kind that produces vulgar laughs. The peasant girl, to her credit did not seem affected by any of it. In fact, she seemed oblivious to everything around her, sights, smells, noises…and this for some reason annoyed him. He moved closer, his face full of menace, then stopped dead. Up till now he'd only seen her from afar. Up close, his eyes near popped from his head.

He gestured to a henchman. 'Are you sure this is the right one, Magnus's girl?'

'Quite sure. Yes.'

'What sorcery is this? 'Tis a damned spell.' William shook his head.

The henchman looked puzzled. 'I don't understand.'

William shooed him away. 'Oh never mind man.' He turned his attention now to Sarah who seemed equally puzzled by the baron's outburst. 'Well speak up girl. Cat got your tongue. What is your name? You cannot be my Greta, and yet, by the devil, I say you look so much like her, it is uncanny.'

'I am no a devil, Sir. And I am no familiar with witchery. I be Sarah Campbell, Magnus's sweetheart.'

Once Sarah opened her mouth to speak, the baron visibly balked. It was as though, the magic was suddenly broken and he was now able to see the simple peasant women before him. 'Dear Lord, still your tongue, child. I cannot bear to listen to you.'

William's head sagged, he suddenly felt exhausted…and confused, disappointed even. Before him was a true likeness of Greta, with Norse cheekbones and a delicate nose. But this devilish pretender had none of Greta's light, or spark. What to do with her he thought? A great weight fell upon his chest, he needed to get away. Yes, he needed space to think. Then a thought came to him. He could take her to the castle towers, give her a tour. Yes, that's what he must do. He held out a hand and flinched at the coarseness of her palm in his own. 'Come on. Follow me.'

'Where are you taking me?' Sarah asked.

'Never you mind. You'll see. Just do as I say.'

A henchman followed them as they climbed the steps, laird and vassal, hand in hand. Near the top of the staircase, Sarah paused for a breath and placed a hand on the wall to steady herself. The baron placed one arm around her and prodded her to continue, impatient with her weariness. The action caused her to shrink away, as though alarmed by his closeness.

'Are you going to claim your *right of first night*?'

The baron choked with mirth and slapped the arm of his henchmen. 'Did you hear that? The wench thinks I want to lie with her. This chicken recently plucked, with a belly full of vassal fancies I want her!'

At the top of the staircase he took Sarah aside and explained: 'You really are a simple girl aren't you? I don't need a law or a right to take you. I am your laird and master. I can do as I please. Do you understand?'

'I think I do Sir. But I am a simple maid, I am not sure…'

'The practicalities are irrelevant, girl. Just try to take heed of this, as Laird of this castle you must submit to my will, or suffer the consequences.' William looked deep into her eyes, searched for Greta's spark, the glitter of wisdom… anything, but what he saw was a vacant expression.

The girl's face sagged. Then after the longest time, her chin lifted and she opened her mouth to speak. 'I submit to your will, my Lord. Do what you must.'

William laughed. 'Do not flatter yourself, girl. On you go.' He gestured for her to continue.

Beyond a crooked doorframe, a passage lead to the castle tower, so high it seemed to touch the clouds. The land seemed to stretch outwards for miles, towards a mass of trees and sparkling water. On the horizon, peasants worked the land, like tiny flies held fast in a spider's web. William signalled for Sarah to look between the turrets. 'Look at the land. The river, the trees. All mine. Beautiful, is it not?'

Sarah stood backwards away from the turrets, her face turning deathly pale.

'Do great heights alarm you? There, there, you are quite safe, girl. Come here.' He held out one hand and prompted her to join him. 'Once the child is born, you and I will return to this tower. Would you like that?'

'Aye, but how did you know I was with child, my Lord?'

William smiled and held her arm tighter. 'Nothing escapes my attention.'

***

After the baron left the tower, two strange women came to collect Sarah. Big, burly women with muscled arms, the like that worked with linen and great sopping washing pots. Washerwomen or was it laundresses? Sarah couldn't remember. She rubbed her arm were the laird had pinched her skin and grimaced, he'd near dragged her down the whole staircase to the bottom of the tower. The baron was not a kind man, Magnus had been right about that.

'May I go home now?'

'Soon child. Baron Bothwell has asked that you stay here for a while, what with the coming child. You will be more comfortable here, or would you rather return to that hovel of a cottage you live in? Come along.'

The washer women took her through a series of long corridors to a good sized chamber. Once in the room, Sarah's mouth gaped open, never had she seen such comfort and finery. Beside a roaring fire, central to the room was a beautiful and ornate wooden bed, framed by silky drapes. As Sarah reached out to caress the silky fabric, one of the women sucked in her breath and slapped away her hand.

'Keep your hands to yourself, hinny – you're filthy. We've orders to strip off your rags, then wash the filth from you. So lift up them scrawny arms and make it sharp. We haven't all day.'

Sarah complained. 'Now? But the stream is so far away and 'tis freezing this time of year.'

One of the washer women laughed. 'What's got into you lassie? They'll be no going to the stream the day. We will scrub you here – in front of the fire until you are spotless clean.'

Sarah's jaw dropped. 'Here? How am I supposed to wash here?'

'Silly goose. You'll see.'

They guided her to the fire and removed her worn clothes. From behind a screen they fetched pail after pail of steamy water to fill a large tub. Instead of jumping straight into it, Sarah gawped at the tub like a dog with its tail between its legs. With trepidation, she raised one leg to test the water with her toe.

''Tis warm.' She beamed an idiot smile.

34

'Aye, go on then – in you go. We need to wash the grime from ya, lassie.'

Sarah faltered, her eyes were huge and her mouth gaped open. 'I can't. I've never seen the likes of that before, what if I drown in there? '

'Nonsense girl, get in. You'll be quite safe.'

In the end they manhandled her into it. Sarah was no competition for their muscular arms. But once in, she yelped with glee and splashed the water. It was a welcome change to bathing in an ice cold stream. It took the two laundresses a good half hour to dissolve the filth from her body, and even longer to dry her hair by the warm of the fire. But once dried, Sarah gawped in amazement as they took a louse trap and combed through her tangled locks, till her hair shone like spun gold.

***

'Lord' Almighty. What on earth was that? That is a devil contraption if I ever saw one. It could have killed me, Robbie.'

'It's a trap for bad men, poachers, trespassers…' Robbie nodded.

Alice gasped, as if unable to comprehend the wicked instrument of torture before her. 'That's evil. Who put it there?'

'Father,' the boy preened.

Alice felt a shiver run down her spine, the boy actually seemed proud of the fact.

'Father has every right to protect his land. Serves the poacher's right if he steps on it - shouldn't be trespassing on private land in the first place, should he?' Robbie declared in a haughty voice.

Alice shuddered and wrapped her arms around her for warmth. 'Never mind that, Master Robbie – we should return to the house. 'Tis getting dark and I don't want you to catch a chill.'

Robbie dismissed her and shooed her away, the muscles in his jaw twitching. 'No. I have to make the trap ready again. Father will be cross if he knows I've tampered with it.' He dropped to his knees to prize the metal springs apart.

Alice took charge and knelt to the ground, taking care not to spoil her dress. 'For goodness sake, move away from it – you'll hurt yourself. Here, let me help you,' Alice wrapped her small fingers around the metal clamps to pull them apart. 'This is very dangerous. Don't come here again. Are you listening to me?'

'You can't order me about, you're just a servant.'

'Do it yourself then,' said Alice before moving away.

Robbie bit his lip and circled the trap. Alice knew that he was all the while taking a wee glance at her – but she continued to ignore him and crossed her arms over her bosom, not afraid to show her displeasure. As anticipated the master soon grew tired, groaned and yelled out loud: 'All right – you do it. You just need to open it up again'

It took Alice just a moment to set up the trap, but in the process she cut herself on one of the trap's sharp teeth. 'See I told you it was dangerous.' She sucked the blood from her finger, and then covered the trap with soil and leaves. When they stood a distance away from it all they could see was hue of colours, red, amber and a yellow-green. Before they reached the boundary wall, Robbie found a withered dandelion and plucked it from the soft earth. With one hand outstretched he offered it to Alice.

'A peace offering.'

'Thank you,' she said before placing it behind her ear.

'Wee the bed, wee the bed,' chanted Robbie.

***

After dinner, William sought out the two laundresses. Each of them stood looking at him like two hounds waiting for a bone. William shivered, they were damned ugly the pair of them, and the size of the muscles in their arms, he wouldn't like to fight either of them.

'The dress?'

The bigger woman answered. 'We did like you said and rolled the dress in herbs, mint and angelica was all we could find, but I think you'll be happy with the result.'

The other woman interrupted: 'Aye, the aroma is really quite pleasant, faint and sweet even, like the peaceful smell of lingering incense.'

William thanked the laundresses and threw each of them a shiny coin, then made his way to his chamber. Through dim candlelight, he peered into the reflection of a looking glass, tilted his head this way and that, picked up some mulled wine and entered a secret door. William knew the passageway well, he often wondered of the priests that fled here during the reformation to hide within the priest's hole. A wave of nausea overcame him near a sword scarred archway; beyond the arch another concealed door loomed in the near distance. He paused, and then turned as though to go back to his chambers, then turned again, in doubt of whether to venture forth, to explore the soft flesh that lay within. Thus, in that dark passageway he paced up and down, conscious of beady green eyes upon him, eyes of providence, watching, waiting – judging. Of a sudden the ancient walls seemed to close in on him, prompting him to follow his destiny, a path of ruin and sin.

'Lord give me strength, a man has needs. Must I always endure this void that plagues me so? I love her still…' His words echoed and bounced off the damp stone walls. He reached the door and pushed.

Silence.

A sickly amber light.

A girl with golden hair, neck bowed, sat quietly upon a bed in one of his wife's old dresses. She was barefoot. Time stood still. He closed his eyes and inhaled deeply, the smell of herbs came to him immediately sending fire into his veins.

'Greta.' He called out.

The girl stood up, stretched out both hands, white palms exposed as though to indicate she is empty handed and possesses nothing.

'I am not Greta. I am Sarah. Where is Magnus?'

The baron winced, so many questions. What to do? For just a moment he faltered. Then he soothed the girl with soft words and empty promises.

'Do not be alarmed. My intentions are entirely innocent.' With steady hands he slipped a vial of valeriana into mulled wine, it always helped if a lassie was docile, disorientated and weak – especially with what he had in mind. As usual, once he allowed himself to think of such things, a delicious tingle began at the tip of his yard. His excitement built, and set William off into a frenzied state – drawing curtains, closing windows and stopping up all key-holes. After a good few hours he untied her naked arms and legs from all four corners of the bed. An empty claret jug lay on the floor beside her, a moth fluttered inside it, its wings furiously beating like a trapped bird. Opposite the jug a birch whip formed an s-shape on the floor, three drops of scarlet blood beside it, each circle bigger than the other.

***

As winter passed, a fresh breeze swept across the Lowlands, and with it came the first flowers of spring, stretching their petals to a golden sun. At Castle Wood, both Magnus and Sarah, were sorely missed, though life with all its disappointments and splendour went on. Sabine cupped a hand over her brow to scan the horizon; her gaze fell upon castle grounds. Twice a day, at dusk and dawn, Sarah's mother stood near the castle wall, waiting for her lassie to reappear. The sight always disturbed Sabine, because with a sickened heart, Sabine feared Sarah's mother waited in vain. Near the boundary wall, Sabine paused before approaching the woman, her face pale and forlorn. Within her arms she carried a child's shawl, no doubt homespun from her own spinning wheel.

Sabine placed a hand upon her shoulder soft like. 'No sign of her?'

'Nae,' Sarah's mother held the shawl to her body and inhaled its scent, her shoulders sagged as she did so, and from the corner of her eye a tear was spent. 'This shawl was hers when she was a wee bairn, a bonny child our Sarah, not the brightest of children mind, but a good lassie all the same. I've mended it for the coming bairn. The child is due in a month or so. I should be helping Sarah now, shouldn't I,' her voice cracked with emotion, 'to prepare her to bring forth the child?' She sobbed.

Sabine shook her head. 'Aye. I can't fathom it. It's like they disappeared, her and Magnus...'

These words of a sudden seemed to have an effect on Sarah's mother, and caused her eyes to brighten and press her hands together in prayer. 'Maybe they've ran off to make a new life together. That's it. They've ran away to Edinburgh or England and now they are free, Sabine. They are free!'

'Aye, maybe that's it.' Sabine said sadly.

CHAPTER 4

The lying-in chamber buzzed with activity. Attendants darted here and there fetching water and linen and more peat for a good fire. Near the hearth, old Getrud, or *Klok Gumma* as she preferred to be called stood open mouthed, examining a parturition chair made from elm and oak, with a removable keyhole seat. With bright, lucid eyes, she examined the hole in the seat, a clear route no doubt for the emerging child. Dead centre of the chair's high back, a religious icon decorated the head rest. Klok Gumma marvelled at the artwork and traced a finger across the smooth woodwork. With an excited wave of the hand, she caught the eye of the senior midwife and gestured for her to inspect it too, and to her surprise, the midwife did so at once.

'What a splendid birthing chair. Look how the icon is positioned just above the point where the mother's head will rest. How ingenious, the Lord will protect her throughout the birth.' Klok Gumma stared at her colleague with beady eyes and waited for her reply. But to her utter amazement the midwife did not even look at the icon, and carried on a conversation across the room with two of her assistants, completely ignoring Klok Gumma. In fact, it took a while for the midwife to acknowledge her at all, and when she did it was to belittle her.
'Aren't you one of the cunning folk, a Scandinavian woman of herbs? Run along now and fetch your black book, we might need it later – perhaps.'
As the senior midwife departed, darkness fell upon Klok Gumma's wizened face. 'Tis always a reason for folk's bad manners, she supposed. For a short while she observed this new midwife with wary eyes, suddenly realising she was a person busy doing nothing at all. From the look of things, she liked the sound of her own voice, barking out this order and that to a small army of maidservants, while completely ignoring the cries of the expectant mother. Klok Gumma picked up her skirts, and with no thought of consequence, contrived to tend to the girl.

'Oh dear Lord, you gave me such a fright. You look so much like my own girl, Greta. Are you all right child? Are the pains coming fast?'

'Aye.'

The poor lassie rested on all fours and had the look of a crazed animal. Alone with no one to help her, she whimpered and wailed and called out for her mother. Every time a new pain came her cries became louder, and still the new midwife and her assistants ignored her. Klok Gumma grumbled and shook her head, this would never have happened in the old days, it was time to take matters into her own hands. As the women folk fetched water, linen and swaddling for the coming child, she reached out to the expectant mother, and offered a comforting hand.

'Sweet girl, I'm going to help you, now take my arm.' With one sinewy arm around the expectant mother, the old wise woman supported the lassie all the way to the birthing chair.

'Breathe away your pains, child. What is your name?'

'My name is Sarah. Have you brought your black book, Klok Gumma? can I see it?'

'No. I've no such thing. Why ever would you think that?.'

'You've a witches book, the women told me…'

'That's nonsense.'

Sarah panted her way through another twinge. 'I do not understand…'

Klok Gumma laughed. 'Nonsense I tell you, the women here are just threatened by my kind. I'm one of the cunning folk, a woman of herbs, with neither witchery or a black book to aid me. The black arts are forbidden here, child. Be careful what you say, I don't want to end up like my mother…'

'What happened to her?'

'They tortured her… and then took her head off with an axe.'

Sarah's eyes near popped from her head. 'They did that to your…' and then another pain began.

'Never mind that now, child, there you go, ease yourself back nicely into the chair…there you go, oh don't grit your teeth like that, you'll bite off yer tongue.'

Klok Gumma dropped to her knees and looked powerfully into the girls' eyes. The lassie looked pale and tired, and there was a terrified expression in her eyes. With each passing moment she became more agitated, and more alarmed at the prospect of her coming child.

'Be brave, child. Try to relax between the pains. You'll need your strength now more than another time in your whole life. Just keep breathing through those pains then rest. It will be over sooner than you think.'

'I will try. I will really. But is it too late to change my mind now? I'm too weak. I cannot do it. I'm so afraid. I want my mither.' A tear rolled down the lassies face. With trembling fingers, she reached for Klok Gumma's bony hand and wept.

Klok Gumma's eyes widened. The lassie reminded her of her own dear daughter, Greta, banished to Hollyrood. The likeness was uncanny. She hoped that if Greta was to become a mother one day, she would be there to support her through the birth. But where was this poor girl's mother? Klok Gumma's brows bunched together, she opened her mouth to question a passing maidservant, but this only drew attention to herself and the expectant lassie.

'Get away from the girl. 'Tis not your business old woman.' Someone shouted.

Klok Gumma's cheeks burned, *oh the shame of it, the old laird would never have allowed the women to treat her so badly*. Once she had been a respected wise woman…now she was just a *useless* old woman, her glory days were long gone. She could hear the whispers, and the disparaging comments. She bowed her head and made her way to the far side of the room, and fought for a space near a couple of kitchen hands preparing a brew. Together they prepared a caudle of wine, warmed with sugar and spices; to lift the expectant mothers' spirits. But Klok Gumma wouldn't let it rest there, once the brew was cooling, she tapped one of the kitchen hands on the shoulder and demanded: 'Who is she? Why hasn't the lassie her family around her – and where are the gossips to witness the birth?'

'That's not our concern. Our instructions are to assist with the birth and that is all.'

Klok Gumma's eyebrows knotted together. It seemed strange the lassie not having her kinfolk around her and no gossips – who ever heard of a lying-in without gossips? Something was definitely wrong. Above the din, as each new pain came, she heard the midwife urging the lassie to press back onto the back of her seat and to grasp the armrests. The birthing, like many other births dragged on and on. Before long, Klok Gumma took to biting her fingernails, the frustration of not being able to help was more than she could bear. She frowned…why had the new baron employed the services of this new midwife anyway? Hadn't she always served them well?

After several hours, to all those present, it became obvious that it was to be a difficult birth, and thus a change occurred in the senior midwife. Not just her manner mind, but in her voice, which became more and more shrill with each passing moment. Suddenly she turned to Klok Gumma and cried: 'You…wise woman, come here please, I need your assistance.'

Klok Gumma stabbed a finger to her chest.

From somewhere in the room, one of the women hissed. 'Hag – witch, she's only fit to wash the lice from peasant's heads.'

The senior midwife took offense to this and waved a menacing finger. 'Klok Gumma has served the Bothwell family for many years. Have some respect. She's a valued wise woman and I will not tolerate you berating her.'

'But you dismissed her earlier…and look at her, she looks like a witch.' One of the women complained.

'Nonsense. Superstitious nonsense. Hold your tongue and be silent all of you. I need Klok Gumma to help me press down upon the mother's stomach. The wise woman might be old, but she is strong. She knows more about childbirth than any of you, so hush!'

Klok Gumma nodded, and the sides of her lips stretched into a smile, no doubt surprised at the midwife coming to her defence. Rolling up her sleeves, she got to work, kneeling upon the floor to observe the midwife at work. She noted that she sat on the floor facing the prospective mother, encouraging her to breathe and push, her face flushed and contorted as though she were in labour herself. The chief midwife did all the things Klok Gumma would have done, but now that all else had failed, she frantically began to massage the young lassie to speed dilation.

After a while the midwife stopped and placed her head in her hands. In a moment she regained her composure and looked up, her face all flushed. 'It's hopeless, I've tried everything and no matter what I do, the child will not come. It must be in a bad position, all that is left is to try a method of version.'

The old wise woman nodded and bit her tongue. With one hand she rummaged through her bag of herbs, keeping one eye on the midwife all the while, who despite several attempts to hasten the birth, invariably failed.

'Oh Lord help us – still she suffers the sins of Eve. Oh what am I to do?' The chief midwife threw up her hands and began to pray, as though to remove herself from the sad state of affairs.

Klok Gumma sighed and remained calm. In all her years of delivering babies she never once panicked, or quarrelled with a fellow wise woman. No matter how rude this woman might have been to her earlier, she was not a woman to hold a grudge, and so she reached out a sinewy hand to the stricken woman and whispered in her ear. 'Can you instruct the others while I attend the girl? We need fresh straw, and the fire is getting low. Get the women to add more peat to the fire?'

The midwife nodded, and then dared to peek at poor Sarah, who looked deathly pale. 'I owe you an apology old woman…'

'No matter. Now please allow me to attend the girl. '

Once alone, Klok Gumma placed a hand to her heart and closed her eyes. She was from a long line of cunning folk and knew the art of magic well. From beneath her petticoats she pulled out her black book and a silver charm. Once her magic was done, with skilful hands she took out two white lily roots and some ergot of rye, then crushed them into a bowl, and then tipped the emetics into the spiced wine.

The girl sagged against the chair, eyes drooping with exhaustion; it took a few slaps to make her alert. There wasn't time for sentimentality. Harsh though it may seem, a good slap to the face could make all the difference between life and death… for a woman and the wean. 'Now then, young lassie, I need you to stay awake because I have a special brew here I need you to drink. That's it, good girl, now drink all of it and then push hard. A few more pushes and all the pain will be gone.'

Within half an hour the child was born.

***

As Sarah delivered her wee baby into the world, the child's father, Magnus, languished in a squat cell, so low in structure, he could barely stand. Like a dwarfed miner, he staggered about, pacing his cell as best he could, fists clenched at his sides, and so alone. Shut off from sun, fresh air and human contact, a couple of his back teeth fell out, and his skin became so wafer thin and pale it appeared to glow in the dark. With the passage of time, a demon took possession of his brain, and caused him to see things, and worse still, hear strange voices. Immersed within a dark underworld, he was now sensitive to the faintest of sounds… the drip drop of water, or a rat scratching for food. One such noise presented itself now, a strange shrieking sound, like the mewing call of a sea gull ashore. Soon the noise grew louder. It triggered another sense, heightened by the pitch dark, a familiar smell - warm, milky, feminine - it reminded him of when he'd held his baby sister when he was a wee bairn. His knee scraped against a rough stone, he ignored the pain and sniffed up again. There it was again, that warm and milky smell, and then in the distance, a glowing torch illuminating the pitch black.

From the darkness emerged the baron, holding a writhing infant in one arm and a torch in the other. As the baby began to squall, Magnus pulled himself up to standing and stretched his hands through the prison bars. He begged, he wept and for a moment Magnus was so confused by what he was seeing, he foolishly believed all would be well, and that the baron would free him and allow him to hold his first born.

'Yes. It is yours. Take a look.'

Magnus cried and managed to blurt out. 'Let me hold it. Please. is it a boy - girl?'

'You don't need to know, Magnus. You're going to rot in here for the rest of your life. You'll never see this baby again.'

Magnus's heart sank as he was plunged once more into darkness.

***

The baron stood outside a small bed chamber, every now and then he moved aside to allow a busy woman to pass. Despite his superiority and curiosity, not once did he chance to venture inside, beyond the door was strictly a woman's domain. It would be foolish to enter now…but soon, well he was willing to take a chance. Several women came and went, usually with linen or pails of water, he even seen one carrying a quantity of bloodied rags.

'Good Lord,' he cried. It looked as though someone had been murdered. He closed his eyes and thought of Matilda and the birth of their son, Robert. William's forehead crinkled, for the life of him he couldn't remember the happy event, no doubt he was away somewhere or other. He rubbed a hand over his stubbly chin, time to face facts…what to do with Magnus's peasant girl and her brat. He signalled to one of the maids leaving the bed chamber.

'You. Has she brought forth the child?'

'Aye.' Nodded the maid.

'Well what is it then?'

The maid trembled. 'A girl child my lord. It is a girl. The mother is too weak to feed it; I've been sent to fetch a wet nurse.'

It wasn't long before a buxom country lass arrived. She followed the sound of wails, and walked right pass the baron into the bed chamber, completely disregarding him. In short, it was as though he wasn't even there. He pushed open the door and stepped inside, the peasant girl lay unconscious on the bed, he ignored her and turned his attention to the wet nurse. She already had the wriggling brat within her arms. Slowly, she brought the child's head toward her breast. It parted its lips a little but did not suckle, so, she squirted a little milk into its mouth and immediately the child latched on. William flushed and turned away, but before he left the room, he called out to her… the wet nurse, and said: 'Please see to it that the child is comfortable. I will make the necessary arrangements for you and the child directly. Everything you need for yourself and the baby will be granted.'

The wet nurse nodded and then returned to her task. After that, for some reason (he could not fathom why) he visited the bairn every day. She was a bonny child, and in truth it brought him great comfort to watch her suckle from the breast of her nurse. And so, as a consequence, the

45

child he decided to keep. But the mother, well he had no further use of her, for obvious reasons she had to be removed. What to do? The dungeon? Banishment? Then the baron had an idea. A few days after the birth of the child, he decided to make a sport of Magnus's peasant girl. And so excited was he at the prospect of this sport, instead of sending someone for the girl, he fetched her himself. The lying in chamber resembled a pigsty when he entered, the peasant girl was such a lazy slut, all she seemed to do was lie about on her bed all day. When he ordered her to dress and vacate the room, she at once cried out in distress.

'Take pity on me, Baron Bothwell, I am still weak from the birth. Can't I stay here a little longer?'

'Nonsense girl. Your kind give birth in the fields and toil not long after. On your feet, I've little time.'

'But I haven't any shoes and this dress, it be tight on me after the birth.. May I have my own clothes returned, and my shoes?'

'All these questions about rags…aren't you curious to know about your child, or have you forgot?'

'I have not. Is it well?

'Yes.'

'May I see it?'

'You may not. Now, follow me.'

The damned girl took an age to climb the stairs to the tower, a couple of times she had to stop to place a hand against the wall to steady herself, as though fearful that she might fall. The baron groaned, and then one eyebrow arched, he resisted the urge to curse, and then continued without her.

'Hurry.' He called out to her.

By the time he reached the top, sweat glistened upon his forehead. He stretched his neck backwards towards a bruised sky, as a murder of cawing crows fluttered and circled above. One of them settled on a pepper-pot turret, its cry ringing into the sultry air. Two henchmen stood stationary at opposite ends of the tower walls. William nodded to one of them before peering down the tower steps.

'Ah here at last, what kept you woman? Look at that sky. A storm is on its way for sure,' he placed two hands upon her shoulders, then removed her cap and reached down to stroke her soft hair, just as he would his hunting dogs. But then he twisted and winded the soft locks around his finger and yanked hard.

'Up you go,' he pulled on her hair again, wrenching her head upwards till tears rolled down her face.

'Up you go – up there,' he gesticulated towards the turrets.

William watched the lassie's face slacken and her mouth gape open like a gormless idiot.

'Up where?'

'Next to the crow, silly girl, hurry now – I haven't all day. Up you go, on top of that turret.' William nodded for one of his henchmen to help her, and then whispered into his ear: 'She's a wee bit unsteady, help her up will you, and then tie her hands.'

The baron shuffled his feet, all the while fidgeting as he waited for the woman to stop snivelling and stand upright on the turret to have her hands tied. His eyes washed over her, for just a moment she lost her balance and with her hands fastened tightly behind her back, she did well to stop herself tumbling off the tower.

'Oops, you nearly fell then, silly girl, nearly spoiled the game. There, there, no need to cry – 'tis only a bit of sport, as long as you listen to what I say, you will be fine. Now take heed, the rules to this game are simple, they have stayed the same for hundreds of years. Once the captive's hands are tied behind their backs, they're obliged to jump twelve-foot gaps between the towers. That's all, very simple. Of you go girl.'

'My name is Sarah, my Lord and I am not your captive. Please let me go, I promise to be good…I'll do anything but this.'

The baron smiled and then leapt up to the turret beside her. He placed two hands upon her shoulders and looked deep into the peasant's eyes. 'You will do as I say.'

'What if I refuse?'

He stroked her hair as though to soothe her and then wrenched her head forward so that they stood near the edge of the turret. Tiny figures moved beneath them in the courtyard below. 'You'll end up down there.' And with a violent jolt he pushed her forward so that she tipped over the edge, the hair in his grip the only thing saving her from imminent death.

Sarah howled like a terrified animal, and as her legs frantically thrashed around in the air, desperately trying to find a footing, the baron and his henchman laughed and cheered her on.

'See how she fights when under pressure, that's the spirit. Better to do as you are told now, girl. Jump the turrets or I'll push you off again by your hair. Understood?' He pulled her back atop the turret by her hair and left her alone upon the tower walls.

The baron turned to his henchmen then and opened out his arms. 'Well that's my fun for today. Get her down.'

***

On dreary days, the master's son liked to explore his ancestral home. In the castle, there seemed to be a never-ending expanse of cob-webbed corridors and locked doors. The fact that some of these chambers were locked and unobtainable made them all the more appealing to a laddie. So, just before noon, young Robbie made his way to the east wing that he had yet to explore. Through a dim, wood-panelled hallway, he shuffled along, every now and then catching a glimpse of the gloomy paintings above. Robbie shivered, the majority were disturbing portraits with dull eyes that seemed to follow his every move. At the very end of the main corridor, deep within the east wing, stood a double doorway decorated with gargoyles and devilish nymphs; at this point he faltered and considered turning back. It wasn't just the creatures see, it was the colour of the door, bog black, that frightened him. After a few deep breaths, he stepped forward, and reached for the doorknob, his heart throbbed as the turned the knob and pushed slowly. Straight ahead was a steep step, just one leading to lower ground. As Robbie stepped downwards, a strange feeling washed over him, a queer sensation as though someone was standing directly behind him, their soft breath tickling the nape of his neck. What a strange fancy, he thought as he entered a darkened chamber. The temperature dropped suddenly, his breath formed puffs of wispy cloud in the cold air. At the end of the chamber, on a huge panelled wall was a large portrait. In the dim light he could just make out the features of his father. But on closer examination he discovered the eyes to be too narrow and the lips less

48

cruel. This must be a picture of my grandfather, the one I was named after, Robbie decided, the first Baron – Robert Bothwell. In less than an hour or so, Robbie sat rubbing his grumbling stomach, covered head to foot in cobwebs and dust. He was tired and bored of his exploring game now, near every room of the east wing he found to be locked. Not a single thing he found, bar one room, in desperate need of repair. Within it a rowan tree sprouted through a hole in the wall, and near every surface crawled with ivy, moss and mice and bat droppings.

***

Matilda's eyes were dull, empty even, like a dead fish. Her hair as always was kept neat but lacked style. She wore no decoration and remained plain and chaste; this is how her husband preferred her. She'd wed William many years ago in a fine Kirk of Scotland, a grand affair, and of course a deeply religious one. On the day they wed, William told her marriage was the culmination of God's plan for man and a woman, and from that day on, he became her husband, and therefore the head of his wife, as Christ was the head of the church. After ten long years of marriage, he had little changed, and in truth she knew as little about him now as she did then. William avoided her. He lacked affection. Matilda tried to pretend she cared not, but in truth she did. Many a time she caught her husband scowling at her, his manner all disenchanted and forlorn. Not once did he consider her feelings, or how his treatment affected her. She stooped, her head sagged low. Matilda of late wept for no reason at all, she felt hopeless, unsightly and alone, Lord she had done since the birth of Robbie. Perhaps that was it? Since the birth of her son there had been no more issue, could she be barren? Perchance William resented the fact that she had not brought forth more children? A wife's music is the cry of children, and here she had failed. What on earth to do, thought Matilda? Dare she venture to sacred springs? Or off to a kirk to rub her belly against the statue of a sacred saint?

Then one morning everything changed. It happened as Matilda drank tea in the great hall. Meticulous as ever, she planned out her day, and then sorted the days' meals. With the aid of her trusted housekeeper she arranged a menu. Taking a quill, Matilda scrawled in long spidery

49

handwriting, recording all provisions to be used. This had to be done, as it was her experience that most cooks, given the chance, sold off surplus and leftover food to peasant folk at the door. Absolutely everything had to be accounted for. Hence, the housekeeper possessed a large set of keys, and was responsible for looking after and locking away the most expensive victuals. Once the menu was completed, Matilda sipped the last of her tea, nodded to her housekeeper and stood to leave.

'Where are you going?' William barred her passage.

'To the garden to take some air.'

'That can wait. Follow me,' he demanded.

William marched off towards the west wing; he took long strides, his favourite hunting dog snapping at his heels. Matilda's short legs stretched to keep up, her dainty shoe heels placed a great strain upon her ankles, and thus her foot twisted beneath her so that she tumbled to the ground. A passing servant offered her a hand; Matilda blushed before taking it, and then carried on towards her husband's private rooms.

'What took you, woman? I turn around and you're gone.' He boomed.

'William, I could hardly keep up with you, I nearly fell…'

'Very foolish. Haven't I told you to wear more sensible shoes? No matter, I have a gift for you, wife.' He produced a small basket and placed it within her arms.

Matilda felt a sinking feeling in the pit of her stomach, since when did William treat her to gifts? Then she remembered a time many years ago when he had brought her a puppy. She didn't even like hounds, the gift had been in fact another dog for him.

'Oh William – not another puppy, haven't we enough hounds? For goodness sake, the mess they make.'

'It is not a puppy. Open it, woman.'

Matilda peeled back a homespun blanket and sucked in her breath. The package contained a tiny infant – a bonny baby girl with wispy blonde hair and clear blue eyes. On impulse she lifted the child from the basket and held it to her bosom, inhaling its milky smell. A tear pooled in the corner of her eye as she kissed its wee head.

'Who is she, William?'

'A foundling child, she needs a mother, Matilda. Would you like to keep it – bring it up as your own?'

Matilda gasped and raised a hand to her mouth. 'Could I?'

'Yes. She already has a wet nurse. I can arrange for the woman and child to be moved nearer to your room.'

Matilda nodded, her dull eyes, brightening like a summer sky.

William clapped his hands together. 'That's settled then, the child will need a name. And Matilda, she is to be brought up in strict attendance of the worship of God'

'Of course, husband. I would like to name her Elisabeth if I may.'

'You may.'

'Oh look how she sucks on my finger, she's hungry, I must go to the wet nurse to feed her at once.'

'Yes in a moment.' He nodded and then held up a hand as though to strike her. 'Do not go yet, I've one more matter to discuss with you...'

Matilda flinched. 'Yes William.'

'I will no longer be visiting your bed chamber.'

CHAPTER 5

Sister Louise, for reasons she'd rather forget, found herself to be in Scotland… it had *not* been her choice. Not long after her arrival, she realised she cared not for this strange land. In fact, ever since setting foot upon Scottish soil, she felt utterly homesick. Everything was strange… the food, words, dialect, smells. Even the poor women at Magdalene Chapel were foreign to her, with their striking Celtic looks, and strange habits. Sister Louise wanted to go home. But here (for a short while at least) she had to remain. The nuns at Magdalene Chapel operated secretly under the protection of the Hammermen of Edinburgh., an amalgamation of men that embraced all those who worked on metal with a hammer. Since the reformation, in England and Scotland, there were no longer any abbeys or priories for women of the Catholic faith (the true faith) to thrive. Most nuns were tolerated and were given pensions even, but the ones who resisted risked execution fled to Europe, but longed to return. It was Sister Louise's task to find out if Scotland could return to the true faith once more, in the hope that the Protestants could be ousted once and for all. But now that she was here, she yearned to return to her own land. She missed her father, and that was odd indeed, as she hadn't missed him at all since entering Abbaye de Notre-Dame. But here, on this strange land, she felt his distance. Nevertheless, Sister Louise was made of stern stuff, from an early age she'd been taught to serve God, obey her superiors and do the Lord's work. So, despite feeling like a fish out of sea, she got on with it.

She took a deep breath. Some places felt peaceful, tranquil and were a pleasure to work in, Magdalene Chapel was not one of them. First of all the women had to hide their Catholic faith (as the Hammermen and benefactors of the chapel demanded it) and secondly, the women here were so melancholy with their sad faces, crooked backs and chapped hands. It was hard to imagine any of these women content once, or happy… not pale-faced and thin, moving silently through long corridors like grey wraiths. Sister Louise shuddered. She had to leave this place.

There was a sombreness here that chilled her bones. She *had* to flee as quickly as possible.

'Sister Louise.'

A feeling of dread swept over the French woman.

Abbess Hoppringle stared at her with watery eyes. 'Didn't the nuns of Abbaye de Notre-Dame teach you anything? You dawdle child. To be idle is to allow Lucifer into your heart. We have a new girl today. Just arrived. I need you prepare her for life at Magdalene. Like all the other unfortunates here, she is of poor moral character. We must wash away her sins. Penance is what the girl needs and strict silence, and what better way to wash a woman's misdeeds away than in the chapel laundry.'

'Yes Abbess.'

'But first you must take this, sister.'

The abbess handed her a knife. Sister Louise's eyes widened. The blade was silver, plain with small wooden handle, it reflected light as she twisted it in her hands. It didn't appear to be particularly sharp.

'What would you like me to do?'

'You'll see.' The abbess clapped her hands together and motioned to one of the sisters hovering near the main door. 'Fetch the new girl.'

A moment later a young woman entered the main hall and approached the abbess. Sister Louise's eyebrows bunched together at the sight of her, something was not right, of that she was sure. The maid was a plain country girl, but she was dressed in fine cloth. How on earth did a peasant afford such luxury? Furthermore, beneath her fine skirts she was barefoot. But before she could open her mouth to declare her confusion, the abbess ripped the serf's white cap from her head.

'Cut it off, all of it, no dawdling and right down to the scalp.'

The peasant girl began to sob like a small child. Sister Louise glanced from her girl's childlike face to the abbess's harsh expression – as though hoping and praying for a change of heart, an act of compassion, but there was none forthcoming. The abbess had a heart of stone, she wouldn't listen to her, a foreign girl from across the channel. Besides, however cruel this might be, wasn't this God's work, and what she was obliged to do, no question? Thus, she nodded to her superior and began. In hindsight, she would have asked for the blade to be sharpened.

'Mademoiselle, please, if you remain still this will not take long.'
With much reluctance, Sister Louise wrapped her fingers around the knife, then picked up a long lock of hair. With her other hand she placed a hand on the girls' shoulder, and rubbed softly in a circular motion until the girl relaxed. To her relief, the girl responded, and soon, the sounds of weeping ceased. Thus, as lock after lock was hacked off, a great golden puddle formed in a halo upon the cold floor.
Sister Louise felt a lump form in her throat. To her disgust, the abbess seemed to take great delight in the indignity of the situation, because once it was over, she even ran her bony fingers across the now stubby head of the peasant girl. 'Not so fine now are we serf? A fancy filly you are no more. Now take off that pretty dress, you'll not be needing it anymore. Don't be shy now girl. You've nothing we haven't seen before.'
The French nun cringed, her mouth twitching at the corners. The sight of the young woman protesting at the indignity of undressing in a communal space was more than she could bear, but her reluctance only served to inflame the abbess, who then slapped the girl across her cheek. The abbess ripped the dress from her and then threw a drab shift and plaid at the girl. 'Now put these clothes on before I take the skin off your back.'
Without thinking Sister Louise muttered beneath her breath. 'Mon Dieu.'
The abbess's neck snapped to face Sister Louise. 'What was that sister? Do you have something to say?'
'No.' Sister Louise closed her eyes as a small part of her soul died inside.
The abbess cleared her throat. 'Make haste girl. What is your name?'
'Sarah.' She replied.
'You are mistaken. *Sarah* no longer exists. From hence forth you shall be known as Sorrow. Is that clear? Speak up, child.'
'Aye.'
'We do not say aye here. We say yes – and Mother is the correct manner in which to address me, do you understand?'
'Yes.'
'Yes what?
'Yes Mother?'

'Sorrow. You are to rise at five in the morning to say your prayers and ask forgiveness for all your wicked sins. After that you shall take breakfast in the great hall. At seven you will go to the laundries and wash away your sins. The other girls will teach you how to scrub till your hands are red raw. After that you will master the iron. And all of this you must do in strict silence. Do you understand?'

'Yes Mother.'

And so, this was Sister Louise's first day at Magdalene Chapel, a day she would rather forget. *It will take time*, she thought to herself...*to fit in*. But in truth, no matter how much time passed, she continued to detest the bland Scottish food, the weather, even the dour sisters. At least at the Abbaye de Notre- Dame there was the joy of singing and her beloved sisters, how she longed to return, but she could not.

Then, just as she contemplated leaving, Sister Louise noticed inconsistencies, and a queerness about the place. For instance, none of the girls at Magdalene were fallen women, except maybe one or two. In truth, most of the women were a mixture of troublesome wives, unmarried mothers, and pretty women considered too flirtatious. A small minority were in fact lunatic women. However, in spite of how or why they arrived there, they all had something in common – they were all admitted to the chapel by a male; either a family member or a priest claiming they were in great moral danger. This was a great cause of concern for Sister Louise, who wondered how many men were committed to institutions – for being too handsome, promiscuous or simply too flirtatious. Not a one she surmised with a cynical heart. For women, the weaker vessels dared not ask such questions – even in private. So for now, she put her concerns aside and got on with good Christian work.

Time passed, more than she thought possible to bear. Thus, Sister Louise became well accustomed to the wretchedness and drudgery that was Magdalene Chapel. The strict regime of morning prayers, the code of silence, and harsh work schedule, all served to break the women's spirits. For the most part the women of Magdalene shuffled around, pallid and exhausted, like beasts of burden. Sister Louise felt pity for them all. Then, at that moment, a young girl passed her, tufts of short yellow hair escaping from her grimy cap. It reminded Sister Louise of the young blonde peasant girl, Sorrow, the one she'd had to hack off her hair. The maid hadn't fared well – of late she resided near the fringes of a dividing wall, an ivy wall separating sane from the insane. At Magdalene it was said that once a poor creature crossed the ivy wall into the lunatic side, there was no going back.

Sister Louise's shoulder's sagged; there was something about Sorrow that tore at her heart. The begging and pleading for her new born child for example, perchance the child existed, perhaps not, for Sorrow was awfully young. Anyhow, regardless of the newborn's existence, to Sorrow the lost child was indeed *real*, so real that she pined for it, night and day until she became quite unwell. Not long after, a physician was sent for. He quickly discovered a problem with the girl's four humours. It was common in those days to have trouble with any one of the four humours; black bile, yellow bile, blood or phlegm. At any rate, the physician quickly deduced that the girl's blood was to blame, and so in order to relieve pressure and calm equilibrium, Sorrow, the peasant girl was bled.

For some reason, unknown to Sister Louise, the physician opened a vein in her throat. To do this, he used a small lancet and bled 20 ounces from her, and not long after, another 10 ounces. As a result, Sorrow became rather pale and unresponsive. During the third bloodletting session, in a seated position, the peasant girl began to shake like a wizened old woman, and then her eyes rolled back in her head. Sorrow was out cold.

'What's wrong with her?' She asked the physician.

'We must prevent inflammation if the girl is to recover. She's sleeping, nothing to worry about. The mind and body know instinctively when to rest.'

He fiddled with his lancet and then shook his head. Sister Louise thought him irritated, especially when he threw down his lancet so that it landed in the bleeding bowl. The physician cursed, then apologised. But instead of retrieving the knife, he began rummaging around in his leather bag.

'Shall I get it for you' Sister Louise pointed to the bowl.

'Nae. Leave it there. I'm not convinced the blade is sharp enough. Besides, I prefer my fleam. Ah here it is.'

Sister Louise glanced at this new device. A horn-handled fleam, made up of three blades, the physician proudly displayed the triangular sharp edges in a fan design. It looked hideous to her mind, just looking at it made her break out into a cold sweat.

'You're not going to cut her neck with that are you?'

'Aye. She must be bled repeatedly.'

Sister Louise swallowed hard. 'Mon Dieu. Is this necessary? She's weak. Too weak I fear.'

The physician shooed her away. 'Nonsense. If her life is to be preserved she must endure this minor discomfort. '

As the triangular blade sliced into the girls' neck vein, Sister Louise felt the room suddenly move, she held out a hand to the wall, steadied herself and tried to focus. But it was no use, she still felt dizzy, she began to sweat. Then a strange ringing began in her ears. The physician called out to her, but her hearing was so bad now, she couldn't hear what he was saying.

'Je dois y aller…I must go…' Then everything went black.

***

When the hallucinations began, Magnus embraced them, such was the depth of his loneliness. Thus, when his dungeon was visited by one of the fairy folk, a cunning little fellow named Ifyn, Magnus made sure to welcome him. They discussed many things together, farming, weather, and Ifyn's favourite subject – food. For hour upon hour they imagined tasty meals together, sweet, sour, hot, cold, baked, boiled or roasted – and all the while Magnus rubbed his growling stomach. How long had he been kept prisoner, and for what? He had no idea. The days and nights all blended into one. With each passing day, despair consumed him, and many a time he contemplated ending it all. But oddly enough, on the very same day he fashioned a long rope to hang himself with, two guards came along and interrupted him.

With his shoulders hunched low, Magnus crouched on the floor and stared into space. He resembled a strange, squat creature, hair and beard overgrown, his fingernails filthy and long, like hawk's talons. It was late afternoon when they dragged him from his cell, pinching his withered arms as they half walked and dragged him to another stony cave. And what a cave it was, a joy to behold, room enough to stand up in, with a chamber pot opposed to a hole. There was even clean water instead of stagnant puddles. Overwhelmed by such luxury, he didn't see the two guards creeping up behind him. He lashed out and then cowered like a beaten dog with his tail between his legs.

'Stop struggling man, we just need to cut your fingernails and hair, then we'll bring you a hearty meal.'

'But why?' Is what he wanted to say, but his lips were stuck together like glue.

After his meal, Magnus slept for the longest time. A hand held to his full stomach, content for the first time in ages. Shortly after awakening, he sat upright with his hand to his heart; a shrill noise frightened him – the sound of iron scraping on stone. Magnus crouched to the floor, curling himself into a ball in the corner of his new cell. Two turnkeys passed by, one either side of a noisy old man. A drunkard perhaps? For what felt like eternity the drunkard babbled on incessantly, though for the life of him, Magnus couldn't understand a word the old man said. Perchance he was a foreigner thought Magnus, an Egyptian or maybe even a Spaniard.

'Hold your tongue, Quaker. Hasn't your blasphemous nonsense brought you enough grief?'

The man continued to rant.

'I'm surprised he can say anything after today.' One guard said to the other.

Across from Magnus's cell, the noises of chains and hammers striking iron made a right din; no doubt they were putting the old man to the gad…or worse, Magnus shuddered to think. For a good half hour the noises continued, until eventually the guards left and at last came silence. Inquisitive by nature, Magnus peered through his bars. The Quaker lay on the floor in sackcloth; his shirt all stained at the front. The old man was all skin and bone.

'Can you hear me?' Magnus rolled up a small piece of bread in the palm of his hand and then threw it across to the old man's cell, luckily it flew through the bars.

No answer.

'Hello, Quaker. Can you understand me? Do you speak English – French? Can you hear me? You must eat, you'll not survive in here unless you eat.'

Silence.

Magnus sat forward, his sanity hanging by a thread, all at once his shoulders drooped to the ground. A low guttural sound emerged from deep in his throat, forming a hearty song. And like all good fairy folk, Ifyn joined in. They sang together till the wee hours of the morning and by the time his oats came Magnus lay fast asleep.

Two or three days went by, and not a sound came from the opposite cell. By now Magnus was indifferent, folk died in gaol all the while, especially the thin ones, in fact to pass on was a blessing. At least in death there was no longer pain, hunger…loneliness. But before long, it became obvious that the old man was alive…Magnus heard his laboured breathing, and every now and then he heard the odd snort. Beyond the iron bars he caught a glimpse of the Quaker, he was very still, but by some miracle he'd survived the first and second night. In the morning the Quaker began to cough…after that he began to choke.

'What is it?' Magnus cried.

'Water.'

Magnus's eyes widened. So the man wasn't foreign after all. 'Have you no pail?'

'It's frozen over.'

'Break the ice; it's most likely just the top layer.' Magnus said.

'No. It's frozen solid.'

'What's wrong with your voice?'

'They drove a nail through my tongue – the swelling has only just gone down.'

That explained the blood on his shirt, thought Magnus. 'But that first night, you never stopped talking, although I couldn't understand a word you said.'

The Quaker laughed. 'I was in agony, but I wouldn't let the bastards have the satisfaction. So I talked and talked till I hadn't a breath left…'

'You're fortunate they didn't rip your tongue out. What's your name?'

'Jacob.'

'I am Magnus.'

'How long have you been here?'

Magnus swallowed hard. 'I don't know. One, two years, maybe longer – I kept track of the days in my last cell, but then they moved me.'

'Why are you here?

'I've not a clue.'

'You must have done something to displease the laird.'

Magnus shook his head. 'No.'

'No man is without sin, Magnus.' Jacob sighed.

'True. But I have done nothing that warrants imprisonment – I am a serf that did not ask permission to marry that is all… oh I lay with my betrothed to ensure she carried my child and not his.'

'You denied him the right of the first night?'

'Aye,' answered Magnus.

Beyond the shadows, Jacob groaned. 'That was foolish, Magnus.' The Quaker struggled to his feet. The sounds of chains rattled as he crossed the cell to take a look at his fellow cellmate. A wizened face pushed up against the bars and sent his scruffy beard sprouting through the gaps like bushy rodents. 'Arh I see. Was she pretty?'

'Aye.'

'Well, well. Women bring a thousand miseries, Magnus. No doubt you've heard the tale of Eve or Jezebel?'

'Adam and Eve, aye, but not Jezebel.'

The Quaker, Jacob stood backwards and bobbed his head. 'Then you have something to look forward to, young man. Tomorrow you shall hear the tale of Jezebel.'

That night, for the first time in a long while, Magnus had something to look forward to.

***

On the subject of the young foundling child, Elisabeth, it is fair to say that young Robbie had little interest. The baby was a real nuisance and the fuss it created – people fawning and cooing all over it just grated his nerves. When the child's cries echoed through the cold corridors, Robbie ventured out-of-doors, and sprinted at top speed to the watchtower. As soon as the dry stone wall and tumbled stones came into sight, Robbie slowed his pace. It was a fine day, and as he strolled along he noticed a bird of prey, high above in a deep blue sky. The bird swooped and plunged; with his neck arched backwards, Robbie observed the hawk's progress, its majestic wings spread out beneath a golden sun. With one hand placed high to his forehead, Robbie followed its flight path, noting how the bird swooped lower and lower, no doubt towards its prey. But all the while, unknown to Robbie, he proceeded towards a patch of softened earth covered in leaves, his feet crunching into the earth, closer and closer, until a macabre snapping noise pierced the air. It happened so fast, his mind had no time to prepare itself. In his mind's eye someone else's leg lay beneath him all bloody and torn, as metal jaws smashed through flesh, muscle and bone. Rapidly his vision failed, the blue sky faded into darkness, the hawk's silhouette imprinted upon his mind's eye – and then everything went black.

When he awoke an old man stared into his face. He looked familiar, but when Robbie tried to talk to ask him who he was, his voice came out all hoarse. Tears rolled down his pale face. He tried to move, but his lower body felt all strange, he couldn't feel his legs and trembled all over.

'Help me.' He managed to mumble. 'I can't get up. I think it's my legs.' My dog can't get up either. No' since ye put an arrow in him.' The old man spat onto the ground.

'Please sir. I don't feel well. I'm cold. How did I get here and why can't I move?' Robbie began to cry then, and between sobs, his teeth chattered.

'God's punished ye boy for taking my animal. What did he ever do tae ye eh? I hope you die like he did.'

***

Serenity and devotion radiated from Jacob's face as he quoted from the bible again. "…and then Jehu went to Jezreel. When Jezebel heard about it, she painted her eyes, arranged her hair and looked out of a window. Throw her down!" Jehu said. "So they threw her down, and some blood splattered the wall and the horses as they trampled her underfoot."

'I don't understand.' Magnus frowned.

Jacob's brows knitted together. 'What is it you do not understand?'

'So Jezebel was a Phoenician princess who married King Ahab, and she converted him from Judaism to worship Baal. But why does that warrant her execution… and why was her corpse eaten by dogs?'

Jacob clapped his hands together and cackled like a wizened old hag. 'Magnus, you are as sharp as a double-edged sword.'

'But that does not answer my question, Jacob.'

'Jezebel was the power behind the throne, not King Ahab, and she believed in a god that was not theirs. Ahab's people were threatened by this. Think about it.'

Magnus nodded. 'No woman should have power over a man.'

'If only that were true.' Jacob nodded with a knowing smile.

'Why have you a 'B' burnt into your forehead, Jacob?'

'B for blasphemer.'

'How can that be when you preach the words of our Lord?'

'Quakers or Friends as we like to be called are a Priesthood of all believers. Many men are threatened by our ways, Magnus – just like Ahab's people. We Quaker's do not worship in kirk, we prefer to worship in the fields or orchards and hold all places to be equally sacred. Sometimes we worship in meeting houses and wait for the Holy Spirit to guide us.'

'You are a foolish man, Jacob – your faith has led to imprisonment and still you preach to the prisoners and guards.'

'Yes. My faith brings me much difficulty and hardship. But I will not abandon my faith, Magnus. To do so would be to abandon who I am, and I must be true to my heart. We must all try to act faithfully in two ways, inwardly to God and outwardly to man – for it is our duty, Magnus.'

'But they beat and punished you.'

'Aye, just like the Romans did to Jesus? *And they know not my pain. They are hurting themselves not me.*'

Through the cold and dark Magnus stretched out his hands, and to his surprise he wept for Jacob. 'You are good man, my friend.'

***

'Twas the ghillies first day, a day he'd never forget…at dusk, as he completed his rounds, he saw on the horizon something lying upon the ground. A creature of sorts, a small deer or hound. But as he got closer, a great pain began to throb beneath his breastbone, as he realised the creature was in fact a human form. Near a dry stone wall, caught in a trap was a young laddie, his legs twisted beneath him at odd angles. The gamekeeper broke into a sprint, his breath whipped away by a howling wind. Once he reached the boy he fell to his knees and cried out in desperation: 'Lord 'Almighty - what evil has befallen ye?' With one ear pressed to the laddie's chest he heard shallow breaths, and the sound though weak and faint gave him hope for the moment. He squeezed the boys hand, it was icy cold. He acted quickly, instinctively knowing that time could mean the difference between life and death. With his face earnest he closed his fingers around the trap, and cursed all the while as he pulled the metal teeth apart. Thank god the lad's still unconscious, he thought as he tied a clout around the wound, before sweeping the boy up into his powerful arms.

He entered the castle entrance near the scullery, shouting out to all and sundry to help him. Maidservants and footmen gathered around, their mouths gaping wide open. The ghillie looked from one face to another, waiting for someone to take charge. When was somebody going to give him an order? For what felt like eternity, he stood dead centre of the room. The ghillie looked down, the boy's body felt limp in his arms, his heart was in his mouth as the boy's blood dripped upon the floor. Then cook arrived.
'Oh dear Lord, what has happened to the wee boy? Lie him on the table. Don't worry about the mess, we've more important things to worry about. How bad is he hurt?'
'It's no' guid, his leg is all crushed. Who is he?' The ghillie asked.
'The young master. We must send word to the baron and his wife, a surgeon must be sent for at once.' With one sweep of her arm, cook

removed all trace of vegetable peelings from the table, then summoned a servant to send news to the master's parents.

The ghillie held onto the table, knuckles white as he gazed down upon the boy. 'I found him near a watchtower caught in a trap.'

'The cook's eyes bulged. 'A trap? Och no he could have been trapped in it for hours.'

'Aye. Aye.'

That's when the screams began, high pitched shrieks of terror. The laddie regained consciousness, and all the ghillie could think to do was keep him still, by placing all his weight upon him. With cooks help, it took both of them to hold him down, all the while taking care to avoid his bleeding limb. But this was no easy task, the boy was strong. In great pains of agony, he thrashed to and fro, while calling out his father's name. But the baron did not come.

***

Matilda doted on the child, Elisabeth. It brought her great pleasure to gaze down upon the wee girl's rosy cheeks and bounce her upon her knee. The babe was such a vision of innocence, she hoped she had a fruitful and merry life ahead of her. Not like hers. Matilda shuddered and wrapped her arms tightly around her precious bundle. No, she wanted more for this wee girl, she didn't want it to mourn a stolen childhood like she did. Her fledgling years had been cut short. Betrothed at a tender age to the future Baron Bothwell of Castle Wood, Matilda was traded like common goods, and left to the mercy of a complete stranger. She wed far too young. But then, she'd had little say in the matter. Her only joy in life henceforth came when Robbie was born, and now he had a sister, Elisabeth, and they were a family at last. Thus, Matilda dared to smile for the first time in years.

The baby girl began to cry, Matilda soothed her and in doing so felt a dampness from her napkin. Her initial reaction was to call for the wet nurse to see to the child, but Matilda detested the woman, and so she decided to attend to Elisabeth herself. She found the act of caring for the child restorative, calming even. Once the child was dry, Matilda held the baby to her body, her chin gently resting upon the wean's head. Back and forth she rocked, oblivious to the fact that her serenity was not to last. A manservant arrived as she sang Elisabeth a lullaby. Matilda took one look at his ashen face and knew something was wrong.

'The young master, Lady Matilda, some ill fortune has…an accident…'

'Dear God, where is he?'

'He is in the scullery, the new ghillie found him near the old watchtower. We have sent for a surgeon….'

'And my husband?'

The servant's face turned vivid red. His eyes darted here and there, and though he opened his mouth to say something, no words came out.

'Speak up man.' Matilda cried.

'The Ma…ma… master. The baron is locked within his chamber; he won't come out.'

'Whatever to do mean you foolish man. Why would he do such a thing? You must be mistaken.'

Before the servant stuttered another word, Matilda pushed the child into his arms, picked up her skirts and raced to the scullery. A great scene of disarray awaited her, servants running here and there, some of them carrying linen and bandages, others water and blankets. In the centre of the room a strapping young man with a long bushy beard stood bent over a table, he appeared to be comforting a young boy, while the old cook, the one with the bad legs, stood beside him. Matilda froze, her mouth became dry. A boy cried out in pain, but it couldn't possibly be her boy, her brain refused to comprehend what played out before her. She simply could not believe it. She closed her eyes, and felt a tear run down her cheek, then jolted. A cold hand touched her elbow.

'Lady Matilda, you must be strong. The boy needs you. Don't stand there like a wet rag woman. Go to him.'

Matilda opened her eyes. The first thing she focused on was cook's face, the elder woman's eyes sparkled with beauty and kindness. What was her name? Eleanor, yes that was it, she was sure of it, she was the missing serf's mother…what was her son's name? Magnus, aye that was it. Could it all be some bizarre dream she wondered. But then the boy…*her boy* began to scream. She rushed to the table with dread in

65

her heart. Blood rushed to her temples, a whooshing noise filled her ears, the situation was dreadful. Poor Robbie's wee leg was all crushed and torn.

'Who did this to him?'

The tall man with the beard took offense to this remark and stood backwards in one swift motion. With just cook to hold him the boy near fell off the table, so Matilda had to act quickly and take the man's place, and as she did so she was amazed at the strength of her wee laddie as he thrashed about in great agony and pain.

'I will ask again, who did this to him?'

The man glared at her. 'What are ye suggesting woman? Nae one did anything tae the laddie. I just found him oot near the watchtower caught in a trap.'

Matilda shook her head, then signalled to a passing servant. 'Fetch something strong, claret, aqua vitae, anything…just be quick. Has anyone sent for Lang Sandy?'

'Aye, he is on his way.' Nodded the servant

Once the spirit arrived, Matilda supported Robbie's head and told him to drink, and as she did so she scolded the man like a woman possessed. 'Well how did this happen? I'm assuming you're the new ghillie. Did one of your hunting dogs attack him?'

'Nae. I've just told ye, I found him caught in a trap.'

Matilda shook her head then wiped the moisture from her eyes with the back of her hand. Her eyes narrowed as she stared into his piercing blue eyes. 'An animal trap?'

'Nae, this was no ordinary animal trap. This was bigger…'

'Bigger. How big?'

'Big enough tae trap a man.'

'That can't be so, we have no such traps at Castle Wood…'

'Gan see it for yerself.' The ghillie shrugged his shoulders and began to walk away.

'I am not finished with you,' Matilda screamed. 'Did I say you could leave?'

The gamekeeper stopped midstride. The muscles in his jaw twitched as he waited for the baroness to speak again.

'Who put the trap there?'

'I've nae got a clue. May I go noo?'

'Yes. Please do. But do not go far. I may need you again and I care not for your insolence.'

The muscles in the gamekeeper's jaws continued to twitch. One of his hands made a fist, but he breathed deep, nodded and left the room. As one man left another entered, and it was rather a spectacular entrance to say the least. One or two servants stopped what they were doing to stare at Lang Sandy as he strutted into the room, and he was quite a sight with his raven upon his shoulder and pet sheep trailing behind him. An apprentice boy came next to relieve him of the raven and sheep, before handing him his bag of surgical tools.

'Lady Bothwell, I came at once, I've brought my new apprentice boy, Donald. He's no bother and very competent. Now how is the wee master? I understand your ghillie found him injured and tied up his leg?'

Matilda nodded. 'Yes. I expect you'll need to speak to him, I'll send for him directly. Fetch the ghillie for me at once, Eleanor.' Matilda gestured to the cook.

'That won't be necessary...' Lang Sandy said as he eyed the old woman's swollen legs.

'No. Our cook doesn't mind, do you Eleanor?'

Cook glared and shook her head. 'Oh my Lady, can't you get one of the maids to fetch him, it's me legs see, they're causing me grief.'

Matilda puffed out her cheeks. 'Oh very well. Tell one of the maids to do it.'

The ghillie returned promptly. His face softened when he seen the boy, but grimaced at the sight of the baroness, he shifted from foot to foot, as though agitated, like a trapped animal. Nevertheless, he answered all of the surgeon's questions.

'Aye. The boy's leg was caught in a huge trap; I released him and tied ma neck chief around the limb tae stop the blood flow. Will that be all for noo? I've work tae be getting on wi'.'

Lang Sandy clapped his hands together. 'Ah do not fret man. Why are all you gamekeepers so keen to be out-of-doors? We won't keep you for much longer. But first we must thank you. We owe him our eternal gratitude, Lady Bothwell, don't we? Because if the ghillie hadn't acted as he did, the wee boy would have slowly bled to death; now let's take a look shall we?'

Matilda felt of a sudden very queer. From then on every noise around her became muffled, like someone had stopped up her ears. As she peered at Lang Sandy and his apprentice boy, their features became all blurred, as though she was viewing them through a great haze of fog. A gasp caught in her mouth as the surgeon lifted one corner of the neck chief around her boy's mangled leg, and suddenly her legs turned to mush. Before Matilda hit the ground, the ghillie caught her.
'Here, take these smelling salts. I think it best you go with this fine young man for a wee while, just till I've finished up here. Your son is in safe hands, I will do the very best I can for him, rest assured.'

In a daze, Matilda took the arm of the ghillie and allowed herself to be half walked – carried out of the room, but before she got through the door she heard the surgeon say to his apprentice: 'The leg has to come off, it's smashed to pieces, there's nothing else we can do.'

***

Once the mother had gone, the surgeon got to work. In spite of his eccentricity, he was a calm and diligent man, and at all times expected discipline and order. Before he even contemplated surgery, he made sure all his surgical tools were neatly set out before him, in preparation for the task ahead. Along with his apprentice boy, he made a checklist, making sure there were enough candles for good light; spirits to dull the pain, and of course plenty of bandages.
'Ready?' He asked the apprentice boy.
'Aye.'

At that moment Robbie stirred from consciousness, prompting Lang Sandy to hold him fast in his arms as he writhed and thrashed in great pains of agony. He beckoned to the apprentice boy for spirits and tipped the injured boy's head back. 'Now then, Robbie, I need you to sip some of this liquid to dull the pain. Do you think you can do that for me?'

Robbie whimpered and cried, face slick with sweat and tears, the black of his eyes huge like black pools. His sobs echoed off the walls, like that of some poor wounded creature, and as his throat grew hoarse his weeping ceased. 'Father,' he croaked.

'Be still, laddie, your father will be here soon. Drink it all up now, son, it will make you feel better,' Lang Sandy fed him more gin. A few sips later, young Robbie's eyes glazed over and held that faraway expression the surgeon had been waiting for. As the boy became limp in his arms he called out to a scullery maid: 'I need a couple of strong men, and be quick.'

The maid nodded and ran off towards an outbuilding. Before long she returned with two stable hands, neither looking too keen to be summoned. With sharp eyes, the physician looked the men over, no doubt wondering if they were strong enough for the job. One of them, the shortest looked queasy for sure.

'You all right, Shorty?'

'As well as can be. Can't the boy assist you?'

The physician laughed and shook his head: 'the boy is hardly strong enough to hold him while I take off his leg now – is he?'

The taller man took sharp, shallow breaths and nodded. 'So we need to hold him down while you…?'

'Aye and I've no time for any nonsense, do you hear me? Mark my word if I do not perform this amputation right now come morning he will be dead. Look away if you have to, but hold him down with all your might.'

The men nodded. And so it began.

First Lang Sandy removed the bloodied scarf from Robbie's leg. Then he picked up his knife and cut through the skin under the knee in one circular motion, through fat and muscle down to the bone, covering the table in sticky blood. The fact that the boy has passed out now made the job much easier, but nevertheless Lang Sandy operated swiftly, to prevent the laddie bleeding to death or perishing through shock. With steady hands, he tied the major blood vessels to prevent haemorrhage. He picked up the amputation saw. The stable hands began to quiver once he began to saw, and was there ever a more macabre or god awful noise? The physician thought not as he hacked through the lower leg. Once again though, the apprentice boy worked diligently and without respite, he would make a fine surgeon one day thought Lang Sandy, nerves of steel the laddie had, and not yet in his twelfth year. Once the leg was off, he gave it to his fearless apprentice boy.

'Donald, wrap it up safely. Put it somewhere safe away from the dogs.' The boy took the leg, swathed it with damp bandages, and then placed it within a hessian sack. While he went off to find it a safe place, his Master got on with pulling the excess skin over the stump of the leg, before bandaging the wound.

Lang Sandy nudged the shorter stable hand. 'That's it – all done. I'll be honest, I didn't think you'd have the stomach for it, Shorty. I'm impressed. Now pass us the gin will you?'

Shorty did as he was told, and handed him the bottle. Lang Sandy thanked him, wiped his hands on his bloody apron, and then took a few gulps of gin. He then returned the bottle to Shorty, who swigged down the whole lot. The other stable hand lay in a heap on the stone floor, out cold he was, beside Shorty's feet, his face the colour of boiled shite.

CHAPTER 6

At the sight of Lang Sandy, the cook, Eleanor grew rather pale, and then walked clumsily backwards into a wall. She loathed barber surgeons and quack doctors, mainly because they always seemed to be caked in blood and carried the stench of death upon their clothes. Eleanor pressed her palms together and prayed for the boy, but most of all she prayed for Lang Sandy to be out of her kitchen.

'Oh Lord, watch o'er the poor wee boy.' Eleanor rested her tired legs, the veins in them seemed to bulge and swell and plagued her so, but she never complained. Upon her chair, she chopped and peeled vegetables in the cold room, set off from the kitchen door. At twilight, an eerie light filtered through a milky pane. A hush descended upon the castle, she lit a candle and contrived to find out if the deed was done. With a tallow candle in hand, and the sound of keys jangling from her waist chain, cook pushed on the kitchen door. An empty bottle of spirits lay on its side on the main table, and at the end of it, all pooled together was a huge amount of blood and pus, a quantity of which spilled down onto the slate floor. The castle dogs lapped it up with excited yelps, tails wagging with glee. Cook screwed up her eyes, as if to block out the image, a hand to her mouth. Then, she took flight, racing towards the dogs to chase them away.

'Be off with you, you dirty hounds,'

With a clout and pail, she washed the mess away as the cursed dogs fought like wolves in the hall. Then a terrible thought occurred to her. The laddie's leg, where was it? Cook's eyes frantically searched the room, she took in every nook and cranny, but the leg was definitely not in sight. Her stomach lurched and caused sour bile to fill her mouth. What if the dogs had eaten the wee master's leg? A cry of revulsion escaped her lips as she bounced around the room in search of the surgeon, she did not have far to go. Lang Sandy had found a settle chair, and now lay slumped within it, legs stretched out in front of him near a blistering hearth.

'Those devil hounds.' She screamed.

'What's the matter?' He near leapt out of the chair.

'The dogs. They've carried away the young master's leg. Oh the very thought of it makes me sick to the stomach.'

'Calm down, woman. You're mistaken. The leg is quite safe. My apprentice has wrapped it for dissection tomorrow and hid it away. I wouldn't let a fresh, healthy limb like that go to waste. Now run along will you and leave me in peace.'

'Very well, if you are sure.'

'I am quite sure, now attend to your duties and bother me no more.'

'I'll not take orders from you.' Eleanor nodded and scurried from the room. 'The devil is at work in this house', she muttered before crossing herself and saying a prayer. Evil came in many forms and she fancied Lang Sandy a horned devil fresh from the fiery pits of hell. The sooner he was out of her kitchen the better.

***

Matilda wept for her son. What would become of him now? She felt numb, and angry… angry that her husband could abandon his son at a time like this. Tears rolled down her face, she choked and hiccupped, till her face became bloated and blotchy. Where was he? She squeezed her eyes shut and pushed her hands together, but what was the use of prayer? It wouldn't bring Robbie's leg back would it. Matilda's stomach lurched, she had barely eaten a thing since the accident, but the thought of food made her feel ill. When her maid brought her a bite to eat, she shooed her away. In her distress she had snapped and chastised the maidservant: 'Take it away, I cannot eat a thing. How could I when my boy lies downstairs crippled?'

The maid fled, but feeling guilty, Matilda decided to find her to apologise. She really shouldn't have snapped at her. But before she'd even reached the scullery, Matilda heard the tittle-tattle.

'What use will he be now, cook? A feeble laddie, and a crippled one, fit for nothing. A burden is what he is now, to his mother and father, one of the lame crew. The baron won't even visit his room…'

'Well at least she still has her boy. Nobody knows where my Magnus is. Just disappeared he has off the face of this earth, but does anyone care?'

Matilda didn't stay to hear anymore. She just walked on with a half stunned gaze, to where she had no idea. Her ears had a strange ringing sound within them, so much so that noises all around her became muffled, and her bosom ached so much she felt sure to die. With her face wet and tearstained, she put one foot in front of the other and kept going till she reached her bed chamber. The room had that hazy glow of filtered sunshine, a bird chirped outside. She tried to identify it, a robin perhaps? Perhaps not. She wrung her hands together, paced the room, then came to a standstill at her favourite sash window. With her face pressed against the cold pane she gazed below. A man worked outside, naked to the waist, she allowed her eyes to sweep over him. It was the bearded upstart, the one who found Robbie. She had not thanked him yet. Perchance she would in time. She averted her eyes and picked up a looking glass, when the tilt of her hat was just right, she put on a brave face and left her room.

It took but a moment to reach Robbie's room. Matilda had a nurse instilled within an adjoining chamber to tend to his needs. With the nurse's care and diligence, Robbie's health improved daily. Matilda greeted him with a kiss on both cheeks and then stood back from the bed. She remained like that for a moment, squinted her damp eyes, and then tilted her head to the right, so that one near touched her shoulder. 'Your bed cushions are not right. Let me prop you up nice and high.' For a moment or so, she fussed with his pillows.

'Leave me be, Mother.'

'Certainly not, I am your mother and I will never leave you be.'

Robbie fidgeted in his bed. An unhealthy pallor upon his face caused her heart to ache; she held a hand to her throbbing chest and swallowed a lump away in her throat. 'Has he been taking food, nurse?'

But before the nurse could answer Robbie said: 'Why ask her? One would think I'm incapable of answering myself. I've lost my leg not my tongue, mother. Aye, the nurse feeds me well, broth near enough every day. Where is father?'

Matilda's heart fluttered, the sensation felt like a tiny moth trapped within her bosom. She affected a smile. 'Has he not been to see you today?'

'No. He has not been to see me at all Mother. Not since the…'

'Never mind dear. You need not speak of it.'

'Oh but I do wish to speak of it. He was the one who put it there see – the trap I mean, but it was meant for poachers, and he might feel like it is his fault, mother. But it was not his fault because I was not looking where I was going and…'

'I know dear. Your father is probably busy.' She said with a tight mouth.

'Yes.' Robbie's shoulders sagged.

An awkward silence followed. Soon noises one wouldn't normally hear became louder to the ear – the sound of a blackbird in song, wind rustling leaves, even the panting of Robbie's mangy dog beside his bed.

'Mr Falmouth came to see me.'

'Falmouth?'

'The ghillie, Mother – you know the man that found me and pulled me from the trap.'

Matilda's body seemed to jolt and twist at the memory. 'Please do not remind me of that horrendous day. I hope you thanked him for saving your life.'

Robbie nodded and pointed to the dog. 'He took Red for a walk; Red hasn't left my side since the accident, he's a good dog. I sometimes save him my broth for him as a reward.'

'Whatever for, Robbie? The food is for you. You need to build up your strength.'

Robbie ignored her and continued. 'Falmouth told me about a man like me.'

'A man?' Matilda frowned.

'A man with one leg. He can walk with a stick. Falmouth says I can be walking in no time with the use of a walking cane or a peg leg…'

'I'm going to have a word with this man Falmouth.' Matilda 's colour reached a deep crimson. 'He has no right to give you false…'

A knock on the door caused them both to freeze, as though caught in some forbidden act. Matilda's eyes locked on her son's face, and then, at that precise moment, she witnessed the spark in her precious boy's eyes fade. Robbie's head remained angled towards the door – waiting, expectant, and bound for despair.

'It'll be the nurse to check on my progress.' Robbie said, his head sagged of a sudden.

But it wasn't the nurse, or his father as the boy had hoped for. It was the ghillie asking to take the dog out for a run in the heather, and it lifted Matilda's spirits to see her son lift his chin from his chest, and thus there was hope for the young Robbie.

***

It started with growths in his groin, tiny hardened nodules. They were, painless, but foolishly he chose to ignore them. Before long, the gravity of the ailment became evident when he developed an irritating rash upon his whole body, a sore throat, and then swollen glands. His weekly pious potion of ground up bible had protected him not, William had the pox! He sank to his knees, two shaky hands pressed together in prayer.

'Lord forgive me,' he said 'if you spare me now I will refrain from all manners of evil and vice.'

To date there were three cures for syphilis. The first required a chicken to be plucked and flayed and pressed against the genitals. The second used the same method but replaced the chicken with a live frog cut in two. When the first two failed, William turned to the third cure - mercury or guaiacum. He groaned, his knees ached upon the cold floor, he quit praying and sank his head into his hands, this was punishment for the accident, he was sure of it. But despite the guilt and turmoil he felt, the baron could not bring himself to face his son. For many days now he'd shut himself up in the castle tower. The walls were closing in on him, he had to get away. As a cock crowed in the distance as he wrote a letter to Morice, instructions for while he was away. He then reached for his valuables, unlocked the door and tiptoed out of the tower. The stables were unattended, one of the ginger grooms lay upon straw near the barn doors. The baron paused for a moment, taking care not to wake him. The man stirred but did not awake. William was glad of that, he knew he must look frightful, the front of his shirt was stained with claret and he was missing his wig. During his time locked away in the tower he'd also grown a rather untidy beard. But his purse full of money could remedy that. Just before dawn, William mounted his horse and rode away like the devil. Not once did he look back.

After half an hour of riding he had a change of heart and pulled on the horse's reins. He jumped off the horse, rolled onto the soft earth and cried like a bairn. Then he screamed at the top of his lungs.

'I must go back.' He held his head in his hands. They shook like a man with barrel fever.

However much he wanted to return, two matters prevented him…guilt and his son. He looked to the skies above, angry grey clouds loomed above him. William frowned, he was being punished for his sinful life, the pox and now Robbie. How could he make amends? How could he? He'd abandoned his laddie when the boy needed him most, and his wife… well he'd never treated her with even an ounce of kindness or compassion. They were better off without him. He wasn't a coward, he told himself, no, he was doing them a great favour by leaving.

***

A cold mist swirled in from the north, covering the hard earth with a blanket of white fog. Winter beckoned, and with it came an icy wind, unyielding, mortal – and for some the kiss of death. At this early hour, Sabine wondered of Magnus, her dull eyes taking on a faraway look as she stared into the distance. Two year had passed since Magnus had gone, Sarah too, and what had become of them no one knew. Sabine shivered, and wrapped her shawl tightly around her, her skirts trailed in the mud as she wandered the fields. Upon the horizon, two figures appeared on horseback; a man and a woman. As the woman came closer, Sabine couldn't help but stare at her; everything about her sparkled, the jewels on her earlobes, her fingers and neck. Even her coat seemed to shimmer and by the look of the material was made from the finest cloth, not the stuff fit for horse blankets, like the fabric peasants wore.

'You - girl. Aren't you the sibling of the missing serf, Magnus?'

'Aye.'

'I thought so.' Matilda shook her head. 'He's sorely missed I expect. Never mind, I am here to speak with you. I'm told you've had a bad harvest, is that correct?

'Aye – 'tis the murrain, we've lost all our…'

'Do not trouble me with the details girl, I've something for you and your family.' Matilda held out a small hamper.

'Thank you, my lady. Much appreciated.'

The bearded man at her side suddenly whispered into the lady's ear, prompting her to ask Sabine a question. 'Have you a stockpile?'

'Nae. Father has been too busy with the animals.'

'Well you may forage for wood and cut some for your winter stockpile.' Sabine shook her head, a frown marred her forehead. 'The baron only allows us to cut a certain amount. We've exceeded our limit already.'

The man, a gamekeeper to Sabine's mind, whispered into the lady's ear again. 'I'm removing all restrictions, feel free to take as much as you wish.'

Sabine felt her cheeks burn and a warm glow envelop her whole body, as much wood as we can take she thought, what fortune. But then her frown returned to spoil her flushed face. 'But the baron, my lady, or his steward… they will surely punish us as they have done in the past.'

'There will be no more punishments at Castle Wood. Besides my husband is abroad, and his steward will be informed of my decision regarding this matter.' And with that said, the couple galloped away.

***

It had been ghillie's idea. He believed that if serfs were well fed and not ill-treated, they would make better workers, and therefore productivity would improve. Of course, this view was contrary to William's…he believed serfs to be beasts of burden, to be exploited and ill-used. He had them all written down in his leather-bound book along with his cattle, horses and equipment – and one thing was for sure, he felt justified in thinking that they were his, to be bought and sold.

At first Matilda wanted to laugh at Falmouth's suggestions, but after a while she came round to his trail of thought. Falmouth believed that folk are all God's creatures, born with the same fingers and toes. Incredible though it may have seemed, he believed that all men and women should be equal. But what impressed her most, happened one day while she visited Robbie. She'd overheard them, discussing the running of the castle and its farms – men talk. But when she entered the room, Falmouth didn't treat her like the weaker vessel William claimed her to be, no, Falmouth included her within the conversation. And so, she watched and learned about ploughing and harrowing, resting fallow land and maintaining and protecting boundary walls. Maltilda was learning.

One day as they walked the castle grounds, Falmouth took the baroness aside, away from prying eyes beneath the leafy branches of an oak tree, a slight tremor in his voice as he said his piece. 'Baroness Matilda - I must speak wi' ye.'
'Very well. Speak your mind.' As usual she had the uncontrollable urge to take a razor to his wild beard and see the man behind all that hair.
'Are ye aware we're taking a huge risk?'
'Risk? What risk?'
'You and I helping the peasant folk. Tongues could start wagging…folk could say I've influenced ye o' late. Persuaded you to assist the serfs. If your husband decides tae return there could be hell to pay. His steward could somehow get wind o' oor changes. Have ye realised that?'
'Morice? He'll not interfere. He may be the steward, but I am Baroness, he must answer to me.'
'Aye, Morice kens his place right enough, but just because you're high born and he isnae matters not a fig. He's a man and you're a woman. The baron's absence makes him King o' the Castle, so we need to be careful. In the meantime, I'll try tae get him on our side.' Falmouth winked.
'All right. But know this Falmouth, I am not a foolish woman, and since my husband has gone I've learned much from you…and Robbie. Do not fret, we will get through this just fine.'
Falmouth's face darkened. 'I know. But I just wanted yae tae be aware of the…'
'When my husband returns, he will find me much changed, an altered woman, and in my opinion, a better woman. Furthermore, if it's your

78

position you're worried about, there is no risk to you, because it is I who have made these changes – not you.'

'All right, all right. It's just…I dinnae want tae gan the same way as the last ghillie.'

Matilda's brow puckered. 'Whatever do you mean?'

'The last ghillie, ye mean ye never heard o' what befell him? Jings, Mistress didn't you hear? The baron declared the poor soul insane, then confiscated his possessions and land. The man's wife and family were banished to God knows where. And then there was what happened tae Magnus and that young lassie…'

'The missing serfs?'

'Aye. There's a rumour he's kept them imprisoned in the castle dungeons.'

'No, that is not possible.' Matilda held her small hand up to her mouth.

'Why not? Open your eyes woman…haven't I told ye all along, your husband is a tyrant…if I find the rumour tae be true, I'll release them all I promise ye that, any living soul in those dungeons.'

'Enough Falmouth. Hold your tongue. I will not be spoken to in that manner, by you or any man…not anymore.' Matilda swallowed hard; the lump in her throat throbbed so hard she felt sure to cry.

'I am sorry, my Lady.'

'No matter. Don't you think I know his failings, his sins, his treatment of his own son? Poor Robbie has spent wasted tears on his useless father night after night since that hideous day…you know… the accident, but does he come? It's as if his son no longer exists. But that man, despite everything is still my husband.'

Falmouth's eyes darted left and right before moving towards her, and though Matilda wished that he would take her hand in his to comfort her, he did nothing of the sort. Of course, it was a foolish thought, hadn't she just reminded him of his place. Thanks to her sharp tongue, cavorting with a noble woman was sadly far from his thoughts.

***

By the time winter came, Magnus had resigned himself to his dingy cell, escape from it seemed impossible. Nevertheless, with Jacob nearby time moved faster, and if his Quaker friend's words were indeed true – one was truly never alone. Jacob often quoted Matthew (28:20) the passage of which claimed Christ was always with you. "I am with you always, even to the end of the world."

But at times Magnus found little comfort in pious words. After all, what use were words when he faded away in the dungeons of Castle Wood, cold hungry, separated from everybody he loved. The child, his and Sarah's – how many years would it have now? Sometimes he felt like pounding his fists upon the walls until his knuckles were red raw, or screaming at the top of his lungs. Life was cruel. What had he done to warrant such treatment? He thought about asking Jacob and then bit his tongue, not wanting another lengthy sermon. How he envied Jacob's tenacity and undoubting religious belief – he had no such piety, what rapture to have such divine faith?

'Do not despair.' Jacob coughed into the cold air.

Magnus tried not to choke; his voice when it came was broken with emotion. 'Leave me be, old man, I must gather my thoughts.'

'No matter how bad you feel someone, somewhere is suffering more than you, Magnus. A man tied to a whipping post, a slave, beaten and shackled and bound for strange lands, a poor insane woman wallowing in her own filth…'

Through the dim light Magnus stretched out his arms to Jacob. And as he did so, a feeling of great warmth and peace grew inside of him. 'I am lucky then, old man in my miserable cell?' A smile formed on his cracked lips and he began to laugh till his belly hurt and his eyes watered.

'Feel better now?' Jacob asked in a quiet voice.

'Well enough, Jacob, thank you, my friend.'

***

William selected the young pickpocket whore from the bagnio again – Lily he thought her name was, but he could not be sure, not with his waning mind. Anyway, Lily, a most wicked and debauched character, always agreed to fulfil even the most depraved and unnatural of desires, so she was perfect for him. Interestingly, he'd heard she catered for women, and was well versed in flagellation, buggery, and all manner of vices. Understandably, Lily was a popular girl, but William wanted her just the same – despite a fixed rule with regards to her price. Lily always measured her customers by a standard of eight inches and expected a shiny coin for every inch that fell short of the mark. In this department William was not a man to disappoint, and he took great pleasure in short-changing Lily following every liaison.

On this occasion, it did not take long for him to have his fill of her. Once sated, he dressed and promptly planted his wig onto his head so that it lay in a rather lopsided fashion, then made for the door. Just one step he had taken out of the bagnio when a man of the cloth accosted him.

'Satan lurks within this house. The flame of lust burns bright within it. Save your soul. Virtue is everything dear man - *everything*.'

William shooed the man away, angry at his pious speech. Didn't he ground up his bible near every day and drink down the sacred liquid? Aye he did… and he gave alms to the poor at kirk. Damn the holy man, he'd already secured his own piece of heaven and William felt sure to survive the Justice of the Lord. For didn't He forgive all sins? William sneered at the minister, his lips curled up as he did so to expose a section of his teeth.

'In order to know virtue, one must first know vice. True happiness can only be achieved through the senses, old man, you should try it. 'William winked and pointed to the bawd house.

The holy man paled and stepped backwards, a hand held up to his chest. 'The seeds of sin are in your nature. You're the devil himself.' He said before he turned and fled.

William threw his head back and laughed.

The gaming hall had none of the profligacy of the bagnio. No strategically placed mirrors or erotic paintings, although everything was lavish and comfortable. At least here, he could take his mind of things, concentrate on dice or cards, and pass some time away. In the wee hours of the morning he staggered from the gaming house to a nearby tavern, and then kicked up an almighty fuss.

'Claret. Bring me claret and a young wench.'

The innkeeper groaned and sent out for a whore.

CHAPTER 7

The damned swellings in William's groin had returned with a vengeance. It was providence he knew it, God's way of punishing him for his sins. As usual he chose to ignore it. Before the baron left the tavern, he caught a glimpse of himself in a pane of glass. His shoulders sagged as he moved closer to the window, a strange creature looked back at him – unfamiliar and obscene. He picked up the bottle of guaiacum, a midnight blue colour fashioned with a human skull, and swigged. It took three attempts to sup the foul liquid, like a tramping man his hands trembled, and so terribly did they shake, he clear missed his mouth and then chipped a tooth. With eyes red rimmed and bloodshot, he staggered downstairs. The innkeeper brought him his usual – a glass of claret and mutton pie. Though halfway through serving him, the meddlesome innkeeper fancied him at death's door and sent out for a barber surgeon. Once the said *quack* arrived, he shook his head, wagged a finger and chastised him – chastised *him*, Baron Bothwell of Castle Wood, so what if he'd near poisoned himself. If he wanted to poison himself, he'd damn well poison himself – to hell and back. The following day, he removed the quack's bandages to examine the scars. The damned barber had opened a vein, and another. He cursed and rubbed a coarse hand over the crisscross notches.

'Fetch me a man-servant and a sedan chair,' he called to the innkeeper below.
'But the surgeon said…'
'Never mind what the idiot quack said, do as I say at once, and bring me more claret.'

It took William a good hour or two to dress. A hopeless manservant trembled nearby, not accustomed to buttons or pins. The baron had to give him instruction in everything from the positioning of his wig to the shining of his silver buckled shoes. A layer of sweat covered the baron's forehead as he descended the tavern stairs. A stout serving-maid carried a tallow candle to light his way – a common strumpet of the lowest kind. He'd seen pigs with more grace and smaller arses. Once the sedan bearers arrived, one opened the door for him, closed it behind, and then tapped on the door.

'Where to, sir?'

'The gaming rooms near the Mile.'

The journey didn't take long. They avoided secluded paths to avoid highwaymen and outlaws and maintained a good speed. Once inside the gaming hall, he ordered a fine wine. William's tastes were extravagant, always had been. He took a snuff mull from one of his pockets, a ram horn with a curled end and hinged lid, then passed it around; he could be generous at times – especially when women were nearby. As candles flickered, he soaked up the atmosphere – watched the dancing, then endured a spot of a tedious chat, politics of course. Then followed an activity well worth his effort – gambling. But even this bored him after a while. Before long, as always, an inevitable compulsion came over William, the desire to prove his virility. He placed a hand to his wig, adjusted it slightly, and then strutted in the direction of fancy French parfum.

A group of women played faro on the farthest table, all of them far too old. He tut tutted, then looked elsewhere, his eyes finally settling on another group, one or perhaps two of them worthy of his attention. He walked towards them, introduced himself. As always, in more sophisticated company, he acted out the role of a gentleman. But William's bold roving eye, and sensualist manner, though not picked up by younger women, did not escape the cautious nature of a more mature and worldly woman. In other words, despite his good looks, title, wealth, in matters concerning the chasing of petticoats, things did not always go to plan.

'Baron Bothwell of Castle Wood, a pleasure.' William aimed his introduction to one woman in particular, one that put powder in his musket for sure – a young blonde, with plump youthful skin. He licked his lips, and began discourse with her. A couple of times he placed a hand upon her shoulder and peered down the deep crevice between her ample breasts. But a clacking hen, (a woman he took to be her chaperone) stood glaring at him the whole time, holding the girl's dancing card in the air, for all and sundry to see. The audacity of the woman thought William, the muscles in his jaw twitched; he ignored the shrew and continued discourse. That is, until her adjourning party suddenly remembered they had a previous engagement elsewhere and promptly left. What a pity, he thought as he knocked back sweet dregs of wine. The lass had been bonny, and had a tiny resemblance to Greta and that daft peasant girl, banished to the Magdalene Chapel. Of a sudden he banged down his crystal glass, causing others to glare at him from beneath their powdered wigs. A whooshing sound filled his ears as he left the gaming rooms to fresh air and the sight of the sedan chair that brought him.

'Oh, you're still here. How fortunate. I've changed my mind see; I don't want to stay here. Take me to the kirk near the Cowgate, the Magdalene one.'

One of the men, the shorter one puffed out both cheeks and glanced at his partner, who had already proceeded to pick up his side of the pole.

'But that's a good hour walk, Sir.'

'Make haste then, young fellow. I've a mind to visit an old friend.'

'Very good, Sir.'

He arrived in the wee hours, slightly inebriated and proceeded to knock hell out of the main door. A cowman soon walked over to him and tipped his hat.

'You won't find anyone up at this hour - except me.'

'They'll be up when I say they are up.' The baron staggered a little and near tripped on his own feet.

'Suit yourself.'

The baron continued to beat on the door with his fists until eventually the door creaked open. If the abbess was surprised to see him she didn't show it.

'What is the meaning of this, Baron Bothwell? This is not a suitable time to call.'

'It suits me, now take me to the girl.' He slurred.

'I'm afraid I cannot allow that. You've made a wasted journey, Baron Bothwell. Your ward is ailing or sickening for something. The girl has been nothing but trouble since she arrived. But rest assured, every effort has been taken to cleanse her soul, wash her sins...'

'Sickening? I'll be the judge of that. I suggest you quit making excuses regarding the girl. She was perfectly healthy the day I left her in your care. Need I remind you of the handsome sum I pay you to keep the girl here? If she's unwell it's because you've neglected your duties, probably overworked her or not fed her. Now take me to her at once.'

The abbess's eyes narrowed, a dangerous glint flickered in them for the longest time. The baron's lips curved into a sneer, the old woman was most definitely struggling to maintain her composure. He despised her type, self-righteous hypocrites the lot of them. 'Very well. Follow me, Baron Bothwell.' The abbess held out a hand and motioned to a door ahead.

For an old woman, she had a brisk step. The baron glanced at her just once as they walked the cold corridors, and when he did he shuddered and imagined hideous gargoyles and other macabre characters carved into the kirk walls. She really was a most repulsive old woman. After they'd exited the great hall, they passed through a series of communal rooms, till they came to an ivy wall. Beyond the wall stood a passageway bathed in dark shadows, with just enough light to make out a number of closed doors. At the very last door she opened a hatch and invited the girl's benefactor to look inside. William's jaw slackened, he exhaled, his breath formed puffs of clouds into the icy air; he hoped there was a good hearth and cheerful fire inside, somewhere to warm his cold hands. He pressed an eye to a latticed hatch and peeked through the shadows. He frowned and stepped backwards. 'That is not her. You are mistaken.'

The abbess shook her head. 'There is no mistake. She has been sickening since she arrived here... I suspect the devil lies in wait for her. It's her head.' the abbess tapped the side of her temple. 'She's sick in her head. That's why I've locked the door. For her own protection.'

'I see.' The baron gazed through the lattice again. Magnus's sweetheart lay upon the dirt floor, a filthy blanket clutched to her delicate body. Upon her thin body she wore a thin cotton shift, her slender limbs sprouted out from beneath it, so that her knees touched her chest. But the thing that irked him was how still she was, and vulnerable. A pang filled his chest and tightened, he pressed a hand to it and stepped back. He alone was responsible for her wellbeing or demise, and yet he was torn, confused even. For a moment he paced outside the darkened room. When he came to a stop he called out in a gruff voice.: 'I would like to spend some time alone with my niece. Can you send for a candle and food?'

'I'll unlock the door when I return.' The abbess nodded and promptly left taking her candle with her, plunging the corridor into darkness. Like an old tree, he remained rooted to the ground – waiting, listening, his heart pealing like kirk bells in his chest. Eventually, with the passing of time, the blacks of his eyes grew bigger, adjusting to the inky black shades of night. And so, as the first rays of sun sliced through the latticed hatch, William could just make out a feminine silhouette, a slight swell of hips, and delicate ankle bones.

The old abbess returned with food and a candle, her watery eyes settling on the sleeping girl. 'No doubt you'll find her much changed. Perhaps I should stay, Baron Bothwell. As I said, she's quite insensible. The girl's succumbed to the devil, she even has a familiar, a cat that sneaks in through the bars at night. She claims the cat is the soul of her new born child.'

'The girl must be delirious. Give me the key to the door. I shall return it directly.'

Once the abbess placed the key within his palm, he took the candle and food, and then dismissed her.

The baron's pulse quickened. Once more, he looked through the lattice and then slowly turned the key in the lock. An eerie creak cut through the silence as it swung ajar. The girl remained still, but he knew she sensed him. A shadow fell upon her as he hovered above, like a black cloud upon a blazing sun. The girl trembled. At the sound of his rustling clothes and jangling coins she began to stir.

'Magnus. Is that you?'

The baron's lips curled upwards and formed a sneer. 'Magnus is gone my dear, far far from here. It is I - your laird.'

William of a sudden was at a loss what to do. For just a moment he stood in the middle of the chamber and just watched her…his eyes never left her as she cowered in the corner of the room, and he noticed how her knees drew up to her body in an effort to become warm. He sniffed up and immediately wished he hadn't, there was a chamber pot in the room, he was sure of it, but in the dim candlelit room he couldn't locate it - Lord he didn't want to step in it. 'That smell.'

'They forgot to change the piss pot.'

William raised his eyes at her vulgar mouth. 'Couldn't you empty it yourself?'

'I'm locked up in here.'

'Ah yes…they think you insensible. Why?'

'I have no idea. I just wish to be reunited with my family, my Lord. I am from simple folk, I won't be a bother and I'll not say a word about anything that's passed between us afore. I promise…'

'Oh hush. Here - before we arrange anything you must eat…you are all skin and bone.' He set the candle down and held out the food.

It amused the baron how she approached him like a beaten dog with its tail between its legs. 'Come, come - I will not bite.'

She took it, thanked him…and once safely away from him, she began to eat.

'Your neck is all scratched?'

'They bled me again. They do that when I get sick.'

He shook his head and as he did so his forehead furrowed. 'Is that the truth? Or did one of those miserable nuns beat you for your sins?'

'No. They treat me well, my Lord.'

'Eat this.' He gave her more food.

He watched her again. William liked to watch. When Greta was around he stared at her all the time, couldn't take his eyes off her. The candlelight softened the serf's angular features. He squinted his eyes and stared, and in the dim light, by some miracle, she looked exactly like Greta. His heart thumped. The girl ate delicately, in fact she had rather refined manners for a peasant girl. The baron liked how she took the food in her open mouth, the tingle began then, and once it did he could not control it. He began to fidget. Dear Lord, the girl inflamed his desire. So much so, that he took the remaining food and returned it to its wrapping.

'You may eat the rest later. '

'But I am hungry…'

'Hush now, Greta. I cannot stay long – but I will return, I promise, and when I do, I will bring more food. But first you must do something for me. Can you do that?'
'But I am not Greta.'

'Oh but you *are*, dear child.' He grasped a lock of her hair and pulled her face to his trembling limbs.

CHAPTER 8

Wrapped within the bosom of the Lord and all of her sisters, Sister Louise knew little of the world and the sins of vile men. In truth, she didn't want to know, and frankly never had. From a small child for some reason, she mistrusted men and had withdrawn herself from the world. Even more so once her dear mother died. Sister Louise's widowed father had done his best, but as soon as she was able, young Louise removed herself from a world of men, and became a bride of the Lord. She much preferred the company of her sisters. Nevertheless, however sheltered her life may have become, she was not a dim-witted woman.

The peasant girl, Sorrow was with child, at least a few months gone – but no matter how many times Sister Louise voiced her concerns to her superior, her fears fell upon deaf ears. Of course, when troubled Sister Louise reverted to the only sense of comfort she knew, she prayed to the Lord, He in his wisdom would guide and prevail – through any crisis. However, after many hours of praying she received two things; sore knees and a raging thirst. At the drinking well, Sister Louise drank her fill before returning to her prayers, her faith in God was absolute, but when her prayers went unanswered, she set off in search of the abbess.

'You are irked for no good reason, child. Did they not teach you anything in France? Sister Louise, I can assure you, there will be a perfectly reasonable explanation for Sorrow's symptoms. A great number of things could have caused her to put weight around her middle... or caused her to retch into a pail. She's a born sinner, probably gluttony...over indulged herself with food.'

Sister Louise placed a hand in front of her mouth and resisted the urge to laugh. 'The women here get nothing but scraps. That could hardly be the case.'

'Well most likely the girl, Sorrow has dropsy and that is all.' The abbess tapped incessantly on her table with a small coin of some sort. The tapping irritated Sister Louise and so she took a deep breath and continued: 'But what of her sickness each morning and ...?'

The abbess stopped tapping, and threw down her coin. 'She has a swelling in the stomach. Now bother me no more with your nonsense and allow me to get on with God's work.'

'Abbess of Magdalene, with respect, I do not think you are listening to me.'

'Need I explain the implications of your insinuations, Sister Louise? The child, Sorrow has but *one* guardian. And this guardian is her *only* visitor, a man of wealth, power and quality. A very generous benefactor of Magdalene Chapel and supporter of the Hammermen – a man of spotless character. Need I say more?'

Sister Louise nodded. A shudder passed along her spine as she awaited further instruction. Compliance, duty, righteousness, all of these qualities are what she subscribed to, she was a child of the Lord. So why did she feel miserable, melancholy even? She felt as though her soul blackened before her watchful superior's wizened eyes. As usual, the abbess was devoid of compassion.

'Should I at least send for a … how do I say – a physician again?'

'We cannot spare the expense.'

'But the girl is ill. If her symptoms worsen she could die. I for one do not want her death on my conscience.'

'Sister Louise, you have a great flair for drama, sometimes I think you might have been more suited to a profession of acting on a great stage. The girl is in not going to die. She merely has a swelling of the stomach, a trifling matter and nothing to fret about. Now take heed of what I have to say. What I suggest is that you reduce her food – this will relieve the swelling.'

'You want me to purge her?'

'Of course not. Why must you always embellish facts? I simply ask that you reduce her food. Now please take heed of my advice. This is not the best solution it is the *only* solution.'

***

When the rains came Robbie grew restless. With the help of the ghillie, Falmouth, Robbie learned to walk on a wooden leg, an ingenious contraption commissioned and successfully constructed by a local carpenter. When the leg was ready, Robbie and Falmouth examined it …it was a classic peg leg design, not dissimilar to a table leg. It had a leather socket to place Robbie's leg stump inside, and lacing for the thigh. With Falmouth's help, Robbie practiced upon it with the aid of a walking stick each day in the privacy of his own room. After a few weeks, Falmouth turned to Robbie and said: 'Master Robbie, it's time ye left this room noo and tried a different terrain. Something uneven tae test your leg further.'

Robbie wiped sweat from his brow. The act of walking on the peg leg still tested him more than he ever anticipated. 'No. I'm not ready to face anyone yet.'

'You cannae hide yourself away forever, laddie. Who are ye hiding from?'

'No one.'

'So, what's stopping you?'

'Folk gawping at my stump. Look at the poor cripple…'

'Och tae hell with them all. Who cares what they think. Get yourself outside. I'll be right beside you, lad. You've come a long way since the accident and I'm proud of ye. You'll be a man soon.'

Robbie felt a tightness in his throat, a choking pain that circled his neck. 'Thank you, Falmouth. You've been like a father to me since…'

Robbie closed his eyes as the door clicked shut behind Falmouth. When he opened them, he peered with a wet face through his chamber window. Anger and frustration bubbled inside of him. To his annoyance, of late, he always seemed on the verge of tears. It embarrassed him profusely. Angrily he wiped away his tears. With a sickened heart he thought of the old man and the dog, the one he shot with the arrow. Had the old man really been there that day or had he dreamt it? Robbie shook his head and pinched the bridge of his nose, he just didn't know. As his eyes scanned the horizon, his vision became blurred, the earth appeared waterlogged and sodden. No doubt difficult to get around on, for the able bodied, never mind the likes of him, a cripple. Suddenly a cry escaped his mouth. Robbie sobbed, a thousand miseries in his eyes, and for all the world, he felt like a caged bird with clipped wings, yearning for flight.

When his tears were spent he shrugged his shoulders, removed his peg leg and picked up a book. The pages were all dog-eared and smelling of dust. He sneezed and stretched out his ugly stump in front of him. Bizarre though it may seem, his leg, severed below the knee felt as though it was still there. It was like a damned phantom limb. A phantom limb that itched – but how does one scratch a phantom limb? Of course one can't. And not only did it itch, it ached too, and when the aching ceased, it felt warm then cold, all the while tightening and squeezing till he felt sure to scream.

His thoughts were dark. What could life possibly offer him now? A cripple, a useless… and then something disturbed his thoughts. A tiny figure, mother's little play thing…a young girl child with a great mop of golden hair. With no grace at all, the child barged into his room and then jumped – well more like forced herself upon his lap. Robbie shrieked. At first, he covered his leg stump with a blanket. But the wee girl yanked it off and laughed as though it was *'find the hideous stump'* game. A smile formed on Robbie's lips – the lassie had spirit and was not disturbed by his deformed leg at all.
'You Bobbie.' She said in her childish voice.
'No. My name is Robbie.'
'You Bobbie. Mama love Bobbie. Lisbeth want play game. What we play?'
'You're too wee to play you little nuisance – and mother will be cross with you for running away from nurse.' Robbie ruffled her hair.
'Lisbeth big girl now. Silly. I like play ball. Ball. I like ball. Catch.'

She was a rascal, Robbie thought for sure, but he liked her… so he stretched out a hand for an apple, one he'd discarded earlier during a meal, it would serve as a ball. Once he had the shiny green fruit in his hands, he waved a hand and ordered her to move further back. 'Open your hands out and get ready to catch, girl.'
The child obeyed but opened her hands wide in front of her. A mischievous expression lit up her little face.
'No not like that, girl. Cup your hands so that you can catch it.'
The girl did as she was told, her pink tongue protruding from her lips.

'What's the matter now?' Robbie pressed his lips together, a great belly laugh threatening to spill out from his mouth. It was the girls face, all scrunched up into a snarl.

'I am Lisbeth, not girl.'

'Well all right – now after three, Elisabeth. Are you ready? One…two…three – catch.'

Elisabeth squealed with delight but dropped the apple; it rolled across the floor until it stopped near nurse's shoe.

'Elisabeth,' cried the nurse, 'I've been looking all over for you. Why are you bothering the master?'

'She's no bother.' Robbie covered his leg quickly and gestured for Elisabeth to throw the apple to him.

'I warned the baroness this would happen. The child needs to be secured within her crib but she keeps climbing out of it. Swaddle her up is what I say, but the baroness will not hear of it. Have you ever seen a child so young toddling around? Barely able to walk and she's running from room to room all over the castle. This won't happen again.'

'Oh don't be ridiculous. She's no bother at all. It's not healthy to be locked away in a room. The girl needs exercise; I will have a word with mother. The child is welcome here anytime – she can keep me company when the rains falls like today. '

Robbie smiled and crossed his arms over his chest. The words played out in his head … *not healthy to be locked away in a room*. Falmouth was right, he must make an effort to get out. It was then, while deep in thought, that an unexpected event happened. The little girl, Elisabeth tottered over to him and embraced him with chubby arms. A wet kiss landed on Robbie's pale cheek – and it was the sweetest moment, so heart-warming that he near shed a tear. And from that innocent hug sprung hope – and warmed Robbie with the spirit of love.

***

Before dawn, he awoke with a familiar itch, a devilish torment that sent fire rushing to his loins - he had to have the peasant girl again. He prepared to depart. Thus, he dressed in haste. To the left of him, upon a wooden nightstand was an enormous full-bottomed wig, freshly powdered; he removed it with shaky hands and placed it upon his head. A manservant helped him to dress, button his attire, and pull on his stockings and shoes. Of late, he had trouble remembering things, the medicine perhaps? So he kept a little notebook of sorts, with lists to do, also a brief diary and names and addresses of acquaintances.

One hour later he instructed his man to hire a post-chaise, one with two horses and a large front with side windows to afford a clear view from inside. The servant did well – a fabulous French carriage arrived, well-sprung and upholstered in the finest velvet. Not only did it shelter him from wind and rain, it also screened off the ugly coachman freezing his hollyhocks off outside. With two sturdy horses it took less than an hour to arrive at Magdalene Chapel, and throughout the journey, he kept a loaded pistol about his person, to safeguard them against highway men.

When the horses came to a stop, the baron pushed on the door and jumped outside. There was a definite spring in his step once he approached the red brick building. At the main door, he made a fist and knocked. Silence. He knocked again, stood back, pressed his lips together and began to whistle. Still nothing. After a good deal of rapping on the hard wood he began to shout. He ranted incessantly and walked on the spot to keep warm. His cold hands plunged into his deep pockets as he wondered what could be the reason for the delay.
'Allow me entry or I shall have your cowman break down the door.' He shouted.

Once he quit shouting the place became tranquil again, and not a sound could be heard except for the odd song bird twittering in the trees. To ward off the cold, the baron continued to shuffle his feet, in the process he stubbed a toe on a sharp stone. He cursed and picked up the offending object, examining it between finger and thumb, in the process an idea occurred to him. Next to the door was a small glazed window, he could break it with the stone and climb inside, damn the nuns and their rules. Thus, with the sharp stone pressed against his palm, he approached the window and peered through the glass. The pane felt cold against his face, he could see a table, and a huge wooden cross fixed to a wall, nothing more, but then an image flashed in front of him, deformed and macabre amidst the rough cuts of glass. A noise filled his ears, resonating from deep within his throat, the sound of his own shriek as he stared into the eyes of an old hag. William jumped backwards, almost losing his balance, at that moment he was sure he'd seen an old witch or a ghoul – but alas, it was the abbess carrying a tallow candle. She opened the window and rested her elbows upon the window ledge. 'Whatever do you want, Baron Bothwell at this ungodly hour? Did I startle you?'

'Yes – dear Lord I thought you were a ghoul.'

'That's a strange fancy, you've more to fear from the living than the dead. What do you want this time?'

'I wish to see my niece.'

The abbess shook her head and wrapped the folds of her habit more closely around her. Every time she spoke an icy cloud formed from her thin lips. 'Impossible. You must return home immediately before you catch the death of cold. The child sleeps – let us not disturb her.'

William's grip tightened around the stone, its smooth surface searing into his palm like a hot coal. He scratched his head and thought, how many times had he visited the lassie now? Seven, eight times at least and every time they have led him straight past the ivy wall to her chamber. Why not now? As he continued with this trail of thought, the abbess began to shut the window; a hard glint in her small, spritely eyes. Before she closed the window, he snapped out an arm, and curled his fingers around the edge of the wooden frame. Thus, the window remained open. But stubborn as she was, the abbess continued to try and close the window… but her strength was no match for his.

'What the devil has got into you old woman? I care not for your impudence. I've a right to visit with my niece whenever I choose, so take me to her now. I demand it.'

'Be reasonable, Baron Bothwell, it's too early. Wouldn't it be more prudent to visit her later when she is fully rested?' The old woman stood her ground.

William scoffed. 'Abbess Hoppringle, you forget yourself.' He added in a haughty tone. 'Need I remind you of the obscene amounts of money I plough into your miserable establishment?'

At the mention of currency all colour drained from the nun's face. 'If you would be so kind to make your way to the main door, I will meet with you directly.'

Once admitted, the abbess took him to the main hall. It was a cold place, no chairs or comforts, its design functional, austere. Upon a stone wall, fixed between two torches, was the crude wooden crucifix he'd seen earlier through the window pane. It reminded him of the cross on his bible, not the one he ground up for holy potion, or the one he pressed against his poxed groin – his family bible.

'Baron Bothwell. My apologies for not having contacting you earlier regarding this matter, but there has been a difficulty with Sorrow.'

'Sorrow? Her name is Sarah to my knowledge.'

'Yes, Sarah, your niece. May I talk with you frankly?'

'Yes.'

'Well I am afraid she has gone.'

William's eyes near popped from his head. 'Gone where?'

'I'm afraid I don't know. There was a swelling in her stomach – dropsy we think. We purged her the night before last, and this morning when it was time for prayers, we noticed she was gone.'

A swelling in her stomach? Every hair upon his head suddenly prickled on his scalp. 'Are you sure it was dropsy?' He could almost see the cogs within her head connect and turn. These holy women could be damned industrious – commerce came before religious conviction, and money meant everything. This one was no exception…he could see it in the way she lovingly handled her silver candlestick, and the way she occasionally caressed the fine ring she wore upon her left hand. Like himself, she was a lover of fine things. He imagined she demanded the finest wine and food, and why not? The dried up old prune probably had little else joy in her miserable life.

'You should have informed me of the girl's condition. You've moved her on because she's in no condition to work, is that it?'

The abbess cocked her head to the side. 'Condition? She had dropsy that is all. I dealt with it as best I could – she was purged, starved.'

'To protect your best interests, it would have been wise of you to keep the girl safe within the chapel walls, abbess. For whatever reason, be it embarrassment or panic, I see you've taken matters into your own hands and moved her to some other miserable wash house further north, no doubt. But that was foolish of you, very foolish. You should have delivered her of child here and sent her bastard to a foundling hospital – then gone on as before. So where is she?'

'I tell you I do not know.'

'You are a damned foolish woman. I've never known such incompetence. How can you not know her whereabouts?'

The abbess sucked in her breath. 'Perhaps you have another niece we could look after for you? We will be sure to treat her with the utmost…'

William's eyes narrowed as he wondered how much lower this holy hypocrite would sink to secure her funds. 'That will not be necessary. My association with the chapel is over. I'm withdrawing my support and will be in touch with the Hammermen.'

'But the daughters of Mary Magdalene need your help, Baron Bothwell, as do our sisters…since the reformation there has been nowhere for these poor souls to go.'

'That is not my concern, all of you can burn in the pits of hell for all I care.'

He stormed off to the dairy and cowsheds to speak to a man, someone who talked sense he hoped. After a while, a cowman appeared, dragging one of his fine beasts behind him. It was milking time, and soon a fresh faced dairy maid arrived carrying a three-legged stool and milk pail.

The baron reached into his pocket and pulled out a shiny coin. 'You. Cowman, I've a question for you. How long have you been here?'

The cowman rubbed his hand together and muttered. 'Since dawn.'

'Anyone leave around then?'

'Not today. But a young lassie and one of them nuns left yesterday around this time.'

'Which nun?'

'The young, bonny one – not from round here mind, one of them foreigner types.' He tapped on the milkmaid's shoulder; the milkmaid had her ear tucked into the cow's hind as she tugged on the cow's udders, and there was a smear of dirt upon her cheek.

The cowman nudged her again. 'Who was the nun with the lassie – yesterday morning?'

The milkmaid wiped the sweat from her brow; she looked up from her stool at the baron, a coquettish tilt to her head at the sight of his shiny coin. 'Och, I dinnae ken, Angus, I was verra busy that morning, I'm no' sure that…'

The baron pulled out another coin from his pocket. 'A coin for each of you provided I am furnished with the nuns name and whereabouts.'

Of a sudden the milkmaid became animated. 'The bonny one ye say, Angus? Was it the one wi' dark hair and skin the colour o' fresh milk, the French lassie, Sister Louise?'

'Aye that's the one.' The cowman stretched out a calloused hand.

William ignored him and looked down upon the milkmaid. 'Can you tell me where they might have gone?'

'I cannae, sir, I dinnae ken where they micht be.' She stretched out her hand for the coin.

'No matter. I'm sure the abbess knows what order of nuns she came from. 'William nodded and tossed them the coins.

***

But before he departed for France, the baron went to see the blacksmith, the one who made the cursed mantrap. He entered the smithy, and leant back against a cold wall, closed his eyes and swallowed hard. Guilt consumed him, it clawed at his insides, he couldn't face him – the smithy that is. Why? By virtue of the fact that he'd instructed the man to build the very device that crippled his son. No matter he thought, as his heart thumped in his chest, he decided to set his shame aside and get done what needed to be done. Once his breathing calmed, William took a deep breath and walked inside.

'I need you to make me…'

The blacksmith's face became deathly pale. 'Not another mantrap surely?'

'Good Lord, man – not that. I want you to make me a collar.'

The blacksmith relaxed. Right away, some colour returned to his face. 'One of your hounds slipped his collar again? You need me to make a new buckle is that it?'

'No. I need you to make me a collar, big enough for a man, a serf collar – brass will do. It will need to be inscribed. Can you do that?'

The blacksmith paled again, a look of sheer incredulity stretched across his face. He stretched out his arms, placed his weight upon his anvil and puffed out both cheeks.

William shuffled from foot to foot. He was nervous and twitchy and just wanted out of here, before folk realised he was near the castle grounds. 'Well how soon can you have it done?'

'I'll start right away.'

'Good.' The baron patted the blacksmith's weak arm.

The following week, William, despite the weather, hoped to be gone before dark. Once in France, he would locate the peasant girl and find peace at last. Who knew what the future held? Perhaps he would take her for a mistress, bring her home and give her rooms in Castle Wood – Matilda would understand, and if she didn't, well too bad. But first he had to deal with Magnus. The damned man hung over him like a black cloud. Just the thought of him brought William out in a cold sweat; he shuddered and found solace in the fact that Magnus would soon be gone.

Within William's secret chamber (a hunting lodge), safely away from the castle, stood a large wooden box.. The box had a small key, he twisted it until it made a clicking noise and lifted the lid, the old hinges creaked in protest. A brass serf collar sat inside, and what a splendid item it was. Once again, the smithy hadn't disappointed. The baron pulled out the item and lifted the collar up to the bright window to turn it this way and that, admiring the way the metal reflected light. Hammered around the rim was an intricately decorated design, all along the top and bottom of the collar. The inscription to his mind was a little crude, but nevertheless he could make out the words: *Magnus Styhr, gifted by Baron Bothwell of Castle Wood as a perpetual servant to Sir John Stuart of Newton Parish.*

Before he departed, he sent a letter to Morice, with instructions for Magnus, and returned the collar to its box.

CHAPTER 9

Once they'd fled the chapel, Sister Louise's first thought had been to return to her homeland. She missed her mother tongue, but most of all she longed for the hills of the Provence and her sisters at the convent near Avignon. To her mind, there was nothing more serene or beautiful, than the divine singing and chanting of the Avignon nuns. For the moment, her return to the Abbaye de Notre- Dame would have to wait, simply because Sorrow needed her. Besides, she didn't know if she was welcome there anymore. Together they travelled on foot and then hay cart towards a ruined priory in North Berwick, close to the English border. A small convent had been established there in clandestine following the reformation, as the nuns had had nowhere to go since King James VI turned the priory lands into a free barony for the Hume family. It was a risk Sister Louise was willing to take...she was fully aware that the order of nuns here were barely tolerated, but what was their alternative? Neither of them had the money to sail to France or Rome...they had to chance Berwick. Along the way, under the shade of a great oak tree, the peasant girl, a rather dim and docile creature now dressed, as Louise was, in the rough clothes of simple travellers began to ask Louise questions.

'Sister Louise, my feet hurt, must we walk further?'
'We must. The old man we just passed thinks there is a small building where the old priory used to be. We need to get there quickly. Hopefully there will be an order of nuns, Benedictine or Cistercian, it really doesn't matter which. What's important is that someone admits us, or else we'll end up cold and alone in the dark, and that's not safe...even for the likes of us.'
'But why couldn't we stay at Magdalene?'
Sister Louise's upper lip raised, at the same time her nose wrinkled as though a ghastly smell filled the air. 'But your Uncle?'
'Aye. What of him?'
The Frenchwoman's eyes widened. 'He took liberties...'
'Aye. But he brought me food and a warm blanket.'

'Sorrow, dear child, your uncle is a wicked man. Lord knows what would have become of you had you stayed. He should not have taken advantage of you. Hopefully there is a better life ahead for you at Berwick. You'll see. Put your faith in the Lord.' She placed a hand upon the girl's shoulder, felt the warm flesh beneath her clothes. The name the abbess gave her, Sorrow, no longer seemed necessary. She asked the girl her real name and vowed to call her that from now on. The girl seemed pleased and proceeded to crinkle up her eyes and show all her teeth in a wonderful smile.

'Will you stay with me once we're there?' Sarah asked.

'Of course, Sarah. But one day I will have to return home. In time my presence will no longer be important to you. Sooner or later you will learn to obey the will of God, and He will become the focus of your life.'

Sarah nodded and kissed the hand upon her shoulder. The Frenchwoman reddened and pulled her hand away.

'A life serving the Lord has much to offer a woman like you, Sarah. If the nuns of Berwick secretly remained in Scotland and the rumours are true, you will benefit from an extended family; and take much comfort from the company of your sisters. *No one* will exploit you. If the life suits you, you could consider taking your religious vows, imagine that. A life given to God brings much happiness. I should know. Do you know why a nun has such an amazing sense of freedom, Sarah? It's because she knows that she is walking towards heaven.'

Sister Louise looked deep into the girl's eyes. She had the purest skin and the most beautiful blue eyes. A lump formed in her throat. She turned away from the girl, disturbed by the intensity of her gaze.

'Would you consider committing yourself to monastic life and taking your vows?'

'Aye,' nodded Sarah. 'But what about this…' She pointed to her swollen stomach.

Once again, the French woman turned away, as though unable to face the sins of wicked men. 'That will be taken care of, Sarah. The nuns will take the child, and rest assured it will be looked after and given a better life than you ever could give it. The good Lord provides for all, trust in Him.'

'I will try…'

'Hush child. Do not fret. I shall guide you. But once you are settled, I must return to France. You've no idea how much I miss my sisters there…'

'Why did you come to Scotland?'

Sister Louise winced, her face contorted with pain. 'Never you mind mon cher, we must think of you and your new life, a life filled with God, Sarah. It matters not why I came to Scotland, I'm here with you and that's what is important for now. Let us take one day at a time, I will remain with you till the child is born…after that we will be sure to set you on the path to true salvation.' Once again, Sister Louise took Sarah's hand in her own.

The blacks of Sarah's eyes ballooned to twice their size. Sister Louise squeezed the girls hand, and felt a warm glow envelope her entire body as the young woman rested her head upon her shoulder. Before long, a damp patch covered her sleeve were the girl had wept silent tears.

Sarah sniffed up and removed her head from the French nun's shoulder. Her speech when it came was rambling: 'I wish with all my heart that you would not leave. Must you return to France? I can't bear to see you go, not after all we've been through. Please stay. How will I cope without you?'

'Nonsense. You will be so busy at the convent you will hardly remember me. I must continue God's work.'

Sarah's bottom lip trembled. She really was a pitiful sight, Sister Louise had to fight the urge to embrace her. There had been quite enough physical contact between them, and now was the time to step back, to strengthen the girl. She knew pampering the girl would do no good.

'I will stay as long as I can, dear Sarah. But now you must try to be strong. You are no longer a child.'

Just before midnight they were admitted to a small building near the ruins of the old convent of North Berwick by sub prioress, Isobel Hume. Due to the late hour, they were given a hasty meal and shown to a small cold cell. In the wee hours, Sister Louise tossed and turned in her bedl, a blanket drawn up to her chin, her nose pressed into her habit, its scent that of the girl.

***

They came at the first sign of dusk, as dogs barked throughout the castle grounds. Around his neck they placed a brass collar, fastening the hasp into one of three slots around his throat with a D shaped rivet. In the opposite cell, old Jacob prayed to the Lord and asked Him to forgive Magnus for his sins.

'Listen to me, Magnus. Peter himself said they promised him freedom, while they themselves were slaves of depravity—for a man is a slave to whatever has mastered him.'

'Silence, Quaker, we've heard quite enough o'yer haverings,' growled one of the gaolers.

Still fettered, they dragged Magnus along a maze of dank corridors, and the only sounds were that of rats scurrying and water drip dripping. For reasons unfathomable there seemed to be an absence of prisoners, perchance they've perished thought Magnus with a sickened heart. The climb up the stairs took a while. The ground was slippery under foot and weakened from captivity, Magnus faltered near every step. In the end, the exasperated gaolers shoved a rough hand under each of Magnus's armpits and half walked – carried him up the steps. At the top he felt a strong draught, like a heavenly caress upon his face. Magnus sniffed up, the air smelled of peat smoke, like smoked bacon, and the aroma made him clutch his shrunken stomach. They tramped along for a while, and with every step the passageway became brighter; Magnus blinked and pinched his eyes, wiping away tears that rolled down his face. And all the while great shootings pains burst beneath his eyelids until he reached the entrance and sank to his knees. It took a while for his eyes to be adjust to the light of day. He squeezed his eyes together, blinked away tears of pain and was able to make out the shadowy silhouette of a wooden cart and horse.

'Up you get, laddie. We've a journey ahead of us.'

'How am I supposed to get up there with these…?' Magnus jangled his chains.

'We'll remove the leg ones, but the ones on your hands stay on.'

'And what about this?' Magnus tugged at the serf collar.

'That's a wee present from the baron.' The gaoler with yellow-brown teeth sniggered and nudged his fellow guard in the ribs.

Once on the cart, they made Magnus lie down on his belly, across the narrowest part of the wooden base, so that his body hunched up. His nose pressed into stale straw, and then a boot kicked him in the back as the cart jolted at the hiss of a whip. How Magnus endured those first breaths upon the cart floor he knew not, his ears pricked up to familiar sounds all around him. Once or twice he fancied he heard his mother's voice and Sarah's, but he couldn't be sure. Thus, as the cart swayed from side to side, he felt his neck and shoulders slacken and his breathing become shallow, and before long he fell into a deep sleep. When he awoke his legs were cramped and the collar around his head cut into his neck.

'My neck hurts.'

'Get him up, said yellow teeth.

They propped him up near the rear of the cart. A long snaking river dominated the horizon. 'Is that the Tweed?'

'Never you mind.'

Before long, they changed course, the cart clattering along an endless winding road, until finally they arrived at one of the most grand and beautiful houses Magnus had ever seen. Nowhere near as big as Castle Wood, it had a square appearance, with symmetrical lines, a large panelled door and huge rectangular windows, and so many of them. Once off the cart, the gaolers nodded to the carter and then dragged Magnus to a back entrance, one for servants and travelling merchants. A sleepy serving maid admitted them, and took them through a small scullery to a large kitchen, before scurrying off to speak to her superior.

'I'm starving. She could have sat us down and gave us some broth first,' said yellow teeth.

'Not as this hour. It wouldn't surprise me if they asked us to come back tomorrow, and we'll have a devil of a time getting a tavern at this hour – we'll have to sleep in the cart...'

'The carter might not permit it; he's probably busy attending his horse in the stables as we speak. He might not want to get his head down with the likes of us.'

'He can easily be persuaded,' yellow teeth produced a shiny coin from his pocket.

Oblivious to his gaolers, Magnus looked around, his mouth gaping open at the sight of the kitchen, a huge turn spit for roasting meats stood in front of a hearth, and a mantle stood above it at a great height, at least one and a half men. The hearth was flanked by two walls, and upon these walls, suspended from hooks were fowl and what he supposed was hare. A fat woman lay curled up on a chair nearby, fast asleep clutching a tea chest and a bunch of keys, most probably the housekeeper or cook.

After what seemed like eternity a rather unassuming little man arrived. Upon his head, he wore a white bed cap, and to Magnus's mind it sprouted from his head like a crude vegetable root, absent of soil. Despite a heavy wool blanket draped around his shoulders, the man's teeth chattered with cold, he proceeded towards the hearth to warm his hands and behind. But before he did, he placed his lantern upon a nearby table. Steam rose off his blanket as he warmed his rump near the fire.

'So what have we here? What has Baron Bothwell sent me? One of his runts no doubt.'

Yellow teeth cleared his throat. 'Aye – this is the man. Go on, laddie, don't keep him waiting – he is your Master now.'

The hairs on Magnus's scalp began to prickle, and his stomach lurched. He looked to the small man, a ridiculous spectacle in his silly hat, and walked forward, ignoring the prods in his back. As he got closer to the hearth, he noticed the cook or housekeeper open one eye and then shut it again.

'That's close enough serf. Stand straight. Lord, he stinks.' The man in the bed cap wrinkled his nose.

Yellow teeth shrugged. 'He's been in the dungeons two year or so, give or take.'

'Open your mouth – nice and wide.'

Magnus frowned and stretched his jaw, his hands forming fists at his side as the man inspected inside his mouth.

'He's lost a few at the back, but good teeth. Take off the leine, I need to see if there are any problems with your back. Come on, laddie don't be shy.'

It was humiliating enough to have to stand there half naked in the kitchen, the cook taking sly glances at him every now and then, but then to disgrace him further, the man began to trace his hands over the sinews of Magnus's muscles.

'Good. Good. A fine specimen, a little scrawny but cook will soon fatten him up. The collar is a nice touch.'

The man peered close to the brass collar, so close Magnus felt his breath upon his skin. Once or twice, the pointed peak of his bed cap poked Magnus in the eye, and this seemed to cause much amusement to the cook and the two gaolers.

'Excellent hammer work but the engraving leaves a lot to be desired. What's your name man, I expect you're wondering what all this is about.'

'Magnus.'

'My name is Sir John Stuart, Magnus, and I am your new master. After today I expect you will not see me again, so there will be no need for any further introductions or pleasantries. Your back looks strong enough, have you had any experience as a pickman hewer?

'I do not understand...'

'Understand what?'

'Why I am here.'

'Ah – of course, you're in no position to inspect the collar, and even if you were, you couldn't read it. Let me explain the situation then, the collar states that you are a gift to me from Baron Bothwell of Castle Wood. He was your laird was he not?'

'Aye.'

'Well Bothwell is no longer your master, I am. In short, I care not for idleness so you will be put to work at once is that understood?'

Magnus nodded.

'I own a mine, well several to be exact and therefore need men to win the coal within them.'

Magnus's eyes widened. 'I'm a peasant farmer. I've worked the land all my life; I've never set foot in a mine.'

'Well that's about to change, Magnus.'

***

The baron and his valet boarded a ship at Leith, bound for France at midday. The weather was not good, he wondered whether to postpone but decided against it. Upon the quarterdeck, he pulled his hat tightly over his face to keep his ears clear of the cold and peered through a thick fog towards his homeland. Shapes shifted in the damp mist, and rolled silently across the dark, restless water of the Forth, It didn't take a genius to realise how cruel and unforgiving the sea was. William clasped the ship rail and leaned over, the sea was frothy, all foam and seaweed. A gull mewed ahead, and sliced through the sea mist to taunt him.

'Filthy creatures.' William stepped back.

'Harmless.' The valet shrugged.

'You wouldn't think so if they shit on you.'

By order of the Captain, the boatswain made the baron his utmost priority, and immediately arranged for him to have his luggage taken to a private cabin. The room, not far from the captain's was small but comfortable, lit by silver lamps filled with whale oil. Before the boatswain departed, he tipped his hat and said: 'I trust the cabin is satisfactory?'

'Adequate thank you.'

'The captain has requested that you dine with him at eight, in his private quarters.'

'Very good – and what of my valet? Where's he to stay during the voyage?'

'He could sleep at the foot of your bed. But if you'd prefer more privacy, I could arrange for him to stay with the able seamen below?'

William shook his head and grumbled. 'No that will not do, Lord knows what manner of pestilence he would contract near the likes of them. He will stay here with me.' The boatswain nodded and pushed the door shut with a soft thud. And the very act seemed to cause the wind to rise and buffeted the ship across a churning sea; William clutched a hand to his stomach and resisted the urge to retch. He never could get his sea legs, a fact his father continually taunted him about for most of his life. After a short nap, William awoke to the loud snores of his manservant. To his relief the passage had become calmer.

'McKenzie.Wake up, man and stop making that God awful noise – you're causing the walls to shake.'

The servant sat up in a daze and wiped the sleep from his eyes. 'I am so sorry, master. I cannae help it.'

William gazed at the wretched man, shivering on the floor with only his plaid to cover him . He threw him a blanket and stretched. 'Here. That should warm you some. Now, how long have you served me, McKenzie?'

'All my life, master. Well since I was a bairn.'

'Do you possess a name?'

The manservant's brows bunched together. 'Aye. McKenzie.'

'A christian name?'

'Blad.'

The baron's eyes narrowed. 'What an odd name. Is that Russian? Come to think of it you do have a Slav look about you…'

'Nae my family originate from Ireland. Whatever makes you think that?'

'Blad – 'tis similar to Vlad, like the Impaler, you know the Romanian Prince…?'

William waited for a response, then almost laughed at his foolishness. How on earth would a manservant, a poor, illiterate man of low standing know who Vlad the Impaler was? Not that McKenzie was dim-witted of course. No, in fact, William had insisted that he accompany him to France purely because he was the best valet around.

'Would you like a wee dram to warm you up, Blad?'

William reached for some whisky and poured them both a good measure, then handed the bewildered servant the drink. The servant held his with shaky hands, his eyes wide with the wonder of a child.

'Well drink up, Blad. Then tell me how you came to have such a preposterous name.'

'Was my sister,' he said wiping his mouth.

'Your sister?' William's forehead wrinkled.

'Aye. She never could say my name. You see my name is Bradley McKenzie. But my sister, Mary, well she could never say it, so she called me Blad instead. I'm afraid the name stuck. Before long, I was just plain Blad.'

William roared with laughter. 'I think I'll stick with McKenzie.'

***

The gaolers left. As light faded, a thin man guided Magnus to a miserable abode not fit for swine…but anything was better than the dungeons. His eyes swept the room, straw pallets lined the floor, and two overflowing piss pots sat in the dark corners stinking the place out. There was no hearth or a place for cooking food. How did folk eat here? Magnus felt like he hadn't ate in days. His stomach growled, he placed a hand upon his belly and rubbed.

'Is there any food?'

The thin man scowled, clearly irritated. 'Workers get rations twice a day here, make sure the rats don't eat it because you'll not be given extra. Do you know who I am?'

'Nae.'

'Your coal master.'

Another master, Magnus thought, *how many am I to have?*

A door banged open and the sounds of disgruntled men entered the room.

'These are your fellow colliers.' The coal master held out an arm.

A motley crew of creatures, a breed apart stared at him. Magnus stared back, such a contrast to healthy men of the soil – of fresh air and sun and plentiful food. If truth be told, due to his imprisonment, Magnus looked much the same, pale, dirty and undernourished. But these miserable creatures carried melancholy within their trembling limbs, their spines curved from labouring in narrow tunnels of putrid air. Magnus dared to gaze upon them, intrigued by their naked torsos, crisscrossed with scars - he soon learned that these marks were made by falling rocks cutting the skin. Coal dust then settled into these wounds to create strange tattoos. Once the men entered the bothy, the coal master ignored Magnus and informed the men of his working in the mine. A trial basis he said. It wasn't long before a discussion began regarding Magnus 'taking up the pick.' For some reason the colliers thought this a ridiculous notion and a quarrel broke out.

The coal master stood with his legs wide apart, hands on hips. 'I don't care if he's never set foot in a mine. My orders are to put him to work in the mine, he's more than capable of taking up the pick.'
One of the senior collier men squared up to the coal master shaking his head. 'That's madness. Haven't we enough to be getting on with down pit? Now you expect us to try and show a man who's never set foot in a mine to immediately win coal? He should be put to the coal wall, he can hold wedges and candles like the bairns. He's never trapped, nor been a putter – he's not even earned the right to be called a half-man.'
The coal master sniggered. 'Stop protesting man. He's more than capable of the work, the man just needs guidance and a muscular pair of arms. He looks strong enough to me.'
'Aye, he's strong enough – but he knows nothing of the dangers of mining; he could take a stoop out and kill us all. Does he even know what one is?'
The coal master groaned. 'All you need to know laddie is dig where you are told to dig and nowhere else. Do not take easy coal from the pillars or everything will collapse. Anything else you want to know ask Jimmy Mole.'

Magnus felt nauseous of the prospect of what lay ahead.
'Ready to go?'
Magnus stared into the coal master's eyes. 'What now?'
'Aye – now is as good a time as any.'
It seemed to Magnus that his heart thumped in his chest, with the rat-a-tat beat of a strange military tattoo. He followed slowly, at the rear of the men, dragging his heels. Magnus was cold, tired and famished. At the pit surface, with much difficulty he climbed into a huge basket suspended above a huge, gaping black hole – the pit mouth. A hand grabbed his arm to steady him as his leg caught in a rope, and to Magnus's surprise it was the very collier who grumbled with the coal

master about his ability to work within the pit. With his neck arched backwards, Magnus took one final glance at the sky above as he made his first descent and then closed his eyes. He loathed the thought of sinking below, though it couldn't be worse than the dungeons...or could it ? As the basket began its descent, he dared to open his eyes once more. He focused on the rope above, the one that held the basket. Would it hold? Was he about to die? He knew the rope passed high over a wheel at the surface and then under another attached to a horse. 'Don't worry, laddie – the horse gin will hold us.'

Magnus placed two hands together in prayer and then clung to the rope, his knuckles white with tension. It was then that he noticed a group of wee boys climbing down the rope above, like four frightened monkeys. 'What on earth are they doing up there? Can't they climb in here with us?

The collier shook his head and grunted. 'Only men are allowed in the basket and you'll do well to curb your tongue. The coal master has asked me to keep a good eye on you, but then where he thinks you can go once we're at the dip-head level is a mystery to me.' The collier pointed to Magnus's serf collar. 'I'll not even ask about that, none of my business. Don't think it'll get you any special treatment, we're all the same here, *all* collier serfs, property of the mine owner – you know the one, lording it up in his grand house while we risk life and limb to extract his black gold. God knows it is dangerous enough with the constant threat of explosions from gases and firedamp, fires, roof fall... and then there's the sepsis following an injury. Am I making myself clear?'

Magnus nodded. Suddenly the basket lurched and caused one of the wee pit boys to scream out and plead to sweet Jesus to spare his life, and then there was nothing but darkness.

CHAPTER 10

A terrible wind blew as William and his manservant crossed the quarter-deck to locate the captain's great cabin. The weather was deteriorating, and as the clouds darkened above, the ship began to roll across a churning sea. The crew reacted, sleeves up, axes in hand to cut away the foremast, to prevent it snapping in two. William wondered whether to return to his cabin. He stepped forward and grabbed the sea rail, then dared to peer below. A howling wind near took the breath from him, as white capped waves slapped the side of the ship and burst into froth, sending a sea spray onto William's face. As he wiped it away he observed Captain Pepper exiting his cabin. The weather seemed of no consequence to him, in fact, the captain seemed more concerned with the position of his fine tricorn hat. William froze, he had an awful feeling, a notion that all was not well. Instead of returning to his cabin, William clung to the sea rail and observed the old sea captain from afar. The man was formidable, a rather stern character with rough features, definitely not a man to be crossed. And so prickly a character was Captain Pepper, he was not a particularly approachable person, so William stayed where he was, clutching the rail, observing the man at war with the sea. Something held the captain's attention... a young cabin boy of young Robbie's age, twelve or thirteen.

The captain flew into a great rage. 'Boy. Why aren't you taking down the studding sails, you know they are the first to come down in bad weather? Get on with it...let's see how you fare this time while the ships rolling. Still haven't got your sea legs have ya, laddie?'
The cabin boy scurried off to help the able seamen take in the mizzen topgallant and studding sails, as the captain decided whether or not to point the ship into the oncoming wind, or away from it so that the storm blew the ship with it, to relieve the pressure. But soon, the captain's focus returned to the boy, and when it did his face took on a look of pure hatred.

Captain Pepper shouted through the shrieking wind: 'You damned scoundrel, have I not told you a thousand times how to take in the sails. I'll take the skin off your back for this…'

A nearby seaman spat tobacco onto the floor as the captain continued to rant and verbally abuse the boy. The seaman didn't bat an eyelid and continued with his work, ignoring the boy's obvious distress. An icy gust roared through the rigging. It was then that William realised the plight of the poor cabin boy, and what meagre clothing the laddie had on, nowhere near good enough for the elements aboard ship. The cabin boy was soaked through, blue with cold and his hands shook as he tried to take in the sails…and then, for no reason, Captain Pepper snatched the length of rope from him and struck him with it so hard, the laddie fell to his knees and began to cry. William's hands curled and formed two fists, never had he seen such cruelty, he stepped forward to intervene, but his valet pulled him back.

'Not our business, Baron Bothwell.'

'Hell and damnation, all the laddie's done is tie up a rope.'

The valet sniggered and opened his mouth to speak, then thought better of it.

William shook his head. 'Well spit it out man. What was you going to say?'

'I cannae say.' The valet's shouldered drooped.

'McKenzie. Just say it.'

'I've seen folk punished for less at Castle Wood. The last ghillie for instance…'

William thought back, aye the ghillie who cut a branch off his covin tree, he'd forgot all about that. Suddenly a cold sweat enveloped him as his gaze returned to Captain Pepper… he narrowed his eyes and thought, *am I like that? Is that the kind of hideous creature I am?* The realisation struck him like a thunderbolt, and caused his legs to turn to mush. His valet luckily supported him until he grabbed onto the ship's rail. And all the while, the captain's rope struck the cabin boy repeatedly until his lips and nose were quite bloodied and swollen. The crew did nothing. Everything carried on as normal, in fact not one of them seemed affected by what had just passed.

After the thrashing, Captain Pepper, despite being rather sweaty and dishevelled from his onslaught upon the wee cabin boy, finally caught sight of the baron and his valet, and swiftly directed them to a room fit for a King... a chamber that would put most Scottish drawing-rooms to shame. A fine dining table graced the middle of the room, carved from gleaming mahogany, atop of it was a selection of silverware. The captain prompted the baron to take a seat, as Mckenzie was shooed away to eat with the other men in the mess. William wished he could join them, instead of having to stomach the company of this detestable man. He closed his eyes and pinched his nose, unpleasant pictures filled his mind. When he opened his eye lids his gaze settled on two silver lamps suspended from the ceiling, dangerously swishing back and forth with the motion of the ship.

'Whale oil if that's what you're thinking, Baron Bothwell.'

'Excuse me?' William said.

'The lamps you are looking at, they are filled with whale oil. Well clear of the stern windows and those fancy drapes.' Captain Pepper chuckled.

'Good to know. Not a good place for a fire I imagine.'

'Disastrous.' The captain replied.

'Is anyone joining us?'

'No.' The Captain rolled up his sleeves.

They dined at once. A splendid meal of meat and vegetables, and fine claret to wash it down. They talked business as they ate. After a while all chat became stilted, and eventually came to a halt, as the two men had little in common, or perhaps neither of them were in a mood for conversation. The whale oil lamps continued to sway, squeaking as they did, competing with the cries of men toiling on the decks outside. After the meal, as William wiped his mouth with a piece of cloth, he noticed the captain's sleeves all smeared with blood.

'May I ask why you punished the cabin boy so severely?'

'Of course. But may I point out first of all, as *Master* of this vessel, I need not explain my actions to you or anyone for that matter, but if you must know the boy was at fault, and therefore needed correcting. A servant of this ship must be corrected at times, and unfortunately this particular boy is in constant need of discipline.'

'For not tying a rope to your liking?'

'Tying a rope correctly on a ship such as this could mean the difference between life and death, Baron Bothwell.'

William nodded, and as he did so the action caused sour bile to fill his throat. He reached for his glass of claret and took a good mouthful, and as the night wore on he had a sinking feeling within the pit of his stomach that he might need a few more stiff drinks before the end of the voyage.

***

It wasn't the dark that alarmed him, it was the heat and lack of air. Magnus felt like he was drowning within the deepest, blackest pond, chest heaving, his breathing laboured – he held a hand to his breast and pressed hard. The collier that took him down lay on his side within a thirty-inch seam of hard rock. A strange device supported his upper body, a wedge of sorts, as he chipped and cut away at the coal.
'I need more light. Bring the candle closer.' He growled.

Magnus staggered in the dark, stupefied by his journey to the dip-level where colliers worked to the rise. Like a dazed and dwarfed animal he'd crawled through dripping wet tunnels, using muscles he'd never used before, till finally they reached a stall. The candle flickered as Magnus moved towards the collier, knees scratched by rock, his muscles twitching. Who would have thought the simple act of holding up a candle could cause such agony and pain?
'I'm so thirsty I'm tempted to lap at that puddle.'
The collier laughed. ''Tis the heat and coal dust clogging up your throat. Once I'm finished here you may fetch my jacket, I've some ale and a bite to eat. Won't be long, just keep the candle here a moment longer will you? Soon be done.'
'Thank you, thank you.' The act of kindness seemed to trigger within Magnus a deep sadness, and suddenly his shoulders drooped and began to shake. *What's the matter with me? Get a grip man.*
'How many tubs now?'
'Three – the third is near the brim.'

'Time for a wee drink and a smoke of me pipe,' the collier twisted his body till he assumed a sitting position, his knees tucked into his bony chest. 'Pass us my coat will you? And don't set it alight with the candle.'

Magnus placed the candle upon the ground, fetched the coat and handed it to the man, already salivating at the prospect of water. But after a while of searching through the coat, the collier groaned out loud. 'Damn rats.'

'What about them?'

'They've taken the food. No matter, I still have the small ale. Here – take your fill.'

Magnus rubbed the coal dust from his eyes and reached for the ale, the liquid tasted like the sweetest nectar, but instinctively he took small sips till his throat burned no more. 'Thank you.'

'You're welcome, Magnus.' The collier held out a hand and gestured for Magnus to help him up. 'Jimmy Mole is the name.'

'Pleased to make your acquaintance, Jimmy.'

As Magnus helped Jimmy to his feet he suddenly realised that the collier was naked as the day he was born.

Jimmy chuckled, and stood with his legs wide apart, as though it was perfectly natural to be naked before a perfect stranger far beneath the ground. 'Pleased to make my acquaintance are you? Well you might change your mind before the end of the day. See our coal master seems to think you'll be handy with a pick – are you ready to try?'

'Aye.'

'Well get those damp clothes off and get yourself ready.'

'Why?'

'You won't slip into the tight spaces with your clothes on, laddie – try it with your clothes on if you like – but see how many times the material snags and traps you to the rock. Believe you me, you will move better down there without your garb on.'

Magnus shrugged, placed down the water and began to tug off his clothes. Once naked, the heat became more bearable and he felt a strange sense of liberty despite the cumbersome collar that scratched his neck.

'Better?'

'Aye. Shall I carry on where you left off' Magnus nodded.

'Oh aye – be my guest.' Jimmy Mole smiled a strange little smile.

On his hands and knees Magnus tried to ease himself into a small black void, at that moment he realised how Jimmy Mole got his namesake. No matter how much Magnus twisted, turned, slithered – he could not manoeuvre himself into the cavity that Jimmy Mole had just worked. Magnus cursed and bit his tongue; the rock cut into his flesh, and scraped away the skin from his back, arms and legs.

Jimmy urged him on. 'That's it, laddie – just twist your shoulder a wee bit and…'

'Aye – go on then hand us the pick.' Magnus lay on his side within a cavity, he felt Jimmy squeeze a wedge beneath his shoulder and hand him the pick. How on earth was he supposed to swing it within this confined place, but somehow he did it – and it was then that he felt a great sense of exhilaration as his first coal was won.

'That's it, son – keep going, use all your might, don't be tempted to rest for too long or you'll seize up.'

Magnus continued to cut the coal with his pick. As he did so, every bone and muscle in his body screamed with agony; hips, back, arms, neck. He toiled for as long as he could, Jimmy Mole all the while guiding and prompting him to work on. Thus, after much sweat, blood and toil, Magnus filled his first hundredweight of coal. The putters and drawers arrived soon after, to take away the tubs of coal. Once they arrived, Magnus cowered in the shadows, his hands positioned in such a way to cover his manhood. This seemed to cause much amusement to Jimmy Mole, who proceeded to imitate him and feign embarrassment.

'Don't be shy laddie, by the end of the day near everyone is naked here, except for their caps – aye if you forget to wear a hat, you'll end up with a bald patch for sure. Wait till you see old Kenny, he's got a head full of thick hair, except for a bald spot where he pushes the tubs with his heid.'

Magnus emerged from the shadows to acknowledge the others. He nodded to all of them, then noticed a beautiful boy with a black face, and when the boy smiled his teeth gleamed like white pearls within a black peat bog. A crude belt was fastened around the laddie's ragged trousers, and a chain dangled between his legs. Magnus turned away, the boy's image disturbed him for some reason, but he knew not why. Like beasts of burden, the boys fastened their chains to the corves, some pushed, thrusting the tubs with their arms and heads, while others (like the beautiful boy) pulled, crawling on all fours, with the chain passing high up between their legs, wearing great holes into their trousers.

'Poor lassies. That's my girl at the front. The pretty one.' Jimmy Mole shook his head.

'What do you mean? No never…lassies?' Magnus squeezed his eyes shut and looked again. His heart thumping in his chest at the memory of the beautiful face – a lass not a boy! And through the dim light, he peered at the departing sinewy figures, and caught a glimpse of a soft swelling curve, and realised Jimmy Mole was telling the truth.

***

Baroness Matilda had a plan, for weeks now the peasant folk had talked of a *hairst,* whatever that was. Every day it had been *hairst* this and *hairst* that. Confused by the meaning of the word, curiosity got the better of her. So, in order to understand she'd arranged for her maid to fetch Falmouth to her private rooms – for a private consultation of sorts. He arrived fresh from the fields. His scent of heather and earth, and was it possible to smell damp rain? She looked him up and down, he was all beard and ruddy cheeks – a young, strapping man in his prime. She blushed, and reminded herself that she was a married woman.

'I wish to ask you a question?'

He nodded. 'Of course. What would you like to ask?'

'What is a hairst?'

'It's the climax of farming. Folk look forward to it all year. If the harvest has been a good one, it's a time for feasts and celebration.'

'And this year… has it been good harvest… or has it been rather hard?' Matilda tilted her head to the side as if straining to hear him.

Falmouth grinned and for a moment he dared to look his mistress in the eye.

'Well Falmouth?' Had Matilda imagined it, or had the gamekeeper's eyes glitter with roguish mirth?

'As you are well aware – it is *very* hard at times, but not now.' Falmouth replied.

Matilda picked up her fan and fluttered it ten to the dozen, as though swatting away a fly. 'Very good. I wish to assist in the celebrations, perhaps you could inform the others of my plans and we can set a time and date.'

'Aye – I'll tell them, no doubt they'll want to uphold the usual customs. The feast can only begin once the last sheaf of corn is cut.'

'Of course. Please keep me informed.' And with that Falmouth was dismissed.

The following Sabbath, as the sun raised itself high into a cloudless sky, one of the farmers took his sickle and cut the cailleach. With much care he took a part of the sheaf (believed to be a fertility symbol), and stuffed it into a sack tucked beneath one of his oxsters, to keep until the first horse foaled, as it was thought to represent new life. The other part of the sheaf, he buried beneath the first ploughed furrow, so fertility would be transferred.

The celebrations began. Upon a bale of hay Matilda sat with her fan in her hand, Robbie sat beside her. She smiled as she observed the dancers swirl around, their crude labouring boots kicking up a cloud full of dust. Matilda wore one of her finest frocks and heavy jewels, not a practical decision on a fine summer's day. Thank heavens her hat shielded her from the onslaught of the powerful midday sun. While Matilda fluttered her fan, a small peasant girl approached her and presented Matilda with one of those awful corn dollies made from a sheaf. She forced a smile, took the doll and shooed the dirty little urchin away.

'Oh mother. She was just trying to make you happy.'

'But I am happy, son. Don't I look happy?'

'No, if anything you look hot and flustered. Why on earth are you dressed up for a ball? A hairst is an informal affair. You stand out like a rose in a dung heap.' Robbie groaned and stretched out his peg leg. His good leg bended at the knee, and seemed to mock the other for not being agile.

'Really Robbie, what would you have me wear? A pair of leather stays and striped petticoats? And why are you wearing those ridiculous peasant's trousers?'

'I think they look rather fetching.' Robbie ran his hands across the coarse plaid cloth.

'Don't be foolish, dear.'

For a while Matilda observed the peasants laughing and dancing, so carefree and merry. 'Why do you suppose they are so happy, Robbie?' Robbie's expression became grave. 'Happy – like a caged bird that sings?'

Matilda stopped fluttering her fan and touched his arm. 'Yes – precisely that. Look at them, they toil in the fields all day and have nothing, and yet they seem full of joyfulness and good cheer.'

'They don't know any different – it's all they've ever known. And because they've never had anything they are thankful for the simplest of things.'

Matilda pondered on that, Robbie was quite an insightful soul for such a young man – she wondered if his true vocation was destined for kirk or the monastery. Lord knew what prospects he had now that he had one leg.

'Mother, are you listening to me?'

Matilda stopped daydreaming and turned to her son. 'Yes.'

'Look mother. Falmouth has arrived.'

Matilda caught a glimpse of the handsome ghillie's broad back, she waved her fan faster, wafting as much air as she could about her pale face. Of late she suffered hot spells, causing her face to glow a vermillion red. Matilda had no control over the matter, and much to her annoyance, once she observed Falmouth; she had one of those blasted hot spells again. With a strange longing in her loins she watched him dance with a wee lassie, his large hands spanning the girl's tiny waist. With confidence, Falmouth twirled her in time to the music, spinning her round and round. Matilda felt a buzzing in her ears as she watched them, neck straining to see who the lass was, she caught a glimpse of the serf girl's weathered face, as brown as berry – ripened by the rays of a harsh sun. 'Do you think she is pretty, Robbie?'

'Who?'

'The serf with Falmouth.'

'Sabine.'

Matilda tutted. 'How do you know her name?'

'He's been walking out with her a few week, she's a nice lassie.'

'Yes, yes. But do you think she is pretty?'

'She's comely. But her face is brown as a berry... she hasn't your beautiful pale complexion, mother.'

Matilda positively beamed, and fanned away another hot flush. 'You are a darling, Robbie.' And with that Matilda did a daring thing, afterwards she would repeat the memory over and over in her foolish head and wonder why she'd acted as she did. In a daze Matilda had thrown down her fan, and picked up her skirts to barge a pathway through a sea of dancers. Once she'd reached the two of them, she'd tapped Falmouth upon the shoulder and held out a hand. And oh the shame – because the two of them, Falmouth and Sabine just stared at her with slack jaws, as if she were a woman with two heads. The longest moment passed before Matilda stuttered: 'I – I – I, I am so sorry.'' And then, with her face crimson red, she'd fled from the feast. What had she been thinking...a lady wanting to dance with one of her servants, she must have been mad. Oh the shame - the shame!

***

At the exact time William dined with the captain, the woman he crossed the English Channel in pursuit of took her vows before Almighty God near the ruins of the old North Berwick Priory. Sister Louise looked on proudly as young Sarah took her vows, her heart swelling beneath her habit, a slight curve to her lips. All thoughts of returning to France she now abandoned, two matters dominated her mind now – achieving the Office of Prioress and Sarah.

In short, Sister Louise was canny. Throughout the whole world, not only Scotland, women, whether high born or of peasant stock were offered little choices in life. Even the top of the heap had little independence, noble women, once married became the property of their husband. Also, once a woman married, all her possessions became their husbands – and the husband... well he became Lord and Master. Peasant women suffered more, milkmaids, street hawkers, whores, servants; all suffered nothing but hard labour and strife. Sister Louise, a woman of humble beginnings, wanted more. A convent (even a secret one) had much to offer. Here a woman served but one Master – an invisible entity, one she could stomach to honour and obey. Furthermore, a nun could choose a vocation, read books, and even pursue an education – in a convent a woman could progress.

To be prioress was the ultimate dream. Prioresses were powerful heads of their communities, and there was no other institution, save perhaps the monastery (a place forbidden to women), that women could partake so fully in shaping their own and other women's destinies. Sister Louise knew this well, a prioress could enjoy considerable freedom in a convent and the outside world; here she would have absolute control over the lives and wills of her sisters. But there was one problem, Scotland was a protestant country now. And yet, this convent seemed to have managed to continue, in a clandestine manner, with an old woman in charge, an ailing woman…but oh what a prestigious position it would be, even during these troubled times, Sister Louise smiled to herself.

The old rules need not apply she thought. How could they when the women shouldn't even be here? The old rules were simple… qualifications for the head of the house, before being presented as a candidate for the Office of Prioress, had to meet certain requirements. Candidates had to be of good name, be legitimately born and a professed nun for at least five years, and be at least twenty years of age – thirty for Cistercian orders. If a candidate did not meet any of the requirements, a special dispensation had to be granted by the Pope, and sadly, in Sister Louise's case, this would have been unavoidable, as she had a defect of birth - in other words she had been born illegitimate. Anyhow, none of this mattered…the priory ran in secret and probably had little contact with Rome now. The nuns had nowhere to go, except abroad…and yet almost all of them preferred to stay, despite the risks, after all it was home. And so, as the last prioress lay on her deathbed, Sister Louise, aware that the women would soon need a new prioress began to scheme. Since her arrival at the convent she had ingratiated herself to everyone. She did this by taking on the role of cellaress, and worked tirelessly in the kitchens and gardens to provide mouth-watering food and wine. Sister Louise grovelled, she crawled, and used every opportunity to make herself the most well-liked and respected sister at North Berwick.

As Baron Bothwell searched for Sarah across Avignon, the old prioress died. And as the nuns mourned her death, an election was conducted to decide who would take her place. In the privacy of her chamber, Sister Louise fell to her knees and pressed her palms together in silent prayer. As she made the sign of the cross upon her person, she hoped her requests would be answered.

***

To Sarah, the Magdalene Chapel and her former home at Castle Wood was a distant memory. She liked the nuns of North Berwick, there was a tranquillity and calmness here that she'd never experienced. it was really quite beautiful. One of the nuns told her that on the eve of the Scottish Reformation there had been 21 sisters and a prioress at the old priory. But now, many years later and following the prioresses death, they were reduced to thirteen in total, a not altogether undesirable figure, because according to the scriptures there had been thirteen present at the last supper. However, the main reason Sarah settled so well at Berwick was because of Sister Louise, her saviour, the rock Sarah attached herself to. Within tranquil cloisters, Sarah looked upon Sister Louise with glazed eyes, just peering upon her face made her feel wholesome and warm. The other sisters said she came from a faraway land, a place she could not pronounce. It was the reason she looked different perhaps. In private, when no one else was around, Sarah admired Sister Louise's glossy black hair, such a contrast to her white skin, and her mouth… the prettiest shape, as though stung by a bee, all swollen and red.

Sometimes, when all was quiet, they stole precious moments together, and promises were made. If Sister Louise became prioress many changes would occur, some good and some bad. Sarah became alarmed at the bad, because she knew that it probably meant that they would have to spend time apart, and she loathed to think of that.
'What will happen if you become prioress?'

'It's too early to say if I will be chosen or not. But if they do pick me, I imagine I will be rather busy. But Sarah, now that you have taken your vows you should be content in your own company, be at peace with God, for He is our one and only saviour.'

Sarah nodded, since the loss of her baby she had felt rather weepy of late. A tear rolled down her face and a pain filled her chest. The feelings she held for Sister Louise frightened and confused her, and at times she became so overwhelmed by them, she had to curl into a ball and place a fist close to her mouth to stifle her sobs. Why hadn't she ever felt this way for Magnus, the father of her lost child, or any man for that matter? 'I forbid you to be cheerless, Sarah – it breaks my heart to see you so. You really are a melancholy girl at times, I do wish you'd lift your spirits, and snap out of it. Take comfort in the fact that we shall always be together, you and I, always, for I have decided to stay here with you. Now embrace me now before we go to the others.'

They clung together, two women – thrown together by chance, and connected for ever more.

CHAPTER 11

The image of the beautiful pit girl and her blackened face disturbed Magnus. At the end of his first day in the mine, he dreamt of the lassie that night, and the next – and near every night after that. It had been so long since he'd bedded a woman. How he longed to see her again, but it would not be for at least a couple of moons before he set eyes on her. Jimmy Mole no longer guided him see, not since the oversman stuck his oar in and fetched him a fremit bearer, and oh and what a pitiful creature she was, this fremit bearer, all covered in cuts and sores with a strap fastened across her forehead to carry her creel. When the lassie removed her 'tug' and placed her creel to the ground, Magnus hesitated before taking her extended grimy hand.

'Effie Hume.' She didn't remove her hat. 'I'm ye fremit bearer.'

'Fremet? What does that mean?'

Effie shrugged. 'Your wife or daughter is usually your bearer. A fremit is a stray…'

His brow furrowed as he tried to figure out her age. 'How old are you?'

'Seventeen. Why are you wearing that collar?'

Magnus ignored the question and looked her over once more; he'd seen more meat on the rats that scratched around the stalls. He hoped she knew what she was doing. Then he almost chuckled to himself, well she was bound to know more than him. Hellfire he was green as could be, unaccustomed to mining work, every muscle in his body burning and screaming with pain. Because if truth be told, he needed a strong woman to carry his coal up top. But really, did he now have to suffer the added inconvenience of an undernourished, ill-kempt child.

'You're thin and just a wee lassie – you're no seventeen.'

'I micht be just a lassie but I've shifted coal since I was a wean. You neednae worry aboot me, I can shift the coal and some back- coal, as much as you could carry hame at the end of the day.'

'Aye – well I hope so or we'll have the oversman breathing down our ear. How long have you been working here?'

Effie lifted her chin from chest and peered into his eyes. 'Ma parents died in an explosion when I was ten. I used taw help look after the other bairns at hame, but I became a bearer after the explosion. The oversman appointed me tae carry coals for any person he thought proper. I've had mony maisters since then. You neednae worry. I am mair than capable.'

The candlelight flickered and cast strange shadows upon her mucky face; she was nowhere near as comely as Jimmy Mole's lassie, but was graced with fine features save for a three inch scar that covered her left cheek. Somehow it gave her character and didn't detract from her looks. Magnus felt compelled to ask her about it.

'The scar – how did you get it?'

'Many years ago, I worked a nine-ladder pit. Have you seen the 22 cwt weights?'

'Aye I think so.' Magnus nodded his head.

'Well a wifie drapped hers above me on wan o' the ladders. Her tug snapped see, it couldnaw be helped. I managed to dodge some but was clattered in the face with great lumps of coal… and had ma shoulder knocked oot for days.'

'I'm sorry lassie.'

'Nae matter – 'tis all part of the work doon here. You're an old woman at forty if ye work the mines.'

Before her chin returned to her chest, Magnus noticed how she stared at his serf collar with curiosity again, but for now any more questions she had, she kept to herself.

'Come on then, Effie. We've work to do.'

Magnus soon realised that Effie spoke the truth. The lass could shift coal. Little Effie had the strength of an ox and never complained, she even shared her food and ale, and not once did she laugh or gawp at him as he toiled naked on the ground. Clumsy, unskilled, but above all…awkward is how Magnus felt amongst the other colliers, men who'd wrought within the coal seams since they were barely old enough to stand. Like Effie, Magnus was an outcast, with no family or friends. But at least Effie had an understanding of the people and ways. The collier class were indeed a breed apart. One day, after a long shift, Jimmy Mole sat with Magnus near the fire and told him all about kirk, and after he'd said his piece, Magnus wondered why anyone bothered to attend a holy service at all.

'Aye colliers are punished both sides of the grave, Magnus. We're no' allowed to be buried on consecrated ground. The collier class are buried on unconsecrated ground, far away from the kirk. We're no' allowed tae worship the Lord alongside decent folk either, for fear we'll contaminate them. Naw, the land owners, coal owners, tradesman and farm labourers worship God from the main part of the kirk, while we brown yins or mining folk, worship from a loft, separate from the main congregation.'

'You're jesting.' Magnus seethed.

'Sadly not.'

'The indignity of it.'

'Aye. They treat us like savages. Set us apart. Tell us to keep our brats 800 yards from the precinct of kirk at all times.'

'Well you'll not catch me there then.' Magnus glowered.

But with time, and because Jimmy Mole's daughter attended kirk, Magnus yielded. It was either that or spend his one free day alone. So, one Sabbath before Martinmas, he succumbed and set off with the others to pray. Kirk bells rang summoning the congregation, the bells peeling till finally there was silence. As Magnus climbed the outside staircase that lead to the separate loft, he took in his surroundings. The heather and ling, twisted trees ravaged by wind…lapwings, blackbirds, God's creations. All of this he savoured and drank in, the vibrant colours, smells, sensations, such a contrast to the black void of the mine. Once seated in the loft he strained his neck to catch a glimpse of Jimmy Mole's girl, she was sat at the back with her friends, and looked different clean…well as clean as could be. Her hair was raven black and her skin had an off yellow tone, she reminded him of an Egyptian, mysterious and exotic, and yet somehow she looked plainer without being stained black with soot.

The sermon began. From the elevated height of the loft folk strained to hear the minister's voice. More than once folk nudged and elbowed the person next to them, to shush one another. Magnus tried to listen for a moment, but the minister's words he liked not, it took all his composure not to walk out as the holy man thumped his bible and chastised the miners from his pulpit, for ungodliness, drunkenness, fornication, debauchery and idleness. The pious speech dragged on. Folk scratched and fidgeted, some yawned. One lassie could hardly keep awake and slumped forward in her seat, her long red hair obscuring her features. The poor lassie had fallen asleep, no doubt exhausted from a day's work in the mines. Some folk tried to wake her up by digging her in the ribs once or twice, but the lassie was not for waking.

Magnus fidgeted but continued to watch the girl when suddenly a noise sounded from behind the kirk door, an almighty screech. What was causing it was a mystery, but then his eyes widened as he watched a huge pole slide through a small hole to prod the sleeping girl, to awaken her. Magnus reacted without thinking and grabbed the pole with both hands, pushing it back to whence it had came.

The sleeping girl came to and suddenly shouted. 'No Magnus. You must not. '

Magnus peered into the lassies eyes, they were the most beautiful shade of sea green. *How had he not noticed that before?* His face suddenly reddened, and when his gaze returned to Effie's face, he focused on her scar instead. 'We should go from here, Effie, far away from this hell hole.'

'We cannot. We're not allowed to be seen by the congregation. We can only leave after the sermon has ended and not before. The minister will signal to us when we may leave.'

'Ah to hell with them all.' Magnus shouted for everyone to hear.

***

Klok Gumma exhaled noisily, cursed in her mother tongue and threw another leek into the cooking pot. She longed for her child, her only daughter, Greta... her beautiful Nordic princess with high cheekbones and clear blue eyes. Ever since the first baron arranged for Greta to be employed at Hollyrood, she felt like her heart had been ripped from her chest. How many years had it been now? She could not remember. Too long. The old baron was long dead, his wife too, and as a result her days of chief wise woman and midwife were well and truly over. These days Klok Gumma was no more than a kitchen hand.

'What ails you?' Cook asked.

'There's nothing for me here anymore, Eleanor. I'm too old.

'That's nonsense Klok Gumma. You're just feeling sorry for yourself.'' Cook grunted.

'I miss my daughter.'

'Aye well I miss my Magnus too. Is Greta a wise woman like you?'

Klok Gumma cackled. Her shoulders shook, but at the end of the laugh she gave a sad little smile. 'What else? 'Tis in her blood. They say she's a respected woman at Hollyrood. A woman of healing herbs and wisdom. '

'You should visit her. I wish I knew where my laddie was. It's been so long now.'

'Visit her, how can I? It's too far. I can't walk so good these days, not even with a stick.'

Eleanor placed a hand upon the wise woman's shoulder. 'Well I know how that feels, my legs are constantly swollen. But don't worry old woman, she'll return one day…to visit you. You'll see. Might even have a couple of bairns trailing after her.'

Klok Gumma's hand went to her face. 'Oh no. She won't come here. Not with *him* about.'

'Him?'

'The baron. Once the old baron sent my Greta away, he made sure his son didn't know of her whereabouts. He has a sickness see, a sickness in his mind and body for my Greta. Oh every day I pray to mother earth that he never finds her. He was obsessed with her see, followed her around all day long and spied on my lovely girl. He thought he loved her. But that was not love. He's not capable of love, a man like him. '

Cook stopped what she was doing and faced the wise woman. 'You talk of him as though he's a bad yin, but I ken him better than that. I fed him from my own breast. They were like brothers my Magnus and the baron once. He's not all bad you know. He did love her terribly though, I remember.'

The old woman's thin eyebrows raised. 'He's a bad egg I tell you. My Greta is gone because of him.'

'Oh quit whining. Go ask one of the carters to take you to see her. Find out which one goes out that way...Hollyrood 'tis not far from Edinburgh isn't it? If you jumped in one of the carts heading out that way, well the baroness probably won't notice you gone...not with her funny turns and her taking to her bed.'

'I might just do that. Oh, before I go, have you tried that potion I gave you for your legs?'

Cook stretched out one swollen leg. 'Aye, but they're still swollen.'

'We must use the arnica again to stop the fluid building up. I'll not have you bled. It's nonsense I tell you, draining the life force out of you it is, I'm convinced.' Klok Gumma sat down, her hands suddenly flopped in-between the folds of her apron, and she began to wring them together, all the while thinking of her canny lassie, so like herself. The fire crackled in front of her, its flames casting strange shadows on the scullery wall. At that moment a great crack and hiss snapped within the blaze and spat out a piece of burning timber. It landed on the floor directly in front of her.

'It's a sign.'

Cook stooped to look at the ember. Her knees cracked as she crouched to inspect it. 'A sign? Is this some kind of sorcery?'

'No. Why must folk always think me a witch? It's just a sign I tell you. Can you see the shape?'

'Aye.' Eleanor shivered. 'But what does it mean?'

'It looks like a mountain, like the one near Edinburgh, Arthur's Seat...'

'Aye I know, I know. I'm no' soft in the heid you know.'

'It's a message from Greta I'm sure of it, I must go at once. My daughter needs me, I can feel it in me bones.'

Cook slapped the old woman's knee and cracked the biggest smile. 'Aye. But not before you've had a hearty meal, old woman. You're all skin and bones. Throw another leek into the pot and give it a stir will you. I'll go and have a wee chat with the carter, see what can be done. All right?'

Cook made for the door and then paused. 'You will tell me if you see my Magnus on your travels though?'
'Yes my dear. I am sure he will return, truly. I can feel it in my bones.'
Cook's eyes pooled with tears.

*****

Magnus descended into the black hole below. It didn't get any easier, every time seemed as daunting as the first. He clung to the edge of the basket, his pale knuckles appearing luminous in the flickering light of a single tallow candle. His heart thumped in his chest, would the rope hold? He looked above into the shadows, took in the slow motion of descent, a passing candle on a ledge, a weed sprouting from a rock, and then a strange black creature…perhaps a bat. The poor laddies dangled above, like jungle monkeys swinging from forest vines, a couple of them had their eyes closed. Effie wasn't amongst them. Women and girls didn't ride in the basket or cling to the rope; she had to climb down four ladders to the stall below. The baskets were for the men.

Just before he reached his stall, Magnus walked past Jimmy Mole, swinging his pick within a twenty-inch seam. He had the knack Jimmy Mole, chipping away with much vigour at the black coal. Magnus watched him for a while, he had this rhythm see, Jimmy Mole, and it was a joy to see, almost soothing, the muscles playing at either side of his spine, along his back and shoulders. He shook his head, it was useless to observe him to try to learn his technique, in his bones he knew he could never match the man. Thus with a heavy heart, Magnus made his way to the stall.

*****

Effie had the monthly curse of women that day. She did not feel well. It was the damned stomach cramps, and her poor back felt like she'd fell from a great height onto a hard floor. She thought of the day ahead and groaned. To reach the pit bottom she had to travel 84 foot with a basket upon her back, about half the height of St Giles from the floor to the steeple. Most of the ladders were around 18ft high, but today they

133

might as well have been mountainous, Effie felt dreadful. At the bottom of the first ladder she proceeded along a main road only three and a half feet high to the second ladder, then a third and fourth. When Effie reached the stall she dropped her empty creel and didn't bother to acknowledge Magnus, she just fell down onto the floor in an untidy heap, too tired to move out of the way of the water that dripped above her. After a while she turned onto her side, and hugged her knees up to her chest. Her eyes opened and looked up, from this position the stall was on its side. Magnus stood hunched in the corner, he was tugging off the last of his clothes.

'What's up with you?'
'Tired.' She said and then struggled to get up.
'You should tell your man to leave you alone.'
'What man?'
'Thought you collier women wed early. Won't be long before you're accepting arles for your first child.'
'Not I. I've nae man and if the Lord answers my prayers, I'll be away from this place one day. Nae bairn o' mine will work the mines. Anyway what business is it o' yours?'

The muscles in Magnus's jaw twitched. Effie frowned. Why did she manage to bring out the worst in him in the mornings? She flinched as he leapt across the stall to haul her up, and not too gently mind. Her teeth ground together and she grimaced, the pain in her back throbbed and her damned stomach cramps plagued her so. *Oh the curse of Eve*, she thought, and for just a moment she closed her eyes.
'It is my business when we toil here together day in day out, both half naked in the dark. What's got into you lass? Curb your tongue, I like not your tone.'
Effie's face twisted with pain. 'Oh can't ye leave me be, Magnus, ma belly hurts. I've an affliction o' sorts.'
'Nothing catching I hope.'
'Naw.' Effie shook her head.
'All right then. Let's start again shall we? 'Bring me the candle and a prop.'

Effie sniffed up, as though she was about to cry, but she was made of sterner stuff and did his bidding at once. She was after all a coal bearer and she knew better than to complain. But the hurt engulfed her, and ached her throat and jaw, and all the while she had to swallow back a lump in her throat.

Magnus worked hard. The sweat dripped off him as he toiled to win the coal. Effie wasted no time and hauled the coal onto her back into a large creel, the basket flattened towards the back of her neck. With near a hundred weight in her basket, she was bent over double so that her body formed a strengthened arch. She winced as the tug dug into her head, and so adjusted the straps as best she could before she was on her way. Once she set off, Magnus laughed at her as she swayed a little, Effie felt like murdering him.
'I'd like tae see you shift this up tae the top, Magnus Styhr.'
Magnus shook his head. 'Aye I'll leave that to you lassie. I'm sorry I didn't mean to laugh.'

Effie grunted and exited the stall. More than once she had to pause as she climbed the ladders, what with the burden she carried upon her back. Her legs and knees trembled, and she felt mighty sorry for herself when they did. But these spells of weakness passed…eventually, as she clung to the rungs, with her fingers curled around the wood like a hawks' talons wrapped around its prey. Once she's tackled the ladders there was another obstacle, one she could so without today. Stagnant water, as high as her knees. She hoped later when it was time to rest that her legs would not swell, and cause her even more pain.

After a dozen or so trips to the surface they stopped for a break, before the day was over Effie would complete at least twenty trips to the surface. But she was used to it. After all she'd worked in the mine most of her young life. Magnus however, was not used to it. He still struggled with the work, and so she took pity on him and helped him as he struggled to escape his confined space on the coal floor. It was an awkward moment, her holding out her hand for him to pull himself to standing. In the flickering darkness she felt his hard torso brush against hers, flesh against flesh, until they sprung apart.

'Lord my back feels as though it's about to cave in, pass me my clothes will you, Effie.'

'It is very sore work I ken. But there's naw need to dress, you'll have tae take them off again in a moment., there is nae cause for embarrassment, I'm quite used tae the sight of a man in the scuddie…'

'Aye. No matter. If it's all the same, I'd rather put them back on for now.'

They ate in silence until Magnus asked about her kin.

'What happened to your brothers and sisters after your parents died?'

'One died of a fever and the other is a trapper here in the mine. A boy.'

'Do you miss him?'

'Aye.'

'Any grandparents?'

'Aye. My grandfather died o' the black spit last winter. And the others passed long before him. I miss them o' course.'

Effie shifted uncomfortably, wondering why he asked so many questions. 'I miss my faither the maist. But if I'm honest the accident was a blessing. He had the black spit ye see, and he was touched in the breath. That's mining for ye. His spine was curved and he spent maist o; his day coughing and howking up a lung. When he went it was a relief. At least he no longer suffers.' She wiped her black face and changed the subject. 'Why dae ye ha'e you that collar roond yer neck?'

Even in the dark she could see his displeasure. His mouth was tight and he seemed to quiver with rage.

'I was a tenant farmer at Castle Wood. The laird there gave it me. A parting gift after throwing me in his dungeons.'

'But why?' Effie asked.

'I offended him for some reason, so he put this collar on me to remind me that I'm his property. He treats his hounds better than his serfs.' Magnus sighed. 'Perhaps he thought I coveted something of his, or the other way around. Either way I will have my revenge…one day.'

Effie shook her head. 'But there must be some reason, Magnus. A laird must ha'e some grounds for punishing his serfs surely?'

136

'Ah Effie. You know nothing child. All you've ever known is this. The baron of Castle Wood can do as he pleases. Take a woman, whip someone, cut off a head. '

'Nae. I thought all that had ended.'

'I wish. That man deserves to suffer. He will suffer.'

'Must ye talk like that, Magnus? You are o'er passionate. The desire for revenge will fester in yer heart like an open wound. It will bring you nothing but sadness.'

'You speak wisely for a young lassie, Effie, but he deserves to be punished. He's the reason I've never got to hear my child's first cries, or hold it within my arms... 'Magnus's voice cracked with emotion. He wiped his damp eyes with the back of his hand, coughed and turned away, in an effort to conceal his distress.

Effie looked away and pretended not to notice. But without thinking, when she returned her gaze, she reached out a hand to him. The candle flickered, he didn't push her away but took her small hand in his own. And then to her surprise he held up his other hand so that his palm faced her bosom. All the pain and cramps within Effie's stomach disappeared and suddenly fluttered and buzzed like a bees nest. She held up her own palm and pressed it against his. The flesh was warm, her fingers dwarfed by his.

'Yours is tiny compared to mine.' He said.

'Aye.' Effie's limbs tingled as he curled his fingers over her own. Her cheeks burned and then out of nowhere she said: 'You like Jimmy's lass don't ye? All the men do. Even the wedded ones.'

'Who?' He snatched his hand back.

'The bonny girl. The one you thought was a boy.' She laughed. 'You thought we were all boys when ye first arrived.'

'Well you're all so thin and covered in coal, it's hard to tell and well...'

Effie was silent.

'You're just as pretty as Jimmy Mole's girl. I just didn't realise it till that day in kirk. '

'Kirk?'

'Aye the day you fell asleep.'

Effie held a hand up to her mouth. 'Oh the shame o' it.'

'Shame? What do you mean? Have I offended...?'

Effie suddenly tensed and shushed him.

'What Effie? I'm sorry.'

'Shush Magnus. 'Hairs stood up on the back of her neck and then her arms. She sniffed up and then grabbed Magnus's arm.

'What are you doing? Effie, you're pinching my arm.'

'Shush. Can't ye feel it? A change in the air…firedamp.'

Magnus shook his head. 'Firedamp?'

The candle flickered and suffered to burn, its flame an odd shade of blue. It happened then, a great rush of wind, sending up a swirl of coal dust into their eyes, followed by a low rumbling noise and then a terrible roar.

'The shaft's caving in, Magnus – grab the candles and run.' Effie screamed.

They ran into the darkness.

CHAPTER 12

After the roar came stillness. Together they ran towards the main shaft, until they reached the road where the tubs of coal were brought. They fell beneath one of the corves full of coal, clear of rock fall. But nowhere was free of coal dust, the air was thick with it. Visibility was nigh on impossible in the choking cloud. Magnus held up his shirt to his mouth to avoid breathing it in, but in spite of it, he was seized with a great bout of coughing. He put a hand to his chest, and spat out some of the black dust on to the ground. Why wasn't Effie coughing, he thought? In haste he stretched out an arm and found Effie's hand. She was quiet and cold, so he shook her roughly, seeking some trace of life and pinched the soft skin on her arm. For his efforts at reviving her, Magnus was rewarded with a sharp clip around the head.

Magnus shouted: 'Is that how you reward folk for helping you? You were too quiet for my liking; I was checking to see if you were dead.'

'I havenae a scratch, no' hurt at all. Just vexed at the sound of you coughing your guts up.'

'I can hardly breathe. How can you stand it?'

'I'm used tae it.'

'Used to it you say. My hands banging, my limbs are trembling and my chest sounds like a set of bagpipes are within it.'

'Ah stop your whining man.'

Despite everything, Magnus laughed and as he did so, a great bout of coughing consumed him again. On Effie's instruction, he placed his head beneath his knees, while Effie patted his back. Before long, as the air cleared, Magnus's coughing ceased. It was only then that they heard cries from other miners in the distance. Magnus's heart thumped at the sound, it was a blessing indeed to know that they were not alone. In the darkness he sighed to himself quietly as a tear rolled down his face, leaving a clean track mark snaking down towards the brass collar around his neck.

'We are not alone, Effie. Thank the Lord. Others have survived.'

Effie lost her composure then and sobbed. 'Aye but I'm fearful for my brother, Magnus, and all the wee bairns who toil in this mine. The trappers sit in the dark here from 4am till 6pm. They're just bairns, Magnus. Is it any wonder they grow tired and scared in this hellish darkness? Sometimes they wait hours for a cart tae come by, tae pass through their trap-door. If a trap-door isn't closed dangerous gases can build up and result in an explosion. Do you think that's what's happened, Magnus?'

'I hope not, but one thing is for sure we will never know if we stay here.'

The pitch black heightened their senses. Each noise became louder, smells more pungent, and the lightest of breeze, an imagined strange and terrible beast. Magnus's heart thumped in his chest, and his bowels felt as though they'd turned to water. What a useless man he was, clinging to a young lass in the dark like his life depended on it. He squeezed Effie's hand and staggered into an inky black void, and as they progressed further into the mine neither of them could see anything, no shapes or silhouettes, just darkness. Then Magnus remembered the candles.

'Are ye all right? Why have we stopped? '

'It's no use, Effie. We're blind as bats here, I can't see a thing. I've a candle, but nothing to light it with.' Magnus began to rummage through his pockets.

'No matter. Quit looking for it.' She sniffed up. 'Better not light it just yet, can't you smell it? The afterdamp. Save the candles for later.'

'But we can't see…'

'The sounds are getting closer. The main shaft must be ahead. Did you hear that? Folks shouting.'

Effie urged Magnus on. They took short tentative steps towards shrieks of terror, moving slowly toward the sound of voices frantically muttering prayers. Hand in hand they kept walking, a hazy light shined ahead in the darkness. Candlelight surely, casting strange shadows of tiny hunched figures, and desperate men in the distance, and even further ahead… a blocked mine shaft. They were trapped. The realisation hit Effie like a lead weight, she almost dropped to her floor, and would have if Magnus hadn't caught her.

'Don't fret, lassie. It will be all right. I promise you.'
'But ma brother. What about oor Thomas? He's all I ha'e. I need tae find him. I *must* find him, Magnus.'
'Don't fret, we will find him.'

Effie's body fell backwards against Magnus, her body sagged and faced forwards as she allowed him to support her. He could feel her soft skin and body trembling against him. The lass was thin, too thin, he could feel her spine pressed against his breast. They remained like that for a while, perfectly still, skin to skin, as though drawing energy from one another. No awkwardness. Not even when he curled his arms around her stomach so that his hands interlinked beneath her bony ribs. It was one moment in time, a respite from the madness. A spell of sorts cast over them, to detach them from the disaster. Insane though it may seem, at that precise moment, Magnus felt content, free of vengeful thoughts, revenge of a sudden erased from his tortured mind. But then, as is the case in life, something happened to break the spell. It happened so fast, they had little time to react, as a great whoosh of air sent a cloud of coal dust into their eyes, followed by the whinny and snorts of a terrified animal.
'It's a pit pony, Magnus. Oh the poor wee thing is frightened tae death.' Effie cried.

Into the weak grey light went the half blind pony, like a demon possessed, at top speed straight into the coalface wall, killing it instantly. Effie turned and buried her head into Magnus's chest. He wrapped his arms around her, and squeezed her slim body before kissing the top of her head. The act seemed to soothe her, but when she pulled away, Magnus's skin was damp with tears.
'Effie, we must have courage, stay strong. Take my hand. You've been brave, lassie, let's keep walking… before you know it we will be with the others.'

With a tight mouth, Magnus squeezed Effie's hand and together they ambled towards the collapsed mine. When they reached the other miners huddled together in prayer, Magnus quickly looked about for Jimmy Mole, for if there was ever a handy man to know at a time like this, it was Jimmy Mole. But he was not there. In desperation he asked one of the young hewers Jimmy Mole's whereabouts. But instead of answering him, the laddie gave him a queer look and stared at young Effie. Magnus felt his cheeks burn, they were still joined in hands.

'Seems you two ha'e been making the maist o' the dark.'

Magnus snatched his hand away. 'Daft thing to say. The lassie was frightened. '

'Effie frightened. Never! There's nae shame in it, the lass no doubt kept you warm afore you found us.' He sniggered.

'Tis none of your business what I dae and he asked you a question, you will do well tae answer it.' Effie sniffed.

'Is that a threat, you gonnae set your brass collar sweetheart on me, Effie? He hasn't the strength of a lamb.' The young hewer laughed.

Mr Moffat, the old pickman spat on to the floor. 'Enough. Pay him no heed, young Effie. Did you pass any others on your way here, anyone trapped?'

'Naw. We didn't see anyone. Has anyone seen my brother, Thomas?'

'No lass, no doubt he's on the other side of that.'

Moffat stretched an arm towards the rock fall that blocked the main mine shaft. A look of desperation marred his wizened face. Magnus rubbed the coal grit from his eyes and looked to where the old man pointed, his eyes frantically searching for weak areas where they might break through. *Why hadn't anyone attempted to clear the way?* He thought. Why on earth not he wondered. What was the use of prayer? Would prayer get them out of this hellhole to the top? As if reading his thoughts, one of the colliers stood atop a pedestal stone and shouted out in a booming voice. 'There'll be no progress while we stand around singing hymns and praying. I say we act now, clear the way to explore all possible exits.'

A woman heavy with child yelled above the din, as men discussed picks and spades and other tools to clear the way. 'But the shaft might cave in further. I say we leave it be. Don't clear it, it could let in more poisonous gas, or fill the area with water. We can't take the chance.'

Magnus answered her. 'I disagree. We must chance it. What's the alternative? Would you prefer we remain here in a blocked shaft? There

142

could be another explosion at any moment… and how long will we last without food, water, clean air?'

The pregnant lassie squatted to her knees and rocked back and forth. Her huge belly protruding in front of her. Many a man grimaced as she began to moan and groan.

Old man Moffat pressed his hands together. 'Ah Jesus, she's not going to bring forth a bairn now is she? That's all we need. Cross your legs will ye lassie. Now isn't the time to drop a wean.'

The pregnant woman cursed and got to her feet. But before she walked away she gave the evil eye to old Moffat who completely ignored her. Effie went over to place a hand upon her shoulder, and as she did, Magnus felt a great swell in his chest. His eyes followed the women as they walked off together, or waddled in the expectant mothers' case. It always surprised him how the mining folk pulled together. In all his life he'd never known such spirit and strength, and they were going to need it now more than ever now… if they were to dig themselves out of this hellhole.

Magnus's collar cut into his neck. The brass felt like teeth devouring his neck, not for the first time he tried to prise the damned thing apart but failed. Effie offered to help him but he shooed her away. He found a pick and took his place among the men, but to his dismay he still hadn't the stamina of the others. As always, he fought a bitter battle and struggled in his toil. His muscles twitched and burned, he gritted his teeth and cursed out loud. 'Lord, give me the strength.' Sweat rolled down his back as his muscles screamed with pain, and yet he toiled on and on, determined to match the other men. Within an hour or so, he could hardly stand, but Magnus refused to give up. He imagined himself in the fields of Castle Wood, a blazing sun shining down upon his back. His pick became a spade; the coal became soft soil. The vision soothed him, but his struggle didn't go unnoticed. As Magnus paused for a breather, an enormous hewer, a man so tall and broad he could be a giant, tapped Magnus on the shoulder.

'Do you want my mell?'

Magnus stopped what he was doing and frowned. 'Mell?'

'Aye my mell hammer. Here, you take it. It cuts through rock easy. It'll be easier. Try.'

'I'll use anything,' Magnus ignored him, his pride wounded. 'I'll use my bare hands if I have to.'

'Dinnae take offense, son. Here, take the mell hammer, I'll use the pick.' He held out his palms, and they were huge like two fleshy paddles.

Magnus took the mell and thanked the giant, then nodded to him before carrying on with his work. But for some reason, the giant stayed close by…at first this irked Magnus. But after a while, he realised the man meant no harm…and Lord, was he as strong as a bear, swinging his pick as though it were a flimsy stick. The man worked like a dog. All of them did. No one slacked and no one complained. Once the larger stones were broken, the women and children carried them away, the smaller stones to be used for wall building, to keep up the roof. The task was not an easy one. Once in a while, a haggard figure fell to his knees in exhaustion, or bent at the waist, so that his face touched his knees. Folk huffed and gasped in the still soot thickened atmosphere, as others guarded the precious candles against the dangers of foul air. Hours passed by, and yet despite their exhaustion, on and on the colliers toiled, cold, damp and hungry, barely a light between them as death crept in from all around.

'Halt.' Yelled old Moffat .' I can feel a gap and a small gush of air.'

A few of the women gasped and began to wail. 'We're all going to die, we will perish. Lord protect us from the bad air.'

Mr Moffat clapped his hands together and shouted. 'Stay calm.'

Before anyone could respond he'd pushed through the hole in the rock fall, slithering on his belly like a snake to the other side. A great hush descended as folk waited with baited breath for the old pickman's voice. After a while, from the gap in the rock fall, there came a muffled shout. 'Pass me a light. It's quite safe here, no bad air at all.'

Magnus scrambled to the opening with a lantern, more than once the skin on his knees cut on the rocks. A bony arm, tattooed by coal dust protruded through the hole, and then disappeared with the lantern in hand.

'Bad news.' Came a cry from Moffat.

'What is it?' Magnus felt a shiver rush up his spine.

'Another rock fall. Even bigger than this one.'

Magnus's shoulders slumped. All around him people groaned with sheer hopelessness and fatigue. How long had they toiled only to discover this, a further blow? And how much longer would the lights last until they were plunged into complete darkness? Death creeping…

'Old man. Stay where you are. How much room is there in there to clear the way?'

'Not enough. It's impossible. We will have to find another way. '

Magnus held out his hand, and pulled Moffat through the hole. 'Another way?'

'There is no other way.' The pregnant woman sobbed.

'But what of the other opening, the ladders?' Magnus suggested.

The woman with child began to sob again. Between sobs she managed to say: 'Why won't anyone listen to me? Water blocks the way you feckless idiots.'

'How high is the water?' Magnus asked her.

To Magnus's annoyance the woman continued to weep, and as she did she stroked the swollen belly that protruded beneath her sagging breasts. A great vein bulged in the hollow of her throat as her wailing echoed and disappeared into the swallowing darkness.

'Jesus. Quit crying will you. How high is the water, woman?' He snapped.

Effie groaned. 'Gan easy on her, Magnus. Dae ye want her tae drop the bairn here and noo?'

Magnus's brows crinkled. He closed his eyes and pinched the bridge of his nose, in earnest he tried to shut out the sounds of feminine woes. He didn't t have time for hysterics. None of them did. In one smooth motion, he smashed his mell hammer down with all his might and shouted at the top of his voice. 'For God's sake, pull yourself together and stop making that awful noise.'

The woman ceased to cry.

'For the last time, how high is the water?'

'Near enough to the top.' She said.

Moffat coughed and spat out some black spit. 'Is it at the low part, lassie. The low tunnel?'

'Aye.'

Moffat rubbed his bald head. 'We'll have to chance it then. Let's hope the water hasn't risen to the top.'

They did a quick headcount, and grabbed as many candles and tools as they could carry. Magnus, Effie, the woman with child - Betty, old Moffat and his missus, the giant, amusingly named Tiny, three more women, six children, and four men. Nineteen of them in total, and by some miracle not one of them injured. They formed an orderly line, each with a hand on the shoulder in front of them, men first, then woman, and children at the back. Before they reached the low tunnel, the ground became wet under foot. If anyone fell or stumbled, the line stopped moving until the injured party regained their footing. In a relatively short amount of time they had reached the water.

The road tunnel was as Magnus imagined it, three feet tall and the water a good few inches from the roof. As fortune had it, the water had not risen. But Magnus's shuddered to think what would happen if it began to rise once they all entered it. In short, they could all drown. The adults of course (being taller) would have to crawl through it. Magnus examined it closely, he surmised the smallest children could possibly crouch through it. The problem was, with the water so close to the roof, they'd have to turn their heads to the side in order to breathe. Everyone was set, all ready to plunge through the black water…but then Betty let out a bloodcurdling scream and ran out of the line.
'I cannae swim. It will be the end o' me and the bairn. I cannae swim. I will drown I tell ye!'
Effie tried to soothe her. 'You don't have tae swim, Betty. Ye just need tae crawl on all fours through the tunnel and turn your head a wee bitty tae the side so you don't swallow the water. It won't take us long. Didn't I tell you this afore? There is nae need tae be feart, we are all here wi' you. We're all together.'
'Naw. I cannae dae it, Effie. Dinnae make me please.'
'Fine. Stay here then.' Magnus said through clenched teeth. '*All alone.* No, foolish me, you'll not be alone. I'm sure there's lots of rats to keep you company, Betty. You and the coming bairn.'

Betty changed her mind then and stopped weeping. But before Effie took her arm and guided her into the line, to wait her turn to enter the tunnel, she scowled at Magnus to show her displeasure.

'All ready?' Someone shouted up front.

As before, the men started the line, Tiny waded through first with his pick hammer, as if to demonstrate that if *he* could squeeze his giant frame through, so could the others. Confident that the tunnel was large enough, the other men followed close by, then the women, and lastly the children at the rear. When Magnus's turn came, he held his breath and plunged into the cold water, dragging Tiny's mell hammer alongside him. The water took his breath away and caused his teeth to chatter, but once he got used to it, it wasn't too bad, if anything it soothed the chafed skin were the brass collar rubbed his neck. As Magnus progressed, a couple of times his knees scraped on sharp stones… and halfway through he forgot to turn his head, only to swallow a mouthful of foul water. At the back of him he could hear the women struggling. He didn't envy them, at least he didn't have to keep a candle alight in six inches of air above his head, with only one arm to support him. Before long, every one of them were in the tunnel, up to their necks in freezing water…even Betty. About three quarters of the way through the watery tunnel Tiny shouted for them all to halt. A big stone blocked the way, the only way Tiny could smash through the stone quickly was with his mell hammer, so Magnus obliged and passed it to the man in front of him. The hammer bobbed above a sea of sopping heads as fading candles hovered dangerously close to the water level. Eventually it reached Tiny.

'Back up, I need room tae work and swing the hammer.' He cried before smashing through the rock with all his might.

All of them, men women and children had backed up in the tunnel. But in the process Betty had dropped her candle and had started wailing, causing many a man to curse out loud.   Tiny, as luck could have it, couldn't hear her, what with all the noise his hammer was making. But as he made progress, Betty became more and more distressed, mainly due to the fact she'd lost her precious candlelight and a keepsake she'd made for her coming baby. Before long, Betty started to make other noises, all too familiar to those who'd witnessed a birth. Effie was

147

directly behind Betty, and her heart sank as dread seeped into her bones. The shock of the situation of a sudden hit her, Betty was having birthing pains.

'What's happening back there, Effie?' Magnus shouted.

Effie shouted into the darkness. 'Oh Lord have mercy on us. It's Betty. She's making strange noises. I don't know what tae do. Her head keeps slipping intae the water. She's gonna drown.'

Magnus asked: 'Who's in front of her?

Effie sobbed. 'Is that you Mrs Moffat? Are you there?'

Mrs Moffat's high pitched voice cut through the air. 'Aye lassie. I'm trying to help her. Can you try to hold her head up?'

'I've still got my candle tae hold up. How am I going tae support her with one hand? D'ye want me tae balance it on ma bastard head? Oh Jesus, she's making growling noises now. Has Tiny nearly cleared the way? Magnus - has he cleared the way? I can't cope here.'

'Not much longer now, lassie. Hold on - pass your candle to Mrs Moffat.'

Tiny worked faster, smashing through the stone with all his strength. The worry was, that once the stone was removed the water level might rise, but luckily this was not the case.

'Nearly done. Tell Betty to cross her legs. 'Magnus shouted.

Effie scoffed and rubbed Effie's back to soothe her. 'Easier said than done. When a bairn wants to come it will come no matter what!'

That's when Betty suddenly became still. 'Betty. B E T T Y ?'

Mrs Moffat cried. 'Don't panic Effie. She's not deid...I can feel her limbs trembling. Support her Effie, take her weight if you can.'

'I am. I am, but there's no room to swing a cat here. Betty are you all right?'

'Aye. Aye. The pain, oh dear Lord - the pain. I just want it to go away.'

Effie cursed under her breath and wished she was anywhere but here. It was pitch dark now that she'd passed her candle to Mrs Moffat. *Perhaps that was a blessing,* she thought. Her arms curled under Betty's armpits and her face pressed into wet hair. 'You're burning up Betty, don't worry I'm here behind you...you'll be all right.'

Betty's head thrashed back and forth as she cried out in distress and pain. Once or twice she banged into poor Effie's face behind her. But after a while she relaxed. Nature had a way of showing folk the way, and soon Betty's chin instinctively dipped so that it dug into her own bosom, as she bore down to push out the child that lay restless inside of her. Short sharp bursts of air suddenly released from her throat …then one final grunt of pain. 'I've changed my mind I don't want a bairn anymore.' Betty sobbed.

And then to everyone's amazement (and relief) the cries of a baby filled the tunnel. Betty had given birth in a two feet tunnel of black water, and with just a few inches of space to hold her baby above her head, Betty's anguish was evident for all to hear.
'I cannae hold ma bairn up - I'm too weak, it will drown. For the love o' God, take it, someone - anyone.'
Mrs Moffat scrambled in the dark to feel for the wean. It's cries bounced off the walls as she managed to scoop it high up into her arms. 'Here take the candle back, Effie - I don't wanna burn the child. The cord is still attached; we'll have to cut it as soon as we can. The afterbirth will come soon. '
'Cord?'
'Aye Effie the birthing cord. Oh never you mind, keep supporting Betty, she's no doubt exhausted from the trials of bringing forth a child.'
'I'm holding her up as best I can, Mrs Moffat but she's like a dead weight. My arms are hurting, I don't know how much longer I can hold her, 'Effie replied.
'Not much longer now pet - think of the bairn, it will need it's mother or it will die. Give her a nudge. The line is moving again now. 'Mrs Moffat said.
Effie nodded and gave Betty a gentle nudge. 'Come on Betty get moving. Be strong, you can do it. Nearly there.'
Betty came to and asked. 'My baby? I can hear it. Is it a lad or lassie, Effie?'
'Mrs Moffat. 'What is it?' Effie called out.
Mrs Moffat laughed. 'How should I ken? I'm balancing it on wan arm while it is howling down my lughole. We'll find out soon enough,

Betty. Keep moving, won't be long now - we need to hurry before you get pains again. '

Then all hell let loose as Betty began to scream again. 'A rat. A huge rat. It'll eat my baby. Kill it Effie will you, before it takes a chunk out of it.'

'For the love o' God Betty, I've nae free hands.' Effie braced herself for what was to come…whiskers, a pointed snout, razor-sharp teeth and then she let out a huge sigh.

'Tis not a rat, Betty.'

'No, what is it then?'

'It's a bloody wig.'

'A wig? What wig?' Betty asked.

'It's my wig and I don't want to hear anymore about it.' Said Mrs Moffat.

Laughter filled the tunnel, then silence… until Mr Moffat shouted from up front: 'And where did you get the money to buy a fecking wig, Mrs Moffat?'

CHAPTER 13

Matilda awoke covered in sweat. She was at her wits end… the hot and cold spells continued to torment her. The night sweats, the mood changes, and the bouts of melancholy were all taking their toll. She sent for the old woman, Klok Gumma, the midwife and wise woman. Matilda knew William disapproved of her, and imagined her to be a witch, but to hell with William, Matilda thought – he was not here - she was going to do as she damn well pleased. The wise woman arrived at dusk carrying a strange little book, bound with animal skin and frayed at the edges. The old hag kept the book clutched to her chest like a magical shield. When Matilda tried to relieve her of it, the old woman near had a fit.

'Please sit down, Klok Gumma. How are you?'

'Middling.'

Silence followed. 'Why have you brought your bible with you? Are you fond of the illustrations?'

Shaking her head she scoffed. 'Hah! 'Tis not a bible and do you think me a fool that cannot read? I may be a poor peasant woman that has fallen from favour, but I've a shrewd mind. This is my black book – my svartebok.'

'Curious you revealing that to me. I would have thought that kind of thing would be kept secret from the likes of me or anyone for that matter, for fear of you being declared a witch.'

Klok Gumma's bright eyes crinkled at the corners. 'Aye, well I can guess why you have summoned me here. This black book will help me cure you. My secret is safe with you I am sure.' The old woman patted the book with one wrinkled hand.

Matilda nodded and frowned, how did the old woman know she needed a cure for anything? Her eyes gazed upon the book once again, imagining the contents within. Matilda decided to trust the old woman, despite her boldness and eccentricity. 'Tell me more about your black book, does it contain spells and the like, is it a book of black arts?'

Klok Gumma sucked in her breath and crossed her arms. 'My lady... with respect, a witch I am not. In Sweden my people are respected and revered. You see, I am of the de Kloka – the wise ones. The svartebok is sacred. Everything a wise woman needs is contained within these pages, and new information, herbs and the like is added each year and passed down from mother to daughter. In time my Greta will inherit this book.'

Matilda's mouth turned down at both sides at the mention of Greta. 'Interesting – so you can read?'

'Aye.'

'Who taught you?'

'My mother, she is of the de Kloka too.'

'Really? How extraordinary. But surely with all this knowledge of herbs and potions you are familiar with the black arts too...and Greta, perhaps that is why my husband had a sickness for her? Greta could have cast a spell upon him.'

The old wise woman shook her head and moved closer, so that her bony knees touched the cloth of Matilda's fine gown. 'No no no. My Greta is not a witch, and neither am I. We shall speak of this no more my Lady. The old baron sent her away a long time ago, and that is the end of it.'

'All right. We shall speak of it no more. In fact, I have wasted enough time as it is, so I will get to the point. Now then, let me see... How should I say this?'

'Spit it out, my Lady. I can't help you if you are keep quiet now can I - cat got your tongue?'

Matilda looked left then right before opening her mouth. 'Hot flushes, it's like a sudden wave of intense heat rushes through my entire body, and then I begin to sweat. Goodness me, it's as though my skin is on fire, and if that isn't bad enough, there's the night sweats too and fatigue throughout the day. It's never ending. Sometimes I think I've lost all my senses.'

'Does your monthly curse sometimes fail to appear?'

Matilda nodded.

'And as well as the hot flushes you are experiencing, do you find that you are sometimes irritable and prone to melancholy?

'Yes.'

'And you say you are having trouble sleeping at night?'

'Yes, yes. Do you know what is causing me to suffer?'

'I think so.'

'Oh thank God. The relief that I feel…' Matilda placed a hand to her bosom and choked up. 'The relief that you might be able to treat me…oh it makes me want to weep. I thought I was going mad…truly, I really did. Of late, well I'm always on the verge of tears and I am simply not myself. Am I possessed? Has the devil…'

'Nonsense. 'Tis nothing to worry about at all. It is just life, the circle of life. A cessation. It happens to all women of a certain age, although I might add you are rather young to be getting your change of life so soon, but that can happen my dear, just as some girls start their monthly courses earlier than expected. 'Tis nature's way of telling you that you're a woman reaching her winter years.'

'What is the cure?'

'It is my experience that the wort flower helps women with this ailment. There is a little flower, a flowers so special, it has tears that are magical. I gather it at midnight on the night of a waning moon. Would you like me to fetch you some?'

'Oh would you? Yes, yes please do. A special flower with magical tears you say? How fascinating.'

'It has five yellow petals, and when picked it cries a crimson liquid – some believe it to symbolise the spilled blood of St John, the saint it's named after.'

'Is that its name – St John?'

'St John's Wort. My mother used to call it *fuga demonum,* in her day it was believed that it could rid a person of the demons haunting them, but of course that's nonsense. To my mind, folk aren't possessed of demons; they've really just a disease of the body or mind.'

Matilda placed a shaky hand to her mouth. 'Oh heaven above, I just want these cursed hot spells to go, and my moods to settle. I'm so relieved I'm not the only one to suffer with this.'

Klok Gumma nodded. 'Yes it's commoner than you think. Some women suffer worse than others. Your change has come early, but do not fret, the wort plant should settle your symptoms. The hot spells will soon cease, and I expect you will begin to feel like your old self again

153

for a while at least. Of course, as you get older the change of life will come full force whether you like it or not...but remember all things pass. Life and Mother Nature have a way of working things out. We must all be thankful for our good health and our time here on earth. Remember it is a blessing.'

Matilda beamed and stretched out a hand to the old woman, and as she rested her own smooth white fingers upon her wizened hand, a feeling of peace descended upon her.

***

Nineteen entered the water tunnel, but twenty exited it. Once they reached a safe area, Effie and old woman Moffat searched for a knife to cut Betty's umbilical cord. Already squeamish from helping with the birth, Effie turned away as the old woman tied the cord, and then waited for the afterbirth. They gathered as many blankets and coats as they could spare, to make Betty a soft bed, and there upon the pit floor she placed a breast to the child's lips for the first time. As the child suckled at Betty's breast, Mr Moffat stepped awkwardly towards the new mother and whispered: 'The candles won't last forever you know. We must get moving soon pet. Do you have the strength to go on, Betty?'
'Aye I just need a wee bit longer.' Betty croaked, her throat was hoarse from a lack of water. 'I'm going to call the bairnie Effie. Without her, I don't think I could have birthed it like that in the water.'

Effie swallowed away a lump in her throat. A child named after her, she was truly humbled and honoured. Her flushed face turned towards the men, her eyes searching for Magnus's silhouette, the contours of his face, and chiselled jaw. Her gaze found his and their eyes locked, an understanding passed between them. At precisely the same moment they both looked away.
'Aw Betty, what an honour. The lassie is bonny, just like her ma. I'm just grateful tae the Lord that you're both safe and well.'
Betty adjusted the child in her arms, holding it high enough to inhale its sweet baby scent. The child's soft skin rubbed against her cheek, and the action caused her body to relax and her eyelids to droop, a welcome

154

respite from the chaotic last few hours. She remained like that for a good few minutes before she came too, cheeks flushed, her eyes searching for the old woman.

'Mrs Moffat, my gratitude to you also, I was torn for a while if I'm honest. Torn between naming the child after you or Effie. Now I'm curious to learn what my lassie might have been called.

Mrs Moffat chuckled and pressed her palms together. 'Oh child, I'm glad you decided on Effie. There's a reason I like to be called Mrs Moffat.'

Effie and Betty turned to one another, curiosity sparkling in their eyes. Effie seemed on the verge of laughter, she bit on her lip and turned to Mrs Moffat.

Go on then, tell us what your christian name is?'

Mrs Moffat feigned indifference. 'What is what? Oh no dearie. I'm not going to tell you that.'

'Please tell us.' Effie and Betty said in unison.

Mrs Moffat shook her head. 'And don't be asking Mr Moffat, he's fiercely loyal when it comes to protecting my...'

'Elspeth Finvall Moffat.'

'Mr Moffat, you are in trouble.'

***

Sister Louise took a moment in the walled garden. The morning had been over long, most of it took up attending the sick and needy in the infirmary. The scent of death seemed to cling to her like barnacles to sea rocks, and the smell turned her stomach. She sat down on a bale of hay, closed her eyes and inhaled deeply, the first flowers were in bloom and gave off a delicious scent. After a while she began to feel a sense of calm, and less anxious...her hands ceased to shake. Sister Louise took her new role as prioress very serious. Since she'd took control, there had been many changes, as she (unlike the older prioress) was willing to embrace change. Yes, the order had to remain secret, but really... who would feel threatened by a group of harmless nuns? She attempted to find wealthy patrons, patrons sympathetic to their cause. How else would they survive? Due to a shortage of competent staff, she'd hired several new servants to help run a small guesthouse. The previous prioress neglected the hostel in favour of other causes, but not Sister Louise, shrewd and resourceful as ever, she could always sniff a profit out. And so, together with her sisters, she distributed alms, and attended the sick as frequently as possible. The tasks were never-ending.

So much had happened since she'd arrived with dear Sarah. It really had been a hectic time. So busy was Sister Louise, she hadn't been able to check on the poor Magdalene girl for days now, what with all her new responsibilities. Suddenly, Sister Louise felt guilty. It was ludicrous really, so ludicrous that she found herself laughing out loud, but why? She owed nothing to the peasant girl, and yet, deep down she knew an invisible thread attached the two of them that could not be severed.

As the sun reached its highest point in the sky, the new prioress picked up her keys and prepared to leave to return to her duties, and would have, had Sarah not burst into the walled garden all flushed and out of breath. Since their escape from the chapel, Sarah enjoyed a safe haven in Berwick, and in this atmosphere she thrived. Gone were the thin arms and legs, the pale complexion…Sarah could have been painted by Lely himself, so lovely was her appearance. Sister Louise smiled, she couldn't help herself…but after just a few minutes she tore her eyes away from the girl and made some excuse or other to leave. As prioress, she no longer had much time to spare…or did she? Sometimes she wondered deep down if she was avoiding the girl, but for what reason she could not fathom.

The new prioress kept her voice soft and low. 'Sister Sarah. It seems you have found me just as I'm about to leave. Please excuse me but I must attend to my duties.''

'But Sister Louise, I was hoping we could sit together. We could enjoy the sunshine for just a little while, oh please say yes. You could teach me more of your language again… I remember our lesson mon amie. Is that correct, did I say it right?'

'Oh dear child. I have so little time. Please forgive me, but can we arrange to meet here tomorrow or the day after that?'

Sarah, being a simple girl, could not feign disappointment. Her shoulders sagged and her bottle lip protruded like a sullen child. 'But you said the same thing last time I found you here.'

'Did I?'

'Aye you did.'

'Well I expect it's forgetfulness due to tiredness. You continue to disturb my sleep, Sister Sarah with your night terrors. Your Magdalene days are long behind you now, you must forget them and banish all thought of it from your mind.'

'I will try, really I will. But it's beyond my control once I am asleep, I have this nightmare see …every night he comes to me in my dreams and…'

'Do not speak of that hideous man, just the thought of him pawing you disgusts me, Sarah.' The prioress raised her voice to such a volume that veins bulged in her neck, and her cheeks reddened to form two huge spots either side of her face. To her surprise her hands began to shake again. If the girl was surprised by her outburst she did not show it.

'I am so sorry that I've disturbed you. Please, I do beg your pardon. I never meant to upset you or keep you awake at night… I beg of you, do not remove me to another chamber. I feel safer near you, do not part us now, please, please… '

It took just a moment to regain her composure, she was prioress now after all…she really ought to control her emotions, but with Sarah around this was always difficult. 'All right mon cher, do not fret, for the time being, we will remain as we are. But now we must pray to the Lord for these night terrors to seize.'

'Aye we must. We must!' Sarah gushed, then stepped forward to clasp the Prioress's hand.

Sister Louise's heart thumped in her chest, she had not anticipated the girl's affection, or had any idea how to react to it. Her natural response was to step backwards and resist the small palm pressed against her own. But then her eyes softened, and not wanting to hurt the young woman, she squeezed the soft hand in her own and jolted the girl to her, so that they stood inches apart.

'I won't be a bother…'

'Hush girl, close your eyes and pray…'

Sarah's voice resonated into her ear... 'You could make me cellaress. I'll manage the domestic servants, sort the food and be close to hand to help you with all your chores.'

'Sarah, I really don't feel you are capable of such responsibilities, you know how forgetful you are. And what of your sisters? The other women will be cross if I give you that position. Bear in mind, child, we are still new here. I cannot give you another woman's position. Can't you see that?'

'Nae.' Sarah shook her head and moved in closer.

The prioress looked anywhere but at Sarah, the girl wrenched at her heart. 'They're still wary of me here you know. It's a miracle I managed to make prioress at all. I'm not a local woman, I've no family here, no local influence at all. Any patrons I've made have come from pure diligence and hard work.' She paused, and then her eyes softened. 'Can't you see my hands are tied when it comes to making changes, trust me when I say it's best to leave matters as they are. It would be better if you stayed with your sisters.'

Sarah tugged on her sleeve and clasped the prioress's hand. 'But you are in charge here, you can do as you wish. You just won't though will you?'

Sister Louise sighed and squeezed Sarah's hand. She winced at the hurt in girl's eyes but continued: 'Yes that is true, but it would be wrong of me to take advantage of my position. Can't you understand that? Oh dear, probably not. Let me explain, I *have* to obey the former rules of the abbey and be mindful of the other sisters.'

Sarah nodded and then her shoulders drooped, with more force than was necessary she released her hand from her dear friend and dipped at the knee. And as she fled from the garden all the flowers seemed to wither and wilt. Not for the first time, Sister Louise placed a hand over her throbbing heart, and wondered why she allowed a simple peasant girl to trouble her so.

***

The baron was vexed. The French nun and the peasant girl were not at the Abbaye de Notre-Dame, Avignon. No one knew of their whereabouts. More infuriating than that, a nun, speaking in broken English, claimed that a sister of this Abbaye would not be permitted to leave for Scotland, and that she had no idea who sister Louise was.

He scratched the stubble on his chin and peered into a narrow opening, a kind of slit in the door at eye level. 'But the mother abbess of Magdalene assured me that this is where she came from. She said the abbey near Avignon - I am sure of it.'
'*Non*. Perhaps you are mistaken, monsieur? Our nuns our not allowed off these premises.' The nun sad.
'Oh to hell with you wretched woman. All this way for nothing. Can't you at least allow me to search the grounds for her?''
The damned nun wouldn't budge. She just glared at him with beady eyes and then closed the opening in the door. The baron stamped a foot and cursed, and then proceeded to knock on the door, all to no avail. And all the while a beautiful chanting sound echoed through the abbey walls. It was music to nourish the soul, an exquisite Gregorian chant, intimate, subtle, God's creation…the voice of the Lord through the sisters of Avignon. It was then that *something* happened. His vision burred, he saw the Lord on his cross, heard the heavenly chants …and then he cried and cried, and suddenly remembered his devotions, his struggle with morality. The baron felt ready, reborn even…ready to serve the Lord - he fell to his kneed and prayed.

In the carriage en route to Calais he pulled out a flask of claret and emptied it out of the window. Mackenzie, his manservant near fell out of his seat. William ignored him and threw himself back onto his chair. His head lolled from side to side as the rickety carriage rocked to and fro in a slow rhythmic fashion. But soon, he was asleep.
He woke groggy and parched, and a little unsteady upon his feet. The chants of the sisters of Avignon continued to ring in his ears, and the noise filled him with such powerful emotions that he felt sure to cry. As the carriage came to a stop, his hands shook so much, he tucked them beneath his armpits to conceal his distress. Oh I am so weak he thought as he struggled to exit the carriage.

159

McKenzie took his arm. 'My Lord, allow me to assist you. You look as though you're about to fall on your arse.'

'All right.' For once he didn't argue and allowed McKenzie to help him exit the carriage and then board the ship. As soon as they stepped foot on the vessel, William had a sinking feeling. He felt dreadful. Upon the quarterdeck, he looked out to sea, his neck twisting this way and that, so that veins bulged beneath his throat. After a while his eyes fell upon the galley, the rigging, the main mast…was that blood spatter upon the deck? Was this the same vessel that brought them across the French La Manche to Calais?

'Is this the…?'

'Aye Master it is.' Mackenzie bowed his head.

William shuddered. 'Oh I do hope we don't have to suffer that awful man's company again.' He placed a hand to his neck, his throat felt raw, and worse still he began to feel green about the gills. With one hand on the ships rail he called out to McKenzie. 'I do hope the passing is not rough like last time. I detest the sea.'

'We've not set sail yet, baron. The anchor is yet to be brought up.'

'Really?' William felt rather foolish then, surely Mackenzie was mistaken. But then they hauled up the anchor, and how he longed for a mouthful of claret to ease his churning stomach at that very moment. The spirits might have helped settle his queasiness. 'McKenzie I must visit a privy at once.'

'Well one must perform his necessaries I am sure.' The manservant looked out to sea.

'Oh dear Lord. I feel nauseous. Never did get my sea legs…' And off he ran to retch into a pail.

Once his stomach was empty, William felt much better. He wiped his mouth on the back of his sleeve and made for the main deck. But before he found McKenzie a wonderful sight greeted him on the starboard side of the ship. A group of seamen looked out to sea, all of them pointing and shouting excitedly. William made his way to the sailors and looked out to the blue horizon. Sea mammals swam and leaped out of the surf, porpoises or the like. Despite the harsh salt breeze, a warm glow filled his body. It really was a sight to behold and affected him for some reason. Damnation, he was acting like a lassie. It was then that he sighted the cabin boy again washing the deck, the one Captain Pepper had flogged with ropes. The boy's clothes were in threads, and his body was covered head to foot in cuts, bruises and sores. William seethed inside, rags weren't adequate for a job that required constant exposure to all natures' elements. The cabin boy really was a sorry sight; it was a miracle he hadn't perished from frost bite. Why hadn't someone helped the boy - gave him warmer attire, and a decent pair of shoes? At that exact moment, William tugged the coat from his own body and held it up for the laddie.

'Here. Take it, laddie - you need this more than I.'

But before he could hand it over, the laddie fled.

***

The baron's steward, Mr Morice, poured himself a generous glass of single malt whisky and lit his pipe. Since the baron had gone life at Castle Wood had been good - more than good, perfect even. In his master's absence Morice had complete control - he alone made all the important decisions. And as steward of Castle Wood, he liked to be in charge. When the baron was absent, as 'House Guardian' he was responsible for running the day- to-day affairs of the castle. And so, he was the overseer of workmen, and a manager of property and financial affairs of sorts…and he was the person cook ran to whenever she had a bee in her bonnet, which was more often than not. Morice chuckled to himself, he liked Eleanor, the cook with the bad legs, but he enjoyed peace more. He slumped back in his chair, sipped the whisky, and savoured the moment. The fire hissed and snapped, he closed his eyes and sucked on his pipe, then heard a loud rap at his door. He ignored it and willed whoever it was to go away. Then he heard it again.

'Who dares to disturb me at this ungodly hour?' He roared and near ripped the door from its hinges.

Morice had thought it was a maidservant or a stable lad, but it was the baroness, stood in the cold and dark corridor, a candle in her trembling hand. She looked different, but he could not fathom why. To his amazement she didn't utter a word and turned to scarper, but without thinking he seized her by the arm and prevented her from doing so. In the flickering candlelight she looked deep into his eyes and then down at the hairy hand that gripped her sleeve. He followed suit and glanced at his hand on her fancy dress, his eyes drawn to the contrast of hairy flesh upon fine silk.

'Take your hand off me.'

'As you wish. But what on earth are you doing here at this time of night?' He released his hand.

She took a deep breath and then produced a bottle of whisky tucked beneath her arm. 'I brought you this.'

Morice's colour deepened, his eyes glittered with pleasure. He lifted an arm and made a sweeping gesture with one hand, then motioned for her to enter the door. He followed close behind, his eyes taking in her contours as she entered the room. Morice liked what he saw. But then, as she set herself down beside his blistering hearth, his forehead crinkled into a deep furrow, she'd never conversed with him before…and why was she bringing him whisky at this late hour?

'Tis very strange to be bringing me whisky now. What on earth have I done to deserve such an honour?' He took the bottle and set it down on his drinks tray along with his pipe.

Matilda blushed and placed a hand to her mouth. 'Just a gift for all your hard work, Morice. The new ghillie speaks very highly of you, and for that you should be rewarded. I'm in rather a vulnerable position you see, what with my husband away on business abroad. It's reassuring to know that with you and Falmouth by my side, I've nothing to fear.'

Morice's eyes twinkled with good cheer, he sneaked a peek at the baroness… she was typical of the quality, all superior and aloof. But every now and then, he caught her glancing at him with flashing eyes. Morice wondered what the hell was going on, he loosened his collar and scratched his head…he was used to dealing with the baron, but he was more than happy to deal with his wife. The baroness was actually quite a handsome woman, how on earth had he not noticed before now. 'You flatter me my lady. Falmouth is a good man. But I am sure you've noticed the wild streak in him. No matter though, he's a good worker and obviously a good judge of character. I hear he's done wonders with wee Robbie.'

'Yes. I owe Falmouth a lot, especially since…' Matilda choked with emotion.

'Oh no, you cannae do that here, dry your tears, woman. Here take this,' he poured out a glass of whisky and handed it to her.

'Oh no I couldn't, Morice. I've never touched spirits in my life, not once.'

'Get it down you, woman.'

His lips curled into a smile at the haughty expression on her face.

'You can't speak to me like that, Morice.'

'And why not?' He laughed.

She took the glass from him, and to his delight she did not remove her hand when his own palm lingered near hers as they sat by the fire.

CHAPTER 14

They'd needed something to bribe the steward, to keep him sweet. Matilda, and Falmouth in particular wanted Morice on their side, so as to not inform the baron of the changes they'd made. *Changes* that benefited the serfs. Only a few mind. Even so, the fact that only a few alterations had occurred mattered not, the baron would not approve of any of them. Not a single one. So Falmouth got to work and asked around...what did the steward like to do? Did he like to hunt, gamble, drink? What brought him pleasure? It wasn't long before the ghillie discovered the man's passion. Morice was a whisky man. Like many Scotsmen, he was partial to a good single malt aqua vitae, and so off Falmouth went in search of Black Friar John who ran a secret underground distillery. And so secret a location it was, only a handful of folk knew its location. Even the old cook, Eleanor, who usually knew everything didn't know. But no matter, Falmouth may not have known where the distillery was, but he did have a plan. He suspected someone at a nearby tavern might know of its whereabouts for a few coin...and indeed he was right. With the knowledge was obtained, off he went in search of the moonshine minister.

Wherever water and peat mixed and flowed plentifully, the distillation of whisky provided an irresistible temptation to the poorer classes. This fact was well known to the minister of Black Friar. He'd been brewing as a result of the dissolution of the monasteries, as many a monk, driven from their sanctuary, had no choice but to put their skills to good use. Black Friar John had learned his trade from one of those very monks. Partial to a few drams a day himself, Black Friar John was more than happy to assist his humble parishioners (and the odd stranger), to the joys of illicit stills, after all it preserved health, prolonged life, and relieved colic, palsy and even smallpox. When Falmouth reached the kirk at noon, he found who he assumed to be the 'illusive' whisky distiller near an old kirk pulpit - and not an illegal distillery there was in sight!

164

The minister stood in a double-lined robe, preaching to a beautiful young widow about the wonders of our Lord and the act of penitence. The woman shuffled her naked feet upon the stone floor… her bony toes blue with cold, and her pretty face lined with angst. She held out a few coins and pleaded for penance. It seemed Black Friar John's speciality wasn't just whisky, he sold kirk forgiveness too. Falmouth watched slack jawed as the woman handed the minister a bag of coins and then, to the ghillie's amazement, allowed herself to be patted on the backside by her minister. If that wasn't odd enough, her bowlegged walk out of kirk was most peculiar to say the least. She seemed to take an age staggering up the aisle, tiny steps, one foot after the other, as though in immense pain.

'You an excise man?'

Falmouth prodded his own bosom. 'Me.'

'Aye you.'

'Nae. I'm ghillie at Castle Wood.'

'Ah you're all right then…one of us. Well it's the sheep bladders.'

'I beg your pardon.'

'You're gawping at the woman and wondering why she's walking like a drunken sailor. Look at the state of her, she looks a sight, I swear every time she walks out of here I have trouble not laughing my head off at the sight of her. Who sent you then?'

'One eye Angus from the Star Tavern.'

'Ah that drunkard. I'm sorry I had to ask you, best to be careful, those excise men are right bastards. 'Tis all right now I know you're not one of them.'

'You mentioned sheep bladders?' Falmouth scratched his head.

'The lassie who just left kirk. She had sheep bladders full to the brim with whisky attached to a band around her waist. Doing a few deliveries for me she is. Penance.' He winked.

'Penance for what?'

'She thinks she should be mourning her dead husband instead of keeping me warm in my bed… life is for the living I say, you're a long time dead. She'll come round.' He winked.

Falmouth was tongue tied. Then he found his voice. 'She could do with something on her poor feet, never mind bladders tied round her waist.'

'She's got shoes don't you worry, she won't wear them though, the widow likes to suffer. I've provided for her in more ways than one…but she won't be helped. Like I said, the lassie likes to suffer. She revels in it.'

'Ah I see. May I ask, aren't you worried the bladders might burst one day…perhaps in front of some of your parishioners? What then?'

Black Friar John chuckled. 'She'll most likely say he's pissed herself.'

'Even a cart house wouldn't produce that amount of water.' Falmouth's brows raised and his jaw dropped.

'Aye. Well these things happen as you know, all that standing about in kirk listening to lengthy sermons, if nature calls - nature calls. Now, may I ask why you are here?'

'I need a bottle of your best malt whisky.'

Black Friar John simply nodded then walked to the kirk entrance to bolt the enormous gothic arch door. With the door closed, the kirk darkened, the only light reflected through dirty stain glass windows. Falmouth shivered, he never did like kirk, particularly when is neared dark. With a pale face he looked around, his pupils dilating in the process. Old kirks gave him the creeps, it was all those hideous carvings of gargoyles and mad monks, and strange beasts with horns. *Why has he locked the door,* he thought? Then it became apparent as Black Friar John sank to his knees near the altar. The minister cursed in a very unholy manner as he stooped to remove a few candles and items from the altar.

'Oh my poor back. Too much bending and kneeling for a man of my age. Bad for the bones all this muddling around on the floor. Help me will you son. I'm not as agile as I once was.'

From his knelt position, the minister extended a hand and beckoned for the ghillie to join him. Falmouth gulped and stepped backwards, he didn't like the look of this, *what on earth was he getting himself into* he thought…but with a sheepish expression he reluctantly dropped to his knees.

'Don't look scared son, you look as though I'm about to jump on your bones. You've seen me with the widow, I'm not one of them lot who chase after altar boys. See this stone lid here below, grab the lip and pull, it's hard to budge mind so put your back into it.'

Falmouth did as he was bid and gripped the altar lip and pulled hard. Stone scraped on stone. Falmouth shuddered, it was like unearthing a corpse. His eyes became riveted on the cold stone as the minister allowed for just a wee gap, then plunged in one hairy arm to pull out his distils. With a bottle now in hand, he urged Falmouth to restore the altar to its former condition.

'I'll warn you now, ghillie, this is gonna cost ye. Betrayed by our own parliament we was, back in 1644, but they were canny - they didn't tax whisky direct, the tax was levied on malt. So now every bugger is trying to illegally distil it, but don't you worry, you won't find a finer whisky in these parts, it's the water see, and the oak barrels we use. None stop it is, I can't keep up with the demand, so I distil even at night, which is handy actually, as while the moon is a shining no one can see the smoke. Get my meaning?' He winked. 'The worry is, if the Excise men find my stash under the altar here, I'm finished. So keep your ears open and your mouth shut.' The minister held the whisky lovingly, like a baby cradled within his arms.

Falmouth opened his hands, palms up. 'Aye. Well you've nothing to fear from me. Excisemen can go to hell is what I say.'

'Good. Good.'

'How much of it do you want? If you want a dozen or so I can smuggle it out in a coffin.'

'Nae I only need the one bottle.'

Black Friar John frowned. 'Oh laddie, that's not near enough, you'll be back for more I can tell you.'

'Nae really I'm no' in need of a coffin full. But I will be back I'm sure. How much do I owe you?'

'Let's just say a couple of plump grouse to cook on the widow's fire. Is that fair? Oh and maybe a pigeon or two, she makes a good pigeon pie she does. Did you get a look at the bonny lass?'

'Aye I did.'

'Aye I expect you did, nice round arse on her. She's quite a looker isn't she? That's settled then. Make sure you drink to my merry widow now. Don't forget…oh and before you go, is it true about the young master, I hear he lost a leg?'

'Aye but not the whole leg. Below the knee had to be amputated, couldn't be saved I'm afraid'
'But how on earth?'
'The wee laddie caught it in a trap. I found him. God knows how long he had been there.'
'A trap?'
'Mantrap set by the laird for poachers.'
'That man never fails to amaze me, his depravity knows no bounds. How is the boy?'
'Not good. Low in spirits and tired of being idle. The laird hasn't seen him since the accident, the lad is broken hearted.'
'Oh that's sad. That is indeed very sad.'

Falmouth nodded and started to walk away, he was keen to return to the castle. But then he stopped, conscious of a change in the minister, the holy man's large shoulders slumped, and his eyes became dull. To Falmouth's mind Black Friar John seemed troubled by the news of young Robbie, perhaps more than troubled, shook up even. Then, of a sudden, the holy man snapped out of his melancholy and stood up straight, and his face lit up as he said: 'Well ghillie, what if I told you spirit isn't all I have to offer you today? I've a proposition for you so take heed. As you may have noticed, I've a head for commerce and I think I might be in a position to help the wee master at Castle Wood. What do you think? I need an extra hand here see, and the boy might be just what I need. Is he a quick learner?'
'Oh aye. Sharp as a knife.'
'The mother…will she be a problem?'
'Nae. I'll take care of that.'
'And the leg. Can he walk?'
'Aye. He's got a good peg leg that gets him about, and he can ride his horse.'
'Tell him to visit me on the sabbath at dusk.'

Falmouth tipped his hat. 'Sabbath at dusk.'

***

Before they reached the port of Leith, the baron found an able seamen and produced a shiny coin. They were a strange breed these seamen, but he looked a decent sort. He was certainly dressed better than the cabin boy that was for sure…he wore baggy breeches, a checked shirt and smelled of tar. Upon his head he wore a strange cap made from coarse braided wool, angled to appear jaunty. William handed him the coin, and as the seaman stretched out one muscled arm for the money his tattoos were on full display, a Jerusalem Cross, an anchor and a seabird of sorts. Exposure to the sun had given him a deep tanned look, and his weathered skin made him look old and wizened before his time.

William placed the coin upon his rope scarred palm. ' I need information.'
'Aye. What do you want to know?'
'Your Captain has a cabin boy…'
'Aye. What of it?'
'Last time I was onboard he scourged him for no reason. Why?'
The seaman became shifty, his eyes darted from left to right, searching for signs of prying eyes or wagging ears. 'I cannot help you.' He tried to return the coin.
William swatted the coin away. 'Your cross, it's a Christian symbol is it not?' William prodded the Jerusalem Cross tattoo with his stubby finger.
'The Captain will whip me if he gets wind of me talking to the likes of you. Leave me be. 'The seaman's eyes bulged from their sockets.
'This will go no further I swear. Look around you, man, no one is about. Now quickly, tell me if the boy is in mortal danger…'
'Danger? Danger is all around you on a vessel such as this, what with the wind and sea, and the sickness that can take you at any given moment. But if you mean has he been punished, well aye, near enough every day of the voyage. The captain has it in for him see. One time, the laddie was tied to the mast for nine days and whipped till he was covered in blood. Afterwards, the Captain got a couple of waisters to smear his wounds with brine and pickle.'
'And all the while everyone turns a blind eye and does nothing to help him?'

'The lash is standard, just a bit of pickling…it's how Captains keep discipline. 'Tis nothing unusual, it's meant to toughen lads up, make sailors out of him. Some can take it, some cannot.'
'But surely someone could help him?'
'Nae. The crew will do nothing. We follow orders and that is all.'
'What are the punishments for?'
'Could be anything, last time he was whipped for arriving on deck with one stocking on. The time before that he tied a rope wrong. *Now,* I've said enough. You sir need to go…before we're seen together.'

William barred the man's way. He stretched out one arm and placed a hand upon the sailor's shoulder. 'One more question if I may. How does the boy fair now?'
'The laddie's every colour of the rainbow. His whole body is covered in stripes and bruises and his head is swollen in size.'
'Do you think…?'

The ship's bell rang to signal the next watch. William jerked his head in the direction of the sound, heard the seamen and waisters scuttling from one part of the deck to another. When he turned his head back, the able seaman was gone.

That night, a thick fog lay on top of the water, as the sea vessel rolled across choppy waves. Once again, William clutched his stomach and willed away the sickness that plagued him at sea. This business was a bad one, and the storm just seemed to add to it. He confided in his manservant, told him all he knew of the cabin boy. The baron sat still, arms folded, noticeably irritable as he waited for Mackenzie's response. But to his annoyance, his manservant delayed in answering him, and instead fiddled with a small wooden pipe, packing tobacco into the damned thing and taking an age.
'Since when did you smoke a pipe?'
'One of the sailors gave me it. It calms me.'
'Well?'
'Well what?
'The boy?'
'Not our business.'

'Now look here, Mackenzie… stop puffing on that damned pipe and give me your thoughts. I'd really like your opinion on this you being a common man…' William puffed out his cheeks and then inhaled. The pipe smoke smelled sickly sweet, but was not at all unpleasant.

'I've just told you. Not our place to interfere, my Lord.'

'But if we do not intervene, he will surely die. Look man, forget we are master and servant for a moment, let's just talk… man to man. What do you think?'

Mackenzie gave off a deep sigh. 'He'll not be the first or the last to suffer at the hands of a cruel captain. But just out of curiosity, how do you propose to help him then?'

William bowed his head. 'That I do not know.'

'Well you'd better think on it quick, the voyage will be soon over.'

William nodded. 'You're right, there isn't much time. I should go at once, fetch the laddie now, this very moment.'

Mackenzie scratched his head. 'Aw you're not thinking this through, the captain is a dangerous man, a violent man…and forgive me, Sir, but can I be frank?'

'Of course.'

'It's just you've never struck me as bothering with the misfortune of others before.'

'Well that's about to change. Come on, follow me, I may need your help.'

***

Mackenzie had to hurry to keep up with him. Like a hunting dog, he ran and snapped at his master's feet. 'Wait, wait,' he cried. 'You need to think this through, my lord, the captain will not just hand him over. It'll not be easy. You're going to have to trick him somehow. The lad's his property to treat as he wishes. If he's punished as harsh as he is publicly, imagine what goes on behind closed doors.''

William stopped in midstride. 'Yes. Yes you're right. My God, Mackenzie, you are right. And you, dear man have given me the most splendid idea.'

'But my Lord, are you sure?'

'Yes quite sure. Come on man. We must find the captain now, before it is too late.' Without hesitation the baron and his valet crossed the slippery quarterdeck to the captain's cabin, and without hesitation he banged on the door. The door flew open, and to William's surprise one of the green hands beckoned for him to come quickly inside.
'The captain will not be long, you can wait in the great cabin, your manservant can wait outside.'

The baron shook his head and stretched a grin. 'He most certainly will not, it's blowing a gale out there, he will accompany me.'
The green hand's face became pale. He looked visibly troubled, at odds with himself, before he sighed and said: 'The captain won't be happy but go on then.'
They waited for what felt like eternity inside the great cabin, and as the ship rolled across the sea the whale oil lamps pivoted on their mounted gimbals and squeaked into the cold night. William swept his eyes across the room, it spanned the whole width of the stern and had huge windows. In the centre of the room, a large map stretched across the dining table, and atop of it sat a quantity of nautical equipment. William's eyes became drawn to a compass…he was just about to pick it up when Captain Pepper appeared from behind a screen.

'Baron Bothwell, how wonderful to see you. What can I do for you? Ah let me guess…the wind, the fog - nothing to worry about, all under control, our voyage is near its end, we will soon drop anchor in Scotland.'
'Yes my valet suspected as much, I never can tell our whereabouts. Anyhow, I will get to the point, I've a proposition for you, Captain Pepper, and I sincerely hope you will be agreeable to it. You see, I would like to employ one of your men. Well not a man as such, a laddie…I was hoping to employ the services of your cabin boy.'
'Angus? The lad is useless, I've better workers than him, any of the able seamen…'
'No. It's the boy I want.' The baron took from his pocket a bag of coins and dangled them beneath the captains' nose.

'Oh aye it's like that is it? Ah, I think I understand now. You're a man that has, how should I say this? You're a man that has unusual tastes...' the captain tapped the bridge of his nose.

The baron's stomach turned. The damned captain thought him a sodomite, just the thought of it left a bad taste in his mouth. William opened his mouth to protest, but before he uttered a word, McKenzie grabbed him by the arm and whispered into his ear. 'Play along, let him think whatever he wants to think... just give him the coins and let's be away from here.'

The baron swallowed hard, his face became hot. It took all his composure to swallow his pride before he said: 'Ah well needs must. We all have our quirks captain. The boy will make a delightful pageboy I am sure. I've a wonderful uniform all ready for him, he'll look just the part.'

The captain eyed the bag of coins greedily and suddenly began to cough, it took a moment of wheezing and spluttering before he cleared his throat. 'Would you like for him to be sent to your cabin at once? You see the laddie is a wee bit clumsy, always bumping into things he is and so I'm afraid he's not at all well. Always was a bit feeble minded and weakly. Had a little bump to the head a few days ago I seem to remember. Nevertheless, if you hand over the coins, I can send him over right away.

The baron placed the bag of coins into the captain's hand and smiled. 'No need. Let the boy rest. At the end of the voyage I wish for him to be sent to us with all his things. Is that a deal?'

The captain took the money and shook the baron's hand. 'Yes. We have a deal.'

CHAPTER 15

Two small figures, a young boy and girl, sat crouched upon coal dust and peered into the pit head below. A huge black hole loomed before them, and the opening was so large it seemed able to swallow them up at any moment. The boy placed a protective arm around the young girl and tried to comfort her, but the girl sobbed in short bursts, occasionally interrupted by the odd hiccup. Teardrops snaked a long white trail through the blackness of coal dust upon the girl's face.

'Oh quit crying, Margaret. You're making my head hurt. Others have found their way to the top, more are bound to follow, I am certain of it. Have faith in our Lord, He will protect us and He will guide us. Press your hands together and let us pray. '
'But Thomas, I want to go hame. It's nae guid, I dinnae ken the time, how long has it been now? I just want to know that my faither is safe.'
Thomas Hume shook his small head. He'd been trapping for a year and a half now and was lucky enough to have a cap and a candle, trappers weren't allowed candles as a rule, but his sister Effie often sneaked him one when folk weren't looking. The candle helped him to stay awake in the pitch dark, and his cap helped to keep him warm and protected his head from the jagged coalface. Trapping was a tedious work, for hours on end he had to open and close a trapdoor to allow coal carts to pass through, and if someone forgot to close the door behind a cart they risked dangerous gases building up. Thomas frowned and scratched his head, he hadn't thought about that, perhaps that was the cause of the explosion.
'Do ye think little Joseph fell asleep again? He let the trapdoor stand open for near on a half hour the other week. This could be all his doing. He'll never be a putter that one, he's useless.' Thomas tapped Margaret on the shoulder.

The little girl named Margaret stopped crying for a moment and lifted her chin up in a defiant way before shouting at the boy. 'Well it's

not his fault, Thomas Hume. He's only wee and he has no candle to help keep him awake like you do, you should mind your tongue.'
'All right keep your hair on, Margaret I was only saying.'
A sudden rumble of sound erupted from the gaping hole below, and caused young Margaret and Thomas to scramble backwards on their heels and elbows. From the pit head emerged a head of black soot, and it seemed to sprout from the earth like a strange shrub with long twisted limbs. Another head emerged, then another, until nineteen of them stood at the pit top…and to their amazement, one of the nineteen carried a new born baby.

Thomas turned to squeeze Margaret's hand, but she was already gone, the giant man, the one they called Tiny had her in his arms and the man cried tears of joy as he held her in a fierce embrace. That's what Thomas was gawping at when his sister, Effie tapped him on the arm, and when she did young Thomas fell to his knees and thanked the Lord, for if ever there was a time to be thankful it was now.

***

They found the remains of a child 300 foot from the pit, shot from the mine like a cork from a wine bottle. What was left of it could not be identified, but of course everyone knew it was young Joseph the trapper, just six years of age. Magnus seethed inside, of course he knew bairns worked just the same as adults, that was normal, but what kind of man profited from little children toiling in the depths of a mine? For sure he knew only too well the kind of man. His fingers went to his neck, Magnus sucked in his breath and traced the engraving of the collar that fastened around his throat. Greed, suffering…all for wealth and power, to the detriment of collier serfs…men, women, children. Where was the humanity, the compassion? He bowed his head and silently wept.

An old woman arrived at the pit head. She gazed wistfully at the pit mouth and fell to her knees. 'Is he no oop yet? My Joseph, where is he? He's the only one not accounted for. 'She cried out his name till her voice became hoarse.

Effie placed a hand around her bony shoulders, but the old woman shrugged her off. It was the dead trapper's grandmother dressed in rags, not a tooth left in her downturned mouth - the trapper boy had been an orphan and was all that the old woman had. The grandmother turned deathly pale and stared at all the folk around her, but not one face could meet her gaze.

'I forbid you to look away.' She cried. 'Look at me.' She began to wail, and then her crazed mind caused her to scramble towards the ladders to climb below, and the sight caused Effie to shudder inside.

'Is he no oop yet?' She continued to cry.

Folk became wary of her now and stepped away. But Effie clutched at the woman's skirts, it was all she could do to stop her climbing down the pit ladders.

Effie cried out to her: 'He's gone. He's in heaven… at peace. You ken you're not strong enough to go down there and he's not down there anyway.'

The old woman stopped in her tracks. 'Well where is he then?' She screamed.

Magnus stepped in then and dragged the old woman up from the ground. And as she wept tears into his broad chest he asked her if she really wanted to see what was left of her grandson. 'You remember him as he was, old woman.'

***

Magnus changed after the explosion. The boy's death affected him deeply. Pent-up hate consumed him and threatened to erupt with a catastrophic force. The unexpressed rage that boiled within him began to fester and darken his soul… and so severe were these feelings that Magnus grew quite dizzy at times and broke out into a sweat. Something had to give…or something had to change, but really in truth, Magnus was lost. He'd lost all hope…and that's when an idiotic idea occurred to him. A notion that Effie could help him find peace. Aye that was it, she could be the answer to all his dreams, and perhaps the end of all his hate… foolishly Magnus put all his faith in a ragged fremit bearer from a mining village he didn't even know the name of. And in truth it was sheer madness on his part, daring to imagine a life for him and Effie…for this conviction was wrong, misplaced, not thought out properly. Effie was *not* for him.

He'd cornered her one Sunday, when the collier folk were preparing to worship in the loft of the local kirk, away from the decent folk. Miners would always be a breed apart…

'Effie, please listen to what I have to say…this is not easy for me. I really do not know where to begin. Look I'll just say it, come away with me, far away from this place and that hellhole of a pit. Just you and I. We can have a life together; I know we can.'

Effie shrugged her shoulders and had the audacity to laugh. 'Have you lost your mind? I'm a collier lassie, I've no business living anywhere else, Magnus. This is my home and always will be, I don't want to go anywhere else. And anyway, what life could you offer me? Have you forgotten that collar o' brass around your neck? You are the property of the coal master, and he's not keen on losing workers. You'll be lucky to escape his clutches for a year and a day, he'll set the dogs on you the moment he knows you've gone.'

Magnus tapped the iron with his fist. 'This will not hinder me, nothing will I tell you…not anymore. I can't stay here anymore, Effie, I must go, and I want you to come with me. How can you bear it? Day after day staggering about in darkness choked for air. Don't you ever want to see your bairns roam free, feel the warmth of the sun on their faces and the wind in their hair? Nae I can tell from your face that you're too afraid to leave, you're a damn coward, Effie Hume.' He shook his head.

'Aye if you say so, if staying here makes me a coward then a coward is what I am. Aye, it'll be an arling ceremony for my child when the day comes… and when he or she is grown it'll go down pit as I did, and my parents and grandparents before me. And why you might ask? Well I'll tell you, not that it's any of your business…it's because we're proud mining folk, we stick together and we're not afraid of hard graft.' She folded her arms across her bony chest.

'You're a fool, Effie Hume. You're settling for a life of slavery for you and your bairns. Don't you want more for them?'

'Oh quit talking of the future and bairns and slavery. Who said I'm to be blessed with any babies? That's out of my hands and something for

177

the Lord above to decide. And you...you were nae more than a serf afore you came here. A serf is much the same as a slave is it not? Your master gave you that lump of metal around your neck and threw you in the dungeons to rot. Then he carted you off to here...I'm surprised you find serfdom preferable to this. '

Magnus put his head in his hands. 'Oh Effie, I displeased my master and that is why he treated me so. I toiled in the fields but it was better than the pit and the darkness and all the ailments that go with it.'

'What ailments?'

'Ah were should I begin? Does everyone spit up black phlegm and have eyes all red and clogged up with coal dust? Is that normal tell me? I've seen your scars from the falling coal, and I've heard the wheezing from your chest...I won't even mention the stunted growth and the curved spines. Have you seen young Douglas's head from pushing the coal tubs with his head? Bald and covered in ulcers and he's not a man yet. Is this what's to look forward to?''

'Oh just go will you, you're not one of us and never will be. All that you speak of is a miner's lot, nothing more, nothing less, that's just how it is. I imagine you became used to the calluses on your hands from digging the fields...well that's nothing to us mining folk, we're not as soft as you field labourers. So now I've said my piece, Magnus, I think it's time you left before I say something I'll regret.'

Magnus looked deep into her eyes. 'So that's it.'

'Aye.'

And that's when he realised Effie was not for him.

***

Sister Louise near jumped from her skin when she felt a cold hand upon her shoulder. A loud shriek escaped her lips. *Did that noise come from me?* She thought, but she couldn't think straight, a thick fog clouded her mind. Sleep lingered in her still... she was in a state of semi consciousness, in that mysterious place between awake and slumber. The prioress rubbed her eyes and looked up in a daze, she could just make out the outline of a young woman. It had to be late, the chapel was in near darkness, and her poor knees...she could no longer feel them. She tried to stand and near fell over, oh the shame… she sniffed up and wiped her wet face and resisted the urge to curse in her mother tongue. The young nun, bless her, helped her superior to her feet, and as she did so the prioress tried to recall her name, but for the life of her she could not remember, not even when she squeezed her eyes shut and mentally reeled off a selection of names.

'Merci. I confess I cannot remember…'

'Sister Alice.'

'Ah yes of course, how silly of me to forget. Have you visited the infirmary?'

The nun nodded but remained silent.

'Well…is there any change?'

'The patient is much the same. There is a healing woman with her now, the one from the village.'

'A healing woman? But I thought one of the nuns had trained as a nurse…why doesn't she attend her?'

'She is; well they are…I mean both women are looking after her.'

'Well I must go to her at once.'

'But Prioress…'

'Oui?'

'Is that wise? Sister Sarah has a terrible fever, the healing woman said that we must limit our contact with her. There is no need for you to concern yourself with the girl, we will make sure she is comfortable.'

'I will decide what is of concern, Sister Alice. As prioress, it is my duty to hold the place of God here at the priory, and it is your job to obey Him in all things, now run along.'

***

Before the old abbey was abandoned, a large infirmary graced the east wing. But now, in the wake of the reformation, and devoid of patrons and donations, all that remained was a small building, set into dense trees near the ruins of the old abbey. Once the true faith was restored, hopefully things could return to their former glory, well that's what the nuns hoped for. Sister Louise paused by the infirmary entrance, she was prioress she told herself, a figure such as her shouldn't dawdle or seem hesitant, she had to appear strong. She took a deep breath and pushed open the door.

The first thing that hit her was the smell. It was something you could never quite prepare yourself for, that sickly sweet odour, almost fruity, with the stench of vomit thrown in and something else…a rotting scent perhaps. Near the door was a bed with poor Sarah upon it, either side of the bed were two women, Sister Agnes and a wise woman. At the sight of the wise woman, the prioress felt ill at ease…she never did trust women of herbs, and she never would. In fact, despite her best intentions, she froze at the infirmary entrance, as though unsure of whether to enter or not… the only reason she didn't flee was Sarah. Her eyes darted here and there, as she searched the room. Three patients in all, Sarah and two men, she frowned - there had been three men the last time she had been here.

'What happened to the cowman?' The prioress seemed to hold her breath as she rushed through the door and crossed the room to the women.

'Died this morning.' Sister Agnes said. 'His wounds did not heal, I tried my best to clean them but they became all yellow with pus… and the skin around the wound became full of red streaks and the smell, well I near lost my morning oats I tell you.'

'All right, some things are best left unsaid. Now then, everything seems to be in order. Both of you can leave now, I will attend to the girl for a while.'

The wise woman left the bedside and approached the prioress. 'The girl has the fever, the kind you see in gaols and ships… you cannot stay, it would be foolish of you to remain here, you could catch it see. Sister Agnes and I can cope.'

'If that is the case then why haven't you caught it or Sister Agnes for that matter?'

The healing woman crossed her arms over her generous bosom and pulled a face. 'Most probably because I've been exposed to it a dozen times or more…and it just can't take a hold of me. Like my mother before me, I am rarely sick. Will Sister Agnes get it? Well that remains to be seen. Some folk believe the gaol fever is spread through the bites

180

of lice and fleas, perhaps the smell of my healing herbs puts them off biting the likes of me…but if Sister Agnes is bitten or yourself… and you scratch those bites, well you're in trouble.' The wise woman paused for breath, uncrossed her arms and scratched her head, a deep frown formed across her forehead. 'I've often wondered why scratching the bites makes it worse, but mark my word it does. I once had a child that was bitten to buggery from her flea pit of a crib, oh excuse the expression, prioress. But aye she was bitten all over…and so I swaddled her in fresh, clean bedding so she was unable to scratch, and guess what? She never even got the fever, and once all her bites had cleared up she was right as a trivet.'

'Surely Sarah has no lice upon her body…the girl is usually clean, and we change our linen as often as we can. Has she any bites upon her person…flea bites?'

'None that I can see. And yes her bedding is clean. But I am told she pets a cat here, one you use to catch rats, perhaps the cat has fleas? Or, if she has worked in the infirmary with Sister Agnes, she may have come into contact with a patient with body lice. There are many possibilities. Who knows how these diseases are spread?'

'What are her chances?' The prioress felt a throb in her temple, and placed a hand to her head.

'Not good, prioress. Sarah is very ill. She has a pink rash, and spots and bumps all over her body. Sometimes her fever causes her to become delirious. I really think it would be better for you that Sister Agnes and I attend her. Most of the time she is away with the fairies anyway. Oh, and there is something else.'

'Yes?'

'The girl has the French pox.'

'French pox you say. Do you mean the filthy disease that effects the privy parts?' The prioress did not blush.

'Aye that's the one. She's in the early stages…'

'Strange how the British blame us for the filthy disease… in France we blame it on the Spanish.' The prioress raised her eyebrows and then inhaled deeply. 'There really isn't much hope for her then is there?'

The healing woman nodded and stepped towards the nun. 'I'm afraid not.'

Time seemed to stand still as a great hush filled the room. The prioress felt dizzy of a sudden and began to look for something to lean against, but there was nothing, and so without thought she bent her knees and sat on the edge of the bed wringing her hands. All morning she had been praying for Sarah but seemingly to no avail. Her heart began to thump in her bosom and then all the colour drained from her face. 'Ah, I can't believe it, this is serious is it not? She could die at any moment...'

The prioress looked up from her seated position and watched the wise woman's face change, and her expression bothered her for some reason. The astute look was long gone, and in it's wake was compassion and something else. The prioress blushed from ear to ear. She had a good mind to slap the wise woman's smug face. In a flash, she stood up so that she no longer sat upon Sarah's sick bed.
'You care deeply for this young woman, Prioress?'
The prioress waved a hand at the healing woman and laughed. 'Of course I do. I care deeply for *all* of my sisters. We share so much in common, it is natural for us to be attached to one another. So yes, I do have deep feelings for Sarah. '
'But you care for her more than most. There is no shame in it. 'The wise woman nodded her head and reached out a hand, but the prioress would not take it.
'As you say, there is no shame in my concern for her. Sarah and I have travelled afar to be here; we have shared a journey. I would be grateful if we could stop this foolish tittle tattle, so I may spend a moment with her alone, is that too much to ask?' The prioress tried in earnest to conceal a tear that rolled down her face.

The wise woman nodded. 'I will attend the men folk while you sit with her. But try not to move too close to her. The risk of you catching the same thing will be less likely then. Remember what I said about scratching. If you feel an itch from a bite, do not be tempted to rub it. I know it sounds odd, but please take heed of my advice. '
The prioress nodded and tried her best to smile as the wise woman walked away. The moment she was alone with Sarah, Sister Louise fell to her knees and snatched the girl's hand and held it in her own. As she

gazed down upon sweet Sarah, as always she was unable to tear her eyes away from her. A great passage of time could go by, and she'd be none the wiser, in another world…the world of Sarah. A terrible cramping filled her stomach, and a sob became trapped in her throat, oh and how it ached and swelled. For a long while she just knelt there beside the girl's bed, with Sarah's hand in her own and prayed to God Almighty. Only when she was quite sure her prayers had been answered did she move closer, and in a quiet voice said: 'Sarah. Sarah. Can you hear me?'

As the peasant girl's eyes fluttered open, a stream of light seemed to fall upon her face and lit the colour of her eyes, so that they appeared languid and tawny. When she realised who attended her a wonderful smile stretched across Sarah's flushed face. 'Oh Sister Louise, I feared you'd never come.' She said.

The prioress placed her arms out in front of her and shrugged. 'Oh mon dieu. I am here now. We have all been so worried about you. I've spent most of my morning praying for your good health. How do you feel?'

'Dizzy. I think I've knocked my head, it hurts and aches. But I mustn't be idle, mother will be cross. I need to fill father's pipe, and there's spinning to be done.' Sarah tried to sit up in her bed, a simple action, but as soon as she tried, she failed and flopped backwards onto the bed.

Sister Louise played along for the girls' sake. 'You are very weak, Sarah. You must remain still. If the wise woman catches you trying to sit up she'll chase me away. Just lie back, the chores can be done later. Do not be troubled, I will speak to your parents and tell them you are busy. Now how about you, should I fetch you a bite to eat or something to drink? '

Sarah shook her head and shivered. A thin layer of sweat covered her whole face. 'I couldn't eat a morsel but I'd like a sip of something cold, I feel as though I'm on fire, I am so hot.'

Next to her bed was a horn beaker with small ale in it. The prioress gently placed it to Sarah's lips and let her drink. 'Enough?'

'Aye. Have you seen my baby, a girl child? She is so beautiful. Will you fetch her for me? I need to cradle her see. They won't let me hold her.'

'You lost the child, Sarah, in childbirth, it came too early remember? We buried it near the priory ruins a few month back.'

'Not that one. The other one, the one I had at Castle Wood.'

Sister Louise sucked in her breath and began to shake with rage. 'You've had more than one baby? Oh how I despise that man, you couldn't have been little more than a child when he...when he. Oh God's teeth, the baron is an absolute brute...'

'Nae. The baron had nothing to do with it. Magnus tricked him see, he made me lie with him before we wed. He made me do it so the baron never got his *right of first night*. My baby girl was not the baron's child.' Sarah squeezed the prioresses hand.

'Then if not the baron. Who?'

'I just told you - Magnus.'

'Who is Magnus?'

'A land serf, the same as I. You must fetch back my wee girl, Sister Louise. I want to see her little face once more before I die. It is my dying wish.'

The prioress's lips curled up in disgust. 'A land serf? Lord above, forgive me for saying this but I despise men and how they treat women. It makes my blood boil to think of him placing his dirty hands on you, Sarah. But if he is indeed the father, I expect he has the child, and there's nothing I can do about it. I may be a woman of God, but I cannot take a child from its father for no good cause.'

Sarah squeezed the prioresses hand so hard she winced. 'Nae, you don't ken what I mean. Magnus doesn't have the child. Magnus was took away, he just disappeared and then they came for me.'

'I'm confused. None of this is making any sense. Who came for you?'

'The baron's men. They locked me in a chamber till I brought forth the child. Then he took it away.'

'Who took the baby away... ah no let me guess - the baron.' The prioress said between gritted teeth.

Sarah began to weep, and the sound of her distress tore at Sister Louise's heart. That's when the cramping returned to her stomach, and a great aching pain tore at her throat. Oh the horror of it all, it really was too much to bear, so all at once, the prioress threw caution to the wind and moved closer to Sarah, so that their noses were merely inches apart.

Blood rushed to Sister Louise's head till she felt quite dizzy, dizzy with longing and something else.

'Do you feel it too?' She whispered.

'I always have. I always will.' Sarah replied.

They kissed then, and when they did the prioress broke into a sweat, as desire seared through her whole body. God help her, at that moment she seemed to lose all reason, and when she did, all the emotions she'd held inside for so long flooded out. She cursed herself out loud, and not just for being weak and denying her true feelings... no, most of all she cursed herself for being a woman, when she so badly wanted to be a man at that moment - so she could take Sarah within her arms and make love to her.

That's when Sarah died.

CHAPTER 16

The sea-port of Edinburgh, Leith, on the southern shore of the Firth of Forth was a welcome sight. The baron stood on deck, his elbows resting on the ship rail. At the sight of land, William cupped one hand over his forehead and looked out to a stone bridge and harbour that divided the townspeople. He took a deep breath and exhaled, for the first time in a very long while, William felt a pang of hope. The air was crisp - there was a good breeze. The captain steered the ship at high water towards the mouth of the harbour, to a very long and well-built pier, free of silt and well preserved so as to maintain a large swell of sea.

The harbour buzzed with activity, what with traders, seamen and men folk loading and unloading cargo into a quay well wharf'd up with stone. The quay was well able to discharge more business than the place could supply. The air smelled of sea coal, smoke and sin…anything could be bought at the port of Leith, the baron was well aware of that. But today, he had other things on his mind.

'McKenzie. The ship will drop anchor any moment now, so be a good man will you… run along and collect the boy. I can't stand the sight of that awful man Pepper. Any nonsense from him just come back to me and I will sort it. '

'Pepper? Do you mean the captain?'

'Who else?'

McKenzie pulled a face and spat out some chewed up tobacco onto the deck, a disgusting habit he'd picked up from the seamen. 'Last time I went to the captain's cabin they wouldn't even let me in, don't you remember? They made me eat in the mess with the other men, and once I was there they all just looked at me like dirt, so they did the bastards. I ken I'm a servant, but there's really no need for that. They're no better than me those jack tars.'

'Oh for goodness sake, I'll do it myself.' William said before storming off in the direction of the great cabin.

***

The boy heard seagulls as he lay upon his bed of dirty straw. The ship cat, the ratter had a cleaner and more comfortable bed, which spoke volumes when it came to the cabin boy. The seabirds were a sure sign of land, but that didn't mean his ordeal was over. He lay in rags shivering and thrashing about in absolute torment. The poor laddie was pale as a corpse, and so weak he could hardly lift his head. So he just lay there in great pains of agony until he heard a creaking noise.

Someone was coming...*it might be him* the boy thought - *the captain*...and just the thought of it caused him to shake and then, to his shame warm liquid ran down his legs.
A door burst open and a stranger walked inside.
'The smell. Jesus it stinks in here. What the hell?' The stranger began to gag.
A seaman piped up: 'Aye well he's been lying there for a while now, Baron Bothwell. The laddie can't get up; his head is all swollen see. Must have drank too much grog and bumped his head hard on the deck or something...'
'This is an absolute disgrace. Why hasn't the boy been seen to? He's lying in his own filth, and look at those rags, I can see the lad's ribs. Fetch my manservant will you. He'll carry the boy; I can't have him spoiling my clothes. I'll wait in my carriage. Hurry now - run long.'

The boy whimpered when the cabin became silent again. Tears of relief trickled down his face. How pitiful he should feel such respite in the state he was in...but that's how he felt, safe in the knowledge that the captain wouldn't have the chance to whip him with the cat again. They would come for him soon, he'd heard them loud and clear. They were going to take him away from here, and that's when his face contorted and formed an expression he hadn't experienced since setting foot on this hellhole of a ship - he smiled, and the act felt almost alien to him.

***

Once McKenzie set eyes on the wee laddie in the cabin he dropped to his knees and gasped. Never in all his life had he seen such a sorry sight, it took all of his composure to refrain from finding the captain at that very moment to knock him senseless. Instead, he touched the boy's face (he daren't touch the boy's swollen head), and as he did so a large tear ran down McKenzie's cheek till it reached his bearded chin. McKenzie coughed and wiped it away before whispering in the boy's ear.

'Can you hear me laddie?' The boy's voice was soft in answer, barely audible. 'Aye I can hear you. You're going to take me away from here aren't you? And I am mighty glad of that, but you won't hurt me will you mister?'

'No son. I won't hurt you. No one will ever hurt you again, I can promise you that.'

'I'm thirsty.' The boy managed to say in a croaked voice. 'May I have a drink?'

McKenzie reached into his pocket and pulled out a flask of the fire water and held it to the boy's lips. 'Better than grog this is. Sup it up lad, it will help with the pain. What's your name?'

'Angus.'

'You're in a bad way, Angus but we're here to help you now. Do you think you could get to your feet?'

'Nae.'

'All right then, that's not a problem, I will carry you. But first we must fetch a blanket to wrap you in.' McKenzie nodded to the ordinary seaman and said in a gruff voice: 'Has the laddie some shoes? Where are his possessions?'

The seamen shook his head and shrugged. 'He has nothing... he owns nothing.'

McKenzie frowned. 'Nothing at all? Surely the lad has something?'

'He's an apprentice boy. Came from one of those foundling homes, you know the places for abandoned children? He has nothing or no one.'

'Well he has now. Your captain has agreed to hand him over to my master, so he's the baron's concern now. So take heed, you better fetch me a blanket at once or there will be trouble. I can't take him outside in those rags he's wearing, he'll catch his death of cold. It's a wonder he hasn't perished already.'

'The lad has no blanket. Like I said, he has nothing.'

188

'Well fetch him a blanket, any blanket - where is yours?'
'He can't have mine. My wages are near spent up as it is what with all the extra supplies they charge us for on here…'
'Gone on extra grog has it?'
'Nae.'

McKenzie stamped his feet. 'You know I've watched you seamen on here, and I know you all toe the line and bow to authority, anything to avoid the cat o' nine tails, that's just how it is. Oh aye, I've eyes in my head and I ken your captain on this ship is a man hell-bent on correction and discipline, but for the love of God, look at the boy. How can you all turn a blind eye to him? For the life of me I cannot fathom how all of you can just stand back and watch a boy be beaten near half to death day after day? You should all be ashamed of yourselves.'
The seaman shrugged. 'It's discipline. It's how a laddie is toughened up and prepared for seafaring life. There's no room for mollycoddling onboard a ship.'
'I may not be a mariner or a seaman… but I recognise cruelty when I see it. That has nothing to do with discipline. I think it's more a you all turning a blind eye, rather him beaten than you. Cowards you are, the lot of you.' McKenzie slipped out of his coat and then placed it across the boy. Once he lifted the lad from the ground he realised just how skeletal he was, light as a feather, the poor wee thing.

'Open the door will you and tell that captain of yours once we are gone that I will be reporting this to the appropriate authorities, you can be sure of that.' McKenzie nodded and stormed off through the door.

***

Once the boy was in the carriage it quickly became apparent that he was in no fit state to travel to Castle Wood. So, they crossed Water Lane to one of the merchant's houses to look for lodgings and enquire after a surgeon or someone who practiced medicine right away. The situation was grave to say the least, the cabin boy was quite ill. Once they found a room, the baron kicked open the door and helped McKenzie get the laddie into a bed.

'I thought we were going to stay in a merchant's house?' McKenzie frowned.

'Me too, but seeing as though we're both covered in piss and vomit, I'm afraid I don't quite look the Lord... so it's a tavern or nothing I'm afraid, Blad.' 'McKenzie's eyes near popped from his head. 'You actually remembered my name. By the Christ, I'd never have believed it before this voyage.

'Aye. Full of surprises I am. Now we must find a surgeon right away...'

'There's a barber surgeon next door.'

'How do you know? You've never been here before.'

'There's a window above master with bloody bandages wrapped round a pole. They do that don't they? They bleed folk and then...'

'Yes yes, McKenzie, just get yourself along there right away before the boy snuffs it will you.'

'Back to McKenzie are we?'

The baron waved an arm at his servant. 'Go on man and be quick.'

***

Once alone, the baron dropped to his knees and prayed at the foot of the boy's bed. He was tired...tired of the images and thoughts that polluted his head. He wanted to be wholesome, good, not a creature driven by base instincts, so he pressed his two hands firmly together, as his body and soul cried out to be heard. William *needed* to be heard... the boy had been sent to him he was sure of that... to test him, to make him a better person. Here was *his chance of real salvation*, if he saved the boy he'd be forgiven by God for all of his sins. Cleansed of every wrong doing... against his wife, his son, his serfs, and all the other countless sins he'd committed over the years. Everything rested on the boy, he was certain of it. Thus he prayed in earnest till his tongue stiffened and his knees ached - before long the room became quite dark.

A knock. Then another rapping on the door.

The baron opened his eyes, got to his feet and opened the door.

'We've been knocking for a while; I've found the barber surgeon.' McKenzie ushered the other man into the room.

'I must have nodded off, I'm sorry, it's been a long, long day. Please look at the boy right away, no expense will be spared to make him well.'

The barber surgeon squinted his eyes in the dim light and looked at the two men before shaking his head. 'I'd very much like to examine the boy to determine his health, but sadly this cannot be done in the dark. One of you must fetch candles at once, oh and make sure you get candles and not those feeble rush lights the women will try to fob you off with here. Oh and get some refreshments too.'

The baron grabbed McKenzie's arm. 'I'll go; I won't be a moment.'

A moment later all three men gathered around the cabin boy's bed as candlelight flickered strange shadows upon the walls. The boy lay still in the bed, and all was quiet. Something was amiss, off kilter…the baron could feel it in his bones, taste it even…impending doom? He hoped not.

The barber surgeon opened his mouth to speak, the examination was over…it was clear that he was about to voice his opinion on the boy, but the baron was not quite ready to hear it. In fact, his inner thoughts were conflicting, he'd invested so much in the boy and yet knew nothing of him. He honestly couldn't remember the cabin boy's name…and furthermore, he wondered why his life or death suddenly had so much bearing on his own life.

'Are you sure your examination is complete? Perhaps you should look him over again before you reach a decision.'

The barber surgeon began to button up his coat. 'No need.'

'I insist.'

'No need. The boy is dying. His head is swollen twice its normal size, he's badly malnourished and judging from all the bruises and stripes on his body, he's been beaten, and not just recently… for weeks, months even. Look at his flesh, it's every colour of the rainbow and if you touch it…well it's as soft as a jelly fish in places - probably putrid. The laddie is at death's door, I'd be surprised if he lasts through the night.' The barber surgeon shook his head at the baron, and as he did his lips curled up in disgust.

'Don't look at me like that. It wasn't me that did that to him.'

'Ach that's what they all say. Apprentice boys, cabin boys, foundlings, beggar boys, link boys…I've seen and heard it all.'

Once the surgeon's coat was buttoned up he made for the door, but the baron stepped in front of him to bar the way. 'No, I don't think you understand. Ask my valet, we saved him see, took him from his captain.'

'A sea captain? Ah no, not Pepper again.' The barber surgeon shook his head.

McKenzie butted in. 'He's done this before? The man's an absolute disgrace. My master is telling the truth. We paid the captain off to save the laddie.'

'Well I'm afraid it's too late for that. The boy is just too weak. It would take a miracle I'm afraid.' The surgeon tipped his hat and made off to leave again.

But McKenzie stopped him in his tracks. 'Something has to be done. The man shouldn't be allowed to treat his crew like that.'

The barber surgeon paused by the door. 'The crew won't talk. If they do they lose their jobs, and that's not gonna happen now is it? Half of them are hooked on grog, the other half need food in their bellies. No work, no food or grog - best to keep your mouth shut.'

McKenzie shrugged his shoulders. 'Well I'm not one of his crew, and neither are you…' He stared at his master.

But William was in a daze now. *'It would take a miracle…it would take a miracle'* was all he could hear in his head, over and over.

***

The surgeon was right. The cabin boy, Angus, didn't last the night. William took it badly.

The baron's valet left his master to grieve alone. McKenzie was so damned angry and outraged over the boy's mistreatment, he hadn't the energy for nothing at all, least of all his master's hysterics. The baron had changed since their trip to France that was for sure. McKenzie pinched the bridge of his nose and thought back, when had he changed? Suddenly it came to him, it was at that French nunnery… the baron's strange reaction to the nun's singing and chanting and then, he almost laughed at the recollection…the baron upon his knees praying to the

192

God above. Then, on the return voyage…his master's strange compulsion to save the cabin boy. It was all completely out of character for the laird of Castle Wood. In all his life, he'd never seen his master abstain from drink…or pray so much, and then there was the crying…crying like a real Jessie. His master had gone plain mad. McKenzie thanked the Lord, he still had all his faculties about him. One thing was for sure, he wasn't about to let the sea captain get away with murder - for that was what it was, pure and simple - murder. The boy's corpse lay stretched across the bed. Someone had covered his face, and already the sweet decaying scent of death lingered in the air. The baron lay on the floor beside the dead laddie, snivelling and muttering nonsense.

'All is lost Blad I tell you. *He* was my last chance. My only salvation. If only I could have saved him…well all could have been well. But now I'm ruined I tell you. Ruined. There is nothing left for me in this world now. I might as well join the corpse here and go to hell.'

McKenzie dropped to his knees and looked down upon his master. The wig he had so diligently powdered earlier that day was half on half off, and his master's face was all puffy and red. What had happened to the man? Where was the wicked profligate he knew so well? He shook his head… perhaps he had truly seen the light and wanted to make amends for past deeds. Was it really possible for a debauched man such as he to change? He knew not. McKenzie took a deep breath and rested a hand upon his master's arm.

'All is not lost.'

The baron stopped snivelling. 'How so, Blad?'

'Can I be blunt?'

'Yes. Go on.'

Well what has Angus the wee cabin boy got to do with any of this really? You hardly knew the lad - you cannae remember his name half the time.'

William huffed. 'I can.'

'What is it then?'

'Allan.'

McKenzie sniggered. 'His name was Angus not Allen. Look it seems to me you'd be happier if you just confronted your past. Why not tackle

193

the true nature of your disgrace - return to Castle Wood, put matters right, make amends.'

'No, I can't just leave the boy like this. There must be a trial and a burial.'

'All right. All of this can be dealt with one matter at a time. If we are patient and calm, we can see this through together. First of all, the boy must be examined again by another surgeon. A description of the boy's injuries needs to be drawn up - evidence see. Then the sea captain must be reported. We must both give a statement to the relevant authorities, and produce the medical evidence. That way the captain will face a trial. A burial can be arranged soon after.'

'How do you know about such things, Blad?'

'I've kin here in Leith that are free folk and know all that legal stuff. For a small fee they can arrange everything. They can't do the courtroom fancy talk and the like, but they can do the paper work, and well to know your letters and numbers is a grand thing.'

'Really, Blad? I thought folk of your station couldn't afford an education.'

McKenzie shrugged. 'Some of the dame schools here are very good.'

'Fancy that.'

McKenzie clapped his hands together. 'All right that is settled then. Once Angus is buried, and our statements are given - we will return to Castle Wood to put matters right.'

'There's something else.'

McKenzie frowned. 'Aye, what?'

'It's not just my wife and son I have wronged, there are others too. The girl we sought in France, and her sweetheart, Magnus, I treated them abominably…and my past with Magnus is a tale in itself.'

'Care to tell it?'

McKenzie cringed as his master became emotional once gain.

In a cracked voice, the baron muttered: 'Greta. It all has to do with Greta.'

'The girl your father sent away?'

'Yes. The moment I set eyes on her I was obsessed. Have you ever loved someone so much it hurt? She was in my blood, my heart. All I could ever think about was her, day in day out…I'd have died for her.

194

Then one day, I caught her with Magnus, and I was furious. We were all so young back then, playing in the woods…Magnus, Sabine, Greta, myself in the watchtower playing hide and seek. It was my turn.' The baron's voice faltered again.

'I found them together.'

'Who?'

'Magnus and Greta kissing.'

'What of it? Greta and Magnus were both serfs.'

'But she was *my* Greta - not his. I hated him then. Worse still, father always seemed to giving Magnus and his mother special treatment - that's when I wondered if Magnus was the bastard son of my father. Once I challenged him, I knew for certain. He had the same murderous expression - the same arrogance… and well that tipped me over the edge. I vowed that day to get my revenge.

'So where is he now?'

'Working the mines for a friend of mine. I gifted him - even had a brass collar made for him to wear around his neck. Before that I locked him in the dungeons.'

McKenzie placed his head in his hands. 'Dear Lord. He's your half-brother and you punished him over a lassie?'

'Well they made fun of me you see and that's what tipped me over the edge, I lost all reason. When I caught them kissing, I fell into a rage and drove them apart… and then I, then I.'

'What did you do?'

'I demanded that she kiss me like she kissed him, but she wouldn't. So I tried to force myself upon her and Magnus ran off and told my father. That's when she was sent away.'

'I see. And this happened many years ago when you were all young?'

'Yes.'

'Don't you think it's time you forgave your half-brother? Did he really mean you any harm? After all he was only trying to protect the girl.'

'Forgive him? I've spent most of my life despising him.But don't you see, all my life there has been a void I've been unable to fill. All because of him. Greta was all I ever wanted and he took that from me.'

'Did he really? Or was he just trying to stop the poor girl from being ravaged by you? Be honest man. Be true to yourself. If you truly want

195

to change and make amends, do good by the boy and start facing up to
your wrongs…then put them right if you can.'

CHAPTER 17

Young Robbie lay upon a bed of stuffed horse hair, two arms above him, so that his hands cradled the back of his head. The bed was uncomfortable and played havoc with his back, but it suited him fine, he loved it here, the smells, the sights. the folk... Castle Wood was a distant memory, he considered Black Friar Kirk and the distillery his home now, and there was harmony here that suited him implicitly. With no mother to fuss over him and worry about his missing limb, Robbie thrived...he may have arrived a boy, but he would be sure to depart a man. But leaving was far from Robbie's thoughts, not since he'd set eyes on the widow.

The widow, Lily, was a ravishing creature, enough to make any man's mouth water. Voluptuous and well formed, Lily was a woman designed to bring pleasure to all those around her. Her skin was pale and her eyes sea green rimmed with sooty black lashes, and they were languid and wide ...and if one looked into them, they were bound to stare. Her hair she kept covered, as pious women should, but if you peeped beneath her cap you could catch a glimpse of the most beautiful auburn hair. But regardless of her allure, her eyes sometimes held a sad glint. Lily had a past, and this past she shared with Robbie in secret one day.

'When I was fourteen I married my childhood sweetheart, Douglas, a local farmer, and soon became with child. But it wasn't meant to be, because sadly not long after I lost the bairn, and for a long while I wondered why the Lord had seen fit to punish me so. But no matter - I was young, I went to kirk every day and the kind minister there told me there was plenty of time for more children. But I grew impatient, Robbie, was that wrong? You see my Douglas he longed for plenty of strapping sons, you know to help him around the farm, and so we were both so happy when I became pregnant again. This time I carried the baby near enough to the end, so you can imagine my distress when I lost a baby for a second time. Oh the pain, Robbie, I cannot tell you

how much pain I went through, and my darling Douglas, because year after year I lost another child. Then one day, my husband came in from the fields, gave me a kiss and sat down at our table to eat. He never blamed me for the bairns, but I'm sure it broke his heart. Like I said, he sat down for his evening meal and off I went to fetch his pipe...but when I came back he was slumped over, face first in his bowl of broth - stone cold dead. All because of me and my inability to give him a son. That's when I went to Black Friar John, to begin my penance.'

Her tale was a sad one, and Robbie was visibly moved when Lily finished revealing the cause of her pain, and so he placed an arm around Lily after her confession and was smitten from that day onward. After all, the lovely Lily had confided in *him*, and not Black Friar John. Robbie was certain it meant something. Lily would no longer need the holy man as a confidant, she would come to him from now - Robbie was more than happy to oblige. To his delight, Lily did just that, near enough every other morning before Black Friar John woke up, and together they would sit beside the fire and join hands as they chatted. One morning, she even allowed him to place shoes upon her feet, as Lily had gone barefoot since the day her husband had died. It was the only sore subject between them, as Robbie loathed to see her punishing herself.

'Wear the shoes. I've saved for these for weeks, the cobbler told me they're the best he has."'

'I can't.'

Robbie takes Lily's hand in his and looks deep into her eyes. 'Why not?'

Lily flushes like a rose. 'I just can't. It's penance.'

'Ever tried to grow things, Lily?'

'Aye of course. Kale most of all.'

'Sometimes there are bad seeds.'

Lily shook her head. 'What do you mean?'

'It may not have been your fault, Lily. Even the best plant won't grow if the seed is weak. Now put on the shoes.' Robbie dropped to his knees and lifted one pretty leg from the ground. And as he knelt before her, his fingers ever so gently encircled one slim ankle with his hand, and kept it there longer than he should have. 'Here, allow me.'

198

Lily was in a trance. 'Aye yes, yes - go ahead, Robbie.'
'Now don't go telling Black Friar John about my wee present.'
'No. 'Tis our secret Robbie.'

All this he savoured and stored in his head, every single moment with Lily, he played over and over. Aye Robbie was smitten. So smitten, he almost forgot to study the morning light that filtered into his room. Robbie could tell the time this way, and he knew that when the sun reached the second to last rafter, Lily would arrive at the scullery door to prepare oats and then clean the kirk.

Today was the only half-day of the week. No sermon or kirk activity at all, it was a day meant for rest, but Robbie had other ideas. The day began at noon, when Robbie made his way to the heady and comforting smell of his work place, to begin steeping barley in water to germinate, before turning twice with a big wooden paddle. Distilling whisky was an ongoing process, what with the mashing and brewing that followed germination, but Robbie enjoyed the labour and took great pride in his work. But that was later... if Robbie could keep quiet now in the wee hours, Black Friar John would remain snoring till it was time to begin distilling. As a cock crowed in the distance, Robbie pushed down on his hands to sit up in his bed and froze. A noise caused the hairs on the back of his neck to stand up...coughing, or more precisely, a great bout of coughing. Oh please don't let the old man wake up, stay asleep, Robbie thought as he pressed his palms together. As luck would have it, the coughing ceased soon after and silence was restored. But not long after, as the sun reached the second to last rafter, Robbie's heart skipped a beat as he rolled off the bed and began to dress.

***

Black Friar John had a mischievous glint in his eyes. Dressed in just his bed shift he'd awoken early to make his way to his apprentice's room... the young man would still be sleeping at this early hour. But before he reached young Robbie, a tickle formed in his throat and caused him to have a great coughing fit. So, with one hand pressed firmly on his chest, and the other held across his mouth, he managed to muffle his coughs so as not to wake him. He knew Robbie had got into the habit of leaving his peg leg in the alcove adjoining his bed chamber, because the alcove possessed a small elm armchair on which he could sit comfortably to take off the wooden leg. Black Friar John's mission that morning was to find the leg and hide it before Robbie awoke. Oh aye he knew what the laddie was up to, poor Robbie was besotted...slavering like a hungry dog over a bone for pretty Lily. But Black Friar John didn't mind at all, he'd had his fill of the widow and there were plenty of pastures new to plough and plunder...he just couldn't resist having a little fun that was all. So off he went into the alcove tiptoeing quietly, he had no trouble finding the peg leg at all, it was on the floor beside the armchair just as he anticipated. But before Black Friar John had even crossed the manse hall, out came Robbie hopping like a demented rabbit shouting at the top of his voice.

'Oh not again. Where you going with my leg this time eh? Come back here you old bugger, I'm not in the mood for your pranks today. Can't you pester someone else? '
Black Friar John roared with laughter so hard he had to hold his large belly. 'What do you need your leg for at this wee hour anyway? Today is our only day for lying in, have you something planned laddie?'
'What business is it of yours?'
'Come on, Robbie, what's going on?' Black Friar John sniffed up. ' And what's that smell?'
Robbie's cheeks reddened. 'Oh just leave me be and give me the leg back will you. You've no right to take it. It was amusing the first time but you're going too far now. I'm tired of you teasing me and pulling pranks.'
But Black Friar John ignored him and sniffed up again, before waving his hands up into the air, as if to capture the scent that he could no doubt smell. 'What is it? Ah I know that smell is, it's lavender or is it lemon balm...the Melissa plant? It smells very fresh laddie, I'm sure she will like it whoever she is...'
Robbie stopped hopping and put a hand to the wall for balance. 'I don't know what you mean. Now give me the leg so I can go back to bed.'

But Black Friar John wasn't about to give in so easy. In fact, he waved the peg leg above his head and grinned like the devil. 'You'll have to catch me.'

'Aw I've no time for these games.'

'Where you going then? You won't get far without your leg *Hoppy*.'

'Nowhere.'

'Nowhere? Why the lemon balm then?'

Robbie pulled a face. 'Perhaps it is because I always reek of yeast and this smell replaces the other, so what! Now hand it over.'

But once again, it was not in Black Friar John's character to give in to the lad. So off he went down the hall at top speed, waving the peg leg in the air, while Robbie hopped after him with a red face screaming at the top of his voice. That's when Lily appeared. The old holy man felt bad then, because at the sight of Lily, young Robbie looked mortified, no doubt to be seen there in the hallway, minus his stockings and even worse without his leg. But Lily was not fazed.

'Give him the peg leg now you old rascal. That was a dirty trick.'

Black Friar John's shoulders slumped as he returned the leg to his rightful owner. 'I'm sorry laddie, I was just teasing you. I knew you were up early to see Lily, and well…'

Robbie took the peg leg and fell down to the floor to attach it. But he was so overcome with emotion, he was unable to do it, and in his frustration and distress he tossed it away and began to sob. Black Friar John stopped in his tracks and groaned. Never in his life had he felt so bad, it was meant to be a bit of sport, a jest, but it had all turned sour. He smacked his forehead with quite a bit of force and sank to his knees beside Robbie.

'I'm sorry Robbie, I really am. I thought you would take it in good spirit, but obviously I hadn't thought it through. I shouldn't have…'

'No matter.' Robbie shook his head and motioned for him to go.

But the holy man remained there on creaky knees and placed a hand on Robbie's shoulder. 'No, no - I'm a damned fool, so listen to me, I am so sorry laddie, it'll no happen again I promise. I'll leave you two alone now. You know I think the world of you, I'd be lost here without you, truly I would. You're like a son to me, you really are, and I'm not just saying that to make you feel better. Oh and before I go, I think the pair of you would make a great match, I really do. 'He said with a wink.

***

Once they were alone, Robbie, without the aid of Lily, managed to stand, and immediately wiped away the wetness from his smooth face. His peg leg lay on the floor not far from Lily, and his eyes fell upon it with disgust…just the sight of it repulsed him to the core. Why me, he wondered for the hundredth time? The self-loathing he felt just then caused him to sink into himself so much, that he didn't notice Lily kneel down to pick up the leg and walk across the hall to him. When they were barely inches apart, he felt her presence and drank up her womanly scent, and for what felt like eternity, they stared into each other's eyes. Lily held up the peg leg. 'Do you think this makes you any less of a man? Because I can tell you, it does not. What makes a man is character and grit, the stuff that drives a person to go on no matter what obstacles are thrown at him. You have that, Robbie - you are a good man, a man with real potential, so don't be downhearted. You're a real catch, and one day one lucky lassie will get to spend the rest of her life with you.' Robbie kissed her then, silencing her words.

'I don't want anyone else. I love you.'

'Oh Robbie, I feel just the same. I have since the very first day you came here… but there are so many difficulties around us. You can do so much better than me.'

'Ah there is complications, Lily, but nothing we can't sort out between us. I've never been so happy in my whole life. I could never return to Castle Wood now. I feel so at ease now, and there is purpose for me here. All I want is to remain here with you, and even Black Friar John, not that he deserves it. So don't tell me I can do better than you, let me be the judge of that. You may be a widow, but you are the bonniest widow in the whole of Scotland.'

'Aye but I'm older than you too.'

'No matter. So what! I'm a wee bit young to get wed no doubt, but I might as well say it now. I want us to be married, Lily, and as soon as possible before my mother finds out about us and tries to intervene.'

Lily gasped. 'Us?'

'Yes us. You and I, and right away. Black Friar John will oblige. He owes me a favour after today.'

And that was that. Lily and Robbie Bothwell were betrothed and soon after wed.

***

The servant's kitchen was as always, all hustle and bustle. Falmouth sat at a trestle table, his legs wide apart eating broth, while cook fussed over him as though he was a small child. Matilda was not given the same treatment, if anything she was treated like a bad smell, not at all welcome. So, the mistress of Castle Wood just stood there with her back to the wall watching the cook at her chores for a while. For someone with swollen legs, cook seemed to get around just fine - at times Matilda wondered if the old woman was playing her the fool just so as to get out of certain tasks.

'I've come to set the menu for the day.'

'Oh aye, but as you can see I'm busy now. Can't you come back in a while? It really isn't necessary, folk have the same set meals here day in, day out. I know them all off by heart.'

Matilda winced. Eleanor had given herself graces ever since she was wet nurse to William, but that wouldn't wash with her. 'No, I most certainly won't come back and watch your tone, woman. I want to deal with this now. Falmouth has shot one of the weaker deer, and it would be nice if we could eat it tonight. Now, the venison I want it cooked rare, and no over boiling the vegetables…'

'Very well, my lady.' Eleanor bowed in a rather sarcastic way.

Matilda looked at Falmouth for support, but all he did was shrug his shoulders and laugh at the top of his voice. 'Oh you really are a disagreeable woman since that son of yours ran away.'

Cook pulled a face. 'He didn't run away, Falmouth. He's in the castle dungeons, that's the rumour here, has been for years.'

'No one is in the dungeons, Eleanor. I've been down there myself. All there is are rats and rusty chains. When *he* left I let everyone go.'

'He?'

'The one you played wet nurse to - the baron.'

'Who was down there then?'

'An old man and a Quaker.'

Eleanor sighed and her shoulders sagged. 'My Magnus would never have ran without saying goodbye to me first. Years he's been gone with no word.'

'You look tired old woman. Rest those legs as soon as you can.'

I'll rest my legs later once the day's toil is done.' She turned to face Matilda. 'Will that be all?'

Matilda smiled. 'Yes. Off you go old woman, and take your time.'

The servant's kitchen was rather cosy. A good fire blazed in its hearth, and the air smelled of broth and freshly chopped vegetables. It seemed a pity to leave, so Matilda sat down beside Falmouth, and listened to him prattle on for a while. He liked to talk did Falmouth, about anything and everything to do with the castle state and all the wildlife and nature that came with it. New farming methods, whether to introduce a new species of fish to the castle lakes …the position and condition of the castle herd of deer, the list went on and on.

'I'm concerned about the deer, what with that sighting of poachers, oh and do you know there's a kite about?'

'Kite?'

'Aye, a bird of prey. It will hunt my pheasants and grouse. I can't have that. I've seen a weasel too.'

'Where?'

'Along the north side, at the top of the brae.'

Matilda hadn't a clue but nodded anyway. She was well aware Falmouth knew the landscape like the back of his hand, but she did not. He pointed beasts out to her sometimes on the moors so far away they were merely dots on the horizon - she hadn't his eyesight. It was uncanny really, his vision was second to none.

It was a surprise when he finally talked of something not related to his ghillie duties. 'Have you seen wee Robbie lately?'

Matilda smiled. 'He's not so wee now Falmouth is he? My son is near enough a man now thanks to you. But no, I've not seen him since his last visit. He is very well, so I'm told.'

'Folk say he is sweet on the widow at…'

Matilda's face contorted and turned very pale. 'Well I really don't listen to hearsay. Now let us change the subject.'

But before either of them could continue the conversation a maid entered the room holding a small brown envelope, and upon the reverse was a distinctive red wax stamped with a familiar seal.

'Dear God.' Matilda near fell from her seat and in the process knocked over a tea cup.

'What is it?' Falmouth asked.

Matilda's hands trembled as she broke the seal and opened the letter to reveal the contents. 'It's from him Falmouth.'

Falmouth scratched his beard and threw up his hands in frustration. 'Who the hell is he? Who?'

'My husband.'

Falmouth groaned. 'Well it was grand while it lasted. But now all our good work will be undone. Well go on woman - what does it say?'

Matilda unfolded the letter, but her hands shook so much she simply couldn't keep the paper still enough to read it. 'Oh Falmouth, I can't read it, will you?'

'I can't read too good.'

'Oh for heaven's sake.'

Matilda placed the letter upon the table and began to read out loud.

My Dearest Matilda,

I beg of you, please give me the chance to explain. So much has happened since I saw you and Robbie last, but before I go any further, please allow me to express my sincere apologies for all the pain I have caused you. There is absolutely no excuse for my despicable behaviour, I realise that now.

Thus, I write to you humbly, and ask that you read my words… I have recently returned from France, and while I was there a curious thing happened (at a French Abbey of all places.) It came about as the nuns sang, an epiphany of sorts, and while they chanted their heavenly music our Father in heaven spoke to me and commanded me to mend my ways, I swear it. Since then, on the life of our son, I am completely reformed? I speak the truth, wife - no falsehoods at all. Divine providence has guided me…I now walk the path of righteousness and am cleansed of

205

all evil thoughts. And yet, I am still a retched soul...every day I repent and lay all of my sins before the cross, but the guilt remains. And the guilt will remain until I have made amends to you and our son...and all the other folk I have wronged.

This Sabbath I shall arrive by carriage, but do not fret...my intentions are entirely honourable, Matilda. I beseech you to hear me out and give me the chance to put matters right - before it is too late. The Lord in all his wisdom has given me the strength to confront my decadent past, and however painful that may be, I intend to see it through. When all is said and done, the truth is, I am entirely to blame for all the sorrow I have caused you - I have been a dreadful husband and a horrendous father. My actions following Robbie's accident were unforgiveable. I wouldn't blame him if he never wanted to see me again. But I implore you, Matilda - give him counsel, for forgiveness is the Christian way, I hope our son will find it in his heart to be there when I arrive.
With much affection,
William

Matilda returned the letter to its envelope. For a short while there was complete silence as the pair of them digested the words, but then Falmouth, unable to conceal his thoughts any longer, pushed backwards on his chair with all his might and made an almighty screeching noise as the legs scraped across the floor. 'Well I've heard it all now. He's turned lunatic.'
Matilda sat there with the letter in her lap, her eyes downcast. Her trembling had now ceased. Before long she was quite calm. After a while she dropped the letter so that it floated to the floor, and then she began to laugh. 'Yes. I think he has, Falmouth. But do you think it's a ploy? It could be the claret speaking...'
'Well nae. He sounded quite sincere to me.'
'Before it is too late...do you think he's ill? By the sound of it he's not fairing very well.'
Falmouth shook his head. 'Well if he is that's a shame, my heart bleeds, excuse my saying but that's the least of your worries. You should contact Robbie and see if he wants to see his father. The laddie mightn't

want to, and like the laird said himself, who would blame him? Not after the way he treated him following the accident. The man hadn't the decency to look in on him once, and the laddie could have died of shock alone, never mind bled to death…and all because of one of his mantraps.'

Matilda nodded and clutched Falmouth's hand. 'Yes it was unforgiveable, but he is his father after all… even he deserves a second chance. Oh, I simply can't believe it, Falmouth, after all of this time he just wants to return as though nothing has happened.'

'Well he did say he wants to make amends.'

'That remains to be seen, Falmouth. Talk is cheap, I'm sure we'll find out sooner or later whether he's truly sorry or not. When all is said and done, the baron abandoned us, and his son when he needed him most. He fled and you stayed. You stuck by me and Robbie, and for that I am eternally grateful.'

Falmouth said with a twinkle in his eye: 'Aye well it is nice to be appreciated. Thank you my lady.'

***

After Sarah passed, Sister Louise arranged for her to be buried within the confines of the walled garden, as it was Sarah's favourite place, and where they had both spent time together. Sister Louise knelt by the flower beds and paid her last respects, and when she'd finished she stood up, brushed off the dirt from her skirts and ripped the nun's veil from her head. Sunshine reflected upon her raven hair. The rays felt so warm and comforting, she turned her white face up towards the sky to bask in the Lord's light. Soon her pale skin turned pink, and her flesh tingled…but she remained still and remembered some of Sarah's final words before she passed.

'Have you seen my baby, a girl child? She is so beautiful. Will you fetch her for me? I need to cradle her see. They won't let me hold her.'

Sister Louise stepped on the veil on the ground and then pressed her foot upon it so that it rubbed into the dirt. She picked up a bag she'd packed earlier and walked towards the garden door…the door represented the outside world, once she stepped through it there was no going back. Her heart beat so fast as her hands pressed against the splintered wood, she pushed and then hesitated… what am I doing, she thought? Her gaze returned to the walled garden, and the ruins of the old Berwick priory, and then the dirty veil that lay upon the ground.

She pushed open the door and stepped outside, not once did she look back. On and on she walked for most of the day, until she arrived at a little market town called Kelso by the banks of the Tweed. Here she found an old farming man that would take her Edinburgh way for a few coins.

And so, Sister Louise hopped upon his cart, not too close beside him mind because of his smell, and listened to his tittle tattle for most of the way.

'Where's that you know, that hood thing that goes over your heid? Your face is as red as this apple here I am eating.'

Sister Louise wished she could stuff something down her lug holes, the noise of him chomping down on the said apple was getting right on her nerves. 'I lost it.'

'That's a funny accent. You're no' frae these parts now are ye? A long way frae hame is my guess.'

'No. I am French.'

'Never mind.' He replied, as if it were something to be endured.

'How much farther?'

'Not long now little lady. But if I were you I'd get something else to cover that pretty head, a young woman travelling alone…'

'Oui. I will be sure to purchase a plaid.'

The farm man smiled at that. 'Aye well you'll find no finer tweed or cloth than in Scotland.'

Sister Louise nodded. 'Have you heard of Castle Wood?'

The farm man nodded. 'Aye. We will pass it on the way, is that where you're going?'

'Oui. I have business with the laird there.'

The carter frowned. 'Last I heard he was abroad, but there's rumours he's about to return. So you might be in luck little lady.'

Sister Louise crossed her arms over her bosom… the look she gave the farm man caused him to shrink in his seat. 'Please do not call me that. You may call me Sister Louise. Is that clear?'
The man nodded and remained silent for the rest of the journey.

CHAPTER 18

The baron arrived by carriage on the Sabbath, as dawn turned the eastern sky soft hues of blue and gold. William stared all around him, as though viewing Castle Wood for the first time. His eyes fell upon the moors, to the dips and peaks - so many colours, moss green and heather as purple as foxglove... he closed his eyes and breathed in the scent of home... earthy peat smoke and the sweet grassy smell of heather. God's finger brushed every nook and valley, and every mystic tree... in a sudden he realised how much he loved his father's land. On the horizon, he noticed a group of serfs working hard on one of the many run-rigs, bent over double digging the earth. He ordered the carriage to stop and peered through the nearest window, one hand cupped above his brows, to somehow filter the harsh sunrays.

'Drive on.' He knocked on the carriage door, and folded his arms across his body. Despite the warm morning, he was cold...he was always cold these days.

Once in motion, the carriage began to rock and sway again as the wheels rolled across a dirt track flanked by weeds and hedges. The clip clop of horses hooves competed with a squeaky wheel, and once or twice William bumped his head on the walls of the carriage, prompting McKenzie to stifle a laugh.

'Does my discomfort amuse you?'

McKenzie struggled to keep a straight face. 'Of course not, master, I'm just happy to be home.'

William let it go. The two of them had formed a strong bond since their voyage to France... and the encounter with the cabin boy. In fact, without his manservant, William felt quite sure he would be lost. The man had been a tower of strength to him, the past few weeks or so. McKenzie was indeed a loyal and valued servant.

'Oh it's good to be back, Blad. I thank the Lord for a life so sweet...I have missed these sleepy hills.'

McKenzie nodded but said nothing. At the best of times he was not a talkative fellow.

Before long they entered the main gate, and eventually came to a halt at the large court-yard with the old covin tree. For a while the baron just sat there, his heart beating frantically like a military tattoo, a cold sweat upon his forehead. This was it, time to face his sins…and perhaps even his son, William swallowed hard, he was terrified all of a sudden. McKenzie had no such hesitation and leapt from the carriage with much dexterity for a man of his years.

'Here take my hand.' Mckenzie stretched out a hand to his master.

William took it and climbed so clumsily from the carriage, the castle folk would most likely suppose he'd been at the claret again - but they'd have been mistaken, for he'd not had a drop since France and would remain an abstainer for ever more. 'All right McKenzie, let go of my hand now, I need your assistance no more.'

'You're about to fall on your arse man you're so weak. Why don't you listen to me and get yourself a walking cane?'

'Don't need one.' William shook his head.

'Stubborn as ever.'

Together they entered the east wing of the castle and carried on walking till they reached the great hall. A couple of times the baron stopped to catch his breath, and when he did many a servant raised their eyebrows before scurrying off to spread their tittle tattle. McKenzie winced and prompted his master sit down…

'Master, perhaps you should take a seat, just for a moment.'

'But they're not here - my wife, my son. They're probably in the solar.' The baron stumbled a little as he made off for the upper stories.

'You're not fit to take the castle steps you old fool. Sit down, I'll have a servant fetch them to us, and do not grumble with me. You know I'm right.'

'Oh go on then man. Fetch them here then.'

***

Matilda stared at the French nun. An odd looking creature in dusty robes but no veil. What became of the veil one could only guess. *Best not to ask*, thought Matilda. Despite her peculiarity, the nun was beautiful though, one of those exotic women of pale skin and ebony hair. She'd arrived a week or so ago and refused to leave, and since then, every morning the holy woman woke Matilda to ask for news…damned nuisance she was with all her questions… *Where is your husband? When will he return?*

It was a mystery. Who on earth was she and what business did she have with her husband? But every time Matilda asked her, the French woman refused to reveal anything. In fact, she just crossed her hands over her bosom and repeated: 'I must talk with your husband, Baron Bothwell.'

And now he was here.

The baron had at last returned. How did Matilda know? His hounds… excited yelps of glee echoed across the castle walls, if anyone on this earth loved the baron it was his hunting dogs. In truth, everyone else couldn't care less if he lived or died. Take the servants for instance, at the first sign of his arrival they buzzed here and there with pale faces, petrified that he might find fault with something or someone. They knew only too well how foul his temper could be.

Matilda wrung her hands and then stared deeply into the woman's eyes. 'As you may have realised, my husband has just this moment arrived. I cannot remember when he was here last, but I do know it was that long ago. So, as you can appreciate we have much to discuss. I do wish you could have confided in me regarding your… well whatever it is you need to speak to him about. But suit yourself…I'll send him to you once I've spoken with him. You may wait here …in the solar. I shouldn't be long.'

The French woman nodded.

A stranger sat at the trestle table in the Great Hall. An old man with paper thin skin and eyes sunken into his skeletal head. On catching sight of her, this unfamiliar person stood up in a rather enthusiastic manner, and that's when Matilda realised who this odd fellow was, and her mouth went dry.

'Matilda - my devoted wife. Please find it in your heart to forgive this sinner before you. I have forsaken you, but I will not again. I promise.' The baron fell at her feet.

Matilda gasped and spied her husband's valet standing nearby. 'William - have you lost your senses? Please stand. There are servants about. You - get out!'

The valet looked mortified and at a loss what to do, but in the end he just turned to the baron and shrugged.

'Do not chastise him, Matilda - McKenzie has been a good friend to me these last few months. Here man, help me up off my poor knees - then leave us alone for a wee while, my wife and I have much to discuss.'

Matilda watched in fascination as the manservant helped her husband to his feet and then to his chair, and ever so gentle like... there was a fondness between them that was plain to see.

'If that will be all.' The manservant bowed his head.

'Yes, Blad. Please take my belongings to the watchtower. I'll be staying there from now on.'

McKenzie frowned. 'But it's not fit to live in...and you're in no fit state to go there!'

Matilda joined in and shook her head in disbelief. 'There's no windows and there isn't a stick of furniture in it.'

The baron smiled and squeezed his wife's hand. A kind gesture so uncharacteristic of him, Matilda's eyes near popped from her head. The man before her was indeed a stranger, and so far removed from the man that left Castle Wood the day of the accident, she hardly knew him at all. Her forehead wrinkled as she wondered if it was too good to be true. The baron held up his hands and laughed. 'No matter. I will not be swayed on this...the watchtower is to be my home now until...well until I go to meet my maker that is. Here, sit beside me wife... I have much to tell you.'

As Matilda took a seat beside her husband, McKenzie left abruptly, no doubt glad to have a moment to himself. Thus, they were alone, just the two of them, and Matilda felt of a sudden self-conscious, her face became quite red, and for one awful moment she thought the dreaded hot flushes had come back. She took a handkerchief and wafted it into the air to mimic a fan, and as luck would have it the moment passed.

'Are you all right dear?' William asked.

'Of course, it's just those dogs. Will they ever stop barking? Perhaps you should go see them, William.'

'That can wait.'

'Really, they used to be your one and only priority?'

'Things have changed, Matilda. You will soon realise that I am quite altered…'tis not a trick. I am no longer afraid of anything, and I will no longer lie to you or our son. Look, I'll just say it, I left that day because I was a coward, a good for nothing coward. Where did I go? Instead of helping my son, I went to Avignon - I chased a woman to Avignon.'

Matilda shook her head and frowned. 'I'm past caring, William I really am. But how curious. That might explain why the French nun is here.'

'What French nun?' William asked.

'A French woman arrived here a few weeks ago, but she refused to speak to me. All she would say it that she wanted to speak to you.'

'Where is she?'

'The solar.'

William's eyes seemed to sink further into his head. 'I'm too weak to climb up there, would you have a servant fetch her?'

Matilda rose from her chair, but before she departed William called out to her. 'My boy…how is my boy?'

'You wish to know of our son?'

He nodded and swallowed hard. 'Yes?'

Matilda took in his expression. It was the same look of anticipation Robbie had upon his face when he lay upon his bed for weeks following his accident, waiting to see if his father would walk through the door. 'He's not here. Robbie doesn't live here anymore.'

William's shoulders sagged but she felt nothing for him, not an ounce of sympathy 'He cried out for you so many times you know that day…' her voice cracked with emotion.

'What do you mean he doesn't live here - where on earth has he gone?'

Matilda shook her head. 'Do you really care?'

'Of course I do. Oh I know I've acted abominably. But that doesn't mean I care nothing for our son. Perhaps he will find it in his heart to forgive me one day…'

'Perhaps.'

'And the foundling child, Elisabeth?'
'She is well.'

***

He'd lost so much weight, the bones in his backside pained him as he sat at the trestle table waiting for the French woman. He fidgeted and shuffled about, till he felt a bit more comfortable. The weight loss was a side effect, of copious amounts of guaiacum and mercury…he was so tired of it all. All the pains and aches that plagued him at night, the ulcers and sores, punishment for his sins, of that he was sure. He could bear it no longer, especially the urethral syringe he had to insert into his urethra in the hope that it would burn off the sores. His privy parts were a disaster.
He looked up as a young woman entered the room and stood before him.
'Baron Bothwell?'
'And your name is?'
Sister Louise.'
'Ah do sit down, my dear - take a chair.'
The woman shook her head. 'I prefer to stand.'
William looked her over. She was a fine looking woman, quite beautiful if pale brunettes were to your taste. 'Very well. I assume you are the woman who took Sarah away from that Magdalene place.'
'Oui.'
'How is she?'
'Dead.'
William felt a pang in his bosom. 'No - how?'
'She had the fever…and you, you gave her a filthy disease.'

He averted his eyes, deeply ashamed of himself. 'I know what you must think of me, but I have atoned for my sins, really I have. All I want is to put matters right, as best I can…it is all that I can do. The good Lord in his wisdom has given me a chance to…'
'You are a backslider. You will always revert to your *true* nature, the habits you possess are too strong to resist.'

215

'A bit harsh don't you think? I fell from grace when I pursued my own desires, but the Holy Spirit can be restored if I repent, in fact the Holy Spirit will lead me, empower me, and fill me with God's love. I may have been lost, but now I am found.'

Sister Louise scowled, and the action contorted her lovely face so that she became quite ugly. 'Ah a sermon on the parables of the lost sheep...or perhaps you fancy yourself the *Prodigal Son*. I'm not convinced, Baron Bothwell.'

'Please yourself, I really couldn't care less what you think.' The baron shrugged.

'You can repent till you're blue in the face, but it will not bring back Sarah. She was little more than a child when you abused her...if you'd left her alone, she'd probably still be here. So tell me, how can you put matters right?'

'I cannot. And there is no excuse. I am a despicable human being.'

'She lost another baby you know - *your* child.'

William groaned and pressed his palms together. 'God forgive me. I am so very sorry.'

'Her firstborn child. Where is she?'

'She's here. My wife has cared for her since she was born.'

'Are you truly willing to atone for your sins Baron Bothwell?'

'Yes I am.'

'Very well. The child will come with me.'

The baron shook his head. 'Not possible, my wife...she will be heartbroken.'

Sister Louise remained aloof and indifferent. 'I insist. The child must return with me to France. It was Sarah's dying wish that she would be reunited with her...I will take the child to her mother's grave and then she will sail with me to France.'

'To Avignon?'

'Oui.'

'I visited the convent. They claimed you were not one of them.'

'That's preposterous. I can assure you that I am.'

William closed his eyes and sighed. 'Look here, the girl child will remain with us and that is the end of it. I am sorry that you have had a wasted journey.' He held out a hand.

At the sight of his outstretched hand the nun stepped backwards and her face turned grey.

Sister Louise blurted out: 'You don't deserve to keep the girl. You took Sarah's baby from her when she was little more a child herself. When she lost the second baby it near broke her heart you know… how can you live with yourself?'
'Most unfortunate. But these things happen.' He paused. 'May I ask …how did the bairn die?''
Sister Louise stopped in midstride. 'Do you mean the child conceived in that miserable abode, Magdalene? Do you really care?'

His face reddened, he knew what she was thinking…*backslider* - she sensed the foul odour of his soul. With all his heart he so wanted to be pure - but now, thanks to her, he doubted whether or not he could be restored…would the Lord embrace him now or would he be damned to hell, a profligate to the core?
'Yes I do want to know. In fact I demand to know…'
'The baby when it came arrived too early, no doubt weakened by your poisonous seed. You are a vile man indeed, Baron Bothwell. Repent till your tongue stiffens and your knees bleed…but you'll never be cured.'

***

Before he met with Matilda again, he visited his hounds, and what a welcome they gave him. If all else perished in the world, he could take comfort in the fact that at least his dogs loved him. If only everyone greeted him like that! All the yelps and wagging tails did much to soothe him before he had to face his wife again. He'd made up his mind concerning the child Elisabeth, and there was no going back. In truth, he'd took great delight in sending the nun away empty handed.
Once he'd finished making a fuss of the dogs, with the help of McKenzie, William returned to the great hall to wait for Matilda. The woman seemed to take the longest time - he took a deep breath and tried to unwind. He waited and waited…soon his fingers tapped impatiently on the trestle table. Then he spied the ghillie, the one who found his

son. What to do? Thank him or just ignore him? So, before the man disappeared from sight, he called him over.

'You - gamekeeper. I forget your name.'

'Falmouth.'

'Aren't you the one who found my boy?'

'Aye.' The man's muscles twitched in his jaw.

'I owe you a great deal.'

The ghillie frowned. 'I couldn't leave him there like that, it was my Christian duty.'

'You did a noble thing. I want to thank you for saving him, I'm told your quick thinking is what probably saved him, and for that you should be rewarded.'

The gamekeeper's mouth gaped open. 'Thank you master. Thank you...'

William looked him over once more, a strong man this ghillie - all beard and muscles. He wondered if they were to fight who would go down first - but alas his fighting days were over. Before the man scarpered, he called out to him again: 'One more thing...'

The ghillie stopped in his tracks and turned quite pale. 'Aye?'

'My steward tells me you have made certain changes - along with my wife. To make life easier for the serfs.'

The ghillie looked nervous. 'Aye master, mainly just a bit of extra fire wood to keep away the cold.'

William smiled. 'Really? It never occurred to me that they were cold.'

The ghillie opened out his hands in front of him, palms up. 'When winter comes many get sick with the cold. The cottages are draughty and many don't have enough blankets and clothes.'

'Perhaps they could have some hay too. Keeps my dogs warm I can tell you.'

The ghillie near tripped up as he rushed away. William knew he probably thought him quite mad. After all, it was his Christian duty to reward him was it not?

'William?' Matilda stared at him. 'Whatever did you say to Falmouth? He looked scared to death, as though he'd seen a ghost.'

'I simply told him he is to be rewarded for saving the life of our son. That is all, I didn't mean to alarm him.'

218

Matilda's eyes grew wide. 'Oh. How gracious of you.'

'Now enough of that. It's time we talked. Here - sit beside me.' He patted the seat of the chair beside him.

'But we've already talked, William.'

He looked at her then with fresh eyes, his wife - the mother of his son and only child. Matilda's forehead crinkled, and at the corner of her eyes he noticed small wrinkles, 'laughter lines' he think folk called them - and yet he'd brought her little laughter. Ironic really, that now in trying to do good, he would probably bring her more misery.

'Matilda. The French woman. Do you know why she is here?'

'No I told you before I have no idea. Why is she here?'

'She came for Elisabeth.'

'What on earth for?'

The baron pinched the bridge of his nose and sighed deeply. 'Ah well I'm about to tell you. Do not fret - it must be said if I am to be cleansed, Matilda, so hear me out.'

Matilda held a hand to her mouth and stood. 'I don't wish to know.'

'Sit down woman, Matilda. You see - Elisabeth is not a foundling child, she is the offspring of Magnus Styhr and a field serf called Sarah. I took Elisabeth from her mother when she was born.'

Matilda's face turned ashen. 'But why on earth would you do that?'

'To punish Magnus. He bedded her without my permission and years ago there was that incident with…'

Matilda began to weep. 'Greta. You've never forgiven him have you? All those years have passed by and you still have a sickness for her. Magnus kissed her first and then you had to have her! William you are possessed I tell you. '

The baron held his head in his hands. 'Don't you think I know? I curse the day I set eyes on her.'

'So what became of Magnus?'

'I sent him to a colliery.'

'You sent him to work the mines?'

'Yes. Before that he was in the dungeons.'

Matilda nodded her head. 'So the rumours are true.'

'Yes.'

'But how is any of this connected to the nun?'

'I banished Magnus's woman to a nunnery. While she was there I took certain liberties with her; that is until the French nun intervened...'
Matilda screwed up her eyes and her face became crimson. Her disgust was plain to see, and William was of a sudden taken aback.
'How could you?'
William shrugged. 'It took my mind of Robbie and his leg.
'You used the peasant girl while your son lay in bed with his leg hacked off?'
The baron swallowed hard. 'Yes. Once the French woman took the girl away she must have learned of Sarah's baby.'
'You're despicable.'
William lowered his head and whispered. 'Aye I know.'
'Where is the girl now?'
'Dead.'
'How?'
'A fever, oh and I gave her the pox.'
Matilda squirmed. 'Lord above, can it get any worse?'

With his head bowed low, the baron tried to ignore her sobs and sniffs, he was trying to be a good person, he really was, but sometimes it was damned near impossible. Try as he could, William couldn't seem to find pity or compassion for his wife. 'Oh do stop weeping, Matilda. Tomorrow I shall be gone. For a little while that is... but once I'm home everything will be different. Upon my return, I will no longer be in charge, Matilda - you will be, and someone else will help you...'
Matilda at last quit weeping and asked who.
'Well, Morice has informed me that you and Falmouth have made great progress here with the land serfs. But Falmouth will remain what he is - ghillie, and Morice - my steward will always be on hand to assist you in certain matters. But the man I am going to fetch tomorrow will take my place - beside you, Matilda.'
'Only our son can take your place, William.'
'I have a half-brother, Matilda.'
'What?'
'Magnus Styhr. He is my brother.'
'The serf you sent to the colliery?'
'Yes, I have wronged him and I'm about to make amends.'

220

Matilda shook her head and laughed. 'A serf has no business as laird of the castle. You cannot be serious?'

'Oh but I am.'

'He'll despise you for taking his sweetheart, his child and his liberty. Not only that he is a simple man, he hasn't the skills, education or bearing. Our son does however.'

'Magnus will accept my offer I am sure of it. Robbie I am informed has no wish to return to castle wood, so until he does, Magnus will simply take my place. In the meantime, perhaps you can talk some sense into our son.

Matilda huffed. 'Oh I intend to. But honestly, surely you don't even know for sure that he is your half-brother? His mother is the cook isn't she, and the supposed father the Norseman?'

'Oh Matilda I am fairly sure - haven't you ever noticed how much he resembles father and I?. Father always had a thing for Magnus's mother…why do you think she was made wet nurse?'

'Because she had a child the same time as your mother I imagine…

'Aye and that's because father took his right of the first night, I overheard him and mother argue about it enough. He had to have her, and so the cook's first born was probably the result of that encounter…Magnus is my half-brother, I am certain of it.'

'You suspect he is your brother, but send him to the dungeons and then the mines? Why do you despise him so much?'

William placed his head in his hands. 'You know why - Greta.'

Matilda shrieked. 'Oh not her again. Just like your father you are, can't keep your hands off the serf women, what is wrong with you all?'

'Matilda - I am truly sorry.'

Matilda threw up her hands. 'Oh I don't want to hear of it anymore, William. Go and fetch your peasant half-brother, I really don't care anymore. This isn't repentance, it's cruelty I tell you. Don't you think I know?'

The baron scratched his head. 'Know what?'

'I'll tell you what I know. You've never truly loved me. I've always known. So I compensated, William. I poured my love into our child, Robbie - the son you maimed due to your monstrous mantraps. Now, because of you, he won't set foot on these lands. So I've lost the only thing I've ever cared about thanks to you!'

Matilda picked up her skirts and fled.

William turned to McKenzie who loitered nearby and shrugged. 'She's a bit emotional. But I think she'll be fine.'

McKenzie grunted something inaudible under his tongue.

'What?

'Pity you're not drinking anymore. Now would be a good time for a dram.'

The baron shrugged. 'Have a glass of the firewater, Blad, and while you're at it, have one for me. I'm told Morice has a good stash of it in his room.'

McKenzie nodded. 'Will that be all now master?' Tis late and time for us to retire. '

'Yes. I can sleep here in the great hall; my legs are too weak for those steps. Will you come with me to the mine tomorrow, it'll be difficult… awkward. I'd appreciate your support.'

'Aye. I'll be there by your side.'

'You're a good friend, Blad. Come to think of it, you're my only friend.'

McKenzie's eyebrows raised. His voice cracked with emotion when he replied: 'Aye well I best be off.'

CHAPTER 19

The baron's night had been uncomfortable. Behind a screen in the dais, he struggled to rise from his makeshift bed to face the morning. With very little enthusiasm he tried to sit upright, and once he did, he immediately buried his face within his hands. William was weary of life - and quite a sorry sight with his eyes all glued together with sleep. The baron never was a morning person. A cockerel crowed, but all William could hear was that damned French woman's words... *'Backslider.'*

Oh what a sorry man he was. A life ruined, all because of his lifelong lust for debauchery, and his missed imagined fate...but Greta hadn't been his destiny, never had been really - he finally realised that now. If only he had had wisdom. But what was Wisdom really? A perpetual and pointless pursuit of happiness, that's all it was. William shook his feverish head, an indescribable feeling of sorrow struck his heart.

'I must get a hold of myself.' He muttered to himself, and then staggered from his bed to find McKenzie.

Beyond the dais he found a serving maid, and despite his attempt of self-salvation and reformation, he forgot himself and commanded her in a rather brusque fashion. 'Wench! Fetch my manservant will you, and no dawdling now, I need him immediately. Try the steward's room. Oh and fetch me the blacksmith too.'

The blacksmith arrived first. He was a great hulk of a man with auburn hair and a bushy beard. Immediately upon seeing him, the baron became fascinated by his over developed right arm - his hammer arm. William's eyes narrowed, his thoughts were odd of late, he wondered if he were to arm wrestle the blacksmith who would win. Of course, it was complete folly on his part, he might have been able to beat him once, but not anymore.

'You - blacksmith. I need you to travel with me to Newton. Bring some tools, a file or something to cut metal with. And before you start complaining about having too much to do, we won't be long and you will be compensated.'

223

The blacksmith scratched his beard. 'What kind of metal?'
In a rather blasé manner William said: 'What kind of metal? Brass. A brass collar. The one you made for me a while back, don't you remember? The serf collar. I need you to cut it off the man I fastened it to.'
The blacksmith to his credit tried to hide his revulsion, but after a while, he eyes widened and his mouth gaped open… 'Lord above. I thought it was for one of your hunting dogs. A wolfhound perhaps?'
 'No. It was for a man. Can you do it or not?'

The blacksmith scratched his beard again. 'Aye, but not with a file. It fastened with a rivet if my memory serves me right…and if that is the case the best way to do it is to strike the end off with a chisel. Aye, that should do the trick. But the man would have to be absolutely still.'
'I imagine he will do anything for it to be removed after all this time.'
The baron's nose wrinkled, the disgust he felt at himself just shook him to the core.

***

Soon afterwards, all three travelled by carriage to Newton to meet with Sir John Stuart of Newton Parish, and what an odd group they made, the laird, the blacksmith and the valet. Not one of them uttered a word during the journey, and instead sat with folded arms as the carriage rocked and swayed across what could not truly be considered a road.
'How much longer?' The blacksmith said.
'Nearly there.' McKenzie answered.

The baron peeked out of his window. The colliery loomed ahead, a remote and gloomy image of men and women sprouting from the earth with crooked backs, and creels of black coal. Beyond the pit face stood a fine Georgian house with huge rectangular windows and a gigantic panelled door. At the sight of the colliery, McKenzie seemed to come to life and sat forward so that he was perched on the end of his seat. A vein bulged from the side of his throat as he twisted his neck around to take in the scene before him.

'He'll be in the colliery - down pit. Shouldn't we go there first?'
William shuddered. 'I won't set a foot down there, McKenzie, and neither shall you, you silly old fool. We must speak to Sir John first anyway. No need to be hasty. Come along now, I should like for you to accompany me - but not you.' The baron stared at the blacksmith.
The blacksmith stammered. 'Shall I wait here then?'
'Yes.'
'Have you the money, McKenzie? We need to pay the man off. He'll not be happy that I'm taking back my gift.'

McKenzie retrieved a bag of coins from his pocket and dangled it in the air.

***

The blacksmith leaned back in the carriage, he'd never been inside a post-chaise before, and in truth it was much too fancy for him. He preferred a good old fashioned horse and cart. At least there was fresh air in a cart, not brocade all covered in dust - more than once he had to sneeze into his oily sleeve. Soon his foot tapped on the carriage floor, he needed to get back to the anvil, he'd nails to make, a knife, a portcullis and a poker for a hearth. But he could only do that once his furnace was at a high enough temperature to do the job. If his apprentice had let the fire die down again, and not used the bellows properly, there would be hell to pay.
His patience was running thin. A blacksmith was a very important man, even the laird knew that…that's why he'd hired him to be castle blacksmith, as well as the local villages. Furthermore, now that the wigmaker had stopped pulling teeth, folk had started to ask him to remove rotten teeth…and then there was the hand fasting ceremonies, which he liked not, as it required his beloved anvil.
A sound startled him.
'Blacksmith? Your name? I never thought to ask it.'
The blacksmith jumped from his skin. 'You near frightened me to death sneaking up on me like that. Angus, my name is Angus.'

'Angus? I knew an Angus once, but for the life of me I cannot remember who I'm thinking of… ah the cabin boy - damned shame, damned shame.'
'Aye, I see.' Angus screwed up his face. The laird was a strange one.
'No matter. Angus the blacksmith, it seems we need to go to something called a horse gin, whatever that is. The serf called Magnus is there. Do you know what a horse gin is?'
Angus bobbed his head. 'Aye I think I ken.'

So off they went, on foot to the colliery till they came to a windlass type contraption driven by a horse… and the closer they got the more interesting the scene became, because tied to the horse's reins was a tall man covered head to foot in coal dust, who he assumed to be the serf. In fact, one look at the brass collar round the man's neck confirmed it. Someone had tied his hands to the face of the horse at the gin, so that he had to walk round backwards.
'Lord have mercy - look at the state of him.' Angus blew out his cheeks.

The three of them stood there for a while just gawping at him until Angus complained that he needed to make water. 'Are we just going to stand here all day looking at him? I need a piss.'
The baron wrinkled his nose. 'We must wait. A man should be here shortly to free the serf.'
A passing mine worker heard the baron's words and piped up: 'You'll have a job. He's being made to go the rown, been like that for days.'
William frowned and turned to the blacksmith. 'Could you translate? I cannot understand a word he says. What's a rown?'
Angus shrugged. 'I'm a blacksmith not a miner. No doubt collier types have their own terms and expressions…'
'Oh just try to find out what's going on.'
So Angus, now pinching the end of his privy parts to soothe the burning sensation that irked him, walked over to the mine worker. 'Why is he tied up to the horse gin?'
'Punishment.'
'For what?'

'He tried to escape a week or so ago. The overseer made him go the rown. Ah there's one of them now. He's untying him, they must be letting him go. '

Angus thanked him and then grimaced - he needed to pee so bad.

'Afore you go, I'd get that seen to if I were you, pox is a damned thing.'

Angus released his grip on his tackle and walked away to find a hedge to make water. 'Pox!' He muttered. All he needed was a damned piss.

Once he'd made water, Angus felt much better. He didn't know what was wrong with his tackle of late, every hour or so he needed a call of nature, especially at night. It was driving his wife mad. Before he made his way back to the two men, he made a promise to himself to visit a wise woman.

The laird and the valet were quarrelling upon his return. After a while, Angus realised the argument concerned the serf called Magnus. The blacksmith shook his head, really - he had better things to do, so he just folded his arms across his strapping chest and waited for them the quarrel to end.

The laird paced up and down nervously. His breathing was laboured and he was rather red in the face. 'I just can't do it. Not after everything that has happened. The man must despise me…'

The valet replied: 'True - true, but I thought you wanted to atone for your sins and put matters right?'

'Oh I haven't the stomach for it and frankly I feel quite ill. Would you sort this out, McKenzie, good fellow? I'll wait in the carriage. Perhaps you could explain the situation and put in a good word for me - smooth it over.'

'Smooth it over you say? My lord, forgive me, but I must be frank with you… you took the serf's woman and child, then you locked him up in the dungeons. You sent him to a mine for God's sake… put a collar around his neck as though he was a dog. I fear this requires more than just a few kind words. I am sorry my Lord but this is for you alone to deal with. Only you know the circumstances and well it's about time you faced this - you'll feel better for it.'

Angus tried to stop his mouth gaping open at the sight of the laird being chastised by his valet. What a rare treat he thought to himself - to see a member of the quality grovel and plead with his manservant!
In desperation, the baron grabbed the manservant by the arm and took hold of his two hands. 'Please just this one last favour.'

'No. Once his collar is removed *you* need to speak to him.' The valet answered.

***

A day and a half he'd been tied to the horse gin, walking backwards till the skin on his feet bled. Every time he fell on his arse the overseer whipped him. But Magnus didn't feel a thing, they couldn't hurt him anymore, because he was already dead. His eyelids drooped and his eyes lost focus, he stared into thin air and sucked back on his lips. Everything became a haze, and then he felt warmth, skin touching skin and rope coming loose. He was free...but why he knew not. In exhaustion he fell to the floor and began to weep. When all his tears were spent he rubbed his eyes and dared to look up at two figures hovering above him.

One of the men, a servant of sorts, held out a flask of ale. 'Magnus Styhr?'
Magnus nodded and took the ale. The amber liquid tasted like nectar is his mouth, so he gulped down more, until soon he was choking.
'Slow down man. There's plenty more.'
Magnus sniggered bitterly. 'They've given me very little in days. I'm parched.' He wiped his mouth.
'This man here will remove your collar.'
Magnus's eyes looked over the blacksmith, and a flicker of recognition sparked in his eyes. 'I know you. You're Ned McCain's son, Angus?'
'Aye, that's right. If I'd have known the collar was for, well if I had ...'
He stammered.
The manservant interrupted. 'Look, we need to move away from the pithead and get that thing off him, all right? Let's just get on with it.'

Magnus's heart beat so fast he thought it would explode. They were going to remove his collar. But why? And why was Angus McCain, the blacksmith at the colliery with this strange manservant? All these thoughts buzzed around in his head as the two men lifted him to his feet and escorted him away from the horse gin towards the river.

'Where are we going?'

The blacksmith pointed to the river edge. 'Up yonder, near the river edge. Magnus isn't it?'

'Aye.'

'I need you to be still so that I can take a look at the collar - I just need to see the rivet. I'm going to knock it off with this chisel. Now take heed, you mustn't move an inch or I will end up taking a great chunk out of your neck. Perhaps it's better if you lie on your side. Try that.'

Magnus did as he was told. Upon the soft earth he lay, with a rather lopsided view of the world, all blue sky and lush green rushes, and sunrays turning his skin pink. He squeezed his eyes shut as the chisel struck metal, once - then twice, and then it was off. Just like that.

The manservant said: 'Angus. Return to the carriage. Inform the baron we will be with him in a moment.'

Magnus remained upon the ground in a daze. He traced the skin around his neck, the flesh was chafed and rubbed raw. But he cared not… until he heard that name. 'You said baron, oh no dear Lord, not laird of Castle Wood?'

'Aye Baron Bothwell. He's the reason we are here. Do not fret man, he wishes you no harm.'

Magnus's lip curled and tightened on one side of his face. Suddenly, he leapt up to standing and looked ready to bolt. 'I'll kill him if he comes near me. He's sent me to hell and back…everything I've ever cared about he's took from me.'

'Calm down man. The laird has changed I promise you. He's made peace with God and he wishes only to make amends now…'

'A man such as that cannot be converted! He's the devil himself. I should run now before it's too late.'

The valet stared deep into Magnus's eyes. 'Run then serf. I won't stop you I can assure you. In fact, if you did I wouldn't blame you - not after everything you've been through.'
'Aye no doubt he'll set his hunting dogs on me - tear me to pieces.'

McKenzie continued. 'The dogs are not here.'
'Nae?'
'No really. Look man, just go - escape, run away if you must, but I can assure you, you will regret it. You'll regret it because if you do you'll always be just a serf, when *freedom* might await you. The baron is about to reward you in abundance. All you have to do is find the strength to stay and face him. Let the Lord guide you, forgive your enemies. Throw away your collar - cast away your past and swallow every last bit of vengeance in your heart. '
'Freedom? He won't make me a free man. All he's ever done is punish me!' Magnus's eyes darted left and right as though scanning the horizon, working out the best escape route.
'There will be no more punishments, Magnus – please... trust me...'
Magnus spat upon the ground. A great glob of black mucus expelled from his body and caused the valet to look away with disgust. 'I find that hard to believe. I've seen what the laird is capable of. For years I've dreamt of placing my two hands around his neck and squeezing until every last breath of air choked from his body. Look at the state of me - that bastard has made me suffer.'
McKenzie laughed. 'I've felt like choking him myself once or twice. But I'm telling you the truth, serf. The laird is no longer the man you once knew at Castle Wood. He's a dying man - his body is ravaged with the pox and he's weak. And look, I'm just going to say it, there's a bond between you and the laird you're not aware of yet. Take your time, think it over...once you're decided either make a run for it, or find the carriage. We won't wait long though. Your decision.'
The valet walked away.

By the river edge, Magnus turned over the serf collar in his blackened hands and peered at it. There was writing inscribed all around it, but Magnus couldn't read it. He wanted to call the manservant over to read out the letters, but the man was gone. Oh what did it matter now anyway? The relief he felt now that the awful contraption was no longer round his neck was a joy to behold. He should run now, find a new life somewhere…but then he remembered the servants' words: '… *there's a bond between you and the laird you're not aware of yet.*'

Magnus was sick of running. He wanted to live - without fear, and without the bitterness that blackened his soul. The valet's talk of freedom had piqued his interest, but he was still wary. Could his fortune change for the better at long last? He doubted it. He flung the brass serf collar as far out into the River Forth as he could and started walking.

***

Inside the carriage, they waited in silence. Knees brushing knees - absolutely no eye contact. For the most part all three men ignored each other. McKenzie shuffled in his seat, as a sourness collected his throat. Without warning, the valet felt quite trapped and in need of air, so he lunged forward and proceeded to stick his head out of the carriage window - that's when he saw the serf approaching the carriage door. Magnus was all clenched fists and flared nostrils - he looked ready to commit murder. McKenzie jerked backwards, striking his head on the top of the window frame.
'Ouch - damnation.' He cursed and immediately sat back in his seat.
'What the devil has got into you' The baron asked.
'My Lord. The serf has arrived - he's outside covered in soot. He looks like a blackamoor!'
'Really - but why?'
McKenzie shrugged. 'Working the mines gets you like that. The blacksmith and I will scarper so that you can have a moment alone. We'll not go far. In fact, we will wait outside the carriage and once you have finished talking, all four of us will return to Castle Wood.'

A great rapping sound occurred as Magnus pummelled on the door with his fists.
'Hold your horse's man. We won't be a moment.' Shouted McKenzie.
'Aye well it's your idea me coming here and all that.' Came the reply from the serf.

The baron looked awful pale. His breathing was heavy and he had one hand clutched to his chest. 'He sounds angry, McKenzie.'

McKenzie grimaced. 'Aye well he's every right to be angry. Are you sure you are all right, master? You don't look fit for this carry-on. Listen to yourself, you sound like a clapped out set of bagpipes! Perhaps we should postpone this meeting till we return to the castle?'

The baron pulled out a blue bottle from his pocket and supped on some medicine. 'I'll be right soon enough - I'm just having trouble getting my breath that's all. This thing must be done. Better to get it over with like you said. Now call him in while I still have the courage - before I change my mind.'

'Aye all right then, if you are sure. But I'll have another word with him first. Get him to calm down.'

The baron nodded and forced a smile. 'Good idea.'

The two men, blacksmith and valet jumped out of the carriage. Their boots crunched upon the earth as they hit the ground. McKenzie wasted little time in taking Magnus aside for a quiet word, leaving Angus outside the carriage gazing up towards grey clouds.

'Take a few deep breaths, serf, I'll not have you speaking to the master until then. Remember what I said, the laird is weak and ailing. He's really in no fit state...'

Magnus interrupted. 'You may have respect for your master but I do not. I couldn't care less about him. But do not fret, I will be calm.'

McKenzie frowned and opened up the carriage door. A frail figure cowered inside. 'You better be on your best behaviour, laddie. Conduct yourself in a civilised manner. The blacksmith and I will be just outside. Now in you go. Your master awaits...'

***

Magnus stared into the carriage, he'd never set foot in one...it would take quite a high step to launch himself through the door. How was he supposed to do it? His fingers wrapped around door frame to pull himself in, when McKenzie tapped him on the shoulder.

'Use the foot plate, it serves as a step! And here you will be needing this.' He held out some sort of blanket or plaid.

Magnus took the plaid from him. 'What do I need this for?'

McKenzie laughed. 'I am sure you will figure it out. In you go and don't try anything stupid do you hear me. Like I said, we are just outside.'

In a somewhat awkward fashion Magnus stepped upon the foot iron and pushed down on his knees to climb through the carriage door. A great weight pressed down on his chest, soon he would face the devil himself, and in truth he truly didn't know how he was going to react.

He was in. But he dared not look at him yet. He kept his head down, submissive - obedient like, the serf collar might have been gone from his neck, but it mattered not! He remained within that murky carriage hunched and crouched like a collier within the mines he'd just left - he didn't presume to sit.

When Magnus heard his voice, an awful sense of dread seeped into his bones. 'Take a seat Magnus - there's no room to stand upright in here! For heaven's sake, I won't be cross with you for sitting down. But be sure to sit on that blanket so you don't spoil the upholstery. '

Magnus lost it then. Before he sat down, he bent low so that his backside bounced off the back of the carriage wall. He inched forward till they were face to face, barely inches apart, and spat straight into the laird's eye.

The laird remained calm - he took a handkerchief from his pocket and wiped the saliva from his face 'Just as I deserve. Now sit down.'

In a daze, Magnus did as he was told. He even remembered to sit upon the blanket, before staring hatefully at his laird. 'You're ill. Good! I hope you suffer as much as I have and more.'

'Your hatred for me is understandable. I don't expect your forgiveness, Magnus. All I ask is for an opportunity to make amends. I know you won't believe this, but I have found God, I really have, and God asks us to forgive our enemies - remember that! I am truly sorry for all the pain and suffering I have caused you - I really am.'

Magnus remained silent, a white mist collected in his eyes and a buzzing sound began to fill his ears.

'Magnus?'

'What?' Magnus forced himself to look at the bastard as hatred filled his heart. How he longed to kill him there and then.

'Magnus, did you hear what I said? I am truly sorry.'

CHAPTER 20

It was finally happening. After everything Magnus had been through, this was it - the moment he had been waiting for. He shuffled atop the blanket and stared down at his sooty hands placed awkwardly in his lap. He closed his eyes, visualised those blackened hands wrapped around the baron's scrawny neck.

The laird called out to him again. But Magnus ignored him, he just couldn't think straight. A strange buzzing sound filled is ears as a great rage built inside of him.

'Magnus. Now that I have apologised... the time has come for us to finally talk.'

Magnus took a deep breath. They were so close their knees were barely inches apart. 'Aye. Let's talk before I lose my composure and knock you from this world to the next. Why? That is what I want to know. *Why* have you treated me so cruelly?'

The baron appeared to shrink in his seat. He raised one hand and covered his face. 'Greta.'

'Greta, the wise woman's daughter?'

'She chose you that day at the watch tower - she never did pay me any attention; it was always you she made eyes at. Don't you remember how I caught you together?'

Magnus slapped his forehead and laughed. 'For the love of God, that was years ago, we were just children!' 'It doesn't matter how long ago it was. Back then, I imagined Greta to be my destiny. I loved her with every being of my soul. And you, my father's bastard son - she preferred you to me!'

Magnus shook his head and sniggered. 'No, no, no - do not play your tricks upon me. I have not a drop of noble blood, I am a serf through and through. Be careful what you say my Lord, I am in no mood for your nonsense - this has gone on long enough - this thing between you and I. I cannot stand it anymore. A man can only take so much.'

Magnus noted his reaction, seen the spark of light that glittered in the laird's eye. Not sadistic pleasure he imagined, but something else…
'Well if you do not believe me, Magnus - I suggest you ask your mother upon our return. She's had not one but two quite privileged positions since you arrived kicking and screaming into this world, I wonder why? Wet-nurse and then cook. Father adored her I seem to remember. But then he always did have an eye for a pretty maiden, especially pretty maidens on their wedding night with white sprigs of flowers in her hair.'
'Shut up - I'll wipe that smirk from your face if you're not careful. Lord forgive me I hate you with every bone of my body. Since I saw you last, there has been many an occasion I prayed for death. But do you know what kept me going? Killing you!' Magnus spat out.

The baron turned all queer, his eyes glazed over. 'Well what are you waiting for? Do it now. Take your vengeance, I'm not long for this world anyway, I want to die.'
'Hah! So I can hang on the morrow? Besides I've more questions for you yet. If you think me your half-brother, why imprison me? Why send me to the dungeons?'
'I told you the reason - Greta. I lost her because of you! Father - *our* father sent her away after that day… and I was so angry, I wanted to murder you. I wanted to murder you for taking her away from me - but no, I had other plans for you. So, I watched and waited for you to find a woman, and when you fell for one, I decided there and then to take her from you! Retribution was mine.'
Magnus frowned. 'But the old baron didn't send Greta away because of me. The girl fled on account of you, my Lord. You was forcing yourself upon her. You were…'
The mask slipped, momentarily. ''Nonsense. Some lassies need a bit of coaxing. Greta would have warmed to me, but you went and spoiled it.'

Magnus sighed out loud. A few days ago he was on his hands and knees in the coal mine - now he was in a fine carriage face to face with the man he'd dreamt of murdering night after night. He truly would have been more content in the mine at that moment.

'Oh let's change the subject. This is all in the past. What is important now is the future. That is why I have fetched you here, Magnus, to make amends…I want to make it up to you. Not just you, your mother and all of your family.'

Magnus was astounded. Was this a trick - another ploy to make him suffer even more? He remembered the valet's words - the talk of freedom. 'Will you give me my freedom?'

The baron seemed surprised at the suggestion. 'Freedom will be yours if you do as I ask and take my life.'

Magnus couldn't believe his ears. This was trickery he was sure of it, one last bit of torturous pleasure for the laird. Freedom, dangled like a bag of gold above him. His tongue felt swollen in his mouth and his throat hurt. He collapsed in the seat behind him, and cried out in despair. 'If only I could trust you…after all I've been through.'

'You have my word on God's honour. No harm will come to you. No one will suspect you - no one at all.'

Magnus took a deep breath. He would swing by the neck no doubt if he dared to see this through. But now the moment was here, he could taste it - revenge for all those months lying in a cell, and all the other cruelties inflicted upon him. From the corner of his eye, he glanced at his master and imagined throttling him, two black sooty hands wrapped tightly round his sorry neck. It would be easy…the laird was weak.

'Do it, Magnus - end my miserable life. I do not deserve to be here. I've punished you, my wife, my son…'

Magnus blinked hard. Had the laird read his thoughts? He growled deep in his throat: 'You long for me to kill you? Hah! I am tempted but not yet - I've too many unanswered questions. For instance, where is my child? What became of Sarah and the child she carried in her belly?'

'Sarah is dead.'

'No. How?'

'A fever I am told. The child lives. You will see her at the castle. We have treated her as though she was one of our own.'

'I have a daughter?'

'God's truth.'

'Is she well?'

'She is in good health. Beautiful girl, my wife adores her.'

Magnus couldn't take it all in. A sob caught in his throat, but he wouldn't give the baron the satisfaction of seeing him upset. 'One more question my Lord.'

'Ask away.'

'You claim to be a changed man. But can a man truly be reformed? A man's true nature is simply that…nothing can change it.'

'We all of us are sinners, Magnus, some of us more than others granted. Have you not fallen from grace once? Admit it…all of us have it in us, this compulsion to follow our base instincts. That is why we must turn to God, because only He can show us the way. I admit I was a bad fellow, my path to salvation for a while seemed a figment of my imagination. But look at me now. Transformed, the Holy Spirit is within me now, God's power in action. I am living proof that it is never too late.'

'You claim to be reformed - at peace with God and yet you urge me to take your life! It is a terrible sin to take your own life.'

The baron smiled. 'That is why you must take it, Magnus. I've seen the way you've looked at me since you stepped in here… you've murder in your heart. I deserve nothing more for all the wrongs I have done. You must have thought about this moment, Magnus…'

'Aye I've thought about it all right. But what then? In taking your life - you are safe in heaven while I am damned to hell - swinging at the end of a rope!'

'There will be no more suffering for you, Magnus - I promise you. That blanket there, the one you are sitting on - it will prevent black sooty marks upon my person - erase all suspicion of foul play. My breathing is laboured; they'll be none the wiser - they will assume that I have died in my sleep. Look at it this way, you will be doing me a great favour… *and* you will be ridding the word of a truly wicked man.'

'Damnation, you continue to plague me even now. Oh to hell with you, it is what you deserve! But I cannot do this, for it is a great sin.'

A vein bulged from the side of the laird's neck. 'Are you a man or not? I've wronged you, took your woman and child from you - not to mention your freedom. Take your revenge now I order you. Wrap that plaid around my head now - smother me now until I am dead.'

'I will not.'

The laird took out from his pocket some papers and wafted them in front of Magnus.

'I cannot read. '

'No matter. I'll tell you what these papers say shall I? They state that you are my own flesh and blood, my half-brother, and as such I have named you in my will and testament. Now the law is clear on bastard rules of inheritance, so I've been crafty and had an advocate ensure that you and your family benefit from my death. That is my parting gift to you, Magnus. One moment.' He held up the papers to the window and tapped on the pane of glass.

'Yes Master?' McKenzie opened the door.

'We are nearly finished here, McKenzie - but I must confess I am quite exhausted. I must be coming down with something. Will all three of you go for a walk before we leave for the castle - just so that I may have a nap for a wee while? Oh and could you take these papers to Morice for me? It's very important.'

'Of course, Master. It will be done. Are you sure everything is all right?' McKenzie asked.

'Perfect. I am just weary that is all. I'll close these curtains and have a wee nap. Magnus will join you in a moment - we have worked everything out; all is well between us now.'

'Very good.' McKenzie said and closed the door.

The door closed with a creak and a bang. After the baron closed the curtains they sat in silence. The two men faced each other like that for a while, until their eyes met and stared deeply at one another. Magnus faltered…he took quick sharp breaths and prayed out loud. The baron nodded and spurred him on, as though willing him to do the deed. Before long, Magnus stood and retrieved the blanket. 'Oh Lord forgive me for what I am about to do…'

EPILOGUE

At Castle Wood, a boy stood on the brae, among harebells and ling, looking down across the wild Scottish moors. The boy's uncle stood to the right of him, and his mother to the left, and all three walked slowly across moorland towards an abandoned watchtower. It was nearing twilight. The air had a crispness to it, and a cold snap that nipped at your fingers and ears… the boy took a deep breath, sucked in one brittle gulp of air and sprinted away. He scampered across the soft earth, trampling heather and gorse, and mud pockmarked by the hooves of dumb beasts.

'Watch your step laddie. There's traps around these parts.' Shouted the uncle.

Every bit of colour drained from Matilda's face. And then she did something quite out of character, she took a swipe at the boy's uncle and near tripped in the process. 'Heaven above, don't ever mention traps again…do you hear me? They're long gone, Magnus. Falmouth removed them years ago. You know why.'

Magnus grimaced. 'All right woman. It won't happen again. I meant no malice, the boy should be careful that's all. Falmouth may have said he's removed them, but he *is* a ghillie - how else is he supposed to trap pests such as foxes and the like?''

Matilda had the decency to blush. 'I beg your pardon, Magnus. I never meant to imply…'

'Didn't Robbie's leg fall off in a trap?' The boy interrupted.

'No Jacob, it did not fall off. Your brother's leg became caught in a trap, and then…well it had to be removed.'

'Did you watch them saw it off, mother?'

Matilda turned pale and waved a hand at her son. 'Oh Jacob you are quite horrid and tactless, no I did not watch any such thing. Now hold your tongue and never you mind with all your questions. Let's get ourselves to the tower quickly, away from prying eyes.'

'What does prying mean?' Whined Jacob.

'Oh Jacob what did I just say? No more questions! Please take heed of me for once. Do as I bid.' Matilda scolded.

'A curious mind is an asset…you should encourage it not stifle it, Mother.' Jacob stared at her.

Matilda closed her eyes for a second before she said: 'My God you remind me of your father at times with your arrogant tone.'

Jacob seemed pleased with this piece of information, but to his mother's delight he remained quiet for once as all three of them walked briskly towards the old watch tower. Once they reached the building, they paused near a large wooden door.

'Jacob, I expect you to behave in here. I'll have none of your nonsense inside, so do as you are told.' Matilda nodded and folded her arms across her bosom.

Jacob nodded and smiled at his mother, but as they entered the door he scowled and cursed under his breath, no doubt vexed at being ordered around. He wished his elder cousin, Elisabeth was there, at least he'd have something to look at! A peat fire burned inside, and it smelled sweet and earthy, with just a hint of marsh leaves. The fire gave a wonderful glow and cast shadows throughout the circular tower. Jacob stretched his head back, and stared at the ancient stones. The bricks crawled with ivy and gave shelter to many a small creature. At one section a rowan tree sprouted from a crack in the wall, and it was here, near the tree, that an old man stood with a white beard, a Quaker man - Jacob the elder.

Magnus nudged Jacob. 'That's old Jacob, the one you were named after.'

Jacob shrugged. 'Yes, I've often wondered why. What is he to me?'

Matilda chastised her son. 'Old Jacob is Uncle Magnus's dearest friend, have some respect. You know if it hadn't been for him, Magnus might have perished in the dungeons or lost his sense.'

'I apologise Mother.'

Matilda gave her son a look and twitched her head in Magnus's direction.

'Sorry Uncle Magnus.'

The watchtower of a sudden became silent. Young Jacob hadn't a clue why.

'Mother. How much longer? I'm hungry.' Jacob rubbed his belly.

'Shush child, we've only just got here. Now sit down and stop fiddling, it's time for silent prayer. '

Jacob huffed and puffed, and fidgeted on the floor. He was bored and famished and didn't want to be in the creepy old watchtower… and he was cold. He stretched out one leg to get nearer to the fire, but had the misfortune to kick his uncle, who in response slapped Jacob on the arm. Jacob pouted his lip and resisted the urge to complain to mother, but then he saw the girl with yellow hair. A girl of seven summers or so with the bluest eyes, and a face so striking that he had to stare. And stare and stare at her he did, till he'd memorised that lovely face forever more, she was *that* beautiful.

On the way home Jacob had to ask: 'Who was the girl? You know the one with the fair hair.'
Uncle Magnus answered. 'Greta's girl. I think her name is Hanne.'
Matilda's face darkened. 'Is that her name, Hanne? How lovely. She's very bonny, but probably much too busy helping her mother to play with you, Jacob. She'll be learning about herbs and healing from her mother and grandmother…you know Klok Gumma now don't you, Jacob? The old lady who heals with her herbs and potions. Greta is Klok Gumma's daughter, and Hanne is her granddaughter.'
'Aye. Falmouth says she's an old witch.'
'How rude of him…'
'Oh Falmouth doesn't mean it, he is just jesting, mother.' Jacob laughed and then he turned to face his uncle. 'Uncle Magnus?'
'Yes laddie?'
'Greta and Hanne didn't always live at the castle did they? I mean where did they live before they came here?'
'Greta worked at a nearby castle for a long time. But Greta missed her mother and returned to Castle Wood around the time your father passed. Oh I am sorry to bring that up.'
'No matter. I never knew him. I am glad Hanne is here. I really am.' Jacob rubbed his hands together and smiled.
Magnus ruffled the boy's hair and winked at him. 'Aye I expect you are, she's a bonny lassie is Hanne. No fairer maiden at Castle Wood I'm sure…except my daughter, Elisabeth… oh and your mother.'
Jacob laughed as Uncle Magnus ruffled his hair, but from the corner of his eye he noticed his mother's displeasure. Jacob watched with

curiosity as she pulled Magnus aside. 'Walk ahead, Jacob, I need a word with Uncle Magnus.'

'Oh but mother…'

'Just do as I say, we won't be a moment. 'Tis near dark and we should be returning home as soon as possible. I just want a word with Uncle Magnus, it won't take long. Now run along.'

***

Matilda and Magnus walked ahead. Once they were sure Jacob could not hear them, the couple moved close to one another and began to talk.

'Don't encourage him, Magnus. I don't want him near that girl. She's bound to be trouble, just like her mother.'

'Little Hanne?'

'Yes. Trouble, always trouble when it comes to the likes of them.'

Magnus reached out and placed one hand softly upon Matilda's arm. 'Greta was never trouble, she was a good maiden and a decent sort. She was sent away because of the actions of your husband, Matilda, you know that. For God's sake she literally waited till the day he died before she set a foot at this place, she was petrified of him. Why punish young Hanne? The lassie has done nothing wrong.'

Matilda nodded and squeezed the hand that held her arm. 'Yes, yes, well I suppose you're right, but I really don't think that … well I mean I'm not comfortable with Jacob associating himself with the likes of her. He shouldn't be familiar with the servants anyway, it isn't right. Perhaps I should arrange for him to play with Sir Edward's daughter, or the Campbell girl at Peebles.'

Magnus removed the hand that covered Matilda's arm. 'Oh you really are a little hypocrite at times my love. Fraternising with servants is not so terrible is it? There's nothing wrong with Hanne or Greta. They're decent people, hardworking and honest. Elisabeth and I are of lower stock - we are serfs too!' He tapped his chest.

'Magnus, Elisabeth may have serf blood but she's my daughter and well she is a gentlewoman…'

'Aye she's my daughter too remember, Matilda.'

'Of course my love. Elisabeth is what brought us together...we've William to thank for that! While you were gone, he gave her to me...of course I had no idea she was yours...or that you were his half-brother.'
'I still find it hard to believe. Me! Son to the old baron. I wonder - if I had not a drop of noble blood would you still find your way to my bed?'
'Oh don't be vulgar, Magnus. Elisabeth brought us together - you know that, and, as a result we have Jacob.'
'Aye. A son who'll forever think me his Uncle and nothing more.'
Matilda placed two hands upon his face. 'That's how it has to be, Magnus - for Jacob's sake. Does it really matter? You're the closest thing he has to a father anyway.'
'Aye I suppose you're right, Matilda, I should be glad. Glad to play uncle to my son, and glad to be bastard son of the laird.'
'Oh stop it, Magnus. You do wallow in self-pity at times and it doesn't become you. You should be glad to be a part of Elisabeth's life at last. Cherish this life we have, I beg of you.'

Magnus touched her arm again and whispered into her ear. 'All right my love, I'll stop whining. I am grateful for all I have now... and these fancy clothes upon my back - however uncomfortable! But in my heart I'll always be the son of a Nordic mariner you know, and that's good enough for me.'
'Oh Magnus, you're so much more than that.'
'Do you really think so lassie? All those years my father took me out on his boat...trying to get me my sea legs, well it was useless I tell you, because I was sick as a dog every time. I think he always knew you know, Matilda...but he never said it once. He's my true father, not the old baron. Besides, mother won't even admit he lay with her that night.'
Matilda shrugged and sighed. 'No doubt she's deeply embarrassed by it all. Magnus, you only have to look at the portrait of the first baron to realise you're his son.'
'Really? I haven't seen it, remind me to look at it one day.'
'I shall take you to it later. Now, getting back to the girl, Hanne... I will not change my mind on this. I forbid Jacob to play her...'
'Oh where is the harm? The laddie's smitten with the girl It's like Greta all over again, boys dropping like flies all around her. '
Matilda grimaced. 'More the reason to keep them apart.'

'The more you keep them apart, the more he'll want to see her. Do not deny him or you'll make her even more desirable. They're children. Where's the harm?'

Matilda nodded. 'Well if you think it'll do him no harm.'

'If it helps I could have a wee word with him, man to man.'

Matilda smiled and looked deep into his eyes. 'Be my guest - you know Jacob, he is positively precocious - the boy listens to no-one but his scholars.'

Before he left her he leaned in close, a smile upon his lips and a glint in his eye: 'I'll see you later then my love - you can teach me a thing or two - I am in need of an education.'

Matilda's cheeks became vermillion red. 'Be off with you, Magnus.' She shooed him away.

***

Young Jacob was a brilliant scholar, and an exceedingly bright boy. This was a great source of pride to Magnus. Jacob had been tutored from a young age - he excelled in all his subjects, devouring book after book. Unfortunately this had some bearing on Magnus and his son's relationship… Magnus at the best of times was at a loss when it came to communicating with him. Only the tutors could hold Jacob's attention, everyone else seemed a frightful bore, too plain for his refined intellect. Nevertheless, whether the boy knew it or not, Magnus loved his son - and that is why he rather foolishly attempted to converse with him on occasions.

At the sight of his uncle, Jacob smiled and asked: 'Ah have you and mother finished your private conversation? Whatever were you talking about?'

'Never you mind.' Magnus said and tapped a finger to his nose.

'Aw I hate secrets.'

'Well if you must know I persuaded mother to let you play with Hanne. But I'm warning you, you must always treat her well, Jacob. She's a good lass.'

Jacob beamed with happiness. 'Oh that's grand. Thank you uncle.'

'Aye. Just because she's a servant doesn't mean she's worth less than the big wigs…you know the quality folk.'

245

Jacob frowned. 'Hanne is not my equal, and she never will be, Uncle Magnus. Servants aren't even allowed to look us in the eye, not if they know what's good for them.'

'Jacob. That's not how your mother and I brought you up...'

Jacob changed the subject. 'Didn't my father place you in a dungeon once - for not knowing your place? That's reason enough to be docile and subservient I imagine... if you're unfortunate to be a member of one of the lower orders that is. Did he torture you there Uncle? Did he try to take out your nails?'

Magnus shuddered. 'No, he took something far more precious.'

'What was that?'

'He took my liberty.'

'Your freedom? But you were his serf - you belonged to him. He could treat you however he saw fit.'

Magnus's heart sunk in his chest, the boy's words cut him...he looked intently at the young man before him, his very own flesh and blood. Jacob's eyes were as cold as a fish, his son seemed to look right through him. A chill ran through his Magnus's body. 'And do you think it was right for your father to treat me the way he did?'

The boy's face softened and his lips curled to form a smile, and for just a moment Magnus forgot the boy's insensitivity 'Of course not, Uncle Magnus, and that's why he tried so very hard to make amends before he died.'

Magnus's forehead creased, the boy was way ahead of his years. 'Aye well let's change the subject shall we?'

'Does it bother you, Uncle?'

'Aye it does. To be a serf is to suffer. Men of wealth don't care about working folk see. All they care about is money and power... serfs are cattle or machinery to them, nothing more! A commodity to be bought and traded. One day you might hold great responsibility, Jacob, and be a laird like your father. If you do I hope that you will be a kind and forward thinking man - one that sees serfs as people not property.'

Jacob nodded his head. 'I will try to be a fair man if the day ever comes. Robert will be Laird of Castle Wood.'

'Aye well Robbie's not here yet. Most likely, he will never come, this castle holds unpleasant memories for him. It might come down to you one day, Jacob, so you might as well get used to the idea. I'll just say

246

one more thing and then I'll hold my tongue. Take heed of your Uncle Magnus for once because this is very important, I might not be a learned tutor, Jacob - but I know a thing or two. If you do become laird one day, realise that men, women and children will work all their lives for you. They'll give you sweat and blood and hard graft till their dying days. Do you understand what I am telling you son? Oh it's foolish of me to think you could, but let me tell you, it means calloused hands, bad backs and the like. Look, what I'm asking you is this, if, and when, your time comes to become laird, treat them well, Jacob. That's all I ask - treat them well because I've walked in their shoes. I know what it is like. *See* them as equals. *See* them as human beings. Can you do that, son?'

***

Jacob tilted his head back and looked up at his uncle. He attempted a soppy heartfelt smile, even squeezed out a tear. The man was a fool. 'Yes Uncle. I will do what is just and fair.'
Mother upon realising their conversation was over, rejoined them and all three began the journey back to Castle Wood. But Jacob walked ahead of the besotted couple, he knew they had eyes for each other, he wasn't an idiot. Jacob fixed his gaze firmly on the castle ahead. One day all of it would be his, and it could not come sooner. His heart began to beat faster just thinking about it! Mother and Uncle Magnus lagged behind, they simply couldn't keep up with him - in more ways than one! He loved them both dearly. But truly, when all was said and done, his mother was weak and Uncle Magnus, well he was of lower stock with simple ways. Brother Robbie should have been laird by now…but he refused to set foot here. Mother couldn't get him to return. More fool him, Jacob thought, Robbie's loss would be his gain. For now he had to hold tight. Mother would hold the fort until he came of age.

Jacob's heart raced as he became deep in thought….
When I become laird, there will be none of this equality nonsense. Things will change, oh aye - they will go back to the way they were before. Father had the right idea. Peasants need a firm hand. Folk will

know their place and will bow to their laird, and if they break any rules they'll be sorry.

Robbie thought of his studies...*Money is in industry now, I am sure of it...a change is upon us. Might be better to be shut of them all - evict every last miserable serf. I owe them nothing!* Oh yes, Jacob was forward thinking all right - but not in the way his uncle hoped. Jacob had modern ideas... and ironically, his forward thinking would prove to be the end of serfdom. As a land owner, Jacob planned to put his money into industry - he had no interest in primitive farming methods, homespun blankets and how much kale a serf could produce...Jacob wanted more. He'd heard from his scholars about new industries... about new methods of mining, and steam that could pump water out of mine shafts now. New inventions and innovations were springing up all over the place. But what really excited Jacob was the trade in black slaves... and the rum, tobacco and sugar that went along with it. That's where the real money was, all he needed was a few wealthy investors. Oh aye, Jacob had an eye for commerce.

FINIS

16181083R00147

Printed in Poland
by Amazon Fulfillment
Poland Sp. z o.o., Wrocław